Escape the winter chill for the sunny, beautiful Loire Valley and the drama and excitement of Naples!

CINDERELLA ON HIS DOORSTEP
by Rebecca Winters

Rebecca Winters has taken readers on many wonderful journeys, and this story, her hundredth book, is no exception. She'll capture your imagination with the smells, sounds and flavours of France…and steal your heart with a romance to treasure!

ACCIDENTALLY EXPECTING!
by Lucy Gordon

Tear-jerking and touching—Lucy Gordon brings you a story that will stay with you long after you've turned the last page… On the shores of the Mediterranean, the majesty of Mount Vesuvius and dangerous, dashing Dante will make your senses erupt!

Dear Reader

My wonderful editor Kimberley Young informed me that CINDERELLA ON HIS DOORSTEP was my one-hundredth novel for Harlequin Mills & Boon. I was presented with a gorgeous heart on a chain. It was an open heart, beautifully sculptured. As I drew it out of the box I realised those one hundred books had been a labour of love. They've taken me to faraway places where I could lose myself for a time.

In CINDERELLA ON HIS DOORSTEP, I immersed myself in the château country of France, where some of the most beautiful vineyards in the world can be found. Alex and Dana are two people both searching for something that has eluded them all their lives. When fate brings Dana to the doorstep of Alex's dilapidated château, they both sense their lives are going to change. They long to put down roots as deep and lasting as the roots of his vineyard. Together, it's more than possible their broken hearts will mend.

Enjoy their journey!

Rebecca Winters

CINDERELLA ON HIS DOORSTEP

BY

REBECCA WINTERS

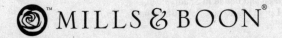

™ MILLS & BOON®

All the characters in this book have no existence outside the imagination of the author, and have no relation whatsoever to anyone bearing the same name or names. They are not even distantly inspired by any individual known or unknown to the author, and all the incidents are pure invention.

First published in Great Britain 2009
Harlequin Mills & Boon Limited,
Eton House, 18-24 Paradise Road, Richmond, Surrey TW9 1SR

© Rebecca Winters 2009

ISBN: 978 0 263 86980 4

Harlequin Mills & Boon policy is to use papers that are natural, renewable and recyclable products and made from wood grown in sustainable forests. The logging and manufacturing process conform to the legal environmental regulations of the country of origin.

Printed and bound in Spain
by Litografia Rosés, S.A., Barcelona

Rebecca Winters, whose family of four children has now swelled to include five beautiful grandchildren, lives in Salt Lake City, Utah, in the land of the Rocky Mountains. With canyons and high Alpine meadows full of wildflowers, she never runs out of places to explore. They, plus her favourite vacation spots in Europe, often end up as backgrounds for her Mills & Boon® Romance novels because writing is her passion, along with her family and church.

Rebecca loves to hear from her readers. If you wish to e-mail her, please visit her website at www.cleanromances.com

To my son, Bill, whom I often call Guillaume, because he speaks French too and loved France and the vineyards as much as I did when we traveled there. I called upon him for some of the research for this book. Once again we had a marvelous time discussing one of France's greatest contributions to the world.

CHAPTER ONE

Sanur, Bali—June 2

"MARTAN?"

Through the shower of a light rain Alex Martin heard his name being called from clear down the street. He paused in the front doorway with his suitcases. The houseboy whose now-deceased mother had been hired by the Forsten Project years earlier to help clean the employees' houses, had attached himself to Alex. Without fail, he always called him by his last name, giving it a French pronunciation.

"Hey, Sapto—I didn't think I was going to see you again." He'd been waiting for the taxi that would drive him to the Sanur airport in Bali.

Before the accident that had killed William Martin, Alex's Australian-born father, William would turn on Sapto. "Our last name is *Martin*! Mar-TIN!"

Sapto had stubbornly refused to comply. In recent months he'd lost his mother in a flood and knew Alex had lost his French mother to an aggressive infection several years back. He felt they had a bond. Alex had been rather touched by the boy's sensitivity and never tried to correct him.

"Take me home with you." His dark eyes begged him. "I've never been to France."

Home? That was a strange thing for Sapto to say. Though Alex held dual citizenship and was bilingual, he'd never been to France, either. As for Sapto, he guessed the fifteen-year-old hadn't ventured farther than twenty miles from Sanur in the whole of his life.

Alex's family had moved wherever his father's work as a mechanical engineer had taken him, first in Australia, then Africa and eventually Indonesia. With his parents gone, he didn't consider anywhere home. After flying to Australia to bury his father next to his mother, he was aware of an emptiness that prevented him from feeling an emotional tie to any given spot.

"I wish I could, Sapto, but I don't know what my future's going to be from here on out."

"But you said your French grandfather left you a house when he died! I could live there and clean it for you."

Alex grimaced. "He didn't leave it to *me*, Sapto." The letter meant for his mother had come two years too late. It had finally caught up to Alex through the Forsten company where he worked.

The attorney who'd written it stated there was going to be a probate hearing for the Fleury property on June 5 in Angers, France. This was the last notice. If Genevieve Fleury, the only living member of the Fleury family didn't appear for it, the property located in the Loire Valley would be turned over to the French government.

After making a phone call to the attorney and identifying himself, Alex was told the estate had been neglected for forty odd years and had dwindled into an old relic beyond salvaging. The back taxes owing were prohibitive.

Be that as it may, Alex had the impression the attorney was downplaying its value for a reason. A piece of ground was always worth something. In fact, the other man hadn't been able to cover his shock when he'd learned it was Genevieve's son on the phone.

Something wasn't right.

At this point the one thing driving Alex was the need to visit the land of his mother's roots and get to the bottom of this mystery before moving on. With no family ties, he was free to set up his own company in the States.

By now the taxi had arrived. Sapto put his bags in the trunk for him. "You will write me, yes?" His eyes glistened with tears.

"I promise to send you a postcard." He slipped a cash bonus into the teen's hand. "Thank you for all your help. I won't forget. Take care."

"Goodbye," Sapto called back, running after the taxi until it rounded the corner.

Hollywood, California—August 2

"Lunch break! Meet back here at one o'clock. No excuses!"

With the strongly accented edict that had been awaited for over an hour, the actors and cameramen left the set in a stampede.

When Jan Lofgren's thick brows met together, Dana knew her genius father was in one of his moods. Most of the time the Swedish-born director was so caught up in the story he wanted to bring to life, he lived in another realm and lost patience with human weaknesses and imperfections of any kind, especially hers.

As his only offspring, she'd been a big disappointment. He'd wanted a brilliant son. Instead he got a mediocre daughter, whose average brain and looks would never make her fortune. When she was a little girl her mother had cautioned her, "Your father loves you, honey, but don't expect him to be like anyone else. With that ego of his, he's a difficult man to love. You have to take him the way he is, or suffer."

The truth was as hard to take today as it was then. Dana had been through a lot of grief since her mother's death five years ago, but had learned to keep it to herself. Especially lately while he was having problems with his present girlfriend, Saskia Brusse, a Dutch model turned aspiring actress who had a bit part in this film. She wasn't much older than Dana's twenty-six years, the antithesis of Dana's mother in every conceivable way.

Privately his love life pained and embarrassed Dana, but she would never have dared articulate her disapproval. The same couldn't be said of her father who'd been outspoken about her disastrous relationship with Neal Robeson, a young actor looking for an in with the famous director, rather than with her. She'd thought she'd found love. Her mistake. It was a lesson in humiliation she would never forget.

Granted she'd made a gross error in getting

involved with anyone in the film industry, but for her father to explode over that when he never seemed to notice anything else she did for him had caused a serious rift between them. It would never heal if left up to him, not when his anger was over the top. Once again she found herself making overtures to breach the gap.

"I brought you some coffee and sandwiches."

Deep in thought he took the thermos from her and began drinking the hot liquid. After another long swallow he said, "I've decided to shoot the rest of this film on location. Then it will ripen into something worthy."

Her father needed atmosphere, that ethereal ingredient the studio set couldn't provide. He flicked her a speculative glance. "Everything's in place except for the most important segment of the film in France. I'm not happy with any of our old options and want something different."

Dana already knew that and was ready for him. Since her mother's funeral, finding the right locations had become Dana's main job besides being chief cook and general dogsbody to her irascible father. She had to concede he paid her well, but the sense that she was invisible to him inflicted a deep wound.

If he wasn't directing one of his award-winning films, he had his nose in a biography. She was a voracious reader, too, and had inherited his love of firsthand accounts of World War II in the European theatre. Over the years they'd traipsed from the coast of England to the continent, pinpointing the exact locales to bring his creations to life.

"I've come across something on the Internet that sounds promising, but I'll need to check it out first. Give me a couple of days." If she could solve this problem for him, maybe he'd remember he had a daughter who yearned for a little attention from him. When she was his own flesh and blood, it hurt to be a mere cipher.

"That's too long."

"I can only get to Paris in so many hours, but once I'm there, I'll make up for lost time. Expect to hear from me tomorrow evening."

"What's your final destination?"

"I'd rather not say." She could hope that if she found what he was looking for, it would ease some of the tension between them, but she doubted it because her mother had been the only one who knew how to soothe him. Now that she was gone, no one seemed to exist for him, especially not his only child.

* * *

Around the next bend of the Layon river, Dana crossed a stone bridge where she saw the sign for Rablay-sur-Layon. So much greenery made her feel as if she'd driven into a Monet painting done at Giverny and had become a part of it. The string of Anjou region villages nestled against this tributary of the Loire gave off an aura of timeless enchantment.

How shocking it must have been for the French people to see soldiers and tanks silhouetted against gentle slopes of sunflowers as they gouged their way through this peaceful, fertile river valley. Dana cringed to imagine the desecration of a landscape dotted with renaissance chateaux and vineyards of incomparable beauty.

A loud hunger pain resounded in the rental car. Between her empty stomach and the long shadows cast by a setting sun, it occurred to her she ought to have eaten dinner at the last village she'd passed and waited till morning to reach her destination. However, she wasn't her father's daughter for nothing and tended to ignore sensible restrictions in order to gratify certain impulses for which she often paid a price.

No matter. She wanted to see how the light played against the Château de Belles Fleurs as it faded into darkness. One look and she'd be able to tell if this place had that unique ambience her father demanded.

Following the map she'd printed off, Dana made a right at the second turn from the bridge and passed through an open grillwork gate. From there she proceeded to the bifurcation where she took the right fork. Suddenly she came upon the estate, but unlike the carefully groomed grounds of any number of chateaux she'd glimpsed en route, this was so overgrown she was put in mind of a *bois sauvage*. Without directions she would never have known of its existence, let alone stumbled on to it by accident.

A little farther now and a *tour* of the chateau's bastion with its pointed cone appeared as if it were playing hide-and-seek behind the heavy foliage. Clumps of plum-colored wild roses had run rampant throughout, merging with a tall hedge that had long since grown wild and lost its shape.

She pulled to a stop and got out of the car, compelled to explore this ungovernable wood filled with wild daisies hidden in clumps of brush. Once she'd penetrated deeper on foot, she peeked through the tree leaves, but was unable to glimpse more.

A lonely feeling stole through her. No one had lived here for years. The estate had an untouched quality. Secrets. She knew in her bones these intangible elements would appeal to her father. If she'd combed the entire Loire valley, she couldn't have found a more perfect spot. He demanded perfection.

"Puis-je vous aider, madame?" came the sound of a deep male voice.

Startled out of her wits, Dana spun around. "Oh—" she cried at the sight of the bronzed, dark-haired man who looked to be in his midthirties. "I didn't know anyone was here." Her tourist French was of no help in this situation, but judging by his next remark, she needn't have worried.

"Nor did I." His English sounded as authentic as his French, but she couldn't place the pronunciation. His tone came off borderline aggressive.

His hands were thrust in the back pockets of well-worn, thigh-molding jeans. With those long, powerful legs and cut physique visible beneath a soil-stained white T-shirt, she estimated he was six-three and spent most of his time in the sun.

"The place looks deserted. Are you the caretaker here?"

He flashed her a faintly mocking smile. "In a manner of speaking. Are you lost?" She had the impression he was impatient to get on with what he'd been doing before she'd trespassed unannounced. Twilight was deepening into night, obscuring the details of his striking features.

"No. I planned to come here in the morning, but my curiosity wouldn't let me wait that long to get a sneak preview."

His dark-fringed eyes studied her with toe-curling intensity. For once she wished she were a tall, lovely brunette like her mom instead of your average Swedish blonde with generic blue eyes, her legacy from the Lofgren gene pool.

"If you're a Realtor for an American client, I'm afraid the property isn't for sale."

She frowned. "I'm here for a different reason. This *is* the Château de Belles Fleurs, isn't it?"

He gave an almost imperceptible nod, drawing her attention to his head of overly long dark hair with just enough curl she wagered her balding father would kill for.

"I'm anxious to meet the present owner, Monsieur Alexandre Fleury Martin."

After an odd silence he said, "You're speaking to him."

"Oh—I'm sorry. I didn't realize."

He folded his strong arms, making her acutely aware of his stunning male aura. "How do you know my name?"

"I came across a French link to your advertisement on the Internet."

At her explanation his hard-muscled body seemed to tauten. "Unfortunately too many tourists have seen it and decided to include a drop-in visit on their 'see-France-in-seven-days' itinerary."

Uh-oh— Her uninvited presence had touched a nerve. She lifted her oval chin a trifle. "Perhaps you should get a guard dog, or lock the outer gate with a sign that says, No Trespassing."

"Believe me, I'm considering both."

She bit her lip. "Look—this has started off all wrong and it's my fault." When he didn't respond she said, "My name is Dana Lofgren. If you're a movie buff, you may have seen *The Belgian Connection*, one of the films my father directed."

He rubbed his chest without seeming to be conscious of it. "I didn't know Jan Lofgren had a daughter."

Most people didn't except for those in the industry who worked with her father. Of course if Dana had been born with a face and body to die for…

She smiled, long since resigned to being forgettable. "Why would you? I help my father behind the scenes. The moment I saw your ad, I flew from Los Angeles to check out your estate. He's working on the film right now, but isn't happy with the French locations available."

Dana heard him take a deep breath. "You should have e-mailed me you were coming so I could have met you in Angers. It's too late to see anything tonight."

"I didn't expect to meet you until tomorrow," she said, aware she'd angered him without meaning to. "Forgive me for scouting around without your permission. I wanted to get a feel for the place in the fading light."

"And did you?" he fired. It was no idle question.

"Yes."

The silly tremor in her voice must have conveyed her emotion over the find because he said, "We'll talk about it over dinner. I haven't had mine yet. Where are you staying tonight?"

Considering her major faux pas for intruding on his privacy, she was surprised there was going to be one. "I made a reservation at the Hermitage in Chanzeaux."

"Good. That's not far from here. I'll change

my clothes and follow you there in my car. Wait for me in yours and lock the doors."

The enigmatic owner accompanied her to the rental car. As he opened the door for her, their arms brushed, sending a surprising curl of warmth through her body.

"I won't be long."

She watched his tall, well-honed physique disappear around the end of the hedge. Obviously there was a path, but she hadn't noticed. There'd been too much to take in.

Now an unexpected human element had been added. It troubled her that she was still reacting to the contact. She thought she'd already learned her lesson about men.

Alex signaled the waiter. "Bring us your best house wine, *s'il vous plaît.*"

"*Oui, monsieur.*"

When he'd come up with his idea to rent out the estate to film studios in order to make a lot of money fast, he hadn't expected a Hollywood company featuring a legendary director like Jan Lofgren to take an interest this soon, if ever.

He'd only been advertising the château for six weeks. Not every film company wanted a place this run-down. To make it habitable, he'd had new tubs, showers, toilets and sinks installed in both the bathroom off the second floor vestibule and behind the kitchen.

Alex needed close access to the outside for himself and any workmen he hired, not to mention the film crews and actors. The ancient plumbing in both bathrooms had to be pulled out. He'd spent several days replacing corroded pipes with new ones that met modern code.

Since then, three different studios from Paris had already done some sequence shots along the river using the château in the background, but they were on limited budgets.

It would take several years of that kind of continual traffic to fatten his bank account to the amount he needed. By then the deadline for the taxes owing would have passed and he would forfeit the estate.

So far, at least fifty would-be investors ranging from locals to foreigners were dying to get their hands on it so they could turn it into a hotel. One of them included the attorney who'd sent out the letter, but Alex had no intention of letting his mother's inheritance go if he could help it.

With the natural blonde beauty seated across from him, it was possible he could shorten the time span for that happening. There was hope yet. She hadn't been turned off by what she'd seen or she wouldn't be eating dinner with him now. Her father was a huge moneymaker for the producers. His films guaranteed a big budget. Alex was prepared to go out on a limb for her.

Dana Lofgren didn't look older than twenty-two, twenty-three, yet age could be deceptive. She might be young, but being the director's only child she'd grown up with him and knew him as no one else did or could. If she thought the estate had promise, her opinion would carry a lot of weight with him. Hopefully word of mouth would spread to other studios.

After spending all day every day clearing away tons of brush and debris built up around the château over four decades, her unexplained presence no matter how feminine or attractive, hadn't helped his foul mood. That was before he realized she had a legitimate reason for looking around, even if she'd wandered in uninvited.

"How did you like your food?"

She lifted flame-blue eyes to him. With all that silky gold hair and a cupid mouth, she reminded him of a cherub, albeit a grown-up one radiating a sensuality of which she seemed totally unaware. "The chateaubriand was delicious."

"That's good. I've sampled all their entrées

and can assure you the meals here will keep any film crew happy."

His dinner companion wiped the corner of her mouth with her napkin. "I can believe it. One could put on a lot of weight staying here for any length of time. It's a good thing I'm not a film star."

An underweight actress might look good in front of the camera, but Alex preferred a woman who looked healthy, like this one whose cheeks glowed a soft pink in the candlelight.

"No ambition in that department?"

"None."

He believed her. "What *are* you, when you're not helping your father?"

The bleak expression in her eyes didn't match her low chuckle. "That's a good question."

"Let me rephrase it. What is it you do in your spare time?"

The waiter brought their crème brûlée to the table. She waited until he'd poured them more wine before answering Alex. "Nothing of report. I read and play around with cooking. Otherwise my father forgets to eat."

"You live with him?"

Instead of answering him, she sipped the wine experimentally. Mmm…it was so sweet. She took a bite of custard from the ramekin, then drank more. He could tell she loved it. "This could become addicting."

Alex enjoyed watching her savor her meal. "If I seemed to get too personal just now, it's because the widowed grandfather I never knew threw my mother out of the château when she was about your age. Both of them died without ever seeing each other again."

Her ringless fingers tightened around the stem of her wineglass. "Since my mother died of cancer five years ago, my father and I have gone the rounds many times, but it hasn't come to that yet." She took another sip. "The fact is, whether we're at home or on location, which is most of the time, he needs a keeper."

Amused by her last comment he said, "It's nice to hear of a father-daughter relationship that works. You're both fortunate."

A subtle change fell over her. "Your mother's story is very tragic. If you don't mind my asking, what caused such a terrible breach?"

Maybe it was his imagination but she sounded sincere in wanting to know.

"Gaston Fleury lost his only son in war, causing both my grandparents to wallow in grief. When my grandmother died, he gave up living, even though he had a daughter who would have done anything for him. The more she tried to love him, the colder he became.

"Obviously he'd experienced some kind of mental breakdown because he turned inward, unable to love anyone. He forgot his daughter existed and became a total recluse, letting everything go including his household staff. When my mother tried to work with him, he told her to get out. He didn't need anyone."

In the telling, his dinner companion's eyes developed a fine sheen. What was going on inside her?

"Horrified by the change in him, she made the decision to marry my father, who'd come to France on vacation. They moved to Queensland, Australia, where he was born."

"Is your father still there?"

"No. He died in a fatal car accident seven months ago."

She stirred restlessly. "You've been through a lot of grief."

"It's life, as you've found out."

"Yes," she murmured.

"My father's animosity toward my grandfather was so great, he didn't tell me the whole story until after mother died of an infection two years ago. Gaston never wrote or sent for her, so she never went back for a visit, not even after I was born. The pain would have been too great. It explained her lifelong sadness."

Earnest eyes searched his. "Growing up you must have wondered," she whispered.

He nodded. "To make a long story short, in May a letter meant for Mother fell into my hands. The attorney for the abandoned Belles Fleurs estate had been trying to find her. When I spoke with him personally he told me my grandfather had died in a government institution and was buried in an unmarked grave."

She shook her head. "That's awful."

"Agreed. If she didn't fly to France for a probate hearing, the property would be turned over to the government for years of back taxes owing. It consisted of a neglected château and grounds. I discovered very quickly the whole estate is half buried in vegetation like one of those Mayan temples in Central America."

The corners of her mouth lifted. "A perfect simile."

"However, something inside me couldn't let it go without a fight. That meant I needed to make money in a hurry. So I came up with the idea of renting out the property to film studios."

She eyed him frankly. "That was a brilliant

move on your part for which my father will be ecstatic. You're a very resourceful man. I hope your ad continues to bring you all the business you need in order to hold on to it."

Dana Lofgren was a refreshing change from most women of his acquaintance who came on to him without provocation. While they'd eaten a meal together, she'd listened to him without giving away much about herself.

Alex couldn't tell if it was a defense mechanism or simply the way she'd been born, but the fact remained she'd come as a pleasant surprise on many levels. He found he didn't want the evening to end, but sensed she was ready to say good-night.

When he'd finished his wine, he put some bills on the table. "After your long flight and the drive from Paris, you have to be exhausted. What time would you like to come to the château tomorrow?"

"Early, if that's all right with you. Maybe 8:00 a.m.?"

An early bird. Alex liked doing business early. *"Bon."* He pushed himself away from the table and stood up. "I'll be waiting for you in the drive. *Bonuit, mademoiselle.*"

* * *

Monsieur Martin not only intrigued Dana, but he'd left her with a lot to think about. In fact, the tragedy he'd related had shaken her. His mother had become invisible to her own father, too. There were too many similarities to Dana's life she didn't want to contemplate.

She finished the last of her wine, upset with herself for letting Monsieur Martin's male charisma prompt her to get more personal with him and prod him for details about his family. That was how she'd gotten into trouble with Neal. He'd pretended to be flattered by all her interest. She'd thought they were headed toward something permanent until she realized it was her father who'd brought him around in the first place—that, and his ambition.

Of course there was a big difference here. Neal had used her in the hope of acting in one of her father's films. She on the other hand had flown to France because Monsieur Martin had advertised his property for a specific clientele. Dana wanted a service from *him*. The two situations weren't comparable.

Neither were the two men….

At her first sight of the striking owner, Dana was convinced she'd come upon the château of the sleeping prince, and *that* before the wine had put her in such a mellow mood. But their subsequent conversation soon jerked her out of that fantasy.

He was a tough, intelligent businessman of substance with an aura of authority she would imagine intimidated most men. Maybe even her own scary parent. That would be something to witness.

Disciplining herself not to eat the last few bites of custard, she left the dining room and went to her room. She could phone her father tonight with the good news. He'd be awake by now expecting her call, unless he'd spent the night with Saskia, which was a strong possibility.

All things considered, she decided to get in touch with him tomorrow after she'd met with Monsieur Martin again.

After getting ready for bed, she set her alarm for 7:00 a.m. She was afraid she'd sleep in otherwise, but to her surprise, Dana awoke before it went off because she was too excited for the day.

She took a shower and washed her hair. Her neck-length layered cut fell into place fast using her blow-dryer. Afterward she put on her favorite Italian blouse. It was a dark blue cotton jersey with a high neck and three-quarter sleeves, casual yet professional.

She teamed it with beige voile pants and Italian bone-colored sandals. Since she was only five foot five, she hoped the straight-leg style gave the illusion of another inch of height. Dana was built curvy like her mother. Being around Monsieur Martin, she could have wished for a few more inches from her father who stood six-one. Barring that, all she could do was keep a straight carriage.

With her bag packed, she headed for the dining room where rolls and coffee were being served. She grabbed a quick breakfast, then walked out to talk to a woman at the front desk Dana hadn't seen yesterday. "*Bonjour*, madame."

"*Bonjour, madame*. How can I help you?"

"I'm checking out." After she'd handed her back the credit card, Dana said, "Last night I drank a wonderful white wine in the restaurant and would like to buy a bottle to take home with me." Her father would love it. "Could you tell me the name of it?"

"*Bien sur*. We only stock one kind. It's the Domaine Coteaux du Layon Percher made right here in the Anjou."

"It's one of the best wines I ever tasted."

"In my opinion, Percher is better than the other brands from this area. Sadly the most cele-brated of them was the Domaine Belles Fleurs, but it stopped being produced eighty years ago."

Dana's body quickened. The woman did say Belles Fleurs. "Do you know why?"

She leaned closer. "Bad family blood." Dana had gathered as much already. There'd been a complete break between Monsieur Martin's mother and her father, but he hadn't mentioned anything else. "It's an ugly business fighting over who had the rights to what."

"I agree."

"The present owner has only lived in the vicinity a month or so," the woman confided. "The château has been deserted for many years."

So Monsieur Martin had told her. "It's very sad."

"*C'est la vie, madame,*" she said with typical Gallic fatalism. "Would you like to buy a bottle of the Percher?"

"I—I've changed my mind," her voice faltered. It would seem a betrayal.

"Is there anything else I can do for you?"

"No, *merci.*"

Dana turned away and left the hotel. She was in a much more subdued frame of mind as she drove the five or so kilometers to the bridge where the trees cast more shadows across the road. The morning light coming from the opposite side of a pale blue sky created a totally different atmosphere from the night before.

This time as she reached the fork in the road, Monsieur Martin was there to greet her. It sent her pulse racing without her permission. She pulled to a stop.

He walked toward her, dressed in white cargo pants and a burgundy colored crewneck, but it didn't matter what he wore, she found him incredibly appealing. It wasn't just the attractive arrangement of his hard-boned features, or midnight-brown eyes framed by dark brows.

The man had an air of brooding detachment that added to her fascination. Combined with his sophistication, she imagined most women meeting him would have fantasies about him.

Under the influence of the wine, Dana had already entertained a few of her own last night. However, because of her experience with Neal, plus the fact that she was clearheaded this morning, she was determined to conduct business without being distracted.

"*Bonjour*, Monsieur Martin."

When he put his tanned hands on the door

frame, the scent of the soap he'd used in the shower infiltrated below her radar. "My name's Alex. You don't mind if I call you Dana?" His voice sounded lower this morning, adding to his male sensuality.

"I'd prefer it."

"Bien." He walked around to the passenger side of her car and adjusted the seat to accommodate his long legs before climbing in. His proximity trapped the air in her lungs. "Take the left fork. It will wind around to the front of the château."

Old leaves built up over time covered the winding driveway. It was flanked on both sides by trees whose unruly tops met overhead like a Gothic arch. Dana followed until it led to a clearing where she got her first look at the small eighteenth-century château built in the classic French style.

Beyond the far end stood an outbuilding made of the same limestone and built in the same design, half camouflaged by more overgrown shrubs and foliage. No doubt it housed the wine-press and vats.

She shut off the engine and climbed out to feast her eyes. He followed at a slower pace.

The signs of age and neglect showed up in

full force. There were boards covering the grouped stacks of broken windows. Several steps leading to the elegant entry were chipped or cracked. Repairs needed to be done to the high-sloped slate roof. It was difficult to tell where the weed-filled gardens filled with tiny yellow lilies ended and the woods encroached.

Dana took it all in, seeing it through her father's eyes. She knew what the original script called for. This was so perfect she thought she must be dreaming.

"It's like seeing a woman of the night on the following morning when her charms are no longer in evidence," came his grating voice. Trust a man to come up with that analogy. "Not what you had in mind after all?"

Schooling herself not to react to his cynicism, she turned to her host, having sensed a certain tension emanating from him. "On the contrary. It will do better than you can imagine. Knowing how my father works, he'll need three weeks here. How soon can you give the studio that much time?"

CHAPTER TWO

FEW things had surprised Alex in life, but twice in the last eighteen hours Dana Lofgren had taken him unawares.

"I have nothing signed and sealed yet. Is the season of vital importance?"

Her nod caused her hair to gleam in the sun like fine gold mesh. "It has to be late summer. Right now if possible," she said, looking all around, "but maybe that's asking too much."

"Don't worry. It's available. My next tentative booking so far is with a Paris studio that won't be needing it until mid-September."

"Good," she murmured, almost as if she'd forgotten he was there.

"Are you ready to see the interior?"

"No." She sounded far away. "I'll leave that to my father. I've seen what's important to him.

The estate possesses that intangible atmosphere he's striving for. I knew it as I drove in last night.

"Over the years of watching him work I've learned he doesn't like too much information. If I were to paint pictures, he'd see them in his mind. They would interfere with his own creative process." She suddenly turned and flashed him a quick smile. "His words, not mine."

Alex couldn't help smiling back. She had to be made of strong stuff to handle her father whose ego was probably bigger than his reputation. "Such trust in you implies a spiritual connection I think."

"I would say it has more to do with our mutual love of history. When I leave, I'll phone him and let him know what I've found. Before the day is out you'll hear from two people."

This fast she'd made her decision? Alex couldn't remember meeting anyone like her before. Did she always function on impulse, or just where her father was concerned? "I'll be waiting."

"Sol Arnevitz handles the financial arrangements. Paul Soleri is in charge of everything and everyone else when we're on location. Paul will go over the logistics and has the ability to smooth out any problem. You'll like *him*."

"As opposed to…"

She made a face. "Who else?"

Meaning her father of course. Dana Lofgren was a woman who didn't take herself too seriously. Despite what he assumed was a ten-year age difference between them, he feared she was growing on him at a time when he couldn't afford distractions.

"What more can I do for you this morning?"

"Not another thing." But her blue eyes burned with questions she didn't articulate, piquing his interest. "Thank you for dinner last night and your time this morning. It's been a real pleasure, Alex. Expect to hear from Sol right away. Here's his business card." She handed it to him. "He'll work out all the details with you."

To his shock she got in her car before he could help her.

"Where are you going in such a hurry?" He wasn't ready to let her go yet.

"A daughter's work is never done. I have to be in Paris this afternoon, then I'll fly back to L.A. Enjoy your solitude before everyone descends on you."

The next thing he knew she'd turned around and had driven off, leaving him strangely bereft and more curious than ever about her association with a father who was bigger than life in her eyes. Alex saw the signs. Ten, twenty, even thirty years from now he had a hunch Jan Lofgren's hold on her would still be powerful.

He stared blindly into space. Whether strongly present in Dana's life, or deliberately absent as Gaston Fluery had been in his daughter's life, both fathers wielded an enormous impact. The thought disturbed Alex in ways he'd rather not examine.

An hour later, after he'd changed clothes and had begun cutting down more overgrowth, his cell phone rang. It could be anyone, but in case it was Dana, he pulled it out of his pants pocket. The ID indicated a call from the States. He clicked on. "Alex Martin speaking."

"Mr. Martin? This is Pyramid Pictures Film Studio calling from Hollywood, California. If it's convenient Mr. Sol Arnevitz would like to set up a conference call with you and Mr. Paul Soleri before he goes to bed at eleven this evening. It's 7:00 p.m. now. Mr. Lofgren heard from his daughter and is anxious to move on this."

Alex was anxious, too, for several reasons. "Eight o'clock your time would work for me."

"Very good. Expect their call then."

After twenty more minutes loading the truck, Alex went back to the château and entered through a side door leading into the kitchen. He washed his hands, then poured himself a cup of coffee before carrying it to the ornate salon off the foyer, which he'd turned into a temporary bedroom-cum-office. He liked living with the few furnishings of his parents he'd had shipped.

The salon's original furniture was still stored on the top floor. Once he'd made inroads on the outside of the château, he would concentrate on the house itself, that is if he made enough money in time. For now he'd supplied himself with the necessities for living here: electricity, cable and Internet, running water hot and cold, a new water heater, a stove, a fridge, washer and dryer and a new bed with a king-size mattress and box springs.

He snagged the swivel chair with his foot and sat down at his desk. No sooner had he booted up his computer than his call came through. Once the other two men introduced themselves, they made short work of the negotiations. The company would be on location from August 8 through 31. Sol quoted a ballpark figure, but left it open because other expenses always accrued.

Alex didn't know if Dana had anything to do with the actual amount, but it was a far greater sum than he'd hoped for. Sol sent him a fax, making the contract official before he rang off.

Paul stayed on the line with him for another twenty minutes. They discussed logistics for the cameramen and staff. Alex e-mailed him a list of hotels, car rental agencies and other businesses in and around Angers such as Chanzeaux.

"Chanzeaux?" the other man said. "Dana mentioned she stayed at a hotel there last night. I believe it was the Hermitage. According to her it's the perfect place for her father."

It pleased Alex she'd given her seal of approval. "The food's exceptionally good there. Mr. Lofgren should be very comfortable."

"Since we're behind schedule as it is, we all want that," he admitted with a dry laugh that spoke volumes about Dana's father. "The crew will arrive day after tomorrow. Everyone else the day after. I look forward to meeting you, Alex."

"The feeling's mutual."

After clicking off, he headed outside again. Dana would be back in a few days, this time with her father. Over the years Alex had been involved in various relationships with women, but he'd never found himself thinking ahead to the next meeting with this kind of anticipation. He had no answer as to why this phenomenon was suddenly happening now.

* * *

During the taxi ride to the house, Dana phoned Sol whose secretary told him the contract with Mr. Martin had been signed. Relieved on that score she called Paul, wanting to touch base with him before she saw her father.

"Hey, Dana— Are you back already?"

"Yes, but only long enough to pack before I leave again. Sol says everything's ready to go."

"That's right. I've got us booked at three hotels fairly close together. Just so you know, the Hermitage didn't have any vacancies, but with a little monetary incentive I managed to arrange adjoining rooms for you and your father for the month."

She smiled. "You're indispensable, Paul."

"Tell your father that."

"I don't need to." Except that nobody told Jan Lofgren anything. Little did Paul know that even though he'd arranged a hotel room somewhere else for Saskia, she'd probably end up staying with Dana's father. "Listen, Paul—I'm almost at the house so I've got to go. Talk to you later."

"*Ciao*, Dana."

After she hung up, her mind focused on her own sleeping arrangements. Since the film studio had the run of the estate until the end of August, Dana decided she would stay in the deserted château away from everyone. When else in her life would she get a chance like this? She'd buy a sleeping bag. It would be a lark to camp out inside.

Her dad wouldn't need her except to do the odd job for him and bring him lunch. Once he settled in for work each day, he hated having to leave with the others to go eat. Maybe he used it as an excuse to be alone with his own thoughts for an hour. Who knew?

What mattered was that she'd have most of her time free to explore the countryside and only come back at dark to go to sleep. Her thoughts wandered to Alex. She wondered where he was staying. The concierge at the Hermitage indicated he lived in the vicinity. Considering the taxes he owed, she imagined he'd found a one-star hotel in order to keep his expenses down. It made her happy that the film company would be giving him a financial boost. He—

"Miss?"

Dana blinked. "Oh—yes! I'm sorry." They'd reached her family's modern rancho-styled home in Hollywood Hills without her being aware he'd stopped the taxi. She paid him and got out.

Just in case her father had brought Saskia home,

she rang the doorbell several times before letting herself in. After ascertaining she was alone, Dana took off her shoes and padded into the kitchen to sort through the mail and fix some lunch.

The clock in the hall chimed once, reminding her France was nine hours ahead of California time. She doubted Alex would be in bed yet. Was he out with a beautiful woman tonight? And what if he was?

For a man she'd barely met, Dana couldn't believe how he'd gotten under her skin so fast. It was that unexpected invitation to dinner with him. He didn't have to take the time, but the fact that he did made him different from the other men she'd known. She found him not only remarkable, but disturbingly attractive.

While she finished the last of her peanut butter and jelly sandwich, she reached for her mother's favorite French cookbook from the shelf. It wasn't a cookbook exactly. It was a very delightful true story about an American family living in France in 1937. Quite by accident they met a French woman who came to cook for them.

Everything you ever wanted to know about France was in it, including French phrases. It was full of recipes and little drawings, so much better than a Michelin guide. Both Dana and her mom had read it many times, marveling over a slice of history captured in the account. Dana would pack this with her.

In the act of opening the cover, warm memories of her mother assailed her. A lump stayed lodged in her throat all the way to the bedroom where she flung herself on the bed to thumb through it. Chanzeaux looked just like the adorable villages in the book with their open-air markets selling the most amazing items. She rolled over on her back, wondering about Alex. Having lived on the other side of the world, did he find France as charming as she did?

There were many questions she'd like to ask him, but she'd already probed too much. Anything more she learned *he* would have to volunteer when they happened to see each other. He could be slightly forbidding. It would be wise to stay out of his way. That went for her father, too, except to feed him.

Oh, yes, and remind him to go to the local hospital for his weekly blood test. No one would believe what a baby he was, which reminded her she'd better check the medicine cabinet and make sure he had enough blood thinner medication to be gone two months. After they left France, they'd finish up the filming in Germany where Dana had already checked out the locations ahead of time.

With a sigh she got up from the bed needing to do a dozen things, but a strong compulsion led her to the den first. Ever since she'd heard that the Fleury family had once produced wine, she wanted to learn what she could about it. The wine she'd had with Alex had left the taste of nectarines on her lips. As she'd told him that night, it could become addicting.

She typed in Anjou wine, France. Dozens of Web sites popped up. She clicked on the first one.

The Anjou is one of the subregions of the Loire Valley producing a variety of dry to sweet dessert wines. The two main regions for Chenin Blanc are found in Touraine and along the Layon river where the soil is rich in limestone and tuffeau. Long after you've tasted this wine, it will give up a stone-fruit flavor on the palate. The Dutch merchants in the sixteen hundreds traded for this wine.

That far back?

Fascinated by the information, Dana researched a little more.

Coteaux du Layon near the river is an area in Anjou where the vines are protected by the hills. It's best known for its sweet wines, some of the recipes going back fifteen centuries. By the late seventeen hundreds, several wine producers became dominant in the region including the Domaine du Rochefort, Domaine du Château Belles Fleurs and Domaine Percher.

There it was, part of Alex's family history. Dana's father would find the information riveting, as well, but for the meantime she'd keep it to herself. The owner was a private person. It would be best if she waited until he brought it up in the conversation, if he ever did.

A few minutes later she'd gone back to her room to do her packing. She had it down to a science, fitting everything into one suitcase. As she was about to leave and do some errands, her father came home and poked his head in the door. "There you are."

She looked up at him. "Hi."

"You just got back. How come you're packing again so soon?"

Dana had anticipated his question. "I'm going to fly to Paris with the camera guys in the morning."

"Why?"

"Because Saskia will be a lot happier if she has you to herself when you fly out the day after tomorrow."

"Saskia doesn't run my life," he declared.

No one ran his life. Dana certainly didn't figure in it except to fetch for him, but the actress didn't like her. "I know that, but it doesn't hurt to keep the troops happy, does it?" She flashed him a smile, hoping to ease the tension, maybe provoke a smile, but all she provoked was a frown.

"You really think you found the right place?" he asked morosely.

The film was on his mind, nothing or no one else. Until he saw the estate, he'd be impossible to live with. Good luck to Saskia. "If I haven't, Paul will switch us back to Plan B outside Paris without problem."

After staring into space for another minute he said, "Have you seen my reading glasses?"

"They're on the kitchen counter, next to the script. Have you eaten?"

"I don't remember."

"I'll fix you some eggs and toast."

"That's a good girl," he muttered, before leaving her alone.

He only said that if he needed something from her. Because he was a narcissist, it was all she would get. She knew that, yet because their natures were exact opposites, a part of her would always want more. Still, when she thought of

Alex's mother being cut off by her father, Dana realized her relationship with her father hadn't degenerated to that extent. Not yet…

Alex was in his bedroom when the phone rang again. He'd just hung up from talking with another Realtor who hadn't heard the estate wasn't for sale and never had been. They never stopped hounding him. With each call he'd hoped it might be Dana.

"Monsieur Martin *ici*."

"*Bonjour*, Alex."

His lips twitched. Her accent needed help, but with a grown-up rosebud mouth like hers, no Frenchman would care. "*Bonjour*, Dana. How are things in Hollywood?"

"I wouldn't know. How are things in that jungle of yours?"

Laughter burst out of him. "Prickly."

"My condolences."

"Where are you exactly?"

"In front of the château."

He felt a burst of adrenaline kick in.

"I was hoping you would let me in, but considering your plight, I'll be happy to come back after you and your machete have emerged."

The chuckles kept on coming. "I'm closer than

you think. Don't go away." He hung up and strode swiftly through the foyer.

As soon as he opened the front door of the chateau, she got out of the car. Today she was dressed in jeans and a white short-sleeved top. If the pale blue vest she wore over it was meant to hide the lovely mold of her body, it failed.

Though she gave the appearance of being calm and collected, he noticed a pulse throbbing too fast at her throat. He knew in his gut she was glad to see him.

"When did you fly into Paris?"

"At six-thirty this morning with the camera guys. When their rooms are ready, they'll crash until tomorrow, then probably show up around eight in the morning to start checking things out."

"What about your father?"

"Everyone else will arrive at different times tomorrow."

"I see. He didn't mind you coming on ahead?"

"Most of the time we do our own thing." She gave him a direct glance as if daring him to contradict her.

Alex had asked enough questions for now. It was almost noon. "Let's get you inside. In case you'd like to freshen up, there's a bathroom on the second floor at the head of the stairs."

"Thank you."

Dana followed him up the steps into the foyer dominated by the central stonework staircase. With no furniture, paintings, tapestries or rugs visible, the château was a mere skeleton, but she seemed mesmerized.

Taking advantage of her silence he said, "The place was denuded years ago. Everything is stored on the third level where the servants used to live."

He watched her eyes travel from the walls' decorative Italianate paneling to the inlaid wood floors. "There's a chandelier packed away that should hang over the staircase. Without it the château is dark at night. I told Paul that if night interiors are called for, he'll need to plan for extra lighting. Your father—"

"My father's very superstitious," she broke in on a different tack. "He gets that from his Swedish ancestry. When he stands where I'm standing, he'll be frightened at first."

"Frightened?"

"Yes." She turned to him. "It's always frightening for a figment of your imagination to come to life, don't you think? At first he won't know if it's a good or bad omen."

When her father saw the château, he would be

speechless. His excitement wouldn't be obvious to the casual observer, but she'd see his eyes flicker and feel his positive energy radiate. For a while it would insulate him from his usual irritations. Even Saskia wouldn't grate on his nerves as much, at least not at first. But that was *his* problem. Dana had done her part.

"Would you mind being more explicit?" Everything she said intrigued Alex. Besides her shape and coloring that appealed strongly to his senses, she had an inquiring mind. It engendered an excitement inside him that was building in momentum.

"My father gave his favorite screen writer some ideas and they collaborated on the script for this wartime film. Your château and grounds could have been made for it. For some time I've had the feeling this is the most important project he's ever taken on."

He folded his arms. "Can you tell me about it, or is it a secret?"

"A secret? No." After a pause. "The film is filled with the kind of angst my father is best known for." He heard her breathe in deeply. "Does that explanation help?"

"About the setting, yes, but I'm curious about the story itself."

She gave a gentle shrug of her shoulders. "That's for my father to decide. I don't think he knows it all yet." As far as Alex was concerned, she was being evasive for a reason. "Dad's had a mind block lately. It's made him more irritable than usual. It will take settling into it here for those creative juices to flow again. But to give you a specific answer to your question, his films always leave the audience asking more questions."

That was the truth, but she was holding back from him and that made him more curious than ever. Evidently she knew better than to give too much away. Was that because her father wouldn't like it? "Why do you think he came up with this particular story?"

"How does any author come up with an idea? They see something, hear something that arouses their interest and a kernel of an idea starts to form."

She angled her head toward him. "Part of it could be the guilt he personally feels for his country's compliance with the enemy in the first days of World War II. Another part might be that deep down he still misses mother and wishes he'd had a son instead of '*moi.*'"

She'd said it with a smile, but Alex felt the words like a blow to the gut. He'd heard empti-ness, sadness in that last remark. It made him want to comfort her. "Still, I have my uses. Thanks to you, I found *this* for him." She spread her hands, as if encompassing the entire château. "Heaven sent."

Alex swallowed hard. "For me, too."

"I'm happy if it helps you. I bet your mother is, too."

She kept surprising him. "You believe in heaven, Dana?"

"Yes. Don't you?"

"After this discussion, I want to."

A faint blush filled her cheeks. "I'm afraid I've rattled on too long and have kept you from your work. Please go ahead and do whatever you were doing. If it's all right, I'll just wander around here for a little while before I take a nap. I picked up a sleeping bag in Angers and brought it with me."

Why would she do that? "If you're that exhausted, I'll call the Hermitage and tell them to get your room ready now."

"No doubt they'd make concessions for you, but I'm not staying there, so it's not necessary. Thank you anyway."

Alex rubbed the back of his neck in an unconscious gesture. "Paul told me he would arrange rooms there for you and your father."

"He already has, but while I'm in France I intend to be on my own most of the time. After everyone goes home at the end of the day's shoot, I plan to stay right here where I can have the whole château to myself."

An angry laugh escaped his throat. "I'm afraid that's impossible."

She flashed him an ingenuous smile. "Don't worry about me. I don't frighten easily and love being alone."

His eyes narrowed. Dana had seemed such an innocent she'd almost fooled him. "I'm afraid you don't understand," he ground out. "My ad didn't indicate the château could be used for anything but the filming."

A long silence ensued while she digested what he'd said. "I assumed that since the company had rented the estate for the filming, it wouldn't matter if I found myself a little spot in the château to sleep at night." Her supple body stiffened. "My mistake, Alex. I'm glad you cleared it up before any harm was done."

"Dana—"

She'd almost reached the front door before turning around. "Yes?"

He started toward her. "Where are you going?"

"To find me a place to stay."

"Wouldn't you be better off with your father?" he asked quietly.

"You want your pound of flesh, don't you." Her cheeks filled with angry color. "First of all, if I were seventeen I'd agree with you, but I'm going to be twenty-seven next week, slightly too long in the tooth to still be daddy's little girl."

His estimation of her age had been way off.

"Secondly, my father isn't in his dotage yet. In fact, his latest love interest is one of the actresses in the film and will be sleeping with him, which makes three a crowd. When you see Saskia, you'll understand a lot of things." She smiled. "If my dad ever found out your impression of him, he'd have a coronary."

Alex hadn't seen that one coming. It knocked him sideways.

"Thirdly, while I'm in this glorious region of France, I'd like to pretend I'm an independent woman who needs to spread her own wings for a change. It must have given you an uncomfortable moment thinking I'd made you my target. Again, I apologize."

He'd anticipated her flight and moved in time to prevent her from opening the door. Their hips brushed against each other in the process, increasing his awareness of her womanly attributes. The tension between them was palpable. She slowly backed away from him.

The last thing he'd wanted was to make an enemy of her, but that's what he'd done. One word to her father and he could kiss this deal goodbye. The hell of it was, he couldn't afford to lose this film studio's business, not when he needed the money so badly. A large portion of his life's savings combined with the modest inheritance from his father were all invested in this venture.

"Dana—it never occurred to me you might want to stay in the château."

She refused to look at him. "You're not a dreamer."

"You'd be surprised, but that's not the point." Trying to gauge what her reaction would be he said, "I live here."

Her gaze flew to his. By the stunned look in those blue depths, he knew instinctively his revelation had come as a surprise.

"The concierge at the Hermitage intimated you lived somewhere in the vicinity. To me that ruled out the château…" Her voice trailed.

Alex's first impression of the French woman in Chanzeaux had been right. She was a busybody. When Dana's father arrived and she learned of his importance, it would bring a flood of unwanted curiosity seekers to the estate. His mouth thinned in irritation. He would have to fit the gate with an electronic locking device to give the film company privacy while they were working. Today, if possible.

"I'm afraid there's been a lot of speculation about me since I flew in from Bali."

"Bali— What were you doing there?"

"My work. I'm an agricultural engineer."

She rubbed her palms against womanly hips, as if she didn't know what to do with them. "Are you taking a sabbatical of sorts then?"

"No. I resigned in order to settle mother's estate before leaving for the States."

Following his remark she said, "Then you're only in France temporarily."

"Very temporarily, even if my business venture should succeed—" he drawled.

"What is your plan exactly?"

"To restore the château and grounds to a point that the estate can be put on display alongside the others in the area. Millions of tourists pour into France each year willing to pay entry fees for a look around. With a couple of full-time caretakers, it could prove to be a smart business investment, leaving me free to pursue my career overseas."

Her expression had undergone a subtle change he couldn't decipher. "It's an ambitious undertaking, but with your work ethic I'm sure you'll make it happen." She glanced at her watch. "I need to go and let you get back to your work."

"Not so fast." He looked around before his gaze centered on her once more. "It does seem unconscionable not to let you live here when this was originally built to house several dozen people. Under the circumstances I *insist* you stay, but it means we share the château."

CHAPTER THREE

INSIST?

The provocative statement was backed by a steel tone, making her tremble. It seemed Alex Martin had changed his mind and was willing to let her stay here. Not willing, she amended. Determined all of a sudden.

Why?

Maybe like Neal he could see himself making a lot more money to save the château if he starred in a film. He was gorgeous enough to be a top box office draw, yet the mere idea that he saw Dana as a stepping stone to influence her father made her so ill, she shuddered.

If she was wrong about his motive, then for the life of her she couldn't think what the reason might be. The man could have any woman he wanted.

Alex's dark brows knit together. "Why so reticent now?"

The question coming from his compelling mouth was like a challenge wrapped up in a deceptively silky voice. It curled around Dana's insides down to her toes. If she didn't have to think about it, the idea of being under the same roof with Alex Martin for the next three weeks was so thrilling, she was ready to jump out of her skin.

But she *did* have to think about it for all the usual reasons of propriety, common sense and self-preservation—self-preservation especially because he could be moody and overbearing like her father, the very thing she'd wanted to get away from for a while.

And then there were the unusual reasons, like the fact that her father was coming here to direct the most important film of his career on her say-so alone. If she made a misstep with Alex now and he decided to renege on the contract, how would she explain it to her dad, let alone the rest of the company?

Money had changed hands. Too much was at stake on both men's parts for there to be trouble at this stage because of her.

When she'd declared that she wanted to be an independent woman and spread her own wings, she'd set herself up to be taken at her word and Alex had acted on it. He was probably laughing at her naïveté right now while he waited to hear that she'd changed her mind and didn't want to stay here after all.

The stakes were too high for her to turn this into a battle. An inner voice warned her there was wisdom in going along with him. Dana knew nothing like this would ever come her way again. Why not take him up on it? She wouldn't be human if she didn't avail herself of such an opportunity.

"Thank you, Alex. I'll do my best not to get underfoot." From now on she could fade into the shadows and be like Diane de Poitiers, Henri II's mistress at Chenonceau, who adored the château and oversaw the plantings of the flower and vegetable gardens.

Dana would glut herself on the history of Belles Fleurs, but wherever she slept, she would make certain it wasn't anywhere near Alex. When she'd called his château small, she'd meant it hadn't been built on the scale of Chambord with its 440 rooms, but it was big enough for her to get lost in.

An odd gleam in his dark eyes was the only sign that her answer had surprised him. "With that settled, shall we go upstairs? You can have your pick of any room on the second floor."

By tacit agreement they both started toward

the magnificent staircase. "How many are there?"

"Six."

While she was wondering where his room was located, he read her mind. "For the time being I've made the petit salon off the main foyer into a combined bedroom and office for me."

They'd be a floor apart. That was good. Of course when she wanted to go out for any reason, he'd be aware of her leaving through the front door, that is *if* and *when* he was around. After a few days of becoming aware of his routine, she'd make sure not to disturb him any more than she could help.

When they reached the long vestibule, she was overwhelmed by what she saw. "This is similar to the rib-vaulting at Chenonceau! It's utterly incredible!"

Alex nodded. "On a much smaller scale of course." She was conscious of his tall, hard-muscled frame as he continued walking to one end of the corridor on those long, powerful legs. "Let's start with the bedroom in the turret round."

"Oh—" she cried the second he opened the door and she took everything in. "This is the one I want!"

A smile broke the corner of his sensuous mouth. "You're sure? You haven't seen the others yet. The turret round on the other end has a fireplace."

"I'm positive. Look at these!" There were fleur-de-lis designs placed at random in the inlaid wood flooring. She got down on her knees to examine them.

"If the original designer of this château could see a modern-day woman like you studying his intricate workmanship this closely, he would be delighted by the sight."

"Go ahead and mock me," she said with a laugh before getting to her feet. For the next few minutes she threw her head back to study the cross-beamed ceiling. There were little white enamel ovals rimmed in gold placed every so often in the wood depicting flowers and various forest creatures. "How did they do that? How did they do any of this?"

She darted to the window that needed washing inside and out, but at least it wasn't broken. The entire room would require a good scrubbing to get rid of layers of accumulated dust. Even so there was a fabulous view of the countryside and a certain enchanted feel about the room. Eventually she turned to him. "Do you think this might have been your mother's?"

Her question seemed to make him more pensive and probably brought him pain. She wished she'd caught herself before blurting it out.

"My mother lived here until her early twenties. I have no idea which bedroom she occupied, but it wouldn't surprise me if it had been this one. The view of the Layon from the window at this angle is surreal."

"I noticed," Dana murmured. "I'm glad she met your father so she wasn't so lonely anymore."

Alex shifted his weight. "*Lonely* is an interesting choice of words."

"She would have been, wouldn't she? To know her father preferred her brother?"

"I'm sure you're right," he muttered. "Mother often seemed melancholy, at least that's what I called it, but you've hit on a better description. Even in a crowded room she sometimes gave off a feeling of loneliness that no doubt troubled my father, too."

"Forgive me for saying anything, Alex. It's none of my business. It must be the atmosphere here getting to me."

"You *are* your father's daughter after all, so it's understandable." She didn't detect anything more than slight amusement in his tone, thank heaven.

"If you'll tell me where to find some cleaning supplies, I'll get started in here before I bring up my sleeping bag."

He tilted his dark head. "I have a better idea. We'll drive into Angers in my truck and eat lunch. I need to pick up some items. While we're there, we'll get you a new mattress and box springs."

"You don't need to do that."

"I wouldn't allow you to stay here in a sleeping bag. After we come back, we'll clean the room together and I'll bring down a few pieces of furniture from storage. By sunset Rapunzel will be safely ensconced in her tower."

She chuckled to hide her excitement at spending the day with him, not to mention the rest of the month. "You're mixing up your fairy tales. I don't have long hair."

He gave an elegant shrug of his broad shoulders. "It's evident you haven't read the definitive version. Her father had her long golden tresses cut off so no prince could climb up to her."

A few succinct words dropped her dead in her tracks. In the tale Dana had grown up with, there'd been a wicked witch. Was he still teasing her, or had this tale suddenly taken on a life of its own. "Then how did the prince reach her?"

He paused in the doorway. "I guess you'll have to read the end of the story to find out."

His cryptic explanation was no help.

"I'll bring the truck around. When you've freshened up, meet me outside. I'll lock the door with my remote."

When she left the château a few minutes later, Alex was lounging against a blue pickup loaded with cut off branches and uprooted clumps of weeds. Dana marveled that he did this kind of backbreaking work without help. Pruning the grounds would be a Gargantuan task for half a dozen teams of gardeners, but he couldn't afford to hire help because the taxes were eating him alive.

She felt his dark fringed eyes wander over her as she came closer. They penetrated, causing her pulse to race. Still, everything would have been all right for the trip into town if their bodies hadn't brushed while he helped her inside the cab. Her breath caught and she feared he'd noticed. With nowhere to run, she had to sit there and behave like she didn't feel electrified.

"This won't take long," he said a few minutes later, jolting her out of her chaotic thoughts. They'd stopped at a landfill to dump the debris. Fortunately there was a man there ready to help him, making short work of it. Soon they were on their way again.

After driving this route several times already, Dana recognized some of the landmarks leading into Angers. The massive castle dominating the town on the Maine came into view.

"Have you been through it?"

She shook her head. "Not yet, but I plan to. What about you?"

"One look at the condition of the estate and any thoughts I had of playing tourist flew out the broken windows."

Dana flicked him a sideward glance. "You know what that old proverb says about Jack working all the time."

He surprised her by meeting her gaze head-on. "Are you by any chance intimating I'm a dull boy?"

"Maybe not dull…" Dana said, before she wished she hadn't.

"You can't leave me hanging now—" It came out more like a growl, but he was smiling. When he did that, he was transformed into the most attractive man she'd ever seen or met. There was no sign of the boy he would have once been, one probably not as carefree with a mother whose heart had been broken.

"As you reminded me earlier, you'll have to read to the end of the story to find out."

"Touché."

Dana was glad when he turned onto a side street and pulled up near a sidewalk café full of locals and tourists. She slid out of the cab before he could come around to help her.

There was one empty bistro table partially sheltered from the sun by an umbrella. Alex escorted her to it before anyone else grabbed it. The temperature had been mild earlier, but now it was hot. A waiter came right over and took their orders for sandwiches.

Alex eyed her. "I could use a cup of coffee, but maybe you'd prefer something cold. The air's more humid than usual today."

"Coffee sounds fine." The waiter nodded and disappeared. She sat back in her chair. "I thought most French people preferred tea."

"I grew up on coffee."

"No billy tea?" she teased, referring to his Aussie roots.

He shook his head, drawing her attention to the hair brushing his shirt collar. In the light she picked out several shades ranging from dark brown to black. "I'm afraid tea doesn't do it for me."

"Nor me." She smiled. "You seem so completely French, I forgot."

"It's a good thing *my* father isn't around to hear that."

After a brief silence she said, "When you want to go home, that's a long flight."

"I have no home in the traditional sense. My father's work took us many places. We globe-trotted. Mother died in the Côte D'Ivoire and father on Bali where we were both working for the same company at the time. They're buried in Brisbane."

Dana took a deep breath. "Well, you have a home now."

One dark eyebrow lifted. "A liability you mean. I'm not certain it's worth it."

She wished she could lighten his mood. "That's right. You have other plans. Where in the States?"

"Louisiana. It's where my particular expertise, such as it is, can be fully utilized."

"Are you in such a hurry then?"

The waiter served them their order before Alex responded. "I wasn't aware of it, but I suppose I am."

While he made inroads on the ham and cheese melt, she took a sip of the hot liquid. "Sounds like your father's lifestyle rubbed off on you."

The gaze he flicked her was surprisingly intense. "From the little you've told me about yourself, I'd say you've been similarly afflicted."

"Afflicted?" An odd choice of word. She stopped munching on her first bite. Of course she understood what he meant. Years of traveling around Europe finding locations for her father prevented her from staying in one spot. But it didn't mean that under the right circumstances, she couldn't settle down quite happily.

"Some people never leave the place they were born," he murmured. "I'm not so sure they haven't figured out life's most important secret."

She chuckled. "You mean, while nomads like us wander to and fro in search of what we don't know exactly?"

An amused glint entered his dark eyes. "Something like that."

"Well, given a choice, I'm glad I'm the way I am. Otherwise I wouldn't be living this fantasy. My own little girl dreams of being a princess in a castle in a far-off land have come true. Never mind that it will all end in a month, I intend to enjoy every minute of it now, thanks to your generosity."

Aware she'd been talking too much, she ate the rest of her sandwich.

"You think that's what it is?" The question sent her pulse off the charts. "Little boys have their fantasies, too," came the wicked aside.

Fingers of warmth passed through her body.

"My mother taught me they're not for a little girl's ears." After drinking the last of her coffee she dared a look at him. "Just how young did you think I was when we first met?"

"Too young," was all he was willing to reveal. He put some money on the table and stood up. "If you're ready we'll get some serious shopping done. Groceries last, I think."

She would pay for her keep, she thought to herself. He might be letting her sleep at the château, but she didn't expect anything else.

After visiting a hardware store, he took her to the third floor of the department store where the mattresses were sold. Alex sought out the male clerk and they conversed in French. Their speech was so rapid she understood nothing. Within a few seconds the younger man looked at her and broke out in a broad smile.

"I don't think I want a translation," she told Alex.

His lips curved upward. "You don't need to worry. When he asked me what kind of a mattress we were looking for, I simply asked him if he knew the story of the Princess and the Pea. He said he had the ideal one for you."

She tried not to laugh. "I see."

The clerk spread his hands in typical French fashion. "Would Mademoiselle like to try it?"

"She says yes," Alex spoke for her. They followed the man across the floor to the sample mattresses on display.

"This one is the best. *S'il vous plait.* Lie down."

"Don't be shy," Alex whispered. "He's not Figaro measuring a space for your marriage bed."

An imp got into Dana. "Maybe he thinks he's measuring yours. Why don't you try it first and humor him?"

With enviable calm Alex stretched out on one side of it, putting his hands behind his handsome head. Through shuttered eyes he stared up at her, jump-starting her heart.

"*Venez, mademoiselle.*" The clerk patted the other side. "He said you needed a double bed. See how you fit."

You said you wanted to spread your wings, Dana Lofgren. But she hadn't anticipated literally spreading out on a bed next to Alex for all creation to see. Several people on the floor had started watching with embarrassing interest. If she waited any longer, she'd turn this into a minor spectacle.

Once she'd settled herself full length against the mattress, she turned her head to Alex. "How does it feel against your sore back?"

He rolled on his side toward her, bringing him

breathtakingly close. "You noticed." His voice sounded deep and seductive just then.

Afraid he knew that she noticed everything about him, she said, "I think we should take it. Look—even this close to me, the mattress doesn't dip."

"I noticed." This time when he spoke, she felt his voice reach right down inside to her core. The way his eyes had narrowed on her mouth, she slid off the bed in reaction and got to her feet on shaky legs.

"Eh bien, mademoiselle?"

She decided to make his day. "It's perfect"

He rubbed his hands together. "Excellent."

"Alex? I'll go to the linen department for the bedding. Meet you at the truck." Without looking at him, she made her way down to the next floor.

When the saleswoman asked what Dana had in mind, she described the beamed ceiling. "There's a mini print wallpaper of gold fleurs-de-lis on a cranberry field. I'd like to follow through with those colors."

"I have the exact thing for you."

Within minutes Dana left the store with a new pillow, pale cranberry sheets and bath towels with tiny gold fleurs-de-lis, a cranberry duvet and matching pillow sham.

Alex had reached the truck ahead of her.

Together with two other men from the warehouse, he put the boxes with the mattress and box springs in the back. Upon her approach, he plucked the items right out of her arms with effortless male grace. While he stowed them, she climbed in the cab, eager to get back to the château and make up her new bed.

Without her having to say anything, he drove straight to a boulangerie where she salivated before loading up on nummy little quiches and ham-filled croissants. Alex bought three baguettes and several tranches of Gruyère and Camembert cheese.

"I already feel debauched and haven't even tasted a morsel yet," she moaned the words.

On the way back to the truck his eyes swerved to hers with a devilish glitter. "That's the whole idea. Earlier today I was accused of being a dull boy."

She quivered. If he got any duller, her heart wouldn't be able to take it. "I might have exaggerated a little."

"Careful, Mademoiselle Lofgren, or I'll get the impression you're trying to kill me with kindness." He turned on the engine and they took off.

She'd never had so much fun in her life and the day wasn't over yet.

* * *

"I'm coming down the hall, Dana. I hope you're ready."

He couldn't tell if she cried in fear or giggled. "Alex—please— It's almost ten o'clock. You've done enough! I don't need anything more." They'd cleaned every inch of the room until it gleamed. She was so genuinely appreciative of everything he did for her, it made him want to do more.

"I think you'll find this to be of comfort." Using his high-powered flashlight so he could see, he entered the turret round and put the heavy bronze floor candelabra near the head of the bed he'd brought down from storage. It was as tall as she was.

Dana held her own flashlight to guide him. She'd taken off her shoes and was in a kneeling position on top of her newly made bed. Using his automatic lighter, he lit the twelve candles in their sconces. Like the sun coming up over the horizon, the room slowly filled with flickering, mellow light.

"Oh—" she cried softly.

His sentiments exactly. The candles illuminated not only the inlaid woods of the Italian armoire and dresser, but the utterly enchanting female who'd worked hard right alongside him all afternoon and evening. Her peaches-and-cream complexion glowed, causing her blue eyes to dazzle him.

"The candles will burn down in an hour or so. Enough time to do some reading before jet lag takes over."

She shut off her flashlight. "I think I'm in a time warp."

"I feel that way every time I come inside the château." *Get out of her bedroom. Now.* "Before I go downstairs, we'd better discuss how you want to handle your father tomorrow."

Something in her eyes flickered that had nothing to do with the candlelight. "What do you mean handle?"

"I thought it was obvious. Sweet dreams, princess."

Dana had no agenda. No place she had to be.

After sleeping in until noon, she spent a long time in the modern bathtub, studying everything. She marveled at the superb job Alex had done of combining contemporary and eighteenth-century decor.

The tile work of the ancient looking floor had been laid in a stunning, stone-green and white checkerboard design. Her eyes followed the lines of the green border also carried out around the window and the door.

Delighted by every inch of work created by a master craftsman, she was loathe to leave her bath. However, the pads of her fingers resembled prunes. Without electricity to blowdry her hair up here, she needed to towel it some more, then brush it dry before she went downstairs.

An ornate, mural-size mirror with a rococo-style gilt frame hung on the wall opposite the tub, another sybaritic element of the château. A gasp escaped her lips when she stood up and saw herself reflected full-size. She had a mirror on the back of the door at home, but it was in her bedroom and seemed miniscule in comparison.

One more look at herself was a reminder that only a few days of enjoying the food they'd bought and she'd put on five pounds just like that! *Discipline, Dana. Self-control.*

On the way back to the room in her robe, she repeated the motto that went for other things besides food. Like other people for instance. No, not other people. Just one person.

She clutched the lapels of her robe tighter. *A man like no one else.*

When she entered the room she could hear her phone vibrating on the dresser. Maybe it was Alex wondering if she was still alive. Suddenly breath-less, she clicked on with a smile. *"Bonjour!"*

"Is that you, Dana?"

Her father's voice. What a surprise! "Hi, Dad. How was the flight?" He hated being closed in for long periods.

"Boring." That meant his girlfriend hadn't been able to keep him distracted.

"And Saskia?"

"She's at the Metropole in Angers."

"You sound tired. Where are you exactly?"

"I'm standing in my room at the Hermitage," he grumbled. "More to the point, where are you? The concierge said you never came in last night." He actually noticed?

"That's right. I've decided to stay at the château. It will save me a lot of coming and going."

Alex had the strange idea she was under her father's thumb. If he only knew the truth, that her father didn't think much about her at all. There was nothing to handle, but her host had insinuated something else and it rankled.

"I thought it was deserted."

"Not completely." She started brushing her hair. "The owner lives here. He's been very accommodating and made an allowance for me. After you've slept a few hours, drive over to the château in your rental car and I'll meet you at the gate."

There was a noticeable silence, then he said, "I'm coming now."

Clearly he couldn't wait to see if she'd pulled through for him. Everything hinged on her find.

"In that case let me go over the directions with you." Without Saskia in tow, he could walk around and think in peace. "See you shortly."

Once she'd pulled on jeans and a short-sleeved cotton top in an aqua color, she finished doing her hair and put on lipstick. Slipping her feet into her favorite leather sandals, she grabbed her phone and left the room. Later, after her father had gotten a feel for the estate, she would feed him a late lunch in the kitchen before he went back to the hotel.

Last evening she'd only had a brief glimpse of the salon. Today the door was closed. Alex could be inside at the computer, but in all probability he was out hacking away at his private jungle.

This was the way it should be. Out of sight, out of mind. Didn't she wish!

She stepped out into a day that seemed hotter than yesterday, but she hadn't noticed because the interior of the château was cooler. It felt like being in a cathedral to walk beneath the trees. Here and there sunlight dappled their branches.

As she continued on, the crunch of her feet on

the leaves must have startled some squirrels. They chattered before she saw them scamper up a trunk and disappear. She was still laughing in pure pleasure when she came upon Alex at the gate.

He was down on his haunches in jeans and another thin white T-shirt, fastening something to the wrought iron. She could see the play of muscle across his shoulders. Her heart thudded so hard she was positive he could hear it.

"Sleeping Beauty at last," he murmured, scrutinizing her from head to toe with eyes so dark and alive this afternoon, it sent a delicious current of desire through her body.

"You're getting your princesses mixed up."

"No—" He went back to fastening a screw with his power drill. "You're a woman of many parts. I never know which one is going to emerge at any given moment."

His comment produced a smile from her. "You're full of it, Alex, but keep it up. By the time I leave here, I'll be taking a whole host of enchanting memories with me."

His hands stilled for a moment. "Where are you going next?"

"To a little town on the Rhine in Germany for a month where the last segment of the film will be made."

He dusted himself off and got to his feet. "Stand back and let's see if I've done this right." Pulling a remote from his pocket, he pressed the button. The gate took its time, but it clanged shut.

"*Bravo*. Too bad you didn't get to work on it sooner. It would have kept me out and forced me to phone you for an appointment."

Before she could take another breath, he shot her a laserlike glance. "As you've already surmised, I didn't mind the surprise or you wouldn't be living here." His comment filled her body with warmth. "But I've decided this was necessary to keep out trespassers while the studio is filming every day." He tossed her the remote. "It's yours. I have more in the office I'll give to Paul for anyone who needs one."

"Thank you."

She felt his gaze linger on her features. "Were you looking for me?"

Dana sucked in her breath. "No. My father's on his way over from the hotel. I told him I'd meet him here."

As if talking about him conjured him up, a red rental car appeared and came to a halt. Before Alex said anything that would remind her of his parting words last night, she pressed the button on the remote and the gate swung open.

"Hi, Dad. Drive on through."

He nodded his balding head and did her bidding. Once he'd passed through, he stopped the car and got out. Solid, yet lithe, he'd dressed in his favorite gray work slacks and matching crew neck shirt. His blue eyes, several shades darker than hers, gave them both a stare that others might consider fierce, but Dana was used to it.

"Dad, I'd like you to meet Monsieur Alexandre Martin, the owner of the estate."

"Monsieur." The two men shook hands.

"Call me Alex. I've seen several of your films which I found remarkable. It's a privilege to meet you."

"Thank you. Your English is excellent."

"He's part Australian, Dad."

"Ah. That explains the particular nuance I couldn't identify."

"Unlike your accent in English that no one could ever mistake for anything but Svenska," Dana quipped.

"Too true." His hooded gaze darted back and forth between her and Alex before he addressed him. "My daughter has convinced me I won't be disappointed with this location."

Alex eyed her father through veiled eyes.

"Why don't you take a walk down this road alone. The left fork will bring you to the front of the château. The door's unlocked. Take all the time you want wandering around. I understand you'd rather do the discovering than be herded."

Dana's father looked stunned. That was because Alex had taken his cue from her. Among his many qualities, he'd just shown he was a master psychologist.

"Hand me the car keys, Dad. I'll drive it to the front courtyard and join you in a few minutes."

His surprised glance switched to her before he dropped them in her hand. After nodding to Alex, he turned and began jogging.

Once he'd disappeared around the curve in the driveway, she turned to Alex who'd started gathering up his tools. She could tell he was anxious to get back to his pruning. Considering he'd spent all day yesterday and last evening seeing to it she had a bedroom worthy of a princess to sleep in, she didn't want to be the reason he was kept from his work any longer.

As soon as she'd climbed in the car, she poked her head out the window. "You handled my father brilliantly, Alex. Congratulations on being one of the few." The last thing she saw was his dark, enigmatic glance as she started the engine.

Get going, Dana!

Afraid if she stayed any longer she'd end up blurting out something incriminating like, did he want help? she followed the driveway while studiously avoiding looking at him through the rearview mirror.

After pulling up next to her rental car parked in front, she gave her father a few more minutes lead before she got out. This was one time she was so confident of his positive reaction, it shocked her when he suddenly emerged from the château with a face devoid of animation. The look she'd expected to see in his eyes wasn't there.

"Follow me back to the Hermitage. We have to talk."

CHAPTER FOUR

ALEX was up in one of the tallest trees, cutting away dead branches, when he saw both cars leave the estate. Jan Lofgren couldn't have been on the premises more than ten minutes. That was quick, but Alex guessed he wasn't surprised. In less time, Dana had made the decision to rent the estate on behalf of the company.

His opinion of her father had been correct before meeting him. He personified conceit. Dana miraculously had none.

Two hours later, Alex was coming back from the landfill after another haul when his cell phone rang. Paul Soleri was calling to make sure he and the crew could get in. They were on their way to the estate.

The timing couldn't be better. Once Alex could welcome them and answer any questions, he'd resume his work. The knowledge that Dana would be coming back to sleep after dark never left his mind.

Before long a car and two minivans pulled up in the front courtyard. Alex stepped out of the château to meet Paul and the dozen light and camera technicians assembled. They all appeared delighted by what they saw. Their enthusiasm escalated as they entered the château.

After Alex introduced himself and pointed out the location of the bathroom facilities, he told them to look around and explore all they wanted. Except for the petit salon on the main floor and the west turret round on the first floor, everything else was available to them.

If they wanted to do any filming in the building housing the winepress or down in the wine cellar beneath the château, they were welcome. Already he could tell they were getting ideas as they left the foyer and darted from room to room checking things out.

Paul, who was probably in his midforties, took him aside. "Has Jan been here yet?"

"Yes. A few hours ago. He didn't stay long, then he left with his daughter."

The dark blond man pursed his lips. "I'm surprised I haven't heard from him yet."

"Perhaps he was tired from the long flight."

"That's not like him," he mused. "I assumed he'd be here."

"I have to admit I thought it strange he left in such a hurry," Alex commented.

"It doesn't matter." A pleasant smile broke out on his face. "We'll go ahead without him."

"Make yourself at home, Paul. As I told you over the phone, all the furniture is stored on the third floor. Nothing's locked. Use whatever you need."

He let out a long whistle. "When David gets here, he'll be floored."

"David?"

"The scriptwriter for this film. He'll be arriving any minute with the set designer and staff from costumes and makeup. They're all going to swoon."

"And that's good?"

"You have no idea. Since Jan wanted something unique for this segment of the film, we've been worried it didn't exist. Only Dana could pull this off. She's always had an instinct for picking the right places for him, but this time she outdid herself.

"Don't quote me, but she'll end up being a more brilliant director than her father."

That piece of information came totally unexpected. "Is directing one of her aspirations?"

"Yes, but the last person to know it is Jan, and that's another good thing."

Alex remembered her answer when he'd asked what she did in her spare time. *Nothing of report. I read and play around with cooking. Otherwise my father forgets to eat.*

"If you'll excuse me, Paul, I have to get back to my work outside. Phone if you need me."

"Will do."

Inexplicably disturbed by what he'd learned, he strode down the hallway leading to the side entrance of the château. Dana had been emphatic about not wanting to be an actress. Now it seemed Paul had supplied him with a viable reason.

Inherited talent happened on occasion, but he had the distinct feeling it would take uncommon courage for her to step out from Jan Lofgren's legendary shadow. When she did break out, she'd be caught up in her own career. The thought caused Alex to grind his teeth.

Dana found a parking space outside the Hermitage and followed her dad inside to his room. On the short drive from the château she'd prepared herself to hear that he wasn't pleased with her find.

She knew the place was perfect for the script, so it had to be something else he objected to. For the life of her she didn't know what it was. That meant his mood had already turned wretched and the whole company would pay for it. If she knew Paul, he'd already assembled the crew over there to get to work.

It would be bad enough if they had to pack up again and leave for the Paris location, but there was Alex to think about. The contract Sol had sent him was standard. There was a clause that said Alex would only receive a percentage of the money if for any reason they chose not to film there after all. That wasn't nearly enough compensation for him.

By the time she entered the hotel room, she was ready to fight her father. If he was going to pull out of this deal due to one of his mystical whims, then she would insist Alex be paid all the money agreed upon in good faith.

As usual his room was a mess, but for once she didn't start automatically straightening things. Instead she shut the door and propped her back against it. While she waited for him to speak first, she folded her arms.

He stood next to the dresser, eyeing her while he lit up a cigarette, almost as if he were daring her to protest. She couldn't remember the last time she'd seen him smoke. Her mother had begged him to stop. As a concession to her, he'd cut down a lot. Dana had hoped he would find the strength to quit altogether. Unfortunately Saskia smoked, too. Dana guessed it was asking too much.

"Tell me about Monsieur Martan." He pronounced Alex's last name the French way.

A red flag went up.

Months ago her father had started out another conversation in the same manner, only the subject in question had been Neal Robeson.

So… This was about Alex—not about the suitability of the château. Relief flooded her body.

No doubt when Alex had told her father to go ahead and explore on his own because of something Dana had confided, he hadn't liked it. She knew her dad enjoyed being a mystery to other people, so it had made him uncomfortable to be more transparent to Alex because of her. That irritation would pass, particularly since Alex wouldn't be around while her father worked.

"Martin is his Australian name," she corrected him.

With one long exhale, the room filled with smoke. "He must want to get into acting very badly to give me free rein to his entire estate."

She moved away from the door. "Have you forgotten I went to him, not the other way around? He wants money very badly to restore the château and make it a viable asset before he resumes his career as an agricultural engineer."

Her father gave her one of those condescending nods. "So that's what he's told you."

Dana refused to let him get to her. "In this case you're not dealing with another Neal type."

"No," he muttered, "Monsieur Martan is older and has far more worldly experience. Inside that supposedly deserted château with no electricity beyond the main floor, your bedchamber has been laid out so exquisitely, it even took *my* breath."

She scoffed. "Careful, Dad. You're beginning to make this sound like Beauty and the Beast. When I told him I was planning to stay there at night in my new sleeping bag, he insisted I have a decent bedroom."

He stubbed out his cigarette. "I forbid it, Dana."

Forbid? "I think you've forgotten I passed eighteen a long time ago." As she turned to leave, she heard knocking on the door.

"Jan? It's Saskia. Let me in, *lieveling*."

The timing was perfect, but her father looked ready to throw something.

"I'll get it," Dana volunteered before opening it.

"Hi, Saskia. Did you have a good flight?"

"So-so." The brunette actress kissed her on both cheeks, a pretense at civility.

Dana went along with to keep the peace.

"I was just leaving. See you later, Dad."

Without hesitation she rushed out of the hotel. It didn't take her long to reach the château.

By the time she'd pulled up next to the cars and minivans parked in front, Dana realized there'd be no peace for her if her father was angry enough to renege on the contract. Alex didn't deserve it, not to mention everyone else who would be put out. It looked like it was up to her if she didn't want this boat to sink.

When she found Alex and told him she wouldn't be staying at the château after all, he would assume it was what he'd thought from the first—that she still answered to her father in everything. But as humiliating as that would be, it wouldn't matter if it meant Alex received all his money.

"Dana?"

She got out of the car in time to see David hurrying toward her from the woods. He was her father's age, a wonderful family man with a great gift for writing.

When he caught up to her, he hugged her hard. "Bless you, Dana. Bless you, bless you for this. Words can't describe."

"I know." She'd felt the same way after seeing the château for the first time. It was how she felt now, only more so. He finally let her go, still beaming.

David's reaction settled it. This film was of vital importance to him, too; therefore she had no choice but to pack up her things and drive to the Hermitage. She checked her watch. It was ten to six. Pretty soon everyone would leave for the night. That's when she'd go inside to get her things so she wouldn't draw attention to herself.

Until then she would walk around the back of the château to find Alex. After what he'd done for her, she owed him an explanation of why she wouldn't be staying here after all. He would never know that because of him, she'd experienced the most exciting day and night of her entire life. A man like him was too good for her, but at least this was a memory she'd hug to herself forever.

After telling David she'd see him later, she followed the path next to the hedge at the side of the château. It led around to the back where she hadn't been before. To her surprise the ground, covered by a mass of tangled vegetation divided by a path, sloped gently toward the river.

She wandered down it a few feet, marveling at the sight. Alex had meticulously cleaned out one half of it to reveal individual fruit trees. Who would have guessed what had been hidden there? In its day, the grounds would have been a showplace.

The other part still needed to be tackled, but he was making inroads. She saw his truck piled with cleared-out vegetation. Nearby were various tools including a power saw.

"Bonsoir, ma belle."

Her heart raced. "Alex?" She'd heard his deep, seductive voice, but couldn't see him anywhere.

"I'm in a tree!" He tossed something small and green at her feet.

She reached for it, then looked up. A long, tall ladder had been propped against the trunk. Hidden by masses of leaves, she only saw parts of his hard-muscled physique. He brushed a few aside, allowing her a glimpse of his disarming white smile. Dana could hardly breathe.

"Are these all apple trees?"

"Blanc d'Hiver" apples," he asserted. "The kind that make the best *tartes aux pommes*. By late October I might be able to harvest a few. The trees behind you yield Anjou pears."

Dana shook her head. "No wonder this place is called Belles Fleurs. When their blossoms come out, the sight from the château windows will be glorious.

"That all depends if I live long enough to make it out of this primeval forest to prune another day."

She chuckled. "How old are you?" She'd been dying to know.

"Thirty-three."

"You've got years yet!"

"Years of what?"

"I'm sure I don't know." Dana didn't want to think about his life when he moved on to other places. Other women… It would take a very special woman to capture his heart. "Tell me something—"

"That covers a lot of territory."

Laughter escaped her lips. "Can you see the vineyard from that altitude?"

"So you noticed the building housing the winepress."

"Yes, but I also heard that the vineyard once produced the famed Domaine Belles Fleurs label."

She heard the leaves rustle. In seconds he'd negotiated the ladder with swift male agility before jumping to the ground, carrying his hand saw. "Someone's been gossiping." He gathered the branches he'd just cut and threw them in the truck bed. "Wait, let me guess—Madame Fournier at the Hermitage."

Nothing got past him. "Who else?" She smiled, but he didn't reciprocate.

"Since my arrival, word has leaked out that a long-lost Fleury is back in Les Coteaux du Layon. It sounds like she was talking out of school again."

Dana had irritated him again; the last thing she'd wanted to do. "Only because I wanted to buy a bottle of the dessert wine we drank the other evening. She told me it came from the Domaine Percher, but she added that the very best Anjou wine used to come from the Domaine Belles Fleurs."

Alex rubbed his thumb along his lower lip. "There hasn't been a bottle produced since 1930."

"That's what she said. Naturally I was curious."

"Naturally," he came back, but to her relief he sounded more playful than upset.

"When I flew back to California, I did a little research on the Internet."

His eyes narrowed on her features. "What did you find out?"

"For one thing, Dutch merchants used to favor the Belles Fleurs brand."

He expelled a breath. "I might as well hear the rest. Knowing Dana Lofgren, you didn't stop there."

Embarrassed to be rattling on, a wave of heat washed over her. "There isn't any more, though I will say this—I'm no connoisseur, but if the Belles Fleurs wine was as good as the kind we had at the Hermitage, then it's the world's loss."

She noticed him shift his weight. "My parents never breathed a word to me about a vineyard."

"You're kidding!"

"My father was so intent on protecting my mother from any more pain, we simply didn't talk about her past. When the letter from the attorney for my grandfather's estate showed up, there was no mention of a vineyard. In fact, he led me to believe the place was virtually unsalvageable."

"Sounds like he was hoping you would forfeit so he could buy it for a song."

He nodded. "I got the distinct impression he was hiding something, but didn't understand until I saw the winepress building and eventually discovered the vineyard. No doubt he'd been bombarded by vintners throughout the Anjou region who wanted to buy it and work it, even if they couldn't afford to purchase the château."

"So he thought he'd buy it first," she theorized, "recognizing the money it could bring in."

"Exactly."

"Is it supposed to be a secret then?"

He put his hands on his hips, unconsciously emanating a potent virility that made her tremble. "Not at all."

"But you wish I'd mind my own business."

"You misunderstand me, Dana. There's something you *don't* know. Come with me while I make this last haul and I'll explain."

His invitation made it possible for her to be with him a little longer. She couldn't ask for more than that, but he paused before his next comment ruined the moment. "Unless of course your assistance is required elsewhere." His brow had furrowed. "Naturally your father has first call on your time."

Between Alex and her dad, she felt like a football being tossed back and forth. Both of them treated her like she was a child who couldn't act for herself. She'd thought she and Alex had been communicating like two adults just now, but she'd thought wrong!

Bristling with the heat of anger she muttered,

"If that were the case, I wouldn't have come out here, would I?"

Turning on her heel, she started to retrace her steps, but Alex moved faster. In the next breath his hands had closed around her upper arms, pulling her back against his chest. "Why *did* you come?" he asked in a silky voice.

With his warm breath against her neck, too many sensations bombarded her at once. The solid pounding of his heart changed the momentum of hers. Aware of his fingers making ever-increasing rotations against her skin through her top, she felt a weakness attack her body. Pleasure pains ran down her arms to her hands.

"I—I wanted to thank you." She could hardly get the words out.

"For what?" he demanded, turning her around, causing her head to loll back. His dark gaze pierced hers. "That sounded like you're leaving on a trip. Mind telling me where you're going?"

"The landfill? It may be a French one, but I can still think of more romantic places."

"Dana." His voice grated.

Of course he already knew the answer to his own question, but his male mouth was too close. Her ache for him had turned into painful desire.

She needed to do something quick before she forgot what they were talking about.

"I should have taken your advice before you went to so much trouble for me." She tried to ease away from him, but he didn't relinquish his hold. "My only consolation is that it's one room less you'll have to clean and furnish once you get started on the inside of the château."

Those black eyes roved over her features with increasing intensity. "You knew your father wasn't going to approve. What's changed?"

Dana moistened her lips nervously. "Remember the old saying about picking your battles?" She noticed a small nerve throbbing at the corner of his mouth. In other circumstances she'd love to press her lips to it. "This one isn't important."

She kept trying for a little levity, hoping it would help. It didn't. Her comment had the opposite effect of producing a smile. Some kind of struggle was going on inside him before his hands dropped away with seeming reluctance.

This was the moment to make her exit. "See you around, Alex."

Needing to put distance between them, she went back to the château to pack. It had emptied except for Paul and David. While they were talking in the grand salon, she hurried out to the car with her suitcase and headed for the hotel.

The same woman she'd talked to before smiled at her. "*Bonsoir*, Mademoiselle Lofgren."

"*Bonsoir, madame.* I need the key to room eleven, please."

Her arched brow lifted. "Eleven? But it is already occupied."

"I know. My father and I have adjoining rooms."

"*Non, non.* A Mademoiselle Brusse checked in a little while ago. I've already given her the key."

Something strange was going on.

"I see. Thank you for your help, *madame*."

"Of course."

Dana grabbed her suitcase and opted for the stairs rather than the lift. Once she reached the next floor, she walked midway down the hall and knocked on her father's door several times, but he didn't answer. No doubt he was with Saskia, but this couldn't wait. She pulled out her cell phone and called him.

"Dana?" He'd picked up on the second ring.

"Hi, Dad. What's going on? I tried to check in my room, but the desk said Saskia had picked up the key."

He answered her question with another one. "Where are you?"

"Standing in front of your hotel room door."

"I'll be right out." The line went dead.

Within seconds he joined her in the hall and shut the door behind him. His famous scowl was more pronounced than earlier in the day. "Saskia and I have been having problems, but I can't afford to end things with her until after the picture's finished. She doesn't know my intentions of course."

Dana was glad her father was coming to his senses for his own sake.

"She begged me to let her stay in the adjoining room while we work out our differences."

Poor Saskia. "That sounds reasonable."

His eyes darted to her suitcase. "Saskia's room is free at the hotel in Angers. I called and told the concierge to have it waiting for you."

"Thank you," she muttered, "but I'll make my own arrangements."

There was a long silence before he said, "If you go back to the château, you do so at your own peril."

Their gazes clashed. "And Monsieur Martin's, too?"

His eyes flashed with temper. "How did that

man get his tentacles into you so fast?" he countered.

Dana stood her ground. "Why won't you answer the question, Dad?"

It took him forever to respond.

"I still forbid you, but as you reminded me earlier with all the carelessness of your culture, you're not seventeen anymore."

He went back in the bedroom. As she turned away, she heard the door close. Despite his hurtful remark, she was confident he wouldn't penalize Alex. Not because he'd had a sudden attack of human decency, but because he knew he'd never find a spot this perfect for his film.

Her throat felt tight all the way back to the château where she discovered the gate had been closed. A symbolic dagger for the trespasser to beware?

She closed her eyes, afraid she was being as superstitious as her father. After a minute, she reached for her purse and pulled out the remote. Once she'd driven on through, she shut it again, then continued on to the courtyard.

After getting out of the car, she tried to open the front door, but it was locked and Alex's truck was nowhere in sight. He might still be around the back, working. Acting on that possibility, she drove to the other end of the château. It wound around to the orchard.

He wasn't there.

A hollow sensation crept through her. She checked her watch. It was already eight o'clock. Disturbed that he might have made plans with a woman and had gone into Angers for dinner, she drove to the front of the château once more.

Of course she could phone him, but he wouldn't appreciate a call if he was with someone else. Besides, he'd thought she'd gone back to the Hermitage for good. The only thing to do was drive to the next village in the opposite direction from Chanzeaux where she wouldn't run into her father by accident. After grabbing a bite to eat, she would come back and wait for Alex.

"*Bonsoir*, Monsieur Martan."

"*Bonsoir*, Madame Fournier. Has Mademoiselle Lofgren checked in yet?" He hadn't seen Dana's car outside.

She shook her head. "*Non, monsieur.* She doesn't have a reservation here."

"Then her father isn't staying here, either?"

"But of course he is! The person in the adjoining room is Mademoiselle Brusse. She's an actress doing a film with *le fameux* Monsieur Lofgren."

His hands clenched in reaction. If Dana hadn't come here, then she'd probably driven into Angers to get herself a hotel room. The last trip to the landfill had cost him time before he'd showered and changed clothes, thus the reason he'd missed her.

"Merci, madame." Before she could detain him with more gossip, he went back outside to phone Dana from the truck. It rang seven times. He was about ready to hang up in frustration when he heard her voice.

"Alex?" She sounded out of breath.

"What's wrong?" he demanded without preamble.

"My left front tire is flat. I've been trying to work the jack, but I've been having problems. Pretty soon I'll figure it out."

The band constricting his lungs tightened. "Where are you exactly?"

"Somewhere on the road between Rablay and Beaulieu."

"I'm on my way." He started the engine and drove away from the hotel. "Stay in your car and lock the doors."

"Don't worry about me."

"What caused you to go in that direction?"

"When you weren't at the château, I decided

to get dinner in the next village, but I never made it."

The blood hammered in his ears. "You came by the château?"

"Yes. Dad and Saskia have been quarreling. It's nothing new, but while they work things out she's going to stay in the adjoining room."

"Why did you come back?"

"In order to ask if I could rerent my bedroom so to speak, that is if you don't mind."

He muttered something unintelligible under his breath.

"What did you say, Alex? I'm not sure we have a good connection."

This had nothing to do with the connection. His hand tightened on the steering wheel. "And your father approves?"

There was a brief silence. "No. Does that mean there's no room at the inn?"

Ciel! "You know better than to ask that question." The fact was just beginning to sink in that she'd come to him whether her father liked it or not.

"You sound upset. In case I've ruined your plans for the evening, please forget about me. If I can't fix the tire, I'll walk to the château and wait until you come home later."

"No, you won't—" A woman who looked like her wasn't safe in daylight. Alex didn't even want to think about her being alone in the dark.

"I realize you think I'm too young to do anything on my own, but I'm not helpless."

"Age has nothing to do with it. I'm just being careful."

"Point taken," she admitted in a quiet voice.

His body relaxed. "Where would you like to eat tonight?"

"You mean you haven't had dinner, either?"

"As a matter of fact, I went to the Hermitage in the hope we could drive into Angers for a meal, but Madame Fournier informed me a certain actress had taken over your room."

"Saskia didn't waste any time announcing herself."

"Madame Fournier lives for such moments."

Her sigh came through the line, infiltrating his body. "I don't want to talk about either of them. I'm too hungry. To be honest my mouth has been watering for one of those quiches we bought in Angers. Are there any left?"

He smiled. "I've saved everything for us. There's more than plenty for several meals." Alex preferred dining in tonight where he didn't have to share her with anyone. While his thoughts were on their evening ahead, he saw her car at the side of the road and pulled off behind her. "Don't be alarmed. I've got your car in my headlights."

"I have to admit I'm glad it's you. I'll hang up."

Alex heard the slight quiver in her voice before the line went dead. Though he had no doubt she could handle herself in most situations, her relief was evident. So was his now that he'd caught up to her.

After shutting off the ignition, he reached in the glove box for his flashlight and got out of the truck. She rolled down the window and poked her beautiful golden head out the opening. He caught the flash of those startling blue eyes in the light.

"Did I do it wrong?"

For a second he was so concentrated on her, everything else went out of his mind. "Let me take a look," he murmured, before shining the light on the tire. It was flat, all right.

She climbed out of the car. "What can I do to help?"

Her flowery fragrance seduced him. "If you'll hold the flashlight right there, I'll have this changed in a minute."

Their fingers brushed in the transfer, increasing his awareness of the warm feminine body standing behind him. He hunkered down to work the jack and remove the tire. Several cars slowed down as they passed before moving on. "You must have picked up a nail."

"I'll get it fixed tomorrow." When he started to get up she asked, "Would you like the light to find the spare?"

"Thank you, but I don't need it."

He opened the car door to trip the trunk latch. Except for her sleeping bag, there was nothing else inside. That made it easy to retrieve the smaller tire and put it on. After he'd tightened the lug nuts, he lowered the car and put the flat in the trunk with the tools.

She walked toward him and handed him the flashlight. "You did that so fast I can't believe it."

"All it takes is practice. Over the years I've gotten a lot of it driving trucks out in areas where you have to do the repairs yourself or walk fifty miles."

"Thank you for coming to my rescue, even if you pretend it was nothing."

"It was my pleasure." Unable to help himself, he briefly kissed those lips that had been tantalizing him. They were soft and sweet beneath his.

He wanted so much more, but not out here on the road in view of any passerby. "Now let's get back to the château. I'll follow you."

He helped her inside the car, then he jumped in the truck. She made a U-turn and headed for Rablay-Sur-Layon only a short distance off. Once they'd turned onto the private road, he pressed the remote so they could drive through the gate.

The noise it made clanking shut was the most satisfying sound he'd heard in a long time. It signaled that they'd left the world behind. For the rest of the night it was just the two of them.

CHAPTER FIVE

ALEX'S unexpected kiss had done a good job of melting her insides. She'd been wanting it to happen, but he'd caught her off guard out there on the road where other people could see them. To make things even more frustrating, he'd ended it too soon for her to respond the way she ached to do.

Dana had almost suffered a heart attack when she'd seen him walk toward her car dressed in a charcoal shirt and gray trousers. His rugged male beauty electrified her senses.

By the time he parked next to her in front of the château, she was feeling feverish with longings she couldn't seem to control. If she didn't get a grip, he'd be convinced he was dealing with a schoolgirl instead of a mature woman.

As she started to get out, he opened the back door and reached for her suitcase.

Being on her own so much, she had to concede it was wonderful to be waited on and taken care of. When she looked back on the dilemma she'd been in before he'd phoned her, a shudder rocked her body. He'd spoken the truth. She wouldn't have been safe inside the car or walking back to the château alone.

Alex used his remote to open the front door. Once they were inside he put down her suitcase and turned on the lights. She felt his dark-eyed gaze rest on her. "Food before anything else, I think."

"I like the way you think."

By tacit agreement she followed him through the foyer past the staircase to a hallway leading to the west wing. He turned on another light. Dana hadn't been in this part of the château before. They passed a set of double doors.

"May I see inside?"

"Of course." Alex opened them for her. "This is a drawing room that opens into the grand dining room. As you can see, boards have been nailed over the broken windows. When they're repaired, they'll look out on the front courtyard."

The beauty of the interior caused her to cross her arms over her chest and rub her hands against them in reaction. "I've never seen anything so lovely. The ornate walls and ceilings make me feel like I'm in a palace. After this, you wonder how your mother adapted to life in a normal house."

"I'm sure my father did his share of worrying about it, but they had a good marriage which hopefully made up for a lot of things." Just then he sounded far away.

"Believe it or not, my parents had a solid marriage, too, albeit an unorthodox one. Mom had to make most of the concessions, but she must have wanted to, otherwise she would have left him because he's quite impossible."

Dana followed his low chuckle back out to the hall and down to a turn that opened up to the kitchen.

"How incredible!" It was massive with a vaulted ceiling and an open hearth fireplace that took up one wall. Modern appliances had been mixed in with the ancient. A long rectory-type table with benches sat in the middle of the room. She estimated sixteen people could be seated there comfortably.

"Through that far door on the right are the steps leading down to the wine cellar. The door at the other end of the kitchen leads to a pantry and an outside door. Another leads to a bathroom."

"You've reminded me I need to wash my hands after ineptly handling that jack. Excuse me for a moment."

She darted through the pantry stocked with supplies. A new washer and dryer had been installed in there. The pantry was big enough to be a master bedroom. Beyond it she found the bathroom Alex had upgraded. It wasn't quite as large as the one upstairs, but it had every accoutrement.

The tiles covering the walls and ceiling were the same as the ones lining the counters in the kitchen. Each was an original and had been hand-painted on a cream background to depict grapes, apples, pears, all the fruits probably grown on the estate.

Continually charmed by everything she saw, Dana was in a daze when she returned to the kitchen. She'd been gone so long, Alex had already put their meal on the table. He was standing next to one end with a bottle of wine in his hand.

"Sorry I got detained, but the tiles were so adorable I had to study them."

"Now that I'm getting to know you better, I find that entirely understandable. Sit down and I'll serve you." As she took her place, he uncorked it and poured the pale gold liquid into their glasses.

Their eyes met. "Is this a special wine?"

"It is now." His deep voice sounded more like a purr. He sat down opposite her and lifted his glass. "To us. May our unexpected month together hold many more pleasant surprises."

He'd just laid down the ground rules. She wasn't to read more into that kiss than he'd intended. After the month was over, this season of enchantment would come to an end. She smiled through her distress at the thought and clinked her glass against his. "To you, *monsieur*. May you outlive any regrets for your magnanimity."

With her emotions in turmoil, she forgot and drank her wine like it was water. Too late she realized her mistake and tried to recover without him noticing, but it wasn't possible considering she was choking. His dark brown eyes smiled while he munched on a croissant. "When you're able to speak again, tell me how you find your wine."

Embarrassed, Dana cleared her throat. "It's sweet like the one we had the other night, but it's not the same domaine, is it? This time I tasted honey."

"That's very discerning of you. When you seemed to enjoy the one we had at the Hermitage,

I bought this bottle for you to try. It's another Layon wine called Chaume from the Domaine des Forges. I'm told it's the sweetest of all."

She got this fluttery feeling in her chest. Anxious not to appear disturbed by him, she bit into the quiche he'd warmed for them. It wasn't just his words, but the way he said them. Here she'd promised herself not to get carried away, but being alone with him like this caused her to think many forbidden thoughts.

"You were very thoughtful to do that. Now that I've sampled both, it makes me wonder what the Belles Fleurs wine tasted like."

"We'll never know…" His voice trailed. "Every bottle has disappeared from the wine cellar. I suppose there are a few connoisseurs who bought them up. They might still have them stored in their wine cellars for a special occasion. Good dessert wines can last for decades."

"It seems so sad there's no more wine being made from the grapes grown on your property."

He stared at her, deep in concentration. "I'm afraid I'm not a vintner. It's a whole other world that requires the best oenologist you can hire. A wine expert doesn't come cheap, nor a vintner and crew."

"What do you suppose happened to the records kept by the vintners of this estate?"

"I have no idea. Possibly they're hiding in one of the tons of boxes holding the contents of the library. You haven't seen that room yet. It's in the right wing next to the music room."

After she finished off her quiche, she asked, "Are the books upstairs with the furniture?"

"They're in one of the third floor turret rounds."

She peeled an orange and ate several sections as she digested what he'd told her. "Alex—aren't you curious about them? About the history of this place?"

He ate some cheese before swallowing the rest of his wine. "Not particularly."

"Why?" When he didn't immediately answer her, she felt terrible. It was clear he didn't want to talk about his family's past. "I'm sorry. I didn't mean to pry. It's none of my business."

Unable to sit there any longer, she jumped up and started clearing the table.

"Leave it, Dana."

Ignoring his edict, she took everything over to the sink. "I want to make myself useful before I go upstairs."

"You're tired then?"

"Yes." She seized on the opening he'd given

her. "You must be, too, considering how early you get up and the exhausting labor you do every day." She found detergent to wash their plates and glasses.

Her heart skipped a beat when he joined her with a towel to dry them. Soon she had the table wiped off and the kitchen cleaned up. They were both standing at the counter.

"Since one of your jobs is to provide your father with his daily lunch, feel free to fix it here."

Surprised by the offer, she lifted her head to look at him. "I would never presume on your generosity like that. I've already made arrangements with the Hermitage to bring them here. When everyone else breaks for lunch, he likes to stay put and eat alone. I always bring him hotel food when we're on location."

He stared at her through veiled eyes. "When I have a perfectly functional kitchen, that's a lot of needless going back and forth."

Dana's attraction to him was eating her alive. "I couldn't."

"Not even if I asked you to make lunch for me at the same time?"

Her heart skidded all over the place. "You mean, and bring it out to you while you're working?"

Something flickered in the dark recesses of his eyes. "It would save me a lot of time and trouble."

Yes, she could see how a cook would make his life easier so he could get on with his business. In that regard he wasn't any different from her father.

"I have to admit doing something for you would make me feel a little better about staying on the premises."

"Good," he said in a voice of satisfaction. "I'm anxious to clear out the debris from the rest of the orchard as soon as possible."

"That's right," she murmured, trying to disguise her dismay. "You're in a hurry to leave for Louisiana." The thought of him not being on his property one day was anathema to her.

She rubbed her palms against her hips in a self-conscious gesture he took in with those dark, all-seeing eyes. "W-what do you like for lunch?" Her voice faltered.

He studied her for a moment. "I'm certain anything you make will be delicious."

His charm caused her breath to catch. "In the morning I'll do some grocery shopping when I go into Angers to get the tire repaired."

"As long as you're doing that, would you mind

buying enough food to cover breakfast and dinner for a week, too? In the end it will save our energy for more important matters."

Except that her job of making sure her father had his lunch wasn't on the same scale of doing it for Alex. The thought was preposterous. "You trust me?"

"Let's just say I'm willing to go on faith."

Her lips curved upward. "That's very courageous of you."

Alex's eyes glimmered. "Just as long as you don't simmer pickled pigs feet in wine sauce and tell me it's chicken, we'll get along fine."

Her chuckle turned into laughter. She would love to freeze this moment with him. To be with a man like this, to be the recipient of his attention and enjoy his company in all the little private ways brought joy to her life she'd never experienced.

Early in the morning she'd take stock of his kitchen to find out what staples were on hand. While her mind was ticking off her plans, he pulled out his wallet and laid several large denominations of Eurodollars on the counter. Dana was too bemused by events to argue over who would pay.

"*Merci, monsieur.*" After gathering them, she

walked over to the bench where she'd been sitting and stashed them in her purse.

"De rien, mademoiselle." When he spoke French his whole demeanor changed, making her wholly aware of the sensual side of his nature. "Let me get some more candles and my flashlight from the pantry and I'll accompany you upstairs. You look sleepy."

As he walked off, she reflected on his words. A woman wanted to hear certain things from the man she found desirable, but *sleepy* relegated her to daddy's little girl status.

Since meeting him she had to concede he'd been protective of her. However, that didn't translate into a *grande passion* on his part. Though he'd brushed his lips against hers earlier, not by any stretch of the imagination would she have called it hunger unbridled or anything close.

Afraid she was already giving off needy vibes, she left the kitchen ahead of him and walked through the château to the foyer. Eyeing her suitcase, she grabbed it and started up the stairs. He caught up to her at the top where there was no more light and guided her down the corridor to her room.

It wasn't really her room, but it's the way she

thought of it. When the flashlight illuminated the interior, she felt she'd come home. The sensation stayed with her while he lighted fresh candles in the floor candelabra.

Avoiding his eyes, she put her suitcase down. "You didn't have to do that. My flashlight is right here next to the bed."

"I wanted to," came the deep velvet voice that was starting to haunt her. "Candlelight brings out the pink and cream porcelain of your skin. I've never met a woman with a complexion like yours."

What was she supposed to say to that? "Lots of people have told me I look like a cherub and pat me on the head."

His gaze narrowed on her mouth. "Don't you know any flesh and blood man seeing you doesn't dare do anything else for fear a bolt of lightning will strike him? Get a good sleep."

After he disappeared, she stood there shaking like the ground under her feet during a California earthquake.

On her return from Angers the next day, Dana parked around the end of the château and carried the groceries and other purchases into the kitchen through the side entrance. She'd purposely unlocked it before leaving.

Her father liked to eat at twelve-thirty sharp.
She checked her watch. It was almost that time
now. She hurriedly put things away, then made
both lunches and packed them in the two baskets
with a thermos of hot coffee each.

As soon as everything was ready she went in
search of her father. He was in the grand salon
opposite Alex's office talking with the two leads.
In no time at all the staff had brought down furniture and everything was starting to take shape.
Under Paul's watchful eye the place had become
a beehive of organized commotion.

Knowing better than to disturb her dad, she
stepped inside the room and put the basket next
to the door. He didn't even glance at her before
she darted back to the kitchen. Now she was
free to deliver the second basket to the unforget-
table male responsible for last night's insomnia.

Once she entered the orchard, the sound of
sawing reached her ears. Alex had put the ladder
against a different tree this time. Slowly but surely
he was making progress. She admired him so
much for doing everything single-handedly, she
wanted to shout to the world how remarkable he
was.

It seemed a shame he had to come down out
of the tree for his lunch. Adrenaline gushed

through her veins at the idea of taking it up to him. Why not? There was so much foliage, he could find a spot to secure the basket while he ate.

Without hesitation she started up the rungs, excited to repay him any way she could for his generosity. Almost to the top she called to him. "Alex?"

The sawing stopped. "Dana?" He sounded shocked. Evidently he hadn't seen her. "Where are you?"

Two more steps and she poked her head through the leaves. "Right here. The mountain decided to come to Mohammed," she quipped, but she didn't get the reaction she'd hoped for. His eyes pierced hers in fury.

In an instant his expression had grown fierce. Lines deepened around his hard mouth, giving him a forbidding expression. "Whatever possessed you to climb all the way up here? If you fell from this height, you could break a great deal more than your lovely neck."

She'd been prepared for a lot of things, but not his anger. "You're right. It was foolish of me. I didn't stop to think how guilty you would feel if anything happened to me and you'd be forced to report it to my father. *My* mistake.

Here's your lunch." She formed a nest of leaves and propped it as securely as she could in front of him. *Bon appetit.*

"Dana—" he ground out, but she ignored him. Without any encumbrance she was able to go back down the ladder in record time. He called to her again, this time in frustration.

"Stop worrying, Alex. You had every right to be angry!" she shouted back before running around the side of the château.

Since the rest of her day was free, she would go sightseeing. After grabbing her purse from the pantry, she made sure the door was locked, then got in her car and backed around to the front.

Her heart didn't resume its normal beat until she'd driven a good fifty kilometers on the repaired tire. At the next village she pulled off the road into a park. In the distance she saw some swans on a lake. The serene scene mocked the turmoil going on inside of her.

After the experience with Neal she'd promised herself she wouldn't get close enough to a man again to expose her deepest feelings. But the pathetic little stunt she'd just pulled revealed holes in her best intentions, forcing her to come face-to-face with her own idiocy.

The need to channel her roiling emotions

drove her from the car. She spent the rest of the afternoon walking around the lake, making plans that had nothing to do with Alex. On the way back to the château she stopped for a meal and didn't return to Rablay until five-thirty.

She was relieved no one had gone to their hotels yet. With everyone still around, Alex would make himself scarce. That gave her time to reach her room without him noticing. She'd hibernate there until tomorrow. New day, new beginning.

No sooner had she started down the upstairs hall than she saw Saskia coming out of her bedroom. The brown-haired model turned actress could turn any man's head, but she didn't have the same effect on Dana. The invasion of privacy infuriated her under any circumstances, but if she'd been snooping around on orders from Dana's father, she was ready to declare war.

"Hi!" Saskia was a cool customer. She didn't have the grace to blush or act embarrassed. Dana couldn't bring herself to reciprocate with a greeting. "What did you have to do for the owner of this fabulous estate to give you special privileges?"

"Why don't you ask him yourself?"

"I haven't met him yet, but the girls in makeup tell me he's beyond gorgeous."

That was one way of describing him. Saskia's jaw would drop when she saw Alex for the first time. "Didn't Paul tell you the petit salon and this bedroom were off-limits?"

"I didn't think he meant me."

"Why not?"

Throwing back another question managed to unsettle her a little. "Actually I was looking for you in the hope we could talk."

"About what?"

"Now you're being obtuse. You know very well your father and I aren't getting along right now. I was hoping you'd be able to tell me what I'm doing wrong."

"I can't fault you for anything, Saskia. I wouldn't presume."

"That's no help."

Dana took a steadying breath. "That's because there is no answer. You're not my mother, but you've always known that, so the truth couldn't be a surprise to you. If it's any consolation, I can't do it right, either."

Saskia flashed her a shrewd regard. "Maybe if I stayed here at the château, Jan would worry about me sometimes? See me in a different light?"

You mean, as mistress of the manor with a real live Frenchman attached? Now things were beginning to make sense. She'd been looking for Alex…

"I'm sure I don't know."

"Do you think the owner of the château would let me stay here?"

"Haven't a clue."

She pursed her lips. "I suppose it helped that you're Jan's daughter. Maybe being his girl-friend would work for me."

"It's worth a try."

Her green eyes gleamed in anticipation of confronting Alex. "I agree. Thanks for the talk."

Dana watched her slender figure disappear before she went to her bedroom. Saskia had been fighting a losing battle when it came to Dana's father. No doubt seeing the eight-by-ten photograph of Dana's mother and a smaller photograph of her parents propped on the dresser underlined the futility of Saskia's relationship with him.

As for Dana, she had her own problem in the futility department where Alex was concerned. He couldn't leave for the States fast enough. How ironic that because she'd seen his ad on the Internet, she'd unwittingly made it possible for him to reach his goal sooner. Saskia could dream all she wanted, but she was in for a shock.

* * *

Alex worked in the orchard until twilight. One more trip to the landfill and he'd call it a night. The delicious, filling lunch Dana had delivered air express without consideration for her personal safety had kept him going through the dinner hour.

Much as he'd wanted to go after her, he hadn't wanted an audience that included her father, *grace a dieu*. Since no one knew what had transpired, he decided it would be better to apologize to her after hours when they were alone.

On the way back from his last haul, he locked the gate for the night and drove on to the front of the château. The sight of her rental car meant she was home. His pulse shot off the charts as he hurried inside and made a quick inspection of the ground floor in the hope he might bump into her.

To his chagrin all he found besides furniture in the grand salon was an empty basket and thermos placed at the foot of the paneled door. It was identical to the one she'd brought Alex. He carried it to the kitchen where he'd put his on the way in from the truck.

A few minutes later after a shower and change of clothes, he phoned her while he was warming some food for his dinner. Maybe she'd come down and join him.

"Alex?" She answered on the fourth ring. "Is there something wrong?"

"Yes," he blurted. At this point in their relationship, nothing but honesty would do.

"Did you lose your remote and can't get in the château?"

"I'm afraid my problem can't be fixed that easily."

He felt her hesitate before she said, "Did the studio from Paris cancel on you for mid-September?"

The strong hint of anxiety in her tone plus the fact that she remembered what he'd told her humbled him. He'd grovel if necessary to get back on the footing they'd had before she'd brought him his lunch.

Alex cleared his throat. "I appreciate your concern, but the truth is, I was rude to you earlier today. It takes a lot to frighten me, but when I saw you appear among the leaves like some impossibly adorable wood nymph and realized how far you were from the ground, I lost any perspective I should've had."

She let out a wry laugh. "The relegation from cherub to wood nymph is a subtle improvement I like, so I'll take it."

Dana...

"As for the rest, I've had all day to ponder my actions over that brainless stunt. Chalk it up to the enchantment of this place."

He had to clamp down hard on his emotions. "I can safely say it was the best meal I ever had in a tree."

"That's another distinction I'll treasure, but to save you from an early heart attack, I'll leave your lunch basket on the fender of your truck from now on."

"Why don't you come downstairs and we'll talk about it over a glass of wine." If he hadn't made the rule that he would never take advantage by going up to her room after dark unless invited, he'd be there now.

"Lovely as that sounds, I'm already half asleep. May I confess something to you?"

"By all means." He had to swallow his disappointment.

"You'll think me more superstitious than my father."

That particular word wasn't on the growing list of adjectives he found himself ascribing to her. The mention of her father in the same conversation didn't improve his mood. "Don't keep me in suspense."

"Somehow it seems sacrilegious to drink

anyone else's wine on Belles Fleurs property. Does that make sense?"

His eyes closed tightly for a minute because deep in his core he'd had the same thought last night. Like the seed of the precious *chenin blanc* grape buried in the soil of the Anjou centuries ago, it seemed to have germinated out of nowhere, reminding him of his mother's roots.

"More than you know," he answered huskily.

Until last night he hadn't felt that emotional connection. Now, suddenly, it tugged at him and he realized it was all tied up with Dana, who had everything to do with this unexpected awakening.

"Alex? Are you still there?"

"Mais oui." He gripped the phone tighter. "Do you remember asking if I could see the famous Belles Fleurs vineyard from the top of the tree?"

"Are we talking about the same question you didn't answer?"

"Meet me out in back in the morning at eight. There's something I want to show you."

"I thought I'd been warned off climbing trees."

Alex rubbed the back of his neck absently. "This requires some walking. Wear boots if you have them."

"I don't. Will trainers do?"

"Those will protect your feet better than your sandals."

"We're not going to be trekking through some snake-infested region are we? I have an irrational terror of them."

A low chuckle rumbled out of him. "Few of the snakes in France are venomous. Even then their bites aren't worse than wasp stings. So far I haven't come across any."

"That's not exactly reassuring, Alex."

"I've survived the snake worlds of Indonesia and Africa."

"But you're—"

"Yes?" he prodded after she broke off talking midsentence. She'd left him hanging, the perpetual state he'd been in since meeting her…and didn't like.

"I was just going to say you're invincible."

"Not quite." She'd been making inroads on his psyche from the moment they'd met, infiltrating his thoughts. No woman he'd known could claim that distinction. "For what it's worth, I promise to protect you."

"Thank you."

He wanted to be with her now. "Are you sure you're too tired for Scrabble? I brought the game with me from Bali. My father and I often played."

"In how many languages?"

He couldn't suppress his laughter. "Why don't we find out?"

"Maybe another night when I'm not worn-out."

"What's your birthdate?" She'd be turning twenty-seven. That wasn't a day he was bound to forget, not after his assumption that she'd been much younger.

"The sixteenth."

"Next Monday. Don't make any plans. We'll celebrate and I'll let you beat me."

"I intend to."

He grinned. "Where did you go today?"

"I don't really know. I kept driving until I saw this park and a lake. There was a mother swan. She had three cygnets who followed her around, matching her exact movements like they had radar. I kept running around the lake, watching them. You've never seen anything so sweet or fascinating."

Yes, he had… The picture he had in his mind of her made his whole body ache.

"No wonder you're tired. If you'd rather make it nine o'clock—"

"I'll probably be out there by seven-thirty before any of the crew arrives. I don't like them knowing my business."

Did that include her father? Alex had the strong hunch there'd been little communication between them by phone since she'd chosen to sleep at the château against his wishes.

"That's understandable."

"To be honest, I don't see how you can stand to have your own privacy invaded by a ton of strangers wreaking havoc."

He drew in a sharp breath. "It's called money."

"I know. Let's hope word has spread throughout the film world and you're flooded with new requests. Nothing would make me happier for you. Good night." The definitive click cut off his lifeline.

While he locked up and turned out lights, it came to him Dana was a gift that might come along once in a millennium *if* you were lucky. Her father had to know that. Perhaps it was the reason he guarded his golden-haired offspring so jealously.

In a very short period of time Dana had brought out the possessive instinct in Alex. Evidently it had been lying dormant these many years just waiting to spring to life when or if the right person ever made an appearance.

For the rest of the night he was taunted by dreams of a certain blue-eyed wood nymph smiling at him through the foliage. If the handsaw and the basket hadn't been in the way, the two of them might still be up there in a bed of leaves while he made love to her over and over again.

CHAPTER SIX

"SALUT, ma belle!"

She waved to Alex, who stood by the truck, dressed in thigh-molding jeans and another white T-shirt that revealed the outline of his cut physique. The sun brought out the black-brown vibrancy of his overly long hair, a style that suited him to perfection.

He'd seen her coming around the back in her white-washed jeans and T-shirt in her favorite mocha color. His eyes followed her progress with disturbing intensity, making her feel exposed.

"It's such a beautiful morning I'm not going to ask if you're fine because you couldn't be anything else." He was freshly shaven and the faint scent of the soap he'd used in the shower permeated the air around them.

"You're right about that," he murmured. She

watched him pick up a pair of long-handled pruning shears. "Shall we be off?" There was a slight curve to his lips she'd only tasted for a brief moment the other night. Unfortunately it had set up a permanent hunger nothing but a much longer repeat of the experience would satisfy.

Dana nodded before following him down the path that bisected the orchard. Maybe she was crazy but she felt something crackling in the air between them, the kind of thing that sizzled during a lightning storm.

He kept walking until they reached the perimeter of the orchard. Juxtaposed was a forest of briars taller than they were. It reached to the river, filling the entire hillside and around the bend. She'd never seen the likes of such a thing before.

A gasp escaped her lips. "The only thing I can compare this to are the briars that overgrew Sleeping Beauty's castle, but that was in a storybook."

He slanted her a mysterious glance. "If you recall, it was a *French* fairy tale." He folded his arms. "Behold the Belles Fleurs vineyard."

"No—"

As she tried to take it all in, her eyes smarted. She turned her head so Alex wouldn't see how it had affected her. Now she understood why he hadn't wanted to talk about it.

"This is what happens after eighty years of neglect," came his gravelly voice.

She shook her head. "When you drive here from Paris and see the rows of gorgeous green vineyards…to think they can look like this…" It was impossible to articulate her horror.

"Oh, Alex—for your family to let all of this die—it's beyond my comprehension." She wheeled around to face him. "How did you bear it when you saw this desecration?"

He put down the shears. "Don't be too sad." Taking a step toward her he wiped one lone tear from her hot cheek with the pad of his thumb. As their gazes fused, his hands cupped the sides of her face. "Believe it or not this vineyard is alive."

"But it couldn't be!"

"I assure you it is. Deep in those trunks are the makings of *chenin blanc* grapes grown on Belles Fleurs *terroir*."

"I—I can't fathom it."

"Vines are unusual creatures. They want to climb. They climb and they climb while the birds eat the fruit and drop the seeds where they will. What you're looking at is a tangled mess of what is probably the best prepared soil along the

Layon. Eighty years lying fallow has made it rich. All the vineyard needs is a little work."

"A little—" she cried.

Chuckling quietly, he removed his hands and reached for the shears again, leaving her dizzy with unassuaged longings. "It would take five years to turn this into a thriving business again. The first year all these trunks would have to be cut down to three feet, like this."

She watched him in wonder and fascination as he shaped it down to size like Michelangelo bringing a figure out of the marble. He threw the castoff briars to the side. Dana crouched down to examine one of them. She lifted her head. "Then what happens?"

"The next year new canes appear." He tossed out another vine. Painstaking work. "They have to be treated like newborn babies."

When she smiled, he smiled back, giving her a heart attack. "You said five years."

He nodded his dark head. "In the third year you'd see buds. In the fourth, the first new grapes would appear. By the fifth year they'd be worthy of making a good wine."

"Five years…" He wouldn't be here in five years. The thought sickened her and she jumped to her feet. "When I asked you why you weren't concerned about the vineyard, it's clear why you chose not to answer me until now. They say a picture is worth a thousand words. In this case it's more like a billion."

"Vineyards are a business and family concern. Without one, or one that can't pull together, it doesn't warrant the effort it takes to make wine." There was a residue element in his voice, maybe sadness. It brought a lump to her throat.

"No. I can see that…" Her voice trailed. "Does this mean you're considering leasing the vineyard or even selling it to a prospective vintner?"

"I'm not sure." They started walking back. She could tell he was eager to get busy in the orchard. It was time to change the subject.

"Alex? You know what a bookworm I am. Would you consider it a horrible invasion of your privacy if I went through some of the boxes in storage, just to see what was in the library? I don't speak French, but I can read enough to understand titles and that sort of thing."

"Be my guest."

Excitement welled inside her. Maybe she'd find some family records or scrapbooks he would enjoy looking at. "You mean it?"

His dark eyes seemed to be searching her very soul. "What do you think?"

"Thank you!" she cried. Without conscious thought she put her hands on his upper arms and raised up on the tips of her sneakers to kiss his jaw. What happened next happened so quickly, she never saw it coming. Alex dropped the shears and crushed her against him, covering her mouth with his own.

She didn't know who was hungrier. All that mattered was that he was kissing her until she felt pleasure pains run through her body clear to her palms. Though she knew she couldn't die from rapture, she felt she was on the verge.

When she moaned, he whispered, "My sentiments exactly. Your mouth tastes sweeter than any Anjou wine in existence."

"Alex—" Her body shook with needs bursting out of control. She circled his neck with her arms in order to get closer and pressed little kisses along his jaw. While Dana couldn't get enough of him, his hands splayed across her back, drawing her up against his chest where she felt the thud of his heart resound.

"You're so incredibly beautiful, Dana. Help me stop before I can't." His breathing sounded shallow.

She hushed his lips with a kiss. "I don't want to stop."

He groaned. "Neither do I, but someone's coming."

Thinking that whoever it was was ruining the moment, she had to force herself to leave his arms. Still breathless from their passion, she turned in time to see Saskia in the distance. She walked toward them with purpose.

Of course. Who else.

"Well, hello," Saskia said on her approach, eyeing Alex in stunned surprise that any man could be that attractive. At thirty years of age, Saskia looked good herself and knew it. She eventually tore her eyes away to stare at Dana. They looked greener than usual. "Aren't you going to introduce us?"

"Saskia Brusse? Please meet Monsieur Alexandre Martin, the owner of the estate. Alex, Saskia is my father's girlfriend. She also happens to be one of the actresses in the film."

"But my part doesn't come until we're in Germany which is lucky for me."

"And what part is that?" Alex asked.

She blinked before staring at Dana. "You mean you haven't told him?"

Dana refused to be put off by her. "We haven't discussed the script."

Alex shook hands with her. "I'm happy to make your acquaintance, Mademoiselle Brusse."

"Thank you. You know, I was hoping to talk to you this morning. That's why I drove over here with Jan this early."

"Why did you want to see me?"

"Didn't Dana tell you about that, either?"

"I'm afraid we've had other matters on our minds. Please enlighten me."

While Dana willed her heart to stop racing, little red spots tinged Saskia's cheeks. She didn't like the way this conversation was going. "Jan told me Dana was staying here at the château. I wondered if I might occupy one of the rooms for the rest of the month, too. While we're here in France I have a lot of time on my hands and this is such a beautiful place."

"I'm glad you think so," Alex said with a smile. "But I don't allow anyone to live here with me except my staff. Dana is helping me put Belles Fleurs' library in order. It's quite a task. Since you're acquainted with her, then you're aware she's an historian like her father. Both are brilliant."

He picked up the shears. "Now, if you ladies will excuse me, I have to get to work. It was nice meeting you, Mademoiselle Brusse. When the film is out, I'll look forward to seeing it."

Dana had never seen anyone think on his feet that fast! Poor Saskia didn't know what

had hit her. For that matter, neither did Dana…
No man had ever shown her the respect or
treated her the way Alex did. To defer to Dana
and compliment her in front of Saskia was a
new experience.

When another man might have let her sleep in
the château using her sleeping bag, he'd gone out
of his way to pamper her like a cherished guest.
The night she'd had car trouble, he'd been there
for her in an instant. He worried about her safety.

Alex was the antithesis of her father.

From the corner of her eye she noticed Saskia
watching his hard-muscled body with a combination of anger at not having gotten her way and
undisguised hunger. Suddenly she turned to
Dana. "I saw you two before you saw me. Mixing
business and pleasure can be risky."

"As you've found out with Dad," Dana drawled.
"Given enough time we all live and learn. Talk to
you later, Saskia." Without staying to listen to
anything else, Dana hurried up the path and
around to the side entrance of the château.

Alex was already up in a tree pretty much out
of sight. Although he'd only claimed that Dana
was working for him to checkmate Saskia, he'd
given Dana permission to rummage through the
boxes on the third floor. He was wonderful!

Because of his generosity, she was determined to find out anything she could about Belle Fleurs's history. Surely there'd come a day when Alex would want to know more. After she'd fixed the lunches, she'd go up and make an initial foray.

In the meantime she needed to keep working on his dinner for tonight. She wanted to cook him something authentically French. Yesterday she'd bought all the ingredients for it and had already done some preparations. On her way into the kitchen, she plucked her mother's French cookbook from the pantry shelf where she'd left it. She opened it to the desired page.

Soak an oxtail, cut in joints, in cold water for several hours.

"I've already done that."

Wipe with a clean cloth, and brown in butter with four onions and three carrots, coarsely chopped. When the meat is brown add two crushed cloves of garlic. Cover for two minutes, then add five tablespoons of brandy. Light this and let it burn for a moment, then add one half bottle of dry white wine, and enough bouillon so that the meat bathes in the liquid. Add salt, pepper, a bouquet garni, and cook slowly for three hours with the cover on.

In a little while she had it cooking on the stove. Next task.

Saute in butter one half pound of mushrooms, a good handful of diced fat bacon and about one dozen small onions.

She'd do that after she made the lunches and delivered them.

Later on in the afternoon she checked the recipe for more instructions.

Add the meat to this and pour over all the liquid which has been strained and from which the fat has been removed. Cover and cook for one hour more in a slow oven. The meat should be soft and the sauce unctuous without recourse to thickening with flour.

During the hour it was cooking, she hurried up the stairs. A few of the crew waved to her, but no one wanted to talk. Her dad was somewhere around, but they didn't bump into each other. That suited her just fine considering that Alex had put Saskia's ski jump nose out of joint. No doubt she'd already reported to Dana's father what she'd seen in the orchard and had distorted it further.

Eager to explore, Dana took one of the side staircases to the third floor and walked the length of the château to the turret round. When she opened the door, all she saw was a sea of boxes in the musty room. Dozens and dozens of them. None were marked. Whoever had packed things up hadn't bothered to take the time to label anything. What a shame.

She tried opening a few, but she would need a knife or scissors to do the job. Some markers to identify what was in the boxes wouldn't hurt, either. And she'd need a chair. And some rags to clean off the dust. Tomorrow when she came up, she'd be prepared.

Once she'd returned to her bedroom, she put a change of clothes and some nightwear in a large bag she'd bought yesterday. It could hold most anything and was a lot easier to carry than a suitcase. A few toiletries and the contents of her purse and she was ready to go.

Dana stood at the top of the staircase and waited until no one was in the foyer, then she descended quickly and darted to the kitchen. It smelled good in here if she said so herself. In fact, it smelled the way a proper French kitchen should.

Pleased with her efforts, she turned off the oven, took the pot out and set it on one of the burners of the stove. With everything in order, she went over to the table and pulled out her notepad.

Monsieur Martin— Better put that in case anyone came in here and read it. *Your dinner is on top of the stove. All you have to do is heat it for a few minutes. Just so you know, I'll be staying in Angers overnight, but I promise I'll be back in the morning.*

D.

She put the note on the counter by the sink where he always washed his hands. That way he'd be sure to see it. With that accomplished she slipped out through the pantry to the side entrance and walked around the front of the château to her car.

Some of the cast and crew were getting in their vehicles. They all said hello to each other before she drove off. If Alex could see her leaving from his high perch in a treetop, so much the better.

After the way she'd responded to him in the orchard, she didn't want him thinking what he was entitled to think. Heat poured into her cheeks remembering how she'd practically devoured him. At eight o'clock in the morning no less!

Last night she'd practiced painful self-control and hadn't joined him when he'd phoned her. Tonight she knew she'd cave if he so much as looked at her. The only wise thing to do was remove herself from temptation in the hope of gaining some perspective. Since meeting Alex, she had absolutely none.

Dana must have brought Alex his lunch while he'd been sawing and couldn't see her. When he came down the ladder, there was the basket sitting on top of his truck. Though disappointed she hadn't called to him, he found himself salivating for his meal.

Tonight he intended to take her out for dinner and dancing. She couldn't plead fatigue two nights in a row! He needed her in his arms and wasn't going to let anything stand in his way.

Making it an early night, he did his last haul at six and slipped into the side entrance of the château with his basket, eager to find her. When he walked through the pantry to the kitchen, something smelled wonderful. His gaze went to a covered pot on the stove.

He set the basket on the counter and drew a fork from the drawer. Dana had cooked something that smelled sensational. He lifted the cover, unable to resist putting one of the pieces of beef in his mouth. It was kind of fatty and mild, but the stock was rich. He needed a spoon for it.

As he reached for one he saw a piece of paper lying near the sink. The note was short and sweet.

He let out a curse. *Dana Lofgren—What are you trying to do to me?*

Before he exploded, he needed to calm down. If she thought she was going to hide from him tonight, she could forget it. He'd find her at one of the hotels Paul had lined up for everyone. After her scare on the road the other night, she wouldn't dare go anywhere else.

His eyes flew to the pot. Alex wasn't about to eat the rest of it without her. Forget dinner and dancing! He made a place for the pot in the fridge and left the kitchen.

By the time he'd showered and changed, the château had emptied. He locked up and left for Angers, driving his truck over the speed limit. This time he wouldn't forewarn her with a phone call. No more of that.

He stopped first at the Beau Rivage, but they had no listing for her. His frustration grew when the Chatelet could tell him nothing. By the time he approached the concierge at the Metropole, he was beginning to wonder if she'd checked in at another hotel altogether.

"*Bonsoir, monsieur.* My name is Monsieur Martin from the Belles Fleurs estate in Rablay."

"Ah…it's a pleasure to meet you. I understand the members of the Pyramid Film Company staying with us are shooting a film at your château."

"That's right, *monsieur*. It's very important that I speak to Mademoiselle Brusse. I understand she's in room 140."

"*Non, non.* The beautiful actress was staying in room 122, but she's no longer with us. Mademoiselle Lofgren, the director's daughter, is occupying that room now."

"You have no idea where Mademoiselle Brusse went?"

He leaned forward. In a low voice he said, "I believe with the director."

It seemed he and Madame Fournier had a lot in common. "You've been very helpful. *Merci, monsieur.*"

"*Pas de quoi.*"

Now that Alex knew where his fetching cook would be spending the night, he left the hotel to do a few errands.

Heat from a hot sun still lifted off the cobblestones. A summer night like this was meant for lovers, but he'd never been affected to such a degree before. He was aware of wants and needs growing beneath the surface. To feel emptiness and dissatisfaction with his life after a hard day's work was a new phenomenon for him.

His jaw hardened. After discovering Dana would be gone until tomorrow, the idea of spending the night alone at the château sounded insupportable. How was it she'd become so important to him in two weeks' time?

Before long she'd be off to Germany. And then what? Paul intimated she had plans to become a director.

Alex should never have insisted she stay. Knowing she was around day and night had him tied up in knots. Yet if he were honest with himself, he'd be just as nuts if she'd stayed at the Hermitage. No hiding place was too far for him to find her, and find her he would, father or no father.

He'd decided to give her until ten o'clock. It was five to now. After putting his purchases in the truck bed, he returned to the hotel. Mademoiselle Brusse's room was on the third floor at the end of the hall. This experience reminded him of musical chairs, a game he'd once played in elementary school. Tonight, however, the adults had decided to make it musical bedrooms minus the accompaniment.

"Dana?" he called to her as he knocked. "It's Alex. I know you're using this room, so it would be useless to pretend otherwise."

"Why would I do that?" came a familiar voice

behind him. He swung around in surprise to see her coming toward him in the same clothes she'd had on that morning.

The humidity had brought a flush to her cheeks. Her hair had little golden curls with more spring when she walked. His fingers itched to play with them. She was clutching a carton in her arms. Her eyes questioned his without flickering. "If you wanted to talk to me, why didn't you phone?"

He sucked in his breath. "Would you have answered?"

"Of course."

Since he hadn't tried, he couldn't accuse her of lying. "Why didn't you tell me you planned to leave the estate tonight?"

"Didn't you get my note?" She could play the innocent better than anyone he knew. "I left it by the kitchen sink."

"I saw it," he clipped out. "I'm talking about this morning."

A tiny nerve throbbed at the base of her throat. "If you recall, we were…interrupted."

"My memory's perfect," he murmured, unable to look anywhere except her mouth. She'd started a fire with it at the vineyard. "What about at lunch when you came and went so fast I wasn't aware of it."

She averted her eyes. "I didn't make the decision to stay in town until later in the day."

He glanced at the carton. "What have you got there? You're holding it like it's a newborn baby."

The color in her cheeks intensified. "Actually it's something very old and priceless."

Alex couldn't imagine. "In that case let's take it home in my truck where it will be safe and we'll enjoy that delicious dinner you made. The aroma that filled the kitchen was mouthwatering."

Her startled gaze flew to his. "Then you haven't eaten it yet?" She sounded disappointed.

"I ate part of it, but when I realized you'd gone, I put the rest of it in the fridge for us. After the trouble you went to, I didn't want to eat all of it alone."

It frustrated him she still wasn't convinced. When he didn't seem to be getting anywhere with her, he tried a different tactic. "Why don't I hold the carton while you gather your things. Tomorrow I'll drive you back for your car. I have to come in town again anyway on business."

She bit the underside of her lip, increasing his desire for her. Hopefully it was a sign she was weakening. "All right," she finally sighed the words, "but please don't drop it. I couldn't replace it for a long time."

That sounded cryptic. At this point he was consumed by curiosity.

"I promise I'll guard it with my life."

It could *be* your life, Alex.

With her heart hammering, Dana handed him the carton. A few minutes later she'd packed everything in her bag and they left the hotel. In truth she hadn't wanted to stay here at all and had dreaded returning to the sterile room after accomplishing her objective. For him to have shown up tonight thrilled her to her tiniest corpuscle.

When they reached the truck, she lowered her bag behind the cab, then took the carton from him while he opened the doors with the remote. "Let me hold it again until you climb inside."

Alex could be so sweet. When she was settled, he gave the carton back and carefully shut the door. After they left Angers he flicked her a penetrating glance. "Did you discover anything of interest when you were opening boxes today?"

"Without tools I couldn't see inside one of them and none are marked. It was very frustrating, but tomorrow's another day. How's your orchard going?"

"Thanks to those lunches, I've accomplished

two more hours of work this week. At this rate I should be finished by the end of the next one."

The days were going by too fast. Dana was starting to panic. "What's your next project?"

"To tackle the undergrowth between the château and the winepress building."

Before long everything on the outside would be done. That left the interior. With his work ethic, he'd have the place ready for tourists in no time.

She felt his eyes travel over her. "What are you thinking about so hard?"

"All the work you've been doing without any help."

"It's the kind I like."

Dana admired him more than she could say. "You obviously love the outdoors."

"I've always needed my freedom."

Oh—she knew *that*. Alex had already defined the boundaries of their relationship to the month of August. How else had he managed to elude marriage all these years? Deep in thought she didn't realize they'd entered the estate until she heard the gate clank behind them. He drove around to the side entrance and turned off the engine.

When he got out of the cab and opened her door, he flicked her what looked like a mysterious smile. "I've been looking forward to a midnight supper with you. It appears tonight's the night."

She'd dreamed of such a night. "Aren't you tired after slaving out in the heat all day?"

"On the contrary, I feel energized." On that exciting note he used his remote to let her in the château and turn on lights. While she hurried through the pantry, he followed with her bag and some purchases of his own.

"Where do you think you're going in such a rush?" He'd taken the pot out of the fridge and placed it on the stove to heat.

"I thought I'd put this away first."

He eyed the carton. "It's dark upstairs. You might fall and break whatever it is you're guarding so jealously."

Dana couldn't afford for that to happen. "You're right." She put it down on the counter.

"Why don't you sit on the bench while I wait on you. After slaving over our dinner, you deserve a rest."

"I'd rather help, but first I need to wash my hands." She walked to the sink where she saw the note she'd left. When she'd written it, she never dreamed Alex would have come looking for her to bring her back. Her pulse was off the charts.

His actions had to mean something, but she

was a fool if she thought he wanted more than a few weeks pleasure with her under his roof. Like this morning when she'd succumbed so easily, she could do it again and that frightened her.

Dana had been the one to ask if she could stay at the château. If anything, she'd been the one to take advantage of Alex, not the other way around. Whatever happened from here on out, she would have to accept the consequences and live with them.

Soon the smell of the meat wafted past her nostrils. When she turned, she noticed he'd already set the table. Along with French bread and the bottle of the wine they'd enjoyed the other night, he'd added an old silver candelabra with new candles.

Once he'd lit them, he turned off the kitchen light, transforming the room into an incredibly intimate setting. His eyes beckoned her to come and sit. The gleam in those dark depths sent a tremor through her body.

She twisted her napkin nervously as he brought the contents of the pot to the table in a wonderful old round bowl with handles. After sitting down opposite her, he ladled a portion for both of them onto their plates. "Bon appetit."

Dana hoped it was good and took a first bite.

To her surprise it didn't taste like anything she'd ever eaten before. She took another, but it needed something. Maybe a baguette would help.

Alex had already eaten most of his. "My compliments to the chef. Among your many talents you're a superb cook, Dana."

She put her spoon down. "No, I'm not."

He flashed her a curious glance. "Why do you say that?"

"Because it's awful. I—I wanted to make you something spectacular," she stammered. "It's not."

"What do you call it?"

"See?" Tears threatened. "Even *you* don't know what it is."

"Isn't it beef?"

"No."

"If you're trying to tell me this is pickled pigs feet, I'm surprised it's this delicious."

"Wrong animal."

One dark brow lifted, giving him a sardonic look. "Cow?"

"No."

"Horse?"

"No!"

"Frog's legs?"

She shook her head. "You'll never guess. I

found the recipe in my mother's French cookbook I brought with me."

He cocked his head. "Then this could cover anything from brains to innards to tongues."

"This is more of an 'end' thing. The *marchand* at the *boucherie* told me it was a great delicacy," she confessed.

"An end thing…" She could hear his brilliant mind turning over the possibilities.

When nothing was forthcoming she said, "It's oxtail. How can the French eat it? I think it's disgusting!"

CHAPTER SEVEN

ALEX'S explosion of laughter echoed off the limestone walls. It was the deep male kind, so infectious her tears turned to laughter, too.

He reached for her hand and squeezed it. His touch shot warmth through her system. "I'm touched that you went to so much trouble for me."

"I should have fixed you something *I* love. Because you're the kind of man you are, you would never say anything to hurt my feelings, but even I can tell this would have to be an acquired taste. It's too mild and fatty, a terrible thing to serve a hungry man."

"Terrible," he teased. His gaze slid to hers. It was alive with emotion. "Let's have some wine with it."

"No—wait—"

Her cry resounded in the room, wiping his sensual smile away. "Why? What's wrong now?"

"Nothing. It's just that I bought us a special surprise while I was in town. Since I didn't think I'd be seeing you before tomorrow evening, I hadn't planned on producing it yet, but under the circumstances I think now is the perfect time."

"Do I get to open it?" He looked and sounded like an excited schoolboy waiting to tear away the wrapping on his long-awaited birthday present.

She nodded. "But please be careful."

In a few swift strides he reached the counter. She got to her feet and moved closer to watch him. The carton encased an old green bottle of wine packed in straw. He drew it out to examine the magenta and cream label. She'd already had the privilege. In fact, she'd stared at it for a long time, hardly able to believe she'd been able to buy anything so precious.

His face paled. "Domaine Belles Fleurs Coteaux-du-Layon Cuvee D'Excellence, 1892, Anjou, France." As he spoke the words, he sounded like a man who'd gone into shock.

Suddenly his eyes shot to hers. They were on fire. "Where did you get this?" His voice trembled.

"I went to an impeccable source. Madame Fournier was able to put me in touch with Monsieur Honore Dumarre, a wealthy businessman and wine connoisseur living in Angers. He had three bottles of Domaine Belles Fleurs from different vintages in his wine cellar. When I explained why I wanted one, he was gracious enough to sell this to me."

She could see Alex's throat working. Even his hand was trembling. "A bottle like this can cost upward of five thousand dollars. Even meeting his full price, he'd have an almost impossible time parting with it."

Dana smiled. "Once in a while it helps that I'm Jan Lofgren's daughter. The fact that he's shooting his latest film on the Belles Fleurs estate went a long way to make up his mind for him. I threw in the fact that the new owner lived on the other side of the world until now and has never tasted his family's wine before."

Alex resembled a war victim suffering shell shock. "I have no words for what you've done," he whispered, "but you have to return it and get your money back."

She took a fortifying breath. "I knew you'd say that, but I did it for the pleasure it gave me. Do you know he wants to meet you? He'll be phoning you to make the arrangements."

Alex's face darkened with lines, revealing the remote quality she sometimes glimpsed, the quality that made her shiver. "Didn't you hear me, Dana? If you don't return it, I will." He'd already taken possession of the bottle and put it back in the carton. It sounded like he hadn't heard anything else she'd told him.

Her chin lifted defiantly. "That was *my* gift. It came from my own savings, not the studio's funds, in case you were worrying."

"If your father knew about this…"

At the mention of her dad, her anger was kindled. "Do you intend to tell him?" she fired. "Go ahead. But if you think blackmail will make me change my mind, then you don't know me at all."

"Dana," his voice grated. "This isn't the kind of thing you give someone."

"Well, pardon me, but I thought I just did. Some friends give cars—jewels—in the profession my father works in, I've seen it all. It pleased me to give you something of your mother's history, the only tangible evidence left of a thriving estate. Where's the romance in your soul?"

His hands knotted into fists. "We're talking about your hard-earned money."

She shrugged her shoulders. "There's money, and then there's money. I've never had anything

I wanted to spend it on before. But I should have remembered that you're in dire straits and need to get the taxes paid, so I tell you what. You go to Monsieur Dumarre. When you get the money back, you use it to make another installment to the bank so you can get out of here sooner and pursue your career."

Blind with pain, she grabbed her bag and flew down the long corridor to the foyer. She didn't need a light upstairs. Dana knew the place blind-folded. The second she reached her room, she threw herself on the bed.

"Dana—"

She might have known he'd be right behind her. Now she couldn't sob into the pillow. "Come back downstairs so we can talk."

"I'd rather not."

"Then I'm coming in. Just remember I gave you a choice."

When she heard the door open, she sat up on the bed and turned on the flashlight next to her bed. At first glance he looked ashen-faced, but maybe it was the starkness of the light against the dark.

Alex pulled the chair away from the writing table he'd provided earlier and sat down. He leaned forward with his hands clasped between his legs and stared at her for several tension-filled moments. "Your gift has overwhelmed me."

She lowered her eyes, too full of conflicted emotions to speak.

"Dana—how can I make you understand I've never known generosity like yours. I'm touched beyond my ability to express what I'm feeling."

His sincerity caused the tightness in her chest to break up. "I guess I wanted us to know what it tasted like so much, I went overboard in your opinion. But honestly, Alex, it wasn't that much money."

"How much?" he demanded quietly. "The truth."

"He gave me a discount as a welcome-to-Anjou gift for you. It only cost three thousand dollars. You see? Not as much as you'd imagined. It's less than what I make a month."

A sound of exasperation came out of him. She wanted to reach him, but how?

"Can't you understand how happy it made me to find a bottle of wine that came from *your* vineyard? After seeing the condition it's in now, it's like—I don't know—it's like finding this amazing treasure."

The torment on his handsome face killed her.

"There's only one way I'd accept it," his voice grated.

She jumped off the bed. "I won't let you pay me for it, so I'll keep it for my own souvenir from France. One day I'll open it for an important occasion a-and I'll remember," her voice faltered. "Now let's forget the whole thing, because I have." She started for the door.

"Where do you think you're going?" He was on his feet in an instant.

"Down to the kitchen to throw out the rest of that awful *Hochepot en boeuf*." Dana had to get out of there before she blurted what she really wanted to say—that she was in love with him, the gut-wrenching kind that went soul deep!

Her father would call it temporary madness, but he would have to be careful because this intensity of feeling had happened to her mother after meeting the enigmatic Swede. Her world had never been the same after that, either.

"The dishes will keep." Alex had caught up to her near the top of the stairs. He swept her in his strong arms like she was weightless and carried her back to the turret round.

"No, Alex—" she cried, trying to squirm out of his tight grasp. "Now you're feeling sorry for me like I'm a little girl who'll be all better with a peck on the cheek and a lollipop."

He laid her on the bed and followed her down so he half covered her with his hard-muscled body. She felt his fingers furrow into her hair, as if he loved the texture. "You don't have any comprehension of what I'm feeling. Would that you were a little girl I could send home to your daddy. But you're not," he muttered in what sounded like anguish.

"You're a big girl I'd like to keep locked up in this tower for my pleasure." His lips roved over her features, setting tiny fires. "Do you understand what I'm saying?"

Her heart leaped. "Then stop tormenting me and really kiss me. I've been in pain since this morning when Saskia interrupted us."

"I've been in pain much longer than that," he confessed.

The way his mouth closed over hers produced such ecstasy, she knew nothing except that this marvelous man was creating a vortex of desire deep within her. No other feeling in the world could compare. They gave kiss for kiss, savoring the taste and feel of each other. Divine sensations held her in thrall.

As time passed she needed to get closer and slid her hands around the back of his head, luxuriating in the freedom of touching and kissing him. He groaned against her tender throat. "You have no idea how much I want you."

The feel of their entwined bodies created heat, making her feverish. His caresses caused her breathing to grow shallow. "Alex—" she cried in a rapturous daze, clinging to him with helpless abandon.

"What's wrong?" he whispered against her swollen lips.

Wrong?

His hands stilled on her shoulders. "Am I frightening you? This is all too new to you, isn't it. Tell me the truth."

In that second while her mind was still capable of hearing him, she felt her heart plummet to her feet. Didn't Alex know she'd cried out his name in a state of euphoria?

The thought came to her that he would never have asked that question if he'd considered her his equal. That was because he didn't see her as a mature woman. It stunned her that his first impression of her still clung to him. In his eyes she was a girl disobeying her father's wishes—a girl so impulsive she thought nothing of sleeping in a château with a stranger and worse—spending $3,000 of her money on a whim.

Dana forgave him for that. Of course she did. She was also aware few men would have been as decent in this situation. But as long as he saw her in that light, it took away some of tonight's joy. Maybe no man would ever take her seriously if she continued to be associated with her father. Neal had been a case in point. Slowly she removed her arms from around his neck.

Tonight this unparalleled experience had given her a lot to think about. Though it killed her, she eased away from him. "You didn't frighten me, but I guess if we're being truthful, I am somewhat nervous that things have escalated so fast."

His handsome profile took on a chiseled cast before he got up off the bed. He stood at the end with his powerful legs slightly apart, away from the flashlight's beam. "I made a vow I'd never cross your threshold while you stayed here. Tonight I broke it, but I swear to you it will never happen again."

"Alex—there's no one to blame. We both lost our heads for a little while. It's human. I'd be lying if I didn't admit I enjoyed every minute of it, but as long as we're being honest, I wish you'd tell me something."

His shadowed eyes swept over her in intimate appraisal, waiting.

"Would you rather I left? Arrangements have already been made for me to stay in Saskia's room at the Metropole."

The way his mouth tightened into a thin line made her shiver. "That decision is entirely up to you. Meet me at the truck at seven-thirty in the morning and I'll drive you to Angers to get your car."

Her heart thudded till it hurt. By asking him that question, she'd proved she was the girl he'd called her, not a woman who acted on her own. Let it be the last mistake she made. "Thank you. Good night."

His dark eyes impaled hers before he disappeared out the door.

She sat on the bed for a long time pondering what to do. A girl would have a meltdown. A woman would brazen her way out of this.

He'd told Saskia that Dana was part of his staff; therefore she'd behave like an employee from here on out. She'd fix the lunches, but beyond that she'd leave him alone until she left the château. The man didn't have time for drama. He was in a hurry.

* * *

At six-thirty the next morning, Alex got up to fill the truck bed with debris. Might as well take another load to the landfill on the way to Angers. When he drove around the front of the château, his pulse sped up to find Dana waiting for him. She looked sensational in white pleated pants and a mini print top of blues and greens on a white background. He'd never known a woman so appealing, all golden and fresh as a piece of summer fruit.

"Good morning." She said it with such a friendly demeanor, last night's fireworks might never have happened. The minute she climbed in the cab, she brought the fragrance of strawberries with her, probably the result of her shampoo.

"You sound rested."

She opened her window. "I had a wonderful sleep."

His fingers tightened on the steering wheel as they headed for the gate. Throughout the endless night his desire for her had never cooled. He could still taste her mouth, feel the mold of her body. Though he'd told her it was her decision about staying or leaving, he hadn't meant it. The château wouldn't be the same without her in it. He'd made up his mind to do whatever was necessary to keep her sleeping on the premises.

"When I came down to the kitchen a few minutes ago, I couldn't find the wine bottle."

He flicked her a shuttered glance, feasting on her lovely profile. "I put it in the wine cellar for sakekeeping."

She flashed him an enticing smile. "That's where it should have been all along. Thank you."

Something was going on in that unpredictable brain of hers. Silence stretched between them. Before they left the landfill he said, "How would you like to tour Angers castle this morning? There won't be as many tourists this early. We'll escape the worst of the heat."

To his surprise she gave a caustic laugh that didn't settle well. "Do you know you're so much like my father at times, it's uncanny?"

His black brows met together in disbelief. "How did he get into this conversation?"

"When has he ever *not* been a part of it in some way or other? Last night you lit in to me. This morning you're trying to placate me. That has been his modus operandi since I was a child. Throw Dana a tidbit and she'll forget."

He gunned the engine and streaked out of there until they were beyond the view of any workers. Then he slammed on the brakes beneath the trees.

Turning to her, he slid his arm along the back of the seat and encircled her warm nape with his hand. He could feel her pulse quicken beneath his fingers.

"I haven't forgotten one second of what happened last night and know in my gut you haven't, either." Unable to stop himself, he kissed her neck, knowing her skin smelled that sweet all over. "The fact is, I want you to stay at the château and was hoping to tell you that while we took a little time off to play. You were right about Jack being a dull boy."

"I wasn't planning to leave," she stated quietly, jolting him in that inimicable way of hers. "As for Jack, it's a well-known secret dull boys are usually the most successful because they never waiver from their goal."

Dana understood him so well, it hurt.

"Knowing how anxious you are to get the estate ready for the public, you won't be doing either of us a favor by taking me through that monster castle. I have my own plans for today. Thank you anyway."

The desire to drag her off to an undisclosed location and kiss her until she cried for mercy was trumped only by the knowledge that she wasn't going to run away from him yet. He bit her earlobe gently before separating himself from her so he could start up the engine.

Neither of them spoke for the rest of the drive into town. He didn't mind. For now it was enough to know she didn't want to leave the château. She loved everything about it including his damn grapes lying dormant inside those gnarled trunks.

It seemed the only drawback in the scenario was Alex.

"There's my car." Her voice jerked him from his torturous thoughts. He maneuvered his truck through the hectic morning traffic and pulled into a parking spot near hers.

She alighted before he could help her down. "You didn't need to get out," she told him as he followed her to the car.

"I'm the one who told you to leave it here overnight. Just looking to make sure everything works." He watched her get in, then shut the door for her. After checking the tires, he told her to pop the trunk. "Everything looks good."

She started the engine. "Thanks for driving me in. See you later." As she backed out and drove off, he waved until he couldn't see her golden head anymore. Turning sharply on his heel, he walked two blocks to the post office to collect his mail.

There were a few bills and letters from his colleagues in Bali, as well as his contacts in Louisiana. He would read them when he got back on the estate. As he finished cleaning out his mailbox, a postcard fell on the floor. He picked it up. The picture of Sanur gave away the name of the sender.

Martan—thank you for the postcard you sent with the big castle on it. One day I want to see it and the house your grandfather left you. I am working hard and am saving my money to come and visit. Maybe work for you one day in the States? Are the French women as hot as they say? How many have you had so far? Write soon, Sapto.

A smile broke out on Alex's face. He walked around the corner to a tourist shop where he bought a postcard with a photograph of the Château de Chenonceau, Dana's favorite. When he returned to the post office, he wrote a message on the back.

Hey, Sapto—I liked your card. It brought back many memories. I'm glad you're working so hard. It'll pay off. Maybe one day we'll see each other again. The French women are definitely hot, but they can't compare to the American woman staying at my château. I have plans for this one. Alex wrote the rest of his thoughts about her in Balinese and signed it, *A. Martin.*

After affixing a stamp, he mailed it, then left for home in his truck. Halfway to the estate it struck him that for the first time since being in France, he thought of it as home. Something was happening to him. Something profound.

Deep in thought about everything that had transpired last night, he almost didn't hear his cell phone in time to answer it. Hoping it was Dana, he almost said her name when he clicked on.

"Monsieur Martin?" a man asked in French. Disappointment swamped him.

"Oui?"

"This is Honore Dumarre. Perhaps Mademoiselle Lofgren hasn't had a chance to tell you about our meeting yesterday."

Alex straightened in his seat. Dana had warned him the other man would be calling, but he hadn't expected it this soon. "As a matter of fact, she presented me with an 1892 bottle of Belles Fleurs wine from your cellar last night."

The man chuckled. "Technically it wasn't from my wine cellar. I was just the keeper of it. Now I know why I held on to this one. It's a great honor for me to know it is now in the hands of the rightful owner. *Soyez le bien venu, monsieur.* I am so pleased to know a Fleury is back among us after all these years."

Something in Monsieur Dumarre's nature caused Alex to warm to him. "Thank you, *monsieur*. I'm touched by your words. As you can imagine, it was such an incredible gift, I'm still overcome. I'd intended to phone you before the day was out and thank you for parting with it."

"Mademoiselle Lofgren was so excited to give it to you, I couldn't have done anything else. Once in a while life offers us something beyond price. I'm not only thinking about the wine, but the beautiful young woman herself. Her soul shines right out of those heavenly blue eyes, doesn't it? What a prize she is."

"Yes," was all Alex could say because emotion had caught up to him.

"To think she's Jan Lofgren's daughter. His films are sheer genius."

"I agree."

"Did she tell you I'd like to host a party?" That was news. Dana probably would have told him if he'd given her half the chance. "All your vintner neighbors will want to meet you. I plan to invite the Lofgrens, too, and hope they can come."

"Thank you, Monsieur Dumarre. I'm sure it will please them to be included."

"*Excellent.* Call me Honore. My wife, Denise, and I were thinking Saturday, the twenty-eighth? Say seven o'clock? Would that be convenient?"

"I'll look forward to it with great pleasure. And please, call me Alex."

"*Bon.* It will be an evening everyone will look forward to."

"You're very kind."

"Not at all. *À bientôt,* Alex."

"*À la prochaine,* Honore."

On Monday morning Dana left the château early to meet with her father. She'd called him ahead of time to let him know she was coming. When she knocked on the hotel room door, he answered in his robe still drinking a cup of coffee.

"Hi, Dad." She moved inside, taking a glance around his messy room. "I'm here to run you to the hospital in Angers for your blood check. While I'm waiting for you, I'll do your wash with mine." She'd brought a laundry bag with her and started gathering up his things.

"I thought you'd forgotten."

How did he dare say that to her? It just proved

how unconscious he was where she was concerned. "Have I ever forgotten anything?"

He eyed her moodily. "I never see you." Oh, brother. "From what I understand you're too busy putting the library in order for Alex."

"I never see you, either." She turned it back on him. "You're so busy directing, the only way I know you've been at the château is to find the empty basket by the door to the grand salon every afternoon."

After a brief silence he said, "Your lunches are appreciated. You cook like your mother." He set the empty coffee cup on the table.

Dana almost dropped the load of clothes she was fitting in the bag. A compliment from him came around about as often as Halley's Comet. "She was the best."

"I miss her, too. Dana—will you sit down? I want to talk to you."

"Why?" She sensed a lecture coming on, his only reason for a talk these days.

"Because I want to give my daughter a birthday kiss. When you're in constant motion, I can't." He put his arms around her and hugged her hard. Emotion welled up inside her. She hugged him back.

"I thought you'd forgotten."

"I could hardly do that now, could I." With a kiss on her forehead, he let her go and pulled a familiar-looking bracelet out of his pocket. It was twisted like fine gold rope, very elegant, very chic. He fastened it around her wrist. "I gave this to your mother on her birthday before she died. Now I want you to have it."

For him to part with something of her mom's was unprecedented. "Thank you," she whispered. "Mother treasured this. I will, too."

"I know." He cleared his throat. "After the hospital, how would you like to spend the day with me? We'll do whatever you want to do and enjoy a meal at some unique restaurant."

Since she'd walked in the room, she'd sensed he had an agenda, but this offer was way too out of character for him. "What about Saskia?"

He frowned. "She's not invited."

"Can you leave your filming that long?"

"They'll get by without me for a day."

No, they won't! "I thought you were on such a rushed time schedule, you couldn't let anything interrupt the shooting of the film. Come on, Dad. Tell me the real reason."

His face clouded. "You need guidance."

"In other words you were going to spend my birthday giving me another lecture!"

"Is it true you purchased a bottle of Belles Fleurs wine for Alex from a Monsieur Honore Dumarre at a cost of $3,000?"

Dana felt like he'd just thrown a pickaxe at her heart. Had Alex betrayed her? She couldn't bear it.

"Yes."

"Yesterday I received a call from him. He invited me to attend a vintner party in honor of Monsieur Martin on the twenty-eighth and asked me to bring my lovely daughter, Mademoiselle Lofgren, with me. He was quick to remind me that true beauty and generosity like yours was rare in this world."

Relief that it wasn't Alex who'd told her father what she'd done filled her with exquisite relief. "How did he get in touch with you?"

"Apparently Madame Fournier at the front desk put you in touch with him in the first place. When he rang the hotel, asking for me, she put him through to my room."

"I see."

"Dana—don't you know Alex Martin is using you?"

Her father would never understand a man like Alex. He was a breed apart from anyone else. "I'm sorry you see it that way."

"Saskia saw you with him in the orchard the other day. From what she told me, I have every reason to be worried about you."

Saskia was furious that Alex hadn't given her the time of day, but her father couldn't see through it. He really was lost without her mother.

"You know what, Dad? It isn't good for us to be working together anymore. I love you very much, but after we're through here in France, I'm going back to California. I want to get myself an apartment and look for a job that can turn into a career."

She picked up the laundry bag. "Shall I wait for you in my car?"

He shook his head. "I'll drive myself to the hospital."

"All right. I'll get a key from the front desk so I can put your clean clothes in the room later. Thank you again for the gift. It's priceless to me."

Two hours later she'd finished all her errands and drove through the gate of the château, anxious to prepare the lunches on time.

Over the last few days she'd been sifting through the library books, labeling the boxes to be put in their proper sections at a later date. There'd been many interesting finds, but so far she hadn't found anything to do with the Fleury family history. Perhaps by the time she left France, she'd come across something valuable to Alex personally.

As for the gorgeous owner of the estate, she'd seen him coming and going, but he'd been more preoccupied than usual and was out in the orchard at all hours. Sensing his urgency to be finished with the outside work, she'd come up with a plan to help him whether he liked it or not.

CHAPTER EIGHT

DANA went upstairs to change into jeans and a T-shirt. After removing the bracelet and putting it away, she slipped on her sneakers and hurried back to the kitchen. As soon as the baskets were ready, Dana took her father's to the grand salon and left it for him, then she went outside the front door with Alex's basket.

While she'd been in town, she'd turned in her rental car on a rental truck. It was only a half-ton pickup, not as big as Alex's, but it could hold a lot. She'd bought some gloves and was ready to roll. After climbing inside the cab, she drove around the back of the château to deliver his lunch.

She saw him loading a huge pile of branches and debris into his truck, more than it could possibly hold. Pleased to have arrived at an opportune moment, she pulled up on the other side of the pile.

Too bad she didn't have her camera so she could capture the stunned look on his burnished face. He paused in his work. "Do I dare ask what this is all about?"

Pleased that he didn't seem angry she said, "I traded in the rental car on this rental. It's my birthday and I want to do something that will make me happy. If you'll just let me help you haul this stuff away, it'll make my day. I'm a California girl and we love the sun."

"I haven't had an offer like that in a long time."

"Good." She slipped on the gloves and climbed out of the cab with his basket. "I'll put this in your truck. You can eat it on the way to the landfill." Dana felt his piercing gaze travel over her body. If he was wondering how long she'd last, she would prove she wasn't afraid of hard work.

Some of the branches were too heavy for her, but for the most part she was able to fill up the back of her truck with hefty tosses. When she saw how fast the pile was disappearing, she wished she'd thought of doing this a week ago.

"You keep up that pace and you'll wear yourself out."

"I'll take a rest when I need to," she assured him. They both continued working until the pile had disappeared. "Let's go dump all this stuff. I'll follow you." She climbed in the cab and started the engine.

The last thing she saw was his dazzling white smile before he got in his truck and took off around the château. This was so much fun, she didn't want it to end. Being with Alex made her happy. It didn't matter what they were doing.

By the end of the day they'd made six more hauls, turning out double the work in half the time. When they returned and she parked the truck in front, he drew up next to her. In two seconds he walked over and pulled her out of the seat into his arms.

"You're hired," he murmured against her neck. His slight growth of beard tickled.

She tightened her arms around his broad chest. "I hope you mean that because I intend to help you until I leave."

His lips roved over her sunburned features before plundering hers. They drank from each other's mouths over and over. Their bodies clung. She relished his warmth that combined with his own male scent. Both were hot, thirsty and tired. Dana had never looked worse, but the way he was kissing her made her feel beautiful. She'd never felt beautiful before.

"You deserve a long soak in the tub, but make it a short one. Meet me in the foyer in a half hour. I've been looking forward to our Scrabble game and don't want you falling asleep on me after dinner."

"I can't give you beautiful in half an hour, but I'll be clean."

"Then you don't mind if I don't shave?"

She smiled up into his eyes. "I like it. With that five o'clock shadow, no one would ever mistake you for our dull boy Jack." She kissed the corner of his jaw one more time before tearing herself out of his arms.

Thirty minutes later she hurried down the staircase in sandals, wearing a khaki skirt toned with a summery tan-and-white striped blouse that tied at the side of the waist. Her hair was still damp from washing it. She'd brushed it into some semblance of order. With an application of tangerine lipstick, she was ready.

Dana's heart was pounding far too fast. She would never be this age again and she would never have a birthday like this again with a man who could thrill her inside and out the way Alex did.

As he stepped out of his office and beckoned her inside, her legs turned to mush because he was so dark and handsome. He'd put on a cream polo shirt and tan trousers. "We match," she quipped to cover her emotions at being invited in the room where he worked and slept.

"I thought we'd eat in here tonight."

The interior came as total surprise because he'd surrounded himself with modern furniture. Amazingly it was like the kind in her parents' home in Hollywood. She glanced at him. "I take it you had all this shipped here?"

He nodded. "From Bali. Pieces of mine and my parents'. When I come in this room, it helps remind me I'm not a seventeenth-century man."

"I see what you mean. The château's atmosphere can swallow you alive. Every time I go to bed upstairs, I feel caught between two worlds."

She wandered over to an end table next to the leather couch where a framed picture was displayed. Dana studied it for a minute. "You get your height and bone structure from your father, but your coloring is all Fleury like your mother. They're very attractive people, Alex."

"Thank you. I think so, too. Will the birthday girl join me?" He held out a chair for her at a round game table made of mahogany. On the top he'd set up the Scrabble board. Next to the table was a tea cart with plates of club sandwiches, fruit and sodas. She noticed there was a supply of chocolate cookies for dessert.

Once she was seated she said, "I'm so glad we're not having oxtail or pickled pigs feet tonight."

He sat across from her, leveling a devilish glance at her. "After the hours of work you put in today, I wouldn't have done that to you. Help yourself to the food and we'll get started on our game."

Alex had made this casual and easy. She loved him for it. "I'll confess I haven't played this in years."

He sent her a sly smile.

For the next two hours they laughed and ate and played and fought over words they both made up when all else failed. Alex won every round.

"You're too good."

"I had to be in order to keep up with my father."

"Do you know my dad and I never played a board game of any kind? He simply didn't have the patience." Since her mother died, he hadn't had the time.

Alex eyed her steadily. "Some minds are too lofty."

"I think he was just scared to lose," she lied.

He chuckled. "It takes all types."

She nodded, wishing she could fall asleep in his arms.

"You look ready to nod off. Before you do, I have a present for you." He reached under the tea cart and handed her a wrapped gift. She assumed it was a book.

"This is exciting. Thank you."

Though Alex lounged back in the rattan chair, she sensed an intensity emanating from him while he waited for her to undo it. At first she didn't know what to think. The book was about an inch thick and bound in a dull red cloth. No title. It reminded her of an old chemistry lab notebook.

Curious, she opened the cover. Inside the paper had a slight yellow tinge. The French writing and notations, many of them numerical, had been penned in bold black ink. If anything it looked like an account ledger of some kind. She lifted her head to stare at Alex. "What is this?"

"You were so anxious to find something from the wine cellar, I rummaged through a couple of boxes upstairs you haven't opened yet and came across this book kept by one of the Belles Fleurs vintners."

"Alex—" she cried with excitement. "So not everything was thrown out."

"Evidently not. If you'll look down the left side, you'll see the notations for 1902. I'm sure there are other books."

"I wish I could read French well enough to decipher this."

"Let me translate a little for you." He got up from the table and came around to stand behind her. With one arm encircling her left shoulder, he used his right index finger to show her each line as he explained in English. His chin was buried in her hair, sending little bursts of delight through her body.

"June—at the critical moment when the buds burst forth, the rain throughout the month produced irregular flowering. Bunches of grapes emerged stillborn.

"July—mildew has been a problem. The rain has continued causing the Layon to flood its banks. We removed the excess leaves from the west side of the plants to allow any sun to shine on the maturing fruit. We eliminated some bunches that flowered improperly in hope that the remaining clusters would ripen completely.

"'August—the hard labor is nearly done. The weather has turned hot and sunny. We have hopes some of the vintage will be saved. God grant us a few more dry weeks. By September we could have fruit. June makes the quantity. August makes the quality. We will see.'"

She shook her head. "I can't believe it. To think he's talking about the vineyard out there. *Your* vineyard! This is like a voice reaching out from the past. It gives me chills."

"Me, too," he murmured deep in his throat. It sent delicious vibrations through her nervous system. "Let's get more comfortable and we'll read a few more pages."

They gravitated to the comfy couch. He pulled her down on his lap, cocooning her so her head lay against his shoulder. Page by page he read to her, giving them insight into the struggles and joys of a vintner's work. The whole process was incredibly complicated. Much more so than she would ever have imagined.

His low masculine voice was so pleasant on her ear, she never wanted him to stop. Her eyelids started to feel heavy. She tried to stay awake, afraid to miss anything he told her.

"You're falling asleep."

"No, I'm not. Please don't make me move."

He pressed his mouth to hers. "I won't."

She yearned toward him. "I love it when you kiss me."

"I love to kiss you. The shape of your mouth is like the heart of a rose. It was made for me."

"Don't leave me." Her need for him had turned into an unbearable ache.

"I don't intend to."

Dana melted into him, trying to absorb his very essence until she knew no more.

The next time she became aware of her surroundings it was morning. She discovered herself on top of her bed in the same clothes she'd had on last night minus her sandals, covered by the duvet. She remembered nothing after she'd curled up against Alex.

It meant he'd carried her all the way up the stairs and down the hall to her room. And *that* after he'd put in ten hours of hard labor and prepared her birthday dinner.

As she sat up, she saw her present on the table next to the bed. Alex intended her to keep it, otherwise he wouldn't have brought it upstairs with her. She was touched beyond words, but at the same time it meant the book didn't have the significance for him it had for her. He had no qualms about her taking it with her when the company left for Germany.

A psychiatrist probably had a term for her wanting Alex to care about his own property when it had nothing to do with her.

She rolled out of bed and changed into another pair of jeans and a jade top. As she put on her sneakers, a few new aches in her arms and back reminded she'd put in some hard physical work yesterday. There would be more today. She couldn't wait. It meant being with Alex.

After she'd freshened up in the bathroom, she went downstairs to get some breakfast. He was already in the kitchen. She felt his gaze staring at her over the rim of his orange juice glass. "Sleeping Beauty awake at last."

"I'm sorry I passed out on you last night. That last long walk carrying me must have been a backbreaker."

His dark eyes were smiling. "Not even love's first kiss could waken you, but I'm not complaining."

For an odd reason she felt shy around him all of a sudden. "Thank you for a wonderful birthday. I'll never forget it." She reached for an apple and bit into it.

"I won't, either. I've never seen a woman work as hard as you do."

"Mother said it's the Swede in me."

She would never know what he was going to say next because Paul came in the kitchen looking for Alex.

"I'm glad I caught you before you went outside to work. For the next two days we'll be shooting some scenes here in the kitchen. They'll be night takes. The set director will want to come in here around 7:00 p.m. each evening to get everything organized. Will that be a problem for you?"

Alex shook his head. "Not at all. It will give me an excuse to play." His probing gaze swerved to Dana. "Mademoiselle Lofgren has accused me of being a dull boy. Two nights should give me enough time to rectify her poor opinion."

Paul winked at her. "Just don't let your dad know."

"What shouldn't I know?"

Dana jerked around in time to see her father enter the kitchen looking like thunder. Paul was quick on the uptake. "It's a joke between your daughter and me. Lighten up, Jan. It's only eight-thirty and we've got a whole day and night to get through." He disappeared out the door.

Her father walked over to her. "I need to talk to you in private, Dana. This is crucial." He flicked Alex a glance. "If you'll excuse us."

"Of course."

Disappointment swamped Dana. She'd planned to help Alex outside until time to fix the lunches. The absolute last thing she wanted to do was damage control for her father. He must have rattled one of the actors. Unfortunately when her father lost his temper, the ground shook and he used Dana to placate injured feelings.

Her gaze darted briefly to Alex before she left the kitchen.

When she found out what her father wanted, she hurried to find Paul. "Do me a favor?"

"Anything if it will put your father in a better mood. He and David don't usually quarrel."

"It's Dad. When he decides he wants something at the last minute, there's no dealing with him on a rational basis. I'm going to be gone for the next few days. Until I'm back, will you arrange for lunches to be brought in for him and Alex? Ask someone to take his out back and put it on his truck where he'll see it?"

"Sure."

"Thanks, Paul. Just hope I come back with good news."

"Amen."

Three more trees and the orchard would be cleared out. Alex drove his truck around the back of the château and got started on the first one. While he worked, he listened for Dana's truck.

When she'd come in the kitchen this morning, she'd been dressed for work and his anticipation was growing.

After yesterday's experience he was spoiled and wanted her around every minute of the day and night, but several hours went by with no sign of her. Being employed by her father, naturally he had first call on her time. Where she was concerned, Alex had no rights at all.

Over the last few weeks he'd been listening between the lines. To his chagrin it appeared she'd be ready to move on to Germany at the end of the month, which was coming up too fast.

Lines bracketed his mouth. Regardless of her wanting to be independent, he noticed how quickly she jumped when her father snapped his fingers. Keeping in mind what Paul had told him, it made sense she continued to work with her father in order to study his directing skills.

Suddenly his saw slipped because he wasn't paying attention. He let go with a curse when he realized a couple of teeth had nicked him on the left forearm. Nothing major, but he needed a cloth to staunch the bleeding.

"Hello, Alex."

He stepped off the ladder to see Saskia Brusse, of all people, waiting for him with a large sack in her hand. "*Bonjour*, Mademoiselle Brusse."

"I'd say this was perfect timing. Did you know you're bleeding?"

"That's why I came down from the tree."

"I think there are some napkins in here that will stop it." She opened the sack and produced several.

"Thank you. Just what I needed." He pressed the paper napkins against it. Just as he thought, the cuts were mere surface wounds.

"You're welcome. Paul asked me to bring you lunch from the Hermitage. Mind if I stay out here and talk to you while you eat?" The brunette flashed him a smile that said she knew she was a knockout. Alex agreed, but he had other plans. He intended to find out why Dana hadn't come.

"I'm sorry, but I'm headed to the landfill." He climbed in the truck and closed the door. "It's been a pleasure talking to you, *mademoiselle*. I thank you and Paul for remembering me. Now, if you'll excuse me, I need to get back to work."

"But you've hardly taken any time off—"

"I can't afford to. There's still the undergrowth around the sides and the front of the château to get rid of."

For the rest of the day he worked steadily until the last tree had been pruned. When he returned from his last haul, it was six-thirty. Dana had to be doing an errand for her father because her truck wasn't out in front.

Paul was just heading out with some others in the minivan. Alex slowed down so they could talk. "I appreciated the lunch."

"No problem. Dana will be back in a few days."

Back? He struggled to control his shock. "Where did she go?"

"Maillé."

Alex had to reach back in his mind. "As in the Maillé massacre?"

The other man nodded. "It's near Tours. At the last minute Jan decided he wants to film a small segment there. She's gone ahead to make the arrangements."

"Understood." Swallowing his bitter disappointment, he drove on around the back of the château.

Dana could have told him. She could have asked him to drive her there, but she wouldn't do that. It wasn't in her nature. If he asked her about it, she'd say that she knew he needed to finish his work.

Before he got out of the truck, he phoned her. With the orchard finished, he'd take the time off. He needed her… But with each attempt to reach her, he got the message "no service." She'd turned off her phone!

In his gut he got the disturbing sensation she was intentionally separating herself from him. Was this her way of letting him down? Cut him off at the ankles and chop away slowly until there was nothing left by the time the company moved on to Germany? Was it of her own free will because she had a career to pursue and didn't need a complication like Alex?

Another colorful expletive escaped his lips.

He could go after her and search until he found her, but that would mean asking Paul to be in charge of the estate until Alex returned. He couldn't do that. The man was under enough stress with Jan in one of his dark moods, but no mood could be as black as Alex's right now....

Thursday morning Dana got up early and left her hotel in Maille for Rablay. It had felt like months instead of three days since she'd seen Alex. By ten o'clock she could hardly breathe as she pulled around the side of the château and saw him making inroads on the vegetation between it and the winepress building. That meant he'd finished the orchard!

Panic set in. Whether he made enough money to pay the back taxes or not, she feared his days in France were numbered.

Trembling with excitement to see him again, she climbed out of the cab and hurried over to the area where he was working on the ladder. She stood at the base and looked up, feasting her eyes on his well-honed physique.

"Pardon, monsieur," she said in her best French, which she knew was terrible. "I'm looking for a man named Prince Charming. Could you tell me where he is?"

His hands stilled on the branch he was cutting before he looked down and slanted her a dark, piercing glance. "I'm afraid he only lives in a fairy tale."

She swallowed hard because that remote veneer he sometimes retreated behind was in evidence. "Spoilsport," she teased, hoping to inject a little levity into the conversation. "You're so grumpy I think you've been missing my lunches."

"Saskia has done her best to make up for them."

Not Mademoiselle Brusse any longer? Somehow Dana hadn't expected that salvo. "She loves to fuss for people who appreciate it. If you'll be nice to me, I have a little present for you. It only cost me ten Eurodollars."

"Is it something to eat?" She thought he might be thawing.

"No."

"To read?"

She smiled. "No."

"I give up. Why don't you bring it to me?"

Flame licked through her. "Am I talking to the same man who terrified me last time I tried it? For self-preservation I think you'll have to wait until you come down later. After I run inside for a few minutes, I'll be back out to help you."

She made it as far as the kitchen when she felt his hands on her arms. He spun her around. Their bodies locked, causing her to gasp. His expression looked borderline primitive. "Why did you turn off your phone?"

They were both out of breath. "So my father couldn't bark at me the whole time I was in Maille. I know when I shouldn't invade his space, but when I'm doing business for him, he doesn't recognize boundaries where I'm concerned."

There was a bluish-white ring around his lips. "You didn't say goodbye." He gave her a gentle shake. "Not one phone call to let me know you were all right."

His words came as a revelation. "I—I wanted to call you, but I hated to bother you."

"Bother me?" he blurted. "By *not* phoning you've caused me two sleepless nights!"

"I'm sorry. I—"

But nothing else came out because his mouth had descended, devouring her with a hunger she'd only dreamed about. He crushed her against him, filling her with a voluptuous warmth. She swayed, almost dizzy from too much passion.

"While you were gone I almost went out of my mind," he whispered against her mouth before plundering it again. His lips caressed her eyes, her nose, her throat. He left a trail of fire everywhere there was contact.

"Don't you know I missed you, too?" She'd been living to be in his arms again.

"I don't even want to think about what it will be like when you're not around here anymore."

Dana heard the words, but their significance took a little time to sink in. If she understood him correctly, no matter how much he was attracted to her—no matter how much he wanted her and would miss her—when the time came, he was prepared to watch her disappear from his life.

His past relationships had never lasted, yet she wagered every woman who'd loved him still bore the scars of a broken heart. She'd known it would happen to her even before her father had warned her of the perils of staying at the château.

Calling on some inner strength, she cupped his arresting face in her hands. "Well, I'm back for now and I'm dying to give you your present."

Those dark eyes played over her features with relentless scrutiny. "Where is it?"

"In my purse."

"I don't see it."

"It dropped to the floor when you caught up to me."

He pressed another urgent kiss to her mouth before releasing her to pick it up.

"Can I look inside?"

"Go ahead."

His hand produced a sack. He held it up. "Is this it?"

She nodded. "I didn't have time to get it gift wrapped." Dana reached inside the sack and pulled out a hat. "Here—let me put it on you."

His brow quirked. "You bought me a beret?"

"Not any beret. This comes from Maille. I came across a shop that makes these in remembrance of the men of the Resistance in the early days of the war. The proceeds go to a memorial fund for the victims' families who were massacred."

She placed it on his head at a jaunty angle.

"You're a handsome man, you know, and the beret adds a certain *je ne sais quoi*." She stared at him for a moment, trying to recover from her near heart attack. "Every Frenchman should look as good."

He paraded in front of her like a French soldier. "You think?" His disarming smile brought her close to a faint.

"You should listen to Dana. She knows what she's talking about."

They both turned to see the renowned French film star standing inside the entrance to the kitchen. Who knew how long she'd been observing them?

Dana smiled at her. "Simone? Please meet Alexandre Fleury Martin, the owner of the estate who made this location possible for us to rent. Alex? This is Simone Laval."

"Enchante, mademoiselle. I saw one of your French films when my family lived in La Cote D'Ivoire. You're an excellent actress, very intense. My mother was a fan of yours. If she were alive today, she'd love to meet you."

As Dana digested that bit of information, the actress's warm, sherry-brown eyes played over him in genuine female interest. "Call me Simone, and the pleasure is all mine."

Simone was still in her 1940s clothes and

makeup. Obviously Dana's father had given everyone a break to use the restrooms or go outside to smoke.

As she shook hands with Alex, their conversation switched to French. Dana could tell he was totally taken with the winning charm of the thirty-eight-year-old divorcée. What male wasn't attracted to her? With her dark auburn hair, she was a natural-born beauty. A real babe, as the guys on the crew referred to her.

The two of them looked good together. Some people meshed on a first meeting. Dana could tell there was a spark between them. Maybe it was their Gallic connection. Whatever, she saw it in the attitudes of both their bodies. They were so intent on each other, Dana slipped unnoticed from the kitchen.

Her father expected a report on the trip. Now that she was back, she might as well do it while he was waiting to resume the filming.

CHAPTER NINE

"SHALL we go?" Alex cupped Dana's elbow and ushered her out of the movie theater to his truck. After a hard day's work hauling more debris, it had been heavenly to drive into town with him for dinner and a film.

"How did you like the *Da Vinci Code*?" Though it had been out for four years, he hadn't seen it. Now that they were headed home from Angers, she was curious to know his reaction.

He flashed her a curious glance. "I found the mixture of fact and fiction riveting, but I'm much more interested to hear what you thought about it."

"Why?"

His hand squeezed hers a little harder. "Come on, Dana. We both know the answer to that."

She heard an edge in his tone and was stunned by it. "We do? Perhaps you better tell me because I've forgotten."

"A while back Paul confided that you have plans to be a director. Today Simone confirmed it."

Dana was surprised Paul had said anything. She was even more surprised the subject had come up in Alex's conversation with Simone. Disturbed in a strange way, she removed her hand from his warm grasp. "What exactly did she tell you?"

"So you don't deny it."

A heavy sigh escaped her lips. "Alex—what's this all about?" How could such a perfect night have turned into something that created so much tension in him?

"Simone said that your input during several of the scenes at the film studio were so insightful, your father didn't contradict you. I've been thinking about that. If he didn't trust your directing instincts, he wouldn't send you off to arrange film locations for him."

"Before Mother died, she and I did it together."

"But you're the one with the talent."

She lowered her head. "Why do I get the feeling you're accusing me of something?" Out of the corner of her eye she saw his hands tighten on the steering wheel.

"Because when we first met, you misrepresented yourself."

The heat of anger prickled. "In what way?"

"You intimated you were at your father's beck and call, nothing more. In reality you're being groomed by him because he accepts directing as your destiny."

What? "Surely you're joking—" she cried in astonishment.

"Not at all. At first I saw his possessiveness as a desperate attempt not to lose you after your mother passed away." She couldn't believe what she was hearing. "However, in light of what I've learned, I've had to rethink that supposition."

"And what conclusion have you arrived at exactly?" came her brittle question.

"He's hated my guts from day one because he doesn't want anything to get in the way of a brilliant career for you. Your father sees me as a possible threat."

Her pain was escalating in quantum leaps. "But since you and I know that's not the case, there's no point to this conversation. I don't understand what you have against the art of film directing. To each his own, I guess."

He muttered something dampening in French.

"As long as it's question time, why didn't you ask Simone to dinner tonight instead of me? Before Paul left the château earlier this evening, he indicated she's more than a little interested in you. I would have thought you'd love to spend time with such a lovely compatriot."

By now they'd arrived at the front of the château. He slammed on the brakes and turned to her. In the semi-darkness his features took on an almost menacing cast. "You'd like that, wouldn't you?"

She jerked her head toward him. "It's not my place to like or dislike what you do. When you said I could stay at the château, it was understood we were both free agents, able to come and go with no strings. You made that emphatically clear when you refused to accept the bottle of wine I bought you out of friendship."

His sharp intake of breath sounded louder in the confines of the cab.

"Why you're coming at me with this inquisition is beyond me. I've had enough. If you don't mind, I'm tired and need to go to bed."

"But I do mind—" He leaned across her to lock the door so she couldn't get out.

"I want the truth." His lips were mere centimeters from hers, but instead of kissing them, he was being relentless with his questions. "Are you planning to direct films in the future?"

Being a director might have appealed to her

once, but after the Neal fiasco she realized she didn't want to be associated with the film world in any sense. Too many narcissists to deal with, too many artistic temperaments, too much blind ambition. But if she told Alex that, he would continue to believe what he wanted, so it wasn't worth the effort.

"I guess when Dad thinks I'm ready." Not only was it the answer he seemed determined to hear, but it would send the message that she had other things on her mind besides him after she left France. "May I get out now?"

Lines had darkened his face. He studied her through narrowed lids as if he'd been gauging the veracity of her words. "Not yet. A few weeks ago I asked you about the plot of this film. You held back on me. Simone told me the film was really your inspiration. She said you know every line and verse of it, that in fact, you helped write part of the script with David."

"What if I did?"

He sucked in his breath. "Why couldn't you have shared that with me?"

If she told him the truth now, that she'd been trying to be a mystery woman to arouse his interest, he would know she was desperately in love with him.

Deep down he already knew it, but she wasn't about to give him the satisfaction of hearing the words. Not when he was prepared to see her drive away from the château next Monday, never to return.

"Most people don't really want to hear the answer to the questions they ask," she theorized.

He sat back with a grimace. "You put me in that category?"

"I didn't know you that well."

She saw his jaw harden. "You do now. I'd like to hear the story."

"Wouldn't you rather see the film when it comes out and be surprised?"

"No," he muttered. "I don't like surprises."

Dana averted her eyes. "I know."

"I wasn't referring to your gifts. I like my hat," he added in a gentler tone.

So did she. On *him*. "Let's go inside first." Their bodies were too close here in the cab.

Once he'd helped her down, she walked to the front door ahead of him. After he opened it and turned on lights, she made a beeline for the kitchen and took a soda out of the fridge. Small as it was, it provided the symbolic armor she needed to keep him at a distance. Or rather, keep her from him.

He made instant coffee, then lounged against the counter to sip it while he stared at her. "I'm waiting."

"Why are you so interested?"

"How could I not be when you picked my estate out of all the French possibilities?"

She supposed he had a point there. "The story calls for a setting where a German soldier, that would be Rolfe Meuller, refuses to be a part of the Maille massacre of August in 1944 in the Loire Valley. It happened on the day Paris was liberated from German occupation.

"His superior shoots him and he's left for dead. Later on he's discovered barely alive, having dragged himself to the garden of a nearby château that has suffered through two world wars and has been raided for its wine. Perhaps now that I've given you a few details, you understand why I knew the moment I glimpsed the château for the first time that it was perfect. Uncannily so."

Alex nodded.

"A young, aristocratic French woman, the second wife of her military husband who's been stationed in Paris for months, comes across his body. That would be Simone.

"He's very attractive. She's never been able to have children and has been trapped in a loveless marriage. The handsome blond German is someone's son and that sentiment causes her to help him.

"As you might assume, when he starts to heal from his wounds, she wants him to become her lover. That places him in a difficult position because he has a wife he loves, yet this French woman could turn him over to the Vichy French or the Germans at any time. He must find a way to placate her until he can walk on his own and escape.

"To stall for time, he uses psychology to get her to talk to him. The film explores both their psyches, exposing their tortured souls. His agony over the senseless murders and killings in the French town is the focus of the story.

"When she agrees to let him go and not tell the authorities, he makes it back to his wife in Germany. That would be Saskia. Their reunion is tragic because she's had a baby and it isn't his. She's burdened by her own guilt. He's broken by man's inhumanity to man at Maille, torn up over her infidelity and mourning his wasted life in a hideous war.

"They can continue on together, bound by their individual Gethsemanes, or they can go their separate ways. The film forces you to decide what they might or might not do. The viewer will have to examine his or her own soul for the most palatable answer."

He drank the rest of his coffee. "It's going to be a powerful film. Where did the kernel of the idea come from?" Alex used her former words to frame his question.

She tossed her empty can in the wastebasket. "There was a picture of Sarkozy in the newspaper. He was in Maille to honor the victims. I showed it to Dad and we discussed the massacre. Before I knew it, he'd dreamed up a basic storyline. That's how it came into being."

"With all your contributions, will your name be listed in the credits?"

"No. Make no mistake. This is Dad's picture. He's getting a masterful performance out of Rolfe Mueller, an unknown. When the film's released, he'll be a star."

She moved to the doorway. "As for you, your estate will be immortalized. By the time you have it ready for the public to visit, the stream of tourists will be never ending and make you a rich man. Good night, Alex. Thank you for dinner and the movie."

He didn't try to detain her. His nonaction sent another jab of pain to her shattered heart.

Dana didn't sleep well. In the early morning, she went up to the third floor with the intention of opening more boxes and labeling them. However, there was still so many to do and Alex appeared so uninterested in her project, she decided there was no point in going on.

She put the chair she'd borrowed back in the other room and took all her tools back to the bedroom. Restless and dissatisfied, she showered and dressed in fresh jeans and a T-shirt.

For the next two hours she would help Alex haul debris before she had to make the lunches. But in that regard she was stymied because his truck wasn't there and he hadn't left any piles for her to work on. She was so used to knowing where he was at all times, it upset her to find him gone.

At noon she packed the baskets, but he still hadn't returned. She left her father's in its usual spot and Alex's in the kitchen. When one o'clock rolled around and he still hadn't appeared, she went back upstairs to scour the bathroom and leave it as spotless as she'd found it weeks ago.

Her bedding and the bathroom towels belonged to Alex. He wouldn't mind if she used his appliances to get them washed and dried. By three she'd housecleaned the bedroom and had packed up everything.

Dana hadn't intended to move out of the château until tomorrow morning, but it was better this way. No goodbye scene.

On her way out of the side entrance to the truck, she thought about the bottle of Belles Fleurs wine resting down in the wine cellar. Much as she wanted to take it home as a souvenir, she knew it belonged here. Alex had given her the vintner notebook. That would have to be enough.

One more day's filming on Monday and everyone would clear out. Alex would get his château back. Dana's part was done. Her father wouldn't be able to fault her for anything, that is if she even figured in the recesses of his mind.

She put her suitcase on the floor of the cab and took off. If by any chance she and Alex crossed paths, she would tell him she had an errand to do for her father. He wouldn't question it. If he wanted to make plans for the evening, she'd tell him she'd get back to him when she knew something more definite.

Part of her was praying she'd see him coming so she could feast her eyes on him one last time, but it didn't happen. She found herself en route to Paris, free as a bird and filled with the most incredible loneliness she'd ever known.

There was a flight leaving Orly airport tonight for St. Louis. From there she'd take another flight to Los Angeles. The trick was to return the truck to the car rental in time to get through the check-in line.

While she maneuvered in and out of heavy traffic, she phoned her father. He'd be through filming for the day. His phone rang several times. Finally, "Dana?"

"Hi, Dad."

"I'm glad it's you. I just received another call from Monsieur Dumarre. He wants to be sure you're coming to the vintner party tomorrow night he's giving for Alex. After the filming is over tomorrow, we'll drive back to the hotel while I get dressed, then we'll go to his home from there."

The vintner party…Alex hadn't brought it up in days. Another hurt.

"Dad—I'm afraid you'll have to take Saskia with you."

"It's over with her. I want to take my daughter."

He wanted her mother. Dana was the next best thing. Her eyes smarted. "You don't understand. I'm on my way back to California as we speak."

A long silence ensued. "What's going on?"

"I told you the other day. I've got to make my own life. It's time. But I'm hoping you'll do me one favor."

He didn't respond because for once she'd shocked him, but she knew he was listening.

"Please go to the party and take Saskia. Do it to support Alex. H-he's a good man. The best there is." Her voice trembled. "Be nice to him."

"Dana—"

She hung up. For the first time in her life she'd cut him off. It was the beginning of many firsts to find her life. One that would never include Alex Fleury Martin.

If you could die from loving someone too much, she was a prime candidate.

After being in meetings all day, Alex arrived back at the château at seven-thirty, anxious to talk to Dana. No vehicles were parked out front. He drove around the side, hoping to see her truck. It wasn't there.

He let himself in the side door. Only when he saw the basket with his lunch still sitting on the counter did he realize he should have called her and told her he'd gotten hung up on business.

She'd packed some plums. He sank his teeth

into one while he waited for her to answer her phone. The caller ID indicated no service. Not to be daunted, he strode through the château to his office and looked up Paul's phone number. He'd know where to find her.

Unfortunately all he got was his voice mail. Alex imagined everyone was out having dinner since it was a Friday night. He left Paul the message to phone him ASAP.

There was a voice mail for Alex from Monsieur Dumarre. The other man had called to remind him of tomorrow's party. He mentioned that Jan Lofgren was coming and would be bringing Dana.

Alex had his own ideas on that score. That was why he needed to talk to Dana. He was taking her to the party and had plans for them afterward. If she insisted she couldn't leave her father, then the three of them would go together and the hostile director would have to handle it!

After making the rounds of the château to lock doors and turn out lights, he returned to the kitchen. He'd had a big meal in Angers with his friend from Louisiana who'd flown in at Alex's request, but he was still craving something sweet, like her mouth. Where was she? Why hadn't she called him?

He poked around in the basket and found a *petit pain au chocolat*. A smile broke out on his face. She had as bad a sweet tooth as he did. In two bites he devoured the whole thing.

Finally desperate, he phoned the Hermitage and asked to be connected to Monsieur Lofgren's room. Again he was shut down when there was no answer and he was told to leave a message. Alex chose not to. If he didn't hear from Dana in another hour, he'd phone her father again.

Maybe the whole company was out celebrating tonight, including Dana. This would be their last weekend in the Anjou before they left for either Maille or the Rhine.

Another film company from Lyon would be arriving in a week for a four-day shoot, followed by the Paris outfit scheduled for mid-September and another for the first two weeks of October.

Every few days he was getting more feelers from his ad. Business was starting to pick up. After talking with his banker today, the outlook was promising that he'd be able to pay the first increment of back taxes by the November deadline.

When he'd come up with this insane scheme, he hadn't really believed it would work, but he'd been out of any other ideas. Then Dana had come trespassing on his property like a mischievous, adorable angel. Her presence had turned his whole life around until he didn't know himself anymore.

The next two hours passed like two years. He was driven to watch TV. No one phoned. He called the Metropole and asked them to ring Dana's room. No answer. Her father wasn't back in his room.

Feeling borderline ferocious over the way his evening had turned out, he took a cold shower before going back to his room. Dana was an early bird. He planned to be up and waiting for her when she drove in from town with the others.

As he entered the bedroom his cell phone rang. It was Paul.

"Thanks for calling me back."

"It sounded important. I'm sorry I didn't check my phone sooner."

"No problem. I was looking for Dana."

"To my best knowledge she's in Paris, seeing about one of the locations there in case Jan decides to add a small scene. He always keeps his options open and nobody negotiates like Dana. She ought to be back some time tomorrow."

All this time she'd been in Paris and unavailable....

"Thanks for the information. Good night, Paul."

The last thing he noticed before turning off the lamp was the beret he'd put on the dresser. Alex comforted himself with the fact that a woman didn't buy a man something like that unless she meant it.

When he awakened the next morning, his first thought was to check his phone in case Dana had called, but there were no messages. Eager to find out if she was back, he got dressed and rushed outside. Still no sign of her truck, either, in front or around the side.

By noon he'd lost all interest in work and decided to quit for the day. On his way down the ladder he heard his name called.

"Paul?"

"Hi. I brought you lunch."

"Where's Dana?" he fired before he realized he'd been rude.

"In Paris. She told Jan she'd meet you at the vintner party tonight. He asked me to pass that along."

Alex took the sack from him. He had to tamp down the surge of negative emotions tearing him apart. "Thanks for the information and the food."

"You're welcome."

* * *

Eight hours later Alex found himself in deep conversation with an enthusiastic crowd of the Anjou's most renowned vintners. Their genuine interest in Alex and their questions concerning his future plans for the estate were heartwarming to say the least.

But by halfway through the evening, Dana still hadn't arrived. Even Monsieur Dumarre, their congenial host who'd brought this very elite fraternity together seemed disappointed. Not even the presence of the famous Jan Lofgren made a difference. However, Dumarre's reaction couldn't match the black state Alex was in.

Dana would never have missed this without a compelling reason. She'd be in her element discussing the Fleury's former contribution to the wine world. Something was wrong. He'd sensed it in his gut since yesterday, but fool that he was, he'd been biding his time because he knew they'd have the rest of the night to themselves.

Being as polite as he could, he excused himself from the crowd and made his way across the room to Jan, who was holding court to a cluster of fascinated listeners. Saskia was circulating with her own following. Without hesitation Alex walked up to him. "Jan? I have to talk to you now. Alone," he underlined.

The older man's frigid blue eyes met his head-on. He nodded and excused himself to everyone. They walked through some French doors to a veranda overlooking the back garden. For the moment no one else was out there.

Alex's hands formed fists. This confrontation had been coming on for a long time. "Where's Dana? I want the truth. So far both Paul and Mademoiselle Brusse have been lying for you so don't deny it."

Jan eyed him pensively. "In California."

Hearing it was like being dealt a body blow, rocking him on his heels. "On another errand for *you*?" His accusatory question hung in the air, sending out its own shock wave.

"No," came the quiet response. "She quit her job yesterday and plans to look for a new one."

"You mean, as an independent film director." No more tiptoeing around the almighty film director. It was past time to lay out the bare bones and be done with it.

To his astonishment, a strange light filled her father's eyes. Alex didn't know they could look like that. "She's good, but that doesn't appear to be her destiny after all."

The words shook him to the core. "What do you mean?"

"I mean, she's got too much of her mother in her—in my opinion the best part of her parents. I hope that answers your question because Saskia's signaling me to rejoin the others."

While Alex stood there in a shocked daze, Jan extended his hand, forcing him to shake it. "If I don't see you again before the company pulls out on Tuesday, I'd like to thank you. Not only for the loan of your magnificent château, but the generosity that went with it."

He cocked his balding head. "My daughter knew a good thing when she saw it."

As he walked away, Alex felt the world tilt. He'd fallen into quicksand of his own making.

When he drove hell-bent through the gate of the château an hour later and saw her truck parked in front, he feared he was hallucinating.

Dana heard Alex's truck before she saw it emerge from the trees. She knew it was impossible, but from the scream of the engine he sounded as if he was going a hundred miles an hour. When he applied the brakes, the truck skidded in a half circle before coming to a stop.

Out of the dust that went flying, he emerged from the cab, looking sinfully handsome in a formal dark blue suit. She'd never seen in him a dress shirt and tie before. He'd gotten a haircut. Not a lot had been removed, but enough to add to his sophistication.

Her mouth went dry because she loved him so much, but he looked terrifyingly angry. In seconds he'd stalked around her side of the truck and flung the door open. He braced his other hand against the frame so she couldn't get out. "I thought you were in California." His voice sounded as if it had come from a subterranean cavern.

Only one person knew her plans. That meant Alex and her father had crossed paths at the party. It would have been a fiery exchange. She shivered, moistening her lips nervously. "I changed my mind, but I got back from Paris too late to come to the party. H-how was it?" she stammered.

His dark eyes studied her with a veiled scrutiny that made the hairs stand on the back of her neck. "Most everyone seemed to have a good time with several exceptions, one of them being Monsieur Dumarre. You made a conquest of him. He was visibly disappointed when you didn't show up."

Dana's hand tightened on the steering wheel. "I'll make it up to him. What I want to know is if *you* had a good time."

"That's a hell of a question to ask since you provided the impetus for him to give the party at all!" he bit out. "Did I have a good time?" His question rent the air. "If you mean did I enjoy getting to meet the prominent vintners in the region and hear stories about the glory days of Belles Fleurs? Then yes, that part was satisfying."

She bit her lip. "Did you take Simone with you? She would have loved it."

Alex made a scathing sound in his throat. "The only star there was Saskia. I had no idea she was such an excellent actress. She managed to convey that you were off doing vital studio business no one else could do. Her performance to cover for your absence did her great credit."

Dana's father had no doubt choreographed Saskia's contribution. He'd actually pulled through for Dana. That was something to be thankful for at least. Alex's rage was another matter altogether.

"Are you always going to be angry with me because of it?"

"I don't know," his voice grated. "You're the one who got me into the predicament in the first place."

His arresting face was so close, she only had

to move her hands a few inches and she could be touching him. "I'm sorry," she whispered.

"No, you're not."

Her head flew back. "You're right. I'm not sorry that because he found out you were a Fleury, he wanted to celebrate your arrival in Rablay with his friends. It was a great honor for you. I wish I'd been there. It's very upsetting to me that I wasn't, but it couldn't be helped." She stirred in place. "I'll find a way to apologize to him, whatever it takes."

The little pulse she'd seen before hammered at the corner of his taut mouth. "Your father told me you quit on him."

With that news out in the open, there were no secrets left. The exchange between them couldn't have been anything but ugly. "True. I'm now jobless and looking for a new career."

"With all your contacts, the field should be wide-open for you in California. Why didn't you get on the plane?"

Dana's lungs constricted. Holding her heart in her hands, she said, "While I was standing in line waiting to check my suitcase, it came to me what I really wanted to do with my life."

"Just like that—" he rapped out, sounding exasperated.

"Yes."

"I guess I shouldn't be surprised," he muttered. "It took you all of ten seconds to decide you wanted to rent the château for your father."

"When something becomes clear, I've found it's better not to hesitate."

"You mean, like charging up a ladder with no regard for your safety?"

Her eyes flashed sparks. "You're never going to let me forget that, are you? I can't help it that I inherited that trait from my mother."

She saw something flicker in the dark recesses of his eyes. "You still haven't answered my question."

"I'm getting to that. After I made my decision not to board the plane, I left the airport terminal and rented the truck back. But by the time I reached Angers, it was midnight. I was so exhausted I stayed at the Metropole and slept in late."

"You've been there all day?" He sounded livid.

"Yes. I had phone calls to make."

"Except to me." His words came out like a hiss.

"I couldn't call you until I'd worked everything out."

He made another violent sound that caused her to quiver. "But it didn't all mesh until it was too late to attend the party. Is that what you're saying?"

She nodded, afraid to look at him. "Could we go inside first?"

"If you'd come to the party, you could have savored dozens of the region's finest wines."

"I could have, but the one I wanted to taste wouldn't have been available. Or was it?" she questioned.

His dark brows lifted. "No. I'm afraid our kindhearted host wasn't willing to give up a second bottle of Belles Fleurs. But who's to say what he would have done if you'd been there…"

On that note he scooped her out of the seat and set her on the ground. In the moonlight she looked so frumpy standing next to him in her jeans and T-shirt, she could have wept. No words passed between them as he pulled her suitcase from the floor of the cab and followed her into the château.

CHAPTER TEN

DANA'S heart skipped a beat when Alex opened the door to the petit salon and turned on the light. "Wait for me in here. I'll be back with your drink."

In this mood, she didn't dare argue with him. Forcing herself not to look at the bedroom end of the room, she moved one of the rattan chairs over to the desk where he'd set up his computer.

Before long he was back. He strolled toward her and set the cola on the desk next to her. Still not saying anything, he shrugged out of his elegant suit jacket. Next came the tie. He tossed them over a nearby chair before undoing the top buttons of his shirt.

The dusting of black hair against his bronzed throat stood out in contrast to the dazzling white of the material. His male beauty caused her to gasp inwardly.

"You wouldn't rather sit on the couch where you'd be more comfortable?"

She'd been there and done that the other night, but everything had changed since then. "This is fine right here for the business I have in mind."

He removed his cuff links and pushed the sleeves up to the elbows, revealing more of his bronzed arms. She saw the gash on his arm. "You cut yourself! When did that happen?"

"Yesterday."

"With the saw?"

"It's nothing. Let's not get off topic. Are you telling me you came back to the château to talk business?"

"Yes. I've had a lot of time to think and—Alex? Will you please sit down? I can't think while you're looming over me like that."

"Is that what I'm doing?"

"Yes."

To her relief he sat down in his swivel chair, extending his long legs so his shoes touched her sneakers. She tucked her feet under her chair. "Is this better?"

"Much."

With one arm on the desk, he gazed at her through shuttered eyes. "How long are you going to keep me in suspense?"

"Not any longer, but you have to promise you won't interrupt until I'm through."

He folded his strong arms. "I'm waiting."

"This is serious now."

"I can see that."

She sat forward. "Please don't patronize me."

"I apologize if that's what it sounded like."

"Sorry. I'm a little touchy about that sort of thing." Dana had thought she could do this, but now that the moment had come, she was in agony. "I have to give you a little background first."

"You mean, there are things about you I still don't know?"

"Exactly. For instance my mother did most of the gardening when I was young. I liked to help her and took pride in the flower beds I planted and weeded. If someone were to ask what was the happiest time of my life, I would have to say it was out gardening, watching things grow. Being in the sun. A lot of beautiful flowers grow in Southern California. It's like a garden of Eden."

So far she seemed to be holding Alex's interest. "But at the time, I didn't consider it important work. Sometimes when I took dad his lunch at the studio, he'd let me stay on the set to watch. What he did seemed very important and I thought, one day I'll grow up to do what he does.

"Over the years I've been studying his technique. One day Paul and I were talking and I expressed my hope to become a director. When I asked him what he thought about it, he was quiet for a while, then he said, 'You're a natural at it, Dana, but I would worry about you because it's not a happy profession.'

"I knew that. My father was living proof he experienced a lot of difficult moments, but directing gave him an outlet for his artistic talent and that seemed very important.

"Little by little, Dad gave me more responsibilities to learn the craft. We often came at an idea the same way. After mother died he trusted me to do more for him. Scouting for unique locations was one example. Editing a script, making changes was another.

"I thought it was what I was truly *meant* to do. Yet in the back of my mind, Paul's comment continued to nag at me. I've kept asking myself if directing was what I *wanted* to do.

"That question got answered for me last week when I started helping you in the orchard. It has taken me back to those times when I helped

Mother in the yard. There's nothing like hands-on experience working in the out-of-doors.

"Lately I've been looking at the overrun vegetable and flower gardens at the other end of the château. So many ideas of how to replant them and make the grounds beautiful is all I think about. When Dad sent me to Maille, I didn't want to go."

She paused to rub her eyes. "After this long, boring speech, what I'm trying to say is that I'd like to be the first person in line for the estate manager job."

He muttered a French imprecation she didn't need translated.

"Believe me, when word gets out you're looking for one before you leave for Louisiana, there'll be lines out to the street hoping for the privilege. I can't think of any career I'd love more than to be put in charge of this place after you've gone."

"It's a lot of hard work, Dana."

"I like hard work. Besides, it's one of the most beautiful spots in France. I'm in love with it. You could trust me to do a better job than anyone else."

Alex stared at her as if he'd never seen her before.

Taking advantage of the silence, she said, "Until that time, I'd like to apprentice for it. I'll do any jobs that need doing. I'll help you clean every room and bring down the furniture. I'd love to put the books in the library and catalog everything.

"I'll plant and weed. I'll pick fruit when the time comes. I realize there are dozens of things I don't know how to do, but I can watch and learn from you."

That remote look she hated crept over his face.

"Please don't close your mind to this, Alex— I know what you're going to say. That you don't have the money to pay me right now, but I don't want pay. One day when it's finally open to the public, we can talk about a salary. Don't you see there's nothing I'd like more than working here?"

He got to his feet.

Though it was nothing tangible, she realized she'd crossed a line with him that probably spelled disaster for her. Dana had known it would be a huge risk, but she'd been willing to take it.

She jumped out of her chair. "Just promise me you'll think about it and give me your answer in the morning. If it's no, I'll understand and leave."

Afraid he might tell her no right now, she grabbed her suitcase placed by the door and hurried out of the room toward the staircase. For the third time in three weeks she lugged it up the steps.

When she reached her room, she turned on the flashlight so she could see to get ready for bed. But she was too worked up to change yet and went over the window. Moonlight had turned the view of the Layon into a river of silver.

For a long time she stood there remembering the night they'd cleaned this fabulous room together, the fun they'd had buying her bed. Her mind was filled with memories of the nights he'd come in here to light the candles, bringing the kind of enchantment you could never find in a storybook.

Hot tears trickled out the corners of her eyes. As she turned away to open her suitcase, Alex appeared in the entry, looking so handsome she almost fainted. He was still wearing the same clothes and carried several things in his arms. Her heart almost leaped out of her chest.

"Don't be startled. I've come to give you your answer now."

It was darker on that side of the room. She moved toward him, but she still couldn't see what he'd put on the table. Maybe it was new candles, but when he walked toward her, carrying two half-full glasses of wine, anything she'd been thinking about left her mind.

The way he was staring at her, she honestly couldn't catch her breath. "As interviews for a job go, yours was extraordinary," he began. "I'm very impressed you would forego a salary in order to learn how to be my manager, therefore, you're hired."

"You mean it?" she cried, hardly daring to believe it.

A ghost of a smile hovered around his lips. "Let's drink to your success, shall we?"

Alex was being very mysterious. It sent chills of excitement through her body. With a trembling hand, she took one of the wineglasses from him. He touched her rim with his and took a drink. She sipped hers, but the second the liquid ran down her throat she realized they weren't drinking Percher, Chaume, or any wine she'd ever tasted before.

Her eyes widened. "What domaine is this?" She took another sip. "The texture is so velvety. How could anything be this incredible? Can you taste that smoky sweetness?"

He nodded. "At the party I was told 1892 was a great vintage year."

When the meaning of his words got through, Dana almost dropped the glass. She stared at him in disbelief. "You opened the bottle!"

"You said you were waiting for an important occasion. I would think taking on a new career constitutes as one. Don't you agree?"

Dana was in shock and could only nod her head. She took another drink. "The wine is out of this world. There's a richness that tastes of the earth itself."

"A nuance from the minerals. That's what comes from a hundred years of aging," he murmured.

Emotion caused her eyes to moisten. "To think we're drinking from your grapes that have been growing on Belles Fleurs soil for hundreds of years." She drank a little more. "Don't you feel a tingling to realize this is a tangible connection to your ancestors?"

"I feel a great deal more than that." He finished his wine and put both their glasses on the table. "While we were downstairs I forgot to tell you I met with my colleague from Louisiana yesterday. He's been anxious to know when I'm going to join him."

How odd she could go cold so fast when the wine had warmed her body clear through. "Did you tell him it won't be long now?"

"No. I informed him he'd have to find another agricultural engineer because France is home to me, permanently. I'm getting married."

Maybe she was dreaming.

"My bride-to-be and I have a life to live and a vineyard to work. Both need love and tender nurturing on a full-time basis."

"Alex—"

Her cry reverberated throughout the tower.

"I'm in love with you, Dana Lofgren. I have been from the beginning, but I sensed a battle with your father and was forced to bide my time before I made my move."

She launched herself into his arms, sobbing for happiness. "Oh, darling, I love you so much, you can't possibly imagine."

He rocked her body back and forth, kissing her hair, her face. "I think you convinced me downstairs."

"I couldn't leave you. When I was standing in that line at the airport, I felt I'd come to the end of my life."

Alex buried his face in her hair. "Try hearing your father tell me you'd gone to California."

She hugged him harder. "I'm sorry. I asked him to be nice to you, but I should have known better."

"You don't understand." He pulled back so he could look at her. "In his way, he gave me his blessing."

"What do you mean?" Her heart had started to thud.

He kissed the tears off her cheeks. "I was ready for a showdown with him until he told me something that changed everything. He said you'd make a good director, but it wasn't your destiny because you were too much like your mother."

"Dad admitted it?"

He nodded.

Dana was delirious with joy.

"Once I heard that, I couldn't get home from the party fast enough to collect a few things and go after you. If I hadn't seen your truck out in front, poor Paul would have gotten a phone call telling him to take care of everything while I was gone."

Dana slid her hands up his chest to his shoulders, relishing the right to touch him like this. "And I sat there terrified you'd drive in with Simone."

"Simone who?" he demanded fiercely, shaking her. "From the night you trespassed on my property, I haven't been the same. Sapto will tell you."

"Who's Sapto?"

"The house boy in Bali who got attached to me. You'll like him. He's saving his money to go to college. I'm planning to fly him over to help us prune the vineyard. That should give his earnings a boost.

"In my last postcard to him, I told him he can stop asking about all the women in my life because I've found the one I want."

Dana pressed a kiss to his lips, too euphoric to talk.

"When I stopped at the post office this afternoon, I discovered another postcard from him. He said that from my description of you, you would give me many beautiful children."

Alex's eyes narrowed on her mouth. "I knew it over dinner that night at the Hermitage. You sat there in the candlelight and your femininity reached out to me like a living thing. It came to me in a flash you were the one I was going to love for the rest of my life, to make babies with."

"I—I knew it before you did." Her voice caught. "From the first moment I laid eyes on you coming out of the shadows. This is going to sound silly, but it wasn't to me. Like Sleeping Beauty in reverse, I felt that I'd come upon the castle of the Sleeping Prince. Everything in me yearned toward you."

His smile turned her heart over. "So now we know the true story of Rapunzel."

She laughed softly, remembering their crazy talk. "She had no shame and moved in on her prince, sleeping bag and all."

"He liked her style." In the next breath Alex kissed her mouth hungrily. "How about taking a walk out to the vineyard with me? We have serious plans to make and fast, because I don't intend to make love to you until you're my wife. I promised your father."

"When?" she half groaned. "I didn't hear you."

"It wasn't anything verbal, but the commitment was just as binding the second you announced your plan to find a spot in the château to sleep."

Dana hid her face in his chest. "You must have thought I was out of my mind."

He tangled his fingers in her hair. "To be honest I thought heaven had dropped a present at my door by mistake, but I wasn't about to give it back and had to think fast."

She gazed up at him, her blue eyes glowing with desire. "So you do believe in it?"

"Since a golden haired woman with a cherub mouth came climbing up my apple tree and peeked at me through the leaves. It was a new sight for this mortal." His dark head lowered. "You are a heavenly sight, *mon amour*," he whispered before his mouth closed over hers, giving her a taste of their glorious future.

ACCIDENTALLY
EXPECTING!

BY
LUCY GORDON

First published in Great Britain 2009
Harlequin Mills & Boon Limited,
Eton House, 18-24 Paradise Road, Richmond, Surrey TW9 1SR

© Lucy Gordon 2009

ISBN: 978 0 263 86980 4

Harlequin Mills & Boon policy is to use papers that are natural, renewable and recyclable products and made from wood grown in sustainable forests. The logging and manufacturing process conform to the legal environmental regulations of the country of origin.

Printed and bound in Spain
by Litografia Rosés, S.A., Barcelona

Dear Reader

When I started writing the first Rinucci books, five years ago, I had no idea what an enjoyable task it was going to be. But as the work developed I discovered that the real joy was not just six attractive heroes, but the feeling of being drawn into a large, united family, where people will do anything for each other. As Dante Rinucci says, 'There's nothing to compare with the feeling that you have the whole tribe behind you.'

So when it came to writing a seventh Rinucci book I was really glad to go back to the Villa Rinucci in Naples, and meet up again with all my old friends.

Dante is a cousin, not a brother, but since his parents died he's lived part of the time at the villa, and has come to see Hope and Toni as extra parents. He's a man practised in keeping secrets, since beneath the laughing exterior he's concealing the tragic knowledge that he might be suffering from an inherited ailment that could lie dormant for years, then suddenly end his life or render him mentally disabled. Of the two, it's the second one he fears.

To cope, he lives for the moment, avoiding long-term commitments, until he meets the one woman he can love deeply enough to risk the future, and whose own love is deep enough to take the risk with him.

So here's the seventh Rinucci, as crazy, charming and infuriating—but also as passionately loving—as the others.

Warmest wishes

Lucy Gordon

Lucy Gordon cut her writing teeth on magazine journalism, interviewing many of the world's most interesting men, including Warren Beatty, Charlton Heston and Roger Moore. She also camped out with lions in Africa, and had many other unusual experiences which have often provided the background for her books. Several years ago, while staying in Venice, she met a Venetian who proposed in two days. They have been married ever since. Naturally this has affected her writing, where romantic Italian men tend to feature strongly.

Two of her books have won the Romance Writers of America RITA® award.

You can visit her website at www.lucy-gordon.com

Other books by Lucy Gordon, featuring the vibrant Italian Rinucci family, are:

WIFE AND MOTHER FOR EVER
  (Justine & Eve's story)
HER ITALIAN BOSS'S AGENDA
  (Primo & Olympia's story)
THE WEDDING ARRANGEMENT
  (Luke & Minnie's story)
THE ITALIAN'S WIFE BY SUNSET
  (Carlo & Della's story)
THE MEDITERRANEAN REBEL'S BRIDE
  (Ruggiero & Polly's story)
THE MILLIONAIRE TYCOON'S ENGLISH ROSE
  (Francesco & Celia's story)

CHAPTER ONE

HORNS blared, lights flashed in the darkness and Ferne ground her hands together as the cab battled its way through the slow-moving Milan traffic.

'Oh no! I'm going to miss the train. *Please!*'

The driver called back over his shoulder, 'I'm doing my best, *signorina*, but the traffic here is like nowhere else in the world.' He said it with pride.

'I know it's not your fault,' she cried. 'But I've got a ticket on the night train to Naples. It leaves in a quarter of an hour.'

The driver chuckled. 'Leave it to me. Twenty years I am driving in Milan, and my passengers do not miss their trains.'

The next ten minutes were breathless but triumphant, and at last the ornate façade of Milan Central Station came into view. As Ferne leapt out and paid the driver, a porter appeared.

'Train to Naples,' she gasped.

'This way, *signorina.*'

They made it to the platform looking so frantic that heads were turned. But suddenly Ferne stumbled and went sprawling right in the path of the porter, who sprawled in turn.

She wanted to yell aloud at being thwarted at the last moment, but miraculously hands came out of nowhere, seized her, thrust her on board, the bags following after her. A door slammed.

'*Stai bene?*' came a man's voice.

'I'm sorry, I don't speak Italian,' she said breathlessly, clutching him as he helped her to her feet.

'I asked if you are all right,' he said in English.

'Yes, but—oh heavens, we're moving. I should have given that poor man something.'

'Leave it to me.'

There was a narrow opening at the top of the window and the man slid his arm through, his hand full of notes which the porter seized gratefully. Her rescuer waved and turned back to face her in the corridor of the train that was already gathering speed.

Now Ferne had a moment to look at him, and realised that she was suffering delusions. He was so handsome that it was impossible. In his thirties, he stood, tall and impressive, with wide shoulders and hair of a raven-black colour that only Italians seemed to achieve. His eyes were deep blue, gleaming with life, and his whole appearance was something no man could be permitted outside the pages of a novel.

To cap it all, he'd come galloping to her rescue like the hero of a melodrama, which was simply too much. But, what the heck? She was on holiday.

He returned her gaze, briefly but appreciatively, taking in her slender figure and dark-red hair. Without conceit, but also without false modesty, she knew she was attractive; the expression in his eyes was one she'd often seen before, although it was a while since she'd responded to it.

'I'll refund you that tip, of course,' she said.

A woman had appeared behind them in the corridor. She was in her sixties, white-haired, slender and elegant.

'Are you hurt, my dear?' she asked. 'That was a nasty fall you had.'

'No, I'm fine, just a bit shaken.'

'Dante, bring her to our compartment.'

'OK, Aunt Hope. You take her, I'll bring the bags.'

The woman took Ferne gently by the arm and led her along the corridor to a compartment where a man, also in his sixties, was standing in the doorway watching their approach. He stood back to let them in and ushered Ferne to a seat.

'From the way you speak, I think you are English,' the woman said with a charming smile.

'Yes, my name is Ferne Edmunds.'

'I too am English. At least, I was long ago. Now I am Signora Hope Rinucci. This is my husband, Toni—and this young man is our nephew, Dante Rinucci.'

Dante was just entering with the bags, which he shoved under the seats, and then he sat down, rubbing his upper arm.

'Are you hurt?' Hope asked anxiously.

He grimaced. 'Pushing my arm through that narrow space has probably left me with bruises for life.' Then a grin broke over his face. 'It's all right, I'm only joking. Stop fussing. It's our friend here who needs care. Those plat-forms are hard.'

'That's true,' Ferne said ruefully, rubbing her knees through her trousers.

'Would you like me to take a look?' he asked hopefully, reaching out a hand.

'No, she would not,' Hope said, determinedly forestalling him. 'Behave yourself. In fact, why don't you go to the restaurant-car and order something for this young lady?' She added sternly, 'Both of you.'

Like obedient little boys, both men rose and departed without a word. Hope chuckled.

'Now, *signorina*—it is *signorina*?'

'Signorina Edmunds. But, please, call me Ferne. After what your family has done for me, let's not be formal.'

'Good. In that case—'

There was a knock on the door and a steward looked in.

'Oh yes, you want to make up the berths,' Hope said. 'Let's join the men.'

As they went along the corridor, Hope asked, 'Where is your sleeping berth?'

'I don't have one,' Ferne admitted. 'I booked at the last minute and everything was taken.'

By now they had reached the dining-car, where Toni and Dante had taken a table. Dante stood up and graciously showed her to the seat beside him.

'Here's the ticket inspector,' Hope said. 'Let's get the formalities out of the way before we eat. They may be able to find you a berth.'

But from that moment things went horribly wrong. As the others showed their paperwork, Ferne scrabbled hopelessly in her bag, finally facing the terrible truth.

'It's gone,' she whispered. 'Everything. My money, the tickets—they must have fallen out when I fell on the platform.'

Another search produced no result. Disaster!

'My passport's gone too!' she gasped. 'I've got to go back.'

But the train was now travelling at full speed.

'It doesn't stop until Naples,' Hope explained.

'They'll stop to throw me off when they find out I've no ticket and no money,' Ferne said frantically.

Hope's voice was soothing. 'Let's see what we can do about that.'

Toni began to speak to the inspector in Italian. After a while he produced his credit card.

'They're issuing you another ticket,' Hope explained.

'Oh, that's so kind of you. I'll pay you back, I promise.'

'Let's not worry about that now. First we have to find you a berth.'

'That's easy,' Dante said. 'My sleeping-car is a double, and I'm only using one berth, so—'

'So Toni can come in with you and Ferne can come in with me,' Hope said, beaming. 'What a splendid idea!'

'Actually, Aunt, I was thinking—'

'I know what you were thinking and you should be ashamed.'

'Yes, Aunt, anything you say, Aunt.'

But he winked at Ferne, and she couldn't help being charmed. The mere idea of this handsome, confident man doing what he was told was so idiotic, and his air of meekness so clearly an act, that she had to smile and join in the joke.

The inspector exchanged some more words with Toni before nodding and hurrying away.

'He's going to call the station now and tell them to look out for your things,' Toni explained to Ferne. 'Luckily you discovered the loss quickly, so they may pick them up before anyone else finds them. But, just in case, you must cancel your credit cards.'

'How can I do that from here?' Ferne asked, baffled.

'The British consulate will help you,' Dante declared, taking out his own mobile phone.

In a few moments he had obtained the emergency number of the Milan consulate, dialled it and handed the phone to Ferne.

The young man on duty was efficient. Quickly he looked up the numbers of the credit-card companies, assigned her a reference number and bid her goodnight. Calls to the finance companies achieved the cancellation of her cards and the promise of new ones. This was as much as she could hope for for now.

'I don't know what I'd have done without you,' she told her new friends fervently. 'When I think what could have happened to me.'

'Don't think about it,' Hope advised. 'All will be well. Ah, here is the waiter with a snack. Hmm, cakes and wine are all very well, but I should like a large pot of tea.'

'*English* tea.' Toni gave instructions to the waiter, who nodded solemnly, evidently familiar with this peculiarity among his customers.

The tea was excellent, so were the cakes, which the others piled onto her plate.

'When did you last eat?' Hope asked.

'Properly? Oh—some time. I left on the spur of the moment, caught the train from London to Paris, then Paris to Milan. I don't like flying, and I wanted to be free to stop and explore whenever I wanted. I had a few days in Milan, shopping and seeing the sights. I meant to stay there overnight and go on tomorrow, but I suddenly changed my mind, packed up and ran.'

'That's the way to live!' Dante exclaimed. 'Here today, gone tomorrow; let life bring what it will.' He took Ferne's hand and spoke with theatrical fervour. '*Signorina*, you are a woman after my own heart. More than a woman—a goddess with a unique understanding of life. I salute you—why are you laughing?'

'I'm sorry,' Ferne choked. 'I can't listen to that guff with a straight face.'

'Guff? *Guff?* Is this a new English word?'

'No,' Hope informed him, amused. 'It's an old English word and it means that you need a better scriptwriter.'

'But only for me,' Ferne chuckled. 'I expect it works wonderfully on the others.'

Dante's face was the picture of outrage.

'The others? Don't you realise that you are the only one who has inspired me to lay my heart at her feet? The only— Oh, all right; I usually get a better reception than this.'

His collapse into realism made them all laugh.

'It's nice to meet a lady with such an adventurous approach to life,' he added. 'But I expect it's only while you're on holiday. You'll go back to England, your sedate nine-to-five life, and your sedate nine-to-five fiancé.'

'If I had a fiancé, what would I be doing here alone?' she demanded.

This made him pause, but only for a moment.

'He betrayed you,' he said dramatically. 'You

are teaching him a lesson. When you return, he will be jealous, especially when he sees the compromising pictures of us together.'

'Oh, will he indeed? And where will these pictures come from?'

'It can be arranged. I know some good photographers.'

'I'll bet you don't know anyone better than me,' she riposted.

'You're a photographer?' Hope asked. 'A journalist?'

'No, I do theatrical work.' Some inexplicable instinct made her say to Dante, 'And he wasn't sedate. Anything but.'

He didn't reply in words, but his expression was wry and curious. So was the way he nodded.

'Let the poor girl eat in peace,' Hope admonished him.

She watched Ferne like a mother hen, finally declaring that it was time for bed. The four of them made their way back along the corridor and said goodnight. Ferne and Hope went into one sleeping car, Toni and Dante went on to the next.

As Ferne hung up the trousers she'd been wearing, a few coins fell out onto the floor.

'I'd forgotten I had some money in my pocket,' she said, holding them out.

'Three euros,' Hope observed. 'You wouldn't have got far with that.'

They sat down on the bed, contentedly sipping the tea they had brought with them.

'You said you were English,' Ferne recalled. 'And yet you speak as though you've been here for some time.'

'Over thirty years,' Hope told her.

'Do you have any children?'

'Six. All sons.'

She said it with an air of exasperated irony that made Ferne smile and say, 'Do you ever wish you had daughters?'

Hope chuckled. 'When you have six sons, you have no time to think of anything else. Besides, I have six daughters-in-law and seven grandchildren.

'When our last son married, a few months ago, Toni and I decided to go on our travels. Recently we've been in Milan to see some of his relatives. Toni was very close to his other brother, Taddeo, until he died a few years ago. Dante is Taddeo's elder son, and he's coming back to Naples with us for a visit. He's a bit of a madman, as you'll discover while you're staying with us.'

'I can't impose on you any further.'

'My dear, you have no money or passport. If

you don't stay with us, just what are you going to do?'

'It just seems dreadful for you to be burdened with me.'

'But I shall love having you. We can talk about England. I love Italy, but I miss my own country, and you can tell me how things are there now.'

'Ah, that's different, if there's something I can do for you.'

'I look forward to you staying with us a long time. Now, I must get some sleep.'

She got into the lower bunk. Ferne climbed to the top one, and in a few minutes there was peace and darkness.

Ferne lay listening to the hum of the train speed through the night, trying to get her bearings. It seemed such a short time since she'd made the impulsive decision to leave England. Now she was here, destitute, reliant on strangers.

While she was pondering the strange path her life had taken recently, the rhythm of the train overtook her and she fell asleep.

She awoke to find herself desperately thirsty, and remembered that the snack bar was open all night. Quietly she climbed down and groped around in the darkness for her robe.

The three euros she'd found would just be enough for a drink. Holding her breath and trying not to waken Hope, she crept out into the corridor and made her way to the dining-car.

She was in luck. The snack bar was still open, although the tables were deserted and the attendant was nodding off.

'I'll have a bottle of mineral water, please,' she said thankfully. 'Oh dear, four euros. Do you have a small one?'

'I'm afraid the last small bottle has gone,' the attendant said apologetically.

'Oh *no*!' It came out as a cry of frustration.

'Can I help?' asked a voice behind her.

She turned and saw Dante.

'I'm on the cadge for money,' she groaned. '*Again*! I'm desperate for something to drink.'

'Then let me buy you some champagne.'

'No, thank you, just some mineral water.'

'Champagne is better,' he said in the persuasive voice of a man about to embark on a flirtation.

'No, water is better when you're thirsty,' she said firmly.

'Then I can't persuade you?'

'No,' she said, getting cross. 'You can't persuade me. What you can do is step out of my way so that I can leave. Goodnight.'

'I apologise,' he said at once. 'Don't be angry with me, I'm just fooling.' To the bartender he added, 'Serve the lady whatever she wants, and I'll have a whisky.'

He slipped an arm about her, touching her lightly but firmly enough to prevent her escape, and guided her to a seat by the window. The barman approached and she seized the bottle of water, threw back her head and drank deeply.

'That's better,' she said at last, gasping slightly. 'I should be the one apologising. I'm in a rotten temper, but I shouldn't take it out on you.'

'You don't like being dependent on people?' he guessed.

'Begging,' she said in disgust.

'Not begging,' he corrected her gently. 'Letting your friends help you.'

'I'll pay every penny back,' she vowed.

'Hush! Now you're getting boring.'

Fearing that he might be right, she swigged some more water. It felt good.

'You seem to be having a very disorganised holiday,' he observed. 'Have you been planning it for long?'

'I didn't plan it at all, just hurled a few things into a bag and flounced off.'

'That sounds promising. You said you're a photographer…' He waited hopefully.

'I specialise in the theatre, and film stills. *He's* an actor, starring in a West End play. Or, at least, he *was* in a West End play until—'

'You can't stop there!' he protested. 'Just when it's getting interesting.'

'I was taking the pics. We had a thing going—and, well, I didn't expect eternal fidelity—but I did expect his full attention while we were together.'

'A reasonable desire,' her companion said solemnly.

'So I thought, but an actress in the play started flashing her eyes at him. I think she saw him chiefly as a career step-up—Oh, I don't know, though. To be fair, he's very handsome.'

'Well known?' Dante asked.

'Sandor Jayley.'

Dante's eyes widened.

'I saw one of his films on television the other day,' he said. 'He's supposed to be headed for even greater things.' He assumed a declamatory voice. 'The man whose embrace all women dream of—whose merest look—'

'Oh, shut up!' she said through laughter. 'I can't keep a straight face at that twaddle, which used to really annoy him.'

'He took it seriously?'

'Yes. Mind you, he has plenty going for him.'

'Looks, allure…?'

'Dazzling smile, more charm than was good for him—or for me. Just the usual stuff. Nothing, really.'

'Yes, it doesn't amount to much,' he agreed. 'You have to wonder why people make such a fuss about it.'

They nodded in solemn accord.

He yawned suddenly, turning so that he was half-sideways and could raise one foot onto the seat beside him; he rested an arm on it and leaned his head back. Ferne studied him a moment, noticing the relaxed grace of his tall, lean body. His shirt was open at the throat, enough to reveal part of his smooth chest; his black hair was slightly on the long side.

She had to admit that he had 'the usual stuff', with plenty to spare. His face was not only handsome but intriguing, with well-defined, angular features, dark, wicked eyes and a look of fierce, humorous intelligence.

Quirky, she thought, considering him with a professional gaze. Always about to do or say something unexpected. That was what she'd try to bring out if she were taking his photograph.

Suddenly he looked at her, and the gleaming look was intense.

'So, tell me about it,' he said.

'Where do I start?' She sighed. 'The beginning, when I was starry-eyed and stupid, or later, when he was shocked by my "unprincipled vulgarity"?'

Dante was immediately alert.

'Unprincipled and vulgar, hmm? That sounds interesting. Don't stop.'

'I met Tommy when I was hired to take the photographs for the play—'

'Tommy?'

'Sandor. His real name is Tommy Wiggs.'

'I can see why he changed it. But I want to know how you were unprincipled and vulgar.'

'You'll have to wait for that bit.'

'Spoilsport!'

'Where was I? Ah, yes, taking pictures for the play. Thinking back, I guess he set out to make me fall for him because he reckoned it would give an extra something to the photographs. So he took me to dinner and dazzled me.'

'And you were taken in by actorly charm?' Dante asked, frowning a little, as though he found it hard to believe.

'No, he was cleverer than that. He made a

great play of switching off the actor and just being *himself*, as he put it, saying he wanted to use his real name because Sandor was for the masses. The man inside was *Tommy*.' Seeing his face, she said, 'Yes, it makes me feel a bit queasy too, but that night it was charming.

'The thing is, Tommy was made to be a film actor, not a stage actor. He's more impressive in close-up, and the closer you get the better he seems.'

'And he made sure you got very close?'

'Not that night,' she murmured, 'but eventually.'

She fell silent, remembering moments that had been sweet at the time but in retrospect felt ridiculous. How easily she'd fallen, and how glad she was to be out of it now. Yet there had been other times that she still remembered with pleasure, however mistakenly.

Dante watched her face, reading it without difficulty, and his eyes darkened. He raised a hand to summon the attendant, and when Ferne looked up she found Dante filling a glass of champagne for her.

'I felt you needed it after all,' he said.

'Yes,' she murmured. 'Maybe I do.'

'So what was the film actor doing in a play?' Dante asked.

'He felt that people didn't take him seriously.'

'Heaven help us! One of them. They make a career out of being eye candy but it's not enough. They want to be *respected*.'

'You've got him to a T,' Ferne chuckled. 'Are you sure you don't know him?'

'No, but I've met plenty like him. Some of the houses I sell belong to that kind of person—"full of themselves", I believe is the English expression.'

'That's it. Someone persuaded him that if he did a bit of Shakespeare everyone would be impressed, so he agreed to star in *Antony and Cleopatra*.'

'Playing Antony, the great lover?'

'Yes. But I think part of the attraction was the fact that Antony was an ancient Roman, so he had to wear little, short tunics that showed off his bare legs. He's got very good legs. He even made the costume department take the tunics up a couple of inches to show off his thighs.'

Dante choked with laughter.

'It was very much an edited version of the play because he couldn't remember all the long speeches,' Ferne recalled. 'Mind you, he made them shorten Cleopatra's speeches even more.'

'In case she took too much of the spotlight?' Dante hazarded a guess.

'Right. He wasn't going to have that. Not that it really mattered, because everyone was looking at his thighs.'

'I don't think you're exactly heartbroken,' Dante commanded, watching her intently.

'Certainly not,' she said quickly. 'It was ridiculous, really. Just showbusiness. Or life.'

'How do you mean?'

'It's all a performance of one kind or another. We each live by pretending something's true when we really know it isn't, or not true when we know it is.'

A strange look came into his eyes, as though her words carried a particular resonance. He seemed about to say something, but then backed off. She had the impression that a corner of the curtain to his mind had been raised, then dropped hastily.

So there was more to him than the charming clown, she thought. He presented that aspect to the world, but behind it was another man who hid himself away and kept everyone else out. Intrigued, she wondered how easy it would be to reach behind his defences.

The next moment he gave her the answer.

Seeing her watching him, he closed his eyes, shutting her out completely.

CHAPTER TWO

SUDDENLY he opened his eyes again, revealing that the tension had gone. The dark moment might never have been. His next words were spoken lightly.

'You're getting very philosophical.'

'Sorry,' she said.

'Were you talking about yourself when you said we each live by refusing to admit the truth?'

'Well, I suppose I really knew that another woman had her eye on him, and I ought to have realised that he'd give in to flattery, no matter what he'd said to me hours before. But it was still a bit of a shock when I went to meet him at the theatre after the performance and found them together.'

'What were they doing—or needn't I ask?'

'You needn't ask. They were right there on the stage, stretched out on Cleopatra's tomb, totally oblivious to anyone and anything. She was saying, "Oh, you really are Antony—a great hero!"'

'And I suppose they were—' Dante paused delicately '—in a state of undress?'

'Well, he still had his little tunic on. Mind you, that was almost the same thing.'

'So what did you do?' he asked, fascinated. 'You didn't creep away in tears. Not you. You went and thumped him.'

'Neither.' She paused for dramatic effect. 'I hardly dare tell you what I did.'

'Have we got to the bit where you're unprincipled and vulgar?' he asked hopefully.

'We have.'

'Don't keep me in suspense. Tell me.'

'Well, I take my camera everywhere…'

Dante's crack of laughter seemed to hit the ceiling and echo around the carriage, waking the barman from his doze.

'You *didn't*?'

'I did. They were wonderful pictures. I took as many as I could from as many different angles as possible.'

'And he didn't see you?'

'He had his back to me,' Ferne explained. 'Facing downwards.'

'Oh yes, naturally. But what about her?'

'She was facing up and she saw me, of course. She loved it. Then I stormed off in a temper, went straight to the offices of a newspaper that specialised in that sort of thing and sold the lot.'

Awed, he stared at her. 'Just like that?'

'Just like that.'

His respect grew in leaps and bounds; a woman who reacted to her lover's betrayal not with tears and reproaches but with well-aimed revenge was a woman after his own heart.

What couldn't she do if she set her mind to it?

Would any man of sense want to get on her wrong side?

But her right side—that was a different matter!

'What happened?' he demanded, still fascinated.

'There were ructions, but not for long. The seats had been selling reasonably well, but after that it was standing-room only. *She* gave an interview about how irresistible he was, and he got offered a big, new film-part. So then he walked out on the show, which annoyed Josh, the director, until the understudy took over and got rave reviews. He was Josh's boyfriend, so everyone was happy.'

'Everyone except you. What did you get out of it?'

'The paper paid me a fortune. By that time I'd

calmed down a bit and was wondering if I'd gone too far, but then the cheque arrived, and, well…'

'You've got to be realistic,' he suggested.

'Exactly. Mick—that's my agent—said some people wait a lifetime for a stroke of luck like mine. I've always wanted to see Italy, so I planned this trip. I had to wait a couple of months because suddenly I was much in demand. I'm not sure why.'

'Word had spread about your unusual skills,' he mused.

'Yes, that must be it. Anyway, I made a gap in my schedule, because I was determined to come here, chucked everything into a suitcase, jumped on the next train to Paris and from there I got the train to Milan.

'I spent a few days looking over the town, then suddenly decided to take off for Naples. It was late in the evening by then and a sensible person would have waited until morning. So I didn't.'

Dante nodded in sympathy. 'The joy of doing things on the spur of the moment! There's nothing like it.'

'I've always been an organised person, perhaps too organised. It felt wonderful to go a bit mad.' She gave a brief, self-mocking laugh. 'But I'm not very good at it, and I really messed up, didn't I?'

'Never mind. With practice, you'll improve.'

'Oh no! That was my one fling.'

'Nonsense, you're only a beginner. Let me introduce you to the joys of living as though every moment was your last.'

'Is that how you live?'

He didn't reply at first. He'd begun to lean forward across the table, looking directly into her face. Now he threw himself back again.

'Yes, it's how I live,' he said. 'It gives a spice and flavour to life that comes in no other way.'

She felt a momentary disturbance. It was inexplicable, except that there had been something in his voice that didn't fit their light-hearted conversation. Only a moment ago he'd shut her out, and something told her he might just do so again. They had drifted close to dangerous territory, which seemed to happen surprisingly easily with this man.

Again, she wondered just what lay in that forbidden place. Trying to coax him into revelation, she mused, 'Never to know what will happen next—I suppose I'm living proof that that can make life interesting. When I woke up this morning, I never pictured this.'

His smile was back. The moment had passed.

'How could you have imagined that you'd

meet one of this country's heroes?' he demanded irrepressibly. 'A man so great that his head is on the coins.'

Enjoying her bemused look, he produced a two-euro coin. The head, with its sharply defined nose, did indeed bear a faint resemblance to him.

'Of course!' she said. 'Dante Alighieri, your famous poet. Is that how you got your name?'

'Yes. My mother hoped that naming me after a great man might make me a great man too.'

'We all have our disappointments to bear,' Ferne said solemnly.

His eyes gleamed appreciation at her dig.

'Do you know much about Dante?' he asked.

'Not really. He lived in the late-thirteenth to early-fourteenth century, and he wrote a masterpiece called *The Divine Comedy*, describing a journey through hell, purgatory and paradise.'

'You've read it? I'm impressed.'

'Only in an English translation, and I had to struggle to reach the end.' She chuckled. 'Hell and purgatory were so much more interesting than paradise.'

He nodded. 'Yes, I always thought paradise sounded insufferable. All that virtue.' He shuddered, then brightened. 'Luckily, it's the last place I'm likely to end up. Have some more champagne.'

'Just a little.'

A train thundered past them, going in the opposite direction. Watching the lights flicker on him as it went, Ferne thought that it wasn't hard to picture him as a master of the dark arts; he was engaging and more than a little risky, because he masked his true self with charm.

She'd guessed he was in his early thirties, but in this light she changed the estimate to late thirties. There was experience in his face, both good and bad.

'What are you thinking?' he asked.

'I was wondering what part of the other world you might have come from.'

'No doubt about it, the seventh terrace of purgatory,' he said, one eyebrow cocked to see if she understood.

She did. The seventh terrace was reserved for those who had over-indulged in the more pleasurable sins.

'That's just what I thought,' she murmured. 'But I didn't want to suggest it in case you were offended.'

His wry smile informed her that this was the last accusation that would ever offend him.

For a few minutes they sipped champagne in silence. Then he remarked, 'You'll be staying with us, of course?'

'As Hope says, I don't have any choice, for a few days at least.'

'Longer, much longer,' he said at once. 'Italian bureaucracy takes its time, but we'll try to make your stay a pleasant one.'

His meaning was unmistakeable. *Well, why not?* she thought. She was in the mood for a flirtation with a man who would take it as lightly as herself. He was attractive, interesting and they both knew the score.

'I'll look forward to it,' she said. 'Actually, Hope wants me to talk to her about England, and it's the least I can do for her.'

'Yes, she must feel a bit submerged by Italians,' Dante said. 'Mind you, she's always been one of us, and the whole family loves her. My parents died when I was fifteen, and she's been like a second mother to me ever since.'

'Do you live here?'

'No, I'm based in Milan, but I came south with them because I think there are business opportunities in the Naples area. So after looking around I might decide to stay.'

'What do you do?'

'I deal in property, specialising in unusual places, old houses that are difficult to sell.'

He yawned and they sat together in companionable silence. She felt drained and contented at the same time, separated from the whole universe on this train, thundering through the night.

Looking up, she saw that he was staring out into the darkness. She could see his reflection faintly in the window. His eyes were open and held a faraway expression, as though he could see something in the gloom that was hidden from her and which filled him with a melancholy intensity.

He looked back at her and smiled, rising reluctantly to his feet and holding out his hand. 'Let's go.'

At the door to her carriage, he paused and said gently, 'Don't worry about anything. I promise you, it's all going to work out. Goodnight.'

Ferne slipped into the carriage, moving quietly so as not to waken Hope, who was asleep. In a moment she'd skimmed up the ladder and settled down in bed, staring into the night, wondering about the man she'd just left. He was likeable in a mad sort of way, and she didn't mind spending some time in his company, as long as it was strictly casual.

But she didn't brood. The rocking of the train was hypnotic, and she was soon asleep.

Next morning there was just time for a quick snack before they arrived. Hope looked eagerly out of the window, wondering which of her sons would meet them.

'Justin's in England and Luke's in Rome,' she said. 'Carlo's in Sicily and won't be back for a couple of days. It'll be one of the other three.'

In the end three sons were waiting at the station, waving and cheering as the train pulled in. They embraced their parents exuberantly, clapped Dante on the shoulder and eyed Ferne with interest.

'These are Francesco, Ruggiero and Primo,' Toni explained. 'Don't try to sort them out just now. We'll do the introductions later.'

'Ferne has had a misfortune and will be staying with us until it's sorted out,' Hope said. 'Now, I'm longing to get home.'

There were two cars. Hope, Toni and Ferne rode in the first, driven by Francesco, while the other two brothers took Dante and the luggage in the second.

All the way home Hope looked eagerly out of the window, until at last she seized Ferne's arm and said, 'Look. That's the Villa Rinucci.'

Ferne followed her gaze up to the top of a hill, on which was perched a large villa facing out over Naples and the sea. She was entranced by the place; it was bathed in golden sun, and looked as though it contained both beauty and safety.

As they grew nearer she saw that the house was larger than she'd realised at first. Trees surrounded it, but the villa was on slightly higher ground, so that it seemed to be growing out of the trees. A plump woman, followed by two buxom young girls, came out to watch the cars arriving, all waving eagerly.

'That's Elena, my housekeeper,' Hope told Ferne. 'The two girls are her nieces who are working here for a couple of weeks, because there will be so many of us—and plenty of children, I'm glad to say. I called Elena while we were still on the train, to tell her you were coming and would need a room.'

The next moment they stopped, the door was pulled open and Ferne was being shown up the steps onto the wide terrace that surrounded the house, and then inside.

'Why don't you go up to your room at once?' Hope asked. 'Come down when you're ready and meet these villains I call my sons.'

'These villains' were smiling with pleasure at

seeing their parents again and Ferne slipped away, understanding that they would want to be free of her for a while.

Her room was luxurious, with its own bathroom and a wide, comfortable-looking bed. Going to the window, she found she was at the front of the house, with a stunning view over the Bay of Naples. It was at its best just now, the water glittering in the morning sun, stretching away to the horizon, seeming to offer an infinity of pleasure and unknown delight.

Quickly she showered and changed into a dress of pale blue, cut on simple lines but fashionable. At least she would be able to hold her head up in elegant Italy.

She heard laughter from below, and looked out of the window to where the Rinucci family were seated around a rustic wooden table under the trees, talking and laughing in a gentle manner that made a sudden warmth come over her heart.

Her own family life had been happy but sparse. She was an only child, born to parents who were themselves only-children. One set of grandparents had died early, the other had emigrated to Australia.

Now her father was dead and her mother had gone to live with her own parents in Australia. Ferne could have gone too, but had chosen to stay in London to pursue a promising career. So there was only herself to blame that she was lonely, that there had been nobody to lend a sympathetic ear when the crash had come with Sandor Jayley.

There had been friends, of course, nights out with the girls that she'd genuinely enjoyed. But they were career women like herself, less inclined to sympathise than congratulate her on the coup she'd pulled off. She'd always returned to an empty flat, the silence and the memories.

But something told her that the Villa Rinucci was never truly empty, and she was assailed by delight as she gazed down at the little gathering.

Hope looked up and waved, signalling for her to join them, and Ferne hurried eagerly down the stairs and out onto the terrace. As she approached the table the young men stood up with an old-fashioned courtesy that she found charming, and Dante stepped forward to take her hand and lead her forward. Hope rose and kissed her.

'This is the lady who joined us on the train and who will be staying with us for a while,' she said.

She began to introduce the young men—first Primo, stepson from her first marriage, then Ruggiero, one of her sons by Toni. Both men were tall and dark. Primo's face was slightly heavier, while Ruggiero's features had a mobility that reminded her slightly of his cousin, Dante.

Francesco had a brooding quality, as though his mind carried some burden. Like the other two, he greeted her warmly, but then said, 'I'd better go now, Mamma. I want to get home before Celia.'

'Doesn't she ever get suspicious about how often that happens?' Hope asked.

'Always, and she tells me to stop, but—' He gave a resigned shrug. 'I do it anyway.' To Ferne he added, 'My wife is blind, and she gets very cross if she thinks I'm fussing over her, but I can't help it.'

'Go on home,' Hope told him. 'Just be sure you're at the party tomorrow.'

He embraced her fondly and departed. Almost at once another car appeared and disgorged two young women. One was dark, and so gracefully beautiful that even her pregnancy-bump couldn't detract from her elegance. The other was fair, pretty in a way that was sensible rather than exotic, and was accompanied by an eager toddler.

'This is my wife, Olympia,' Primo said, drawing the pregnant woman forward to meet Ferne.

'And this is my wife, Polly,' Ruggiero said, indicating the fair young woman.

At this distance she could see that Polly too was pregnant, possibly about five months. Her husband's attitude to her seemed protective, and again Ferne was pervaded by the feeling of contentment that she'd had earlier. Just being here, among people so happy to be together, was enough to create it.

It was soon time for lunch. Hope led the way indoors to inspect the meal Elena was preparing, taste things and give her opinion. In this she was joined not only by her daughters-in-law but her sons, who savoured the dishes and offered advice freely—sometimes too freely, as their mother informed them.

'So it's true what they say about Italian men,' Ferne observed, amused.

'What do they say about us?' Dante murmured in her ear. 'I'm longing to know.'

'Why, that you're all fantastic cooks, of course. What did you think I meant?'

He gave a disillusioned sigh. 'Nothing, nothing. Yes, we're all interested in cooking. Not like Englishmen, who eat sausage and mash on every occasion.' Suddenly he looked closely at her face. 'What is it?' he asked. 'Why are you looking troubled?'

'I just suddenly thought—perhaps I should

telephone the consulate. They might have some news by now.'

'This afternoon I'll drive you into Naples and we'll visit the consulate here. They can get onto the Milan consulate. Now, let's forget boring reality and concentrate on the important things—enjoying ourselves.'

'Yes, let's,' she said happily.

Dante was as good as his word, borrowing Toni's car after lunch and driving her down the hill through the streets of the old town until they reached their destination near the coast.

There the news was bleak. Neither her passport nor her credit cards had been recovered.

'Considering how quickly they were reported, it looks as though someone made off with them,' Dante observed. 'But hopefully they won't be any use to them.'

'We can arrange a temporary passport,' the young woman at the desk said. 'But it will take a few days. There's a kiosk over there for the photograph.'

'No need, I'll take it,' Dante said. Eyeing Ferne's bag, he added, 'If you'll lend me your camera.'

She handed it to him. 'What made you so sure I had it?'

'You told me you always had it. And the woman who was smart enough to record her lover's infidelity wouldn't miss a trick like this.'

She showed him how to work it, and they spent a few minutes out in the sun while she turned this way and that at his command.

'Pull your blouse down this side,' he said. 'You've got pretty shoulders; let's see them. Good. Now, shake your head so that your hair fluffs up.'

'This is no good for passport pictures,' she objected.

He grinned. 'Who said anything about passport pictures? Maybe I have a wicked purpose of my own.'

Back inside, they switched the camera to 'view' and showed the results to the woman at the desk, who regarded them with saintly patience.

'None of these are suitable. I think you should use the kiosk,' she suggested.

'We could have done that to start with,' Ferne pointed out.

'But then my wicked purpose wouldn't have been fulfilled,' Dante said unanswerably. 'Come on; go into that kiosk and take some shots that make you look dreary and virtuous.'

'Are you suggesting that I'm *not* dreary and virtuous?'

'Which part of that question do you want me to answer?'

'Let's just get on with it,' she said hastily.

When the formalities were complete, Dante took her to a café by the beach and they relaxed over coffee.

'If you think the villa's a madhouse now,' he said, 'wait until tomorrow when the rest of the family get here.'

'There's quite a lot of them, isn't there? Six, I think Hope said.'

'That's right, although they don't all live around here. Luke and Minnie will be coming from Rome. Justin and Evie from England, with Mark, Justin's son, and their baby twins.'

A terrible thought struck Ferne. 'Where will they be staying?'

'At the villa, of course.'

'And you're there too, so whose room have I been given? Someone will end up sleeping on the sofa because of me, and I can't have that. I've got to go.'

'And stay where—in a hotel? With no money or paperwork?'

'Well, if you could lend me some money I'll pay it back…'

Dante shook his head firmly. 'Sorry, no. To tell

the hotel that you're a trustworthy person, when actually I don't know if you are, would be most improper. And we must always behave with propriety, mustn't we?'

Despite her agitation, she couldn't help laughing.

'You,' she said in a slow, deliberate voice, 'wouldn't recognise *propriety* if it came up and whacked you on the nose—which I am strongly tempted to do right now.'

'Curses!' he said theatrically. 'She's seen through me. All right, I'll admit my true motive. I plan to keep you here, a prisoner, subject to my will. Cash would help you to escape, which doesn't suit my evil purpose.'

'I wonder if I can guess your evil purpose,' she said dryly.

'Well, I'm not exactly subtle, am I? But do I need to be? You're in my power.'

'In your dreams!' she chuckled.

'In those too,' he said with a yearning look.

'No, I didn't mean— Oh, you know what I meant.'

'Well, a man can dream, can't he?' he asked, eyeing her significantly.

'He can dream all he likes, as long as he doesn't confuse dreams with reality,' she said, also significantly. 'And you didn't answer my question. Whose room have I been given?'

He didn't reply, but his mouth twisted.

'Oh no, please, don't tell me…?'

'If you feel that way, we could always share it,' he suggested.

'Will you just stop, please?'

'All right, all right, don't eat me. You can't blame a man for trying.'

'I can. I do.'

'You wouldn't if you could sit where I'm sitting, looking at you.'

She gave up. How could you talk sense to a man who had that wicked glint in his eyes?

But it could be fun finding out.

CHAPTER THREE

'IF YOU'RE going to reject me, I'll just have to console myself with those pictures of you that I took,' Dante remarked.

'I deleted them,' she said at once.

'Like hell you did! If you didn't delete the evidence of your lover misbehaving, you aren't going to wipe out the pics of you looking like every man's dream of sexy.'

'Will you stop talking to me like that?'

'Why should I?'

What could she say? *Because it gives me a fizz of excitement that I'm not ready for yet.*

He was a clever man, she reckoned; he made it clear beyond doubt that he was sexually attracted to her, yet with such a light touch that she could relax in his company, free from pressure. She didn't doubt that he would jump into her bed in an instant, if she gave him the barest hint.

But without that hint he would sit here talking nonsense, biding his time.

She wondered how many other women had been beguiled into his arms, and what had happened to them when it was over. She suspected that Dante would always be the one to say goodbye, treating love easily, never lingering too long. But there was more to him than that; instinct, too deep to be analysed, told her so.

His tone changed, becoming what he would have called 'prosaic'.

'While I think of it—' he reached into his wallet and handed her a wad of notes '—you can't walk around without any money.'

'But you just said you wouldn't—'

'We're back in the real world. You must have something. Here.'

Staggered, she looked at the amount. 'So much? No, Dante, please—I can't take this.' Accepting some of the notes, she tried to thrust the rest back at him.

'You don't know what you may need,' he said firmly, pushing her hand away. 'But what you will definitely need is your independence, and with that you'll have it. Put it away safely.' He sounded like a school master.

'But what about keeping me in your power?' she asked, tucking it into her bag. 'Making me independent isn't going to help your evil purpose.'

'True,' he mused. 'On the other hand, nothing gained by force is really satisfying. It's better when she knocks on his door and says she can't live any longer without his wild embraces. Much more fun.'

'And do you think I'm going to do that?'

He seemed to consider this. 'No, I think you'll go to the stake before you yield an inch. But, as I said before, a man can dream.'

They regarded each other in perfect, humorous understanding.

Afterwards they drove back to the villa slowly, where supper was just being prepared.

'Some people only turn up just before a meal,' Francesco jeered, giving Dante a friendly thump on the shoulder.

He'd gone home and returned with his wife, Celia, whom he now drew forward.

Ferne would hardly have guessed that Celia was blind. She was bright and vivacious with a way of turning her head, clearly aware of what was happening around her. They fell easily into conversation, sitting on the terrace and chatting about their work. Celia's career was making the world accessible to the blind.

'I'm working on a scheme to make theatres more friendly,' she said. 'It involves an ear-piece with a description of the action. Francesco and I were in London a couple of months ago, going to lots of shows so that I could get some ideas, and we went to a performance where everyone was going crazy over the star, Sandor Jayley. They said he looked incredibly sexy in a little Roman tunic.

'But Francesco wouldn't tell me that, and I had to find out afterwards when apparently there were some deliciously scandalous pictures of Sandor in the papers. Why, what's the matter?'

Dante had drawn a sharp breath. The sight of his appalled face made Ferne burst out laughing.

'Have I said something wrong?' Celia begged.

'No, not at all,' Ferne choked. 'It's just that…'

Briefly she told the story and Celia covered her mouth in horror.

'Oh no! What have I done? I never meant— Please, please—'

'It's all right,' Ferne hurried to say. 'I saw the funny side of it ages ago. Oh heavens!' She went off into gales of laughter again, then calmed down and tried to reassure Celia that she wasn't in a state of collapse. It took a while, but at last she managed it.

When she looked up Dante was observing her with a strange smile and a look in his eyes that might have been admiration.

From inside the house they heard Hope's voice.

'Ferne, dear, are you there? I need your help.'

'I'll be back in a minute,' Ferne said, hurrying away.

Celia listened as Ferne's footsteps faded, then turned to Dante.

'She's gorgeous,' she said. 'You're a lucky man.'

'What makes you think she's mine?'

'Francesco says you can't take your eyes off her.'

'And with reason. She's worth looking at.'

'I think her face is gentle and kind, like her voice, when she went to so much trouble to reassure me. She sounds lovely.'

'She is lovely,' Dante murmured.

'Is she really all right about that man—the one they call "sexy legs"?'

'Would you mind not saying that?' Dante said in a strained voice.

'You've really got it bad, haven't you?'

'I decline to answer,' he said after a moment. 'Shall we go in to supper?'

That evening was one of the most pleasant Ferne had ever spent. As the sun faded, lights came on in the garden and at last everyone drifted away from the table to drink their wine under the trees.

'I think your family has found the secret of happy marriage,' Ferne murmured. 'They all look like courting couples—even Hope and Toni, after all these years.'

Dante nodded. 'Hope says that's all down to Toni, the sweetest-natured man in the world. He's always been very kind to me. I'm glad he has happiness now, even if it's in the sunset rather than the sunrise.'

'I wonder if that could be better.'

'I doubt it. Who can ever tell what their own sunset is going to be?'

'Perhaps wondering about it is one of the pleasures of life?' she suggested.

He gave a little shrug. 'Perhaps. Let's go where we can watch the Naples sunset.'

Totally content, she let him lead her to a place where they could stand beneath the trees and watch the miracle that was happening over the bay. For a dazzling moment the light was deep red, seeming to set the sea on fire, and they watched it in awed silence.

'No matter how often I see that,' he murmured, 'it never fails. As long as there's so much glory in the world…' He fell silent.

'Have you spent much time here?' Ferne asked.

'Since my parents died I've kind of moved around the family, living with aunts, uncles, grandparents. This was where I came in the summer, and I loved it. It felt more *home* than anywhere else.'

'But it sounds sad to be moving around the family, not really having a settled base.'

'I like having a big family. There's nothing to compare with the feeling that you have the whole tribe behind you.'

'Isn't there one member of the tribe you need more than the others?'

'Hope and Toni have been like second parents. Apart from them, no. Like you, I'm an only child, but I thrive on having plenty of cousins.'

At last everyone drifted back to the house. There were children to be put to bed, and Hope wanted an early night. Ferne was glad of the chance to go to her room to be alone and think about everything that had happened to her.

To think about Dante Rinucci.

He was attractive, amusing, sexy and clearly in the mood for a diversion. Since she felt the same, there was really no problem, except for the little voice in her head that kept saying, *Beware*!

But beware what? she asked herself.

There's something about him that doesn't add up.

Nonsense. I'm just being fanciful.

She put on a night-gown, took out her laptop and connected it to her digital camera. In a moment she was looking at the pictures Dante had taken of her, trying to recognise herself.

Who was this woman with the come-hither look, giving the man that teasing smile because she was basking in his attention? It was an illusion. Dante had summoned that look from her in the joking spirit that seemed natural to him, and somehow he'd persuaded her to glance sideways, smiling, to intrigue him as he intrigued her. This man was a natural showman with the gift of luring everyone else into the show. There was no more to it than that, and she mustn't forget.

There was a knock on the door and Dante's voice called, 'It's me.'

She drew a slow breath of dismay. She'd half-expected him to appear at her door, but not so soon. Where was the skilled, sensitive man with the light touch that she'd pictured? Was he going to be vulgarly obvious after all? Her disappointment was severe.

As she was preparing the words of rejection, he knocked again. 'Can I come in?'

'Yes,' she said hastily, reaching for her robe and whisking it on as his head appeared cautiously around the door.

'Ah, you've got the pictures on-screen,' he said. 'I was hoping to see them. Am I any good as a photographer?'

'Er, yes, some of the pictures are very nice,' she said, trying to marshal her thoughts.

He was still fully dressed and didn't seem to notice that she was attired for the night. He studied the computer screen eagerly.

'Nice,' he said. 'You photograph well, and the light was good just then.'

He ran through to the end of the pictures, then back, then forward again, until he found one that seemed to please him especially. She had just shaken her hair so that it fell in soft curls about her face, framing her laughter.

'I'd like to have a copy of that one,' he said. 'You look just great.'

Here it was: the first move. *Be careful.*

But it was hard to be careful when she was suddenly conscious of her nakedness beneath the flimsy night-gown. Her whole body seemed alive to him and oblivious to her efforts at control.

'I'm afraid that may take a while,' she said. 'I don't have a printer with me.'

'No problem. Here's my email address. Send it to me as a file attachment and I'll take care of the printing. Now, I should get to bed if I were you. You've had a long day, and tomorrow is going to be even busier.'

He turned in the open door.

'Sleep well. Sorry I disturbed you. Goodnight.'

The door closed behind him.

Just down the corridor, the sound of that door closing was heard by two who lay contentedly in each other's arms.

'Leaving so soon?' Toni observed. 'Dante's losing his touch. Usually he can have any woman he wants—for a little while.'

'I know,' Hope sighed. 'As soon as it looks like getting serious, he vanishes. But how can we blame him? Think what it must be like for him, living with the knowledge that— Oh, it's terrible! Of course he can't be like other people.'

'He won't let anyone mention the subject,' Toni said sombrely. 'If you try, he becomes cold and angry. He wants to pretend that nothing is wrong, but if you catch him off-guard it's there in his eyes, the knowledge and the fear.'

'Should we tell Ferne?' Hope said. 'Just in case?'

'Warn her, you mean? Not now. Perhaps later. Dante would be furious to know that his secret was out.'

'Won't it have to come out in the end?'

'I don't know,' Toni said sadly. 'Perhaps it will never be spoken of at all—until it's too late.'

Dawn was the best part of the day, when the bright, clear air gave the view across the bay to Vesuvius a new vividness. How peaceful the volcano looked now it was sleeping, and how hard won that peace must be. The previous night had taught Ferne that.

She'd thought herself so well prepared, so ready to fend off any advance from Dante. But when he'd bid her a gentlemanly goodnight she'd been ill prepared for any of the reactions that had coursed through her.

Starting with disbelief, they had exploded through to outrage, deprivation and finally insult.

At the mere prospect of making love with him, her body had flowered. And he hadn't been interested. It was sheer bad manners.

She could cheerfully have hurled something at the door he'd closed behind him. It had taken the rest of the night to calm the volcano inside her, and now the sight of the real one in the distance didn't improve her temper.

Had he suspected her moment of weakness? The thought made her go hot and cold.

She felt an urgent need to get away from where he might be. He'd come out last night to watch the sunset. Suppose he came out again at dawn?

Turning to hurry inside, she saw him standing behind her. How long had he been there?

'Good morning,' she said hurriedly, trying to get past him.

But he detained her with a light hand on her arm. 'Stay.'

'You're very free with your commands,' she said tersely.

'Have I offended you?'

'Of course not. But I expect you want to be alone.'

'Not alone from you.'

He turned her so that she faced the sea and

then he stood behind her, his arms crossed over her breast, holding her gently against him. Mysteriously his touch seemed to soothe her annoyance, and Ferne put up her hands, not to push him away but to hold his forearms.

'So near and yet so far,' he murmured.

'How far is Vesuvius really?'

'Only about six miles in earthly distance, but it comes from another universe. Once, years ago, I heard it rumble, and it was like magic. I'm always hoping for another one.'

'No luck?'

'Not yet. It keeps you waiting.'

'Maybe it can't decide what it wants.'

'Or maybe it knows what it wants and can't decide what to do about it,' he mused. 'Even when you want something badly, the way isn't always clear.'

Now she had her answer about the night before. He didn't want to keep his distance from her, but for some reason seemed to feel that he should. So the next step was up to her. Nothing else mattered now; she was content.

They returned to find the villa already awakening. Everyone was agog at the arrival of the two remaining sons, Justin from England, Luke from Rome. As many of the family as possible were going to the airport to meet Justin, his wife and children. Dante and Ferne remained at the villa to greet Luke.

In the early afternoon Primo and Olympia arrived, soon followed by another car, out of which stepped a powerful-looking man and a petite, fair-haired young woman.

'Luke and Minnie,' Dante said.

It was clear from the interested looks Ferne was getting that her story had spread throughout the family. When Minnie came downstairs from settling into her room, she commandeered Ferne's company, demanding to be told everything. But before there was time to say much there was a shout and everyone hurried outside to welcome the party from England.

Justin, Hope's eldest son, was an austere-looking man who at first seemed out of place in this convivial gathering, but Ferne noticed that his eyes followed his mother with a possessive look that contrasted curiously with his bearing. He had the same look for his wife, Evie, a brisk young woman with an air of friendly efficiency.

They were accompanied by Mark, Justin's son by his first marriage. He was twenty, handsome, with dark wavy hair and brilliant eyes that made both the young maids give him yearning looks.

'He's just discovering his powers as a lady-killer,' Justin said with a groan, yet also a touch of fatherly pride. 'It makes him very difficult to live with.'

'Don't be hard on him,' Evie protested. 'It's not his fault he's good-looking. He's just finished his first love affair with a girl who teaches ballroom dancing. He started learning as a way of getting close to her, and now he's really good.'

The young man's presence changed the atmosphere, making it livelier. Later, when the meal was over, Toni rummaged through some old tapes, made in the days before rock 'n' roll, and played them on an ancient tape recorder.

'Go on,' he told Mark. 'Let's see how good you are.'

Without hesitating, Mark extended a hand to Ferne, whom he'd been admiring across the table all through supper.

'Dance with me?'

Pleased, she accepted. She was a good dancer, and Mark was an expert. Soon they were spinning around in perfect time.

'Let's go really fast,' he said suddenly, swinging her around and around.

Gasping, she just managed to keep up. When

they finished there was applause from the others, who had retired to sit down and watch them with admiration.

'What is that dance?' Dante asked, coming forward hastily. 'Could you teach it to me?'

'It's basically the quick-step,' Mark told him. 'You do it like this.'

Someone switched the music on again, and there were more cheers and applause as Mark gave a dazzling demonstration, with Ferne as his partner. Then Dante took possession of her and proceeded to show how well he'd learned.

Ferne had to admit that he was a natural, mastering the fastest steps with ease, and taking her flying across the floor as if they had been doing this all their lives.

With this partner the most intricate steps became easy to her, and her feet flashed in and out, sometimes between his own feet, so that she felt they must surely trip each other, yet never did. She had the glorious sensation that no mistake was possible while Dante held her. He was a powerful man, but that power lay not in muscles and brawn but in quicksilver.

That was how he lived his life, she was sure. If trouble loomed, he would dance around it, or over it, or past it, then vanish into the shadows, leaving everyone wondering if he'd ever really been there. It made him both enchanting and dangerous.

At last Toni changed the tape, and they slowed into a waltz.

'I'm impressed,' she gasped. 'Have you really never done the quick-step before?'

'No, but I love dancing; the faster, the better.'

'Waltzing's too dull for you, huh?'

'Much. Who needs it? You have to hold her close.'

'As you're doing with me?'

'Naturally. And you have to pay her compliments, like she's the loveliest woman in the room.'

'But you're not doing that!' she protested indignantly.

'Why should I bore you with what you've heard a hundred times before? Besides,' he added more slowly, 'you know exactly what you look like.'

He was right. She'd taken time over her appearance, and was pleased with the result. The honey-red of her hair was perfectly set off by the floaty chiffon dress with its mixture of autumnal colours. It was knee-length, revealing that her legs were long and elegant, her ankles perfect, and she had a natural balance for the high-heeled sandals that many women couldn't have risked wearing.

In the arms of this tall man, those heels were an advantage, helping her match his height and see his face more closely.

'Maybe I know and maybe I don't,' she teased. 'That's for me to say.'

'So you want me to tell you that you're a dream of beauty, a goddess of the night?'

'Oh, shut up!' she chuckled.

'I'm just trying to do the proper thing here.'

'And you're always so proper, aren't you?'

'Well, somebody did once say that I wouldn't recognise propriety if it came up and whacked me. I can't recall her name just now.'

'Ah! One of those instantly forgettable females. She was probably just trying to provoke you to get your attention.'

He gave a self-mocking smile. 'I wish I could believe she wanted my attention.'

'Or she might be playing cat-and-mouse with you.'

'I'd like to believe that too. You don't know what fun cat-and-mouse can be.'

'You think I don't?' she asked, eyebrows arched sardonically.

'No, forget I said that. Of course you do.' He

added hopefully, 'You could probably teach me a thing or two.'

'No, I don't think I could teach you anything about playing games.'

'The game of love has many different aspects,' he suggested.

'But we're not talking about love,' she whispered. 'This is a different game altogether.'

It was a game that made her pulses race and her whole body sing from the close contact with his. Reason argued that her physical excitement was due to the movement of the dance, but reason fell silent before the pleasure of his clasp about her waist and the awareness of his mouth near hers.

'What do you call the game?' he whispered.

'I'm sure we each have our own name for it.'

'Tell me yours.'

She glanced up, murmuring, 'I'll tell you mine if you'll tell me yours.'

'I asked first.'

This time she didn't reply, but her look was full of mischief.

'You're going to tease me, aren't you?' he said. 'You're a wicked woman.'

'I know. I work at it.'

'No need. I reckon a certain kind of wickedness comes naturally to you.'

'True. It's one of the great pleasures of life.'
Exhilarated, she provoked him further. 'Almost
as much fun as cat-and-mouse.'

A gleam of appreciation came into his eyes.
'Cat-and-mouse; I wish I knew which one I was.'

'I'll leave you to work that one out.'

He gave a shout of laughter that made
everyone stare at them, and began whirling her
fast again until they spun out onto the terrace,
where she broke from him and darted away,
running down the steps and under the trees. She
was high on excitement, and the sound of him
pursuing her was a delight. She ran faster, challenging him to follow her, and he accepted the
challenge.

'Woman, are you crazy?' he demanded,
winding his arms around her waist in a grip of
velvet and steel. 'Just how much do you think a
man can take?'

She responded not with words but with
laughter, that rang up to the moon until he
silenced her mouth with his own. Somehow the
laughter continued, because it was there in the
kiss, passing from her to him and back again. It
was there too in the skilful movements of his
hands that knew how to coax without demanding, persuade without insisting.

He had the gift which so many men lacked, of kissing gently. Her return kiss was joyful, curious, teasing just a little.

'I'm not crazy,' she whispered. 'And perhaps a man should exercise a little self-control.'

'Not while you're making it hard for him,' he growled, moving down her neck.

She was unable to say more, because his lips had found the spot where she was most sensitive. Shivers went through her, defying her efforts to control them as his mouth caressed the hollow at the base of her throat, touching it softly again and again while she clung to him and her head whirled.

He was wicked. Even with all her nerves shouting warnings, he could still make her want him. Her hands had a will of their own. They clasped his head, drawing him closer against her so that his lips continued their skilled work. She should push him away, but, just another minute…

She felt the ground beneath her. She didn't know when he'd drawn her down, but suddenly she was lying in his arms, and he was looking at her with an expression on his face that she couldn't see through the darkness.

That was so like him, she thought feverishly—always keeping one part of himself a secret. And right now she wanted to know his secrets, wanted to know everything about him, to feel his hands on her body, all over, wanted everything there was to want.

His fingers were at the neck of her dress, trying to draw it lower. When it would go no further, he drew the shoulder down and laid his lips against it. Now she could feel his hair brushing her face and she ran her hand deliciously through it, sighing with satisfaction.

But then she heard something that froze her blood: laughter, soft and merry, coming from a little distance away. The family was appearing in the garden, getting nearer.

CHAPTER FOUR

'DANTE,' she hissed. '*Dante*! Get up.'

Frantically she pushed at him and he drew back, frowning.

'They're coming,' she said. 'They mustn't find us like this.'

Muttering a curse, he wrenched himself away and got to his feet, drawing her up with him. He would have run, but Mark's voice came through the trees.

'Ferne, Dante, are you there?'

'I'm going to murder that boy,' Dante muttered. 'He's doing this on purpose.'

'Don't be paranoid.'

'I'm not paranoid,' Dante said in a soft, enraged voice. 'He fancies you.'

Despite her jangling nerves, she nearly laughed.

'Nonsense. His heart's given to his dancing-girl friend.'

'He's twenty,' Dante snapped. 'He forgot her the minute he left England.'

'You don't know that.'

'Of course I know. I've been twenty.'

'So *that's* what young men of twenty do. And thirty. And thirty-five.'

Dante flung her the look of a man driven to madness.

Now the others were calling them. There was no choice but to walk back into the light, looking as cheerful and natural as possible. Ferne had a worrying feeling that her voice was shaking and she was sure that her smile looked unnatural.

But, more than that, she was shaking inside. She felt like someone who'd found herself unexpectedly on the edge of a cliff, and had backed off without knowing how she'd got there.

The family settled down for final drinks under the stars. Mark tried to get close to Ferne but was deterred by a scowl from Dante. If Ferne's nerves hadn't been jangling, she might have felt flattered and amused.

Hope ordered a pot of tea and Ferne drank it thankfully, feeling the warm liquid soothe her. Hope was looking at her kindly, and her eyebrows raised in surprise when Ferne took four sugar-lumps instead of her usual one. She needed them.

'I'm feeling a little tired,' she said as soon as she decently could. 'You won't mind if I go to bed?'

'I'm tired too, after the flight,' Evie said, and the party began to break up.

Ferne escaped upstairs, unable to meet Dante's eyes. Once in her room, she plunged into an icy-cold shower. That would soon put her right.

It did, to the extent that it cooled down her flesh, but her mind remained as disturbed as before. She was accustomed to thinking of herself as calm and collected. Even in the throes of passion for Sandor she'd felt in command—something which their grande finale had surely proved.

But Dante had upset that unruffled composure, making her wonder if it was really such a virtue. Had she perhaps become a trifle smug? If so, he was rescuing her from that danger, surprising her again and again.

He insisted on haunting her mind, despite her stern orders for him to depart. But that was Dante: awkward. When she stepped out of the shower and caught a glimpse of herself in the

mirror, he seemed to be there, eyeing her nakedness longingly, making her regret that she hadn't
allowed him to see her, because he would have
liked her so much.

She pulled on her nightdress and in her mind's
eye his face fell.

'Get out!' she told him. 'Go away and leave
me alone.'

He obeyed, but not without a final glance over
his shoulder.

There was a soft knock at her door.

'Who is it?'

'It's me,' said Dante.

She nearly said, 'Are you back already?' but
stopped herself in time.

'What do you want?'

'Can I come in? There's something I need to
talk about.'

She stood back to let him in, first making sure
that her robe was securely fastened. Even so,
she felt as though her garments were transparent.

He was still in shirt and trousers, but now the
shirt had been torn open at the throat, showing
several inches of his chest. It was an attractive
chest, she had to admit that, but now she was
trying to be cautious. In his arms tonight she'd

almost lost her head. There had been a moment in the grass when she would have done anything he wanted, because he could make her want it too.

She was sure he knew it. This was one clever, manipulative man, and she must never let herself forget that.

'What did you want to talk about?' she asked demurely.

'Us,' he said at once. 'And what you're doing to me. I don't think I can stand it much longer.'

Now she was glad she'd taken the cold shower, for her body had regained its equilibrium and her mind was able to view him rationally.

'If you can't stand being with me, it was hardly wise of you to come here,' she pointed out.

'I didn't say that,' he replied, imitating her tone of reasoned argument. 'It's the "so near and yet so far" aspect that's shredding my nerves. It should be one or the other, and I thought we might discuss it sensibly and come to a rational decision.'

The bland innocence of his face might have fooled anyone less alive to his tricks than Ferne. But by now she was back in command.

'I quite agree,' she said seriously. 'One or the other. And, since I'll be gone fairly soon, I think it we should opt for the second choice.'

'Pardon?'

'It would be wise for you to leave my room.'

He nodded. 'It would be wise, wouldn't it? If I were a wise man I'd flee and never look back. But I was never wise.'

'Then this would be a good time to start.'

He slid an arm around her waist.

'I know I shouldn't have come,' he murmured. 'But I had to. You were so wonderful tonight. I watched you and knew I had to dance with you—and then I danced with you and knew I had to hold you in my arms and kiss you and love you…'

He drew her close as he spoke in a grip that was gentle and implacable together.

'That's going a little too far, surely?' she asked lightly.

'But I want to go too far with you. How could I want anything else when you're so beautiful and you fire me up? I want to go too far and then further—'

'Hush,' she said suddenly. 'I thought I heard a noise in the corridor. Could anyone have seen you?'

'Not a soul. Don't worry, I'll be as quiet as a mouse.'

'You, a mouse?' she jeered softly. 'Who do

you think you're fooling? Dante, I like you a lot, I really do, but I am not some daft little bimbo to be overcome by your charm. Don't forget, I've been seduced by an expert.'

'Are you suggesting I'm not an expert?' he asked in outrage.

'Well, you're not doing brilliantly right now.'

He gave a sigh and a rueful look, much like a schoolboy caught playing truant. She almost capitulated there and then, but thankfully managed to hold firm.

'It was worth a try, wasn't it?' she teased.

'I don't know what you mean.'

'Like hell you don't! You came in here saying to yourself, "Go on, give it a whirl. She might say yes, she might say no, she might slap my face. Let's find out".'

His sheepish expression confirmed her suspicions.

'Well, I found out, didn't I?' he said. 'But at least I didn't get my face slapped.'

'That's the next stage. Now, depart while we're still friends.'

'Friends? Is that really all you—?'

'*Go!*'

He went. Hastily.

* * *

As an attractive woman working in the entertainment business, Ferne had had a fair amount of experience in saying no to over-enthusiastic gentlemen, and she'd discovered that you could tell a lot about a man by how he behaved at the next meeting, assuming there was one. Some behaved well, some badly, some pretended that nothing had happened.

Dante, of course, had to be original, hopping behind her from tree to tree as she walked through the garden, darting out of sight when she turned until she cried, exasperated, 'Come out, you idiot.'

'If you're calling me an idiot, does that mean I'm forgiven?' he asked, presenting himself hopefully before her.

'I guess it does.'

From behind him came a shout. 'Dante, are you coming?'

'On my way,' he yelled back. 'I'm going into town with Carlo and Ruggiero, but I couldn't go until I knew I was back in favour.'

'I didn't say you were back in favour,' she told him sternly. 'I said you were forgiven—just.'

'Yes, of course, there's a difference. I'll work on it when I get back. Bye.'

He kissed her cheek and fled, leaving her

laughing and wondering what she had to do to get the last word.

But then, she reflected, did she really want the last word? It had a melancholy sound.

She spent an enjoyable day with Hope and the other women, talking about England and fussing over the children. Dante's behaviour to her that evening was restrained and impeccable. He seemed completely oblivious to her as a woman, which was how she preferred it, she tried to tell herself.

Ferne had said she was never without her camera, and it was true, so when she came across Toni playing with Ruggiero's baby son she hurried into action and produced some swift, spontaneous shots that had everyone exclaiming with delight.

'I've been thinking what I can do to thank you for your kindness,' Ferne said to Hope. 'And now I know. I'm going to take pictures, dozens of them—everybody alone, in couples, with their children, without their children. Then I want you all to gather in the garden so that I can take a big one.'

'And I'll always have a memento,' Hope cried, overjoyed. 'Oh, yes please.'

Ferne started at once, going around the house,

working on her idea until everyone had a solo shot, down to the tiniest child.

To these she added pictures taken secretly, when people had been unaware of being photographed and were therefore more natural. The final result was a triumphant collection that made Hope weep with joy, and give a special dinner in Ferne's honour.

'That was a very kind thing you did,' Dante said as they sipped wine together. 'Hope's family is everything to her.'

His praise made her slightly embarrassed.

'I did it for myself, really. Taking pictures is a kind of compulsion, and when I can't do it I get restless.'

'Why do you put yourself down? Who are you hiding from?'

'Since when were you an expert in psychoanalysis?' she asked, amused. 'I'm not hiding.'

'Some people would say you were hiding behind the camera, getting everyone else into focus but staying safely concealed. I'm just playing with ideas. If you want some good pictures, let me take you into town and show you old Naples, where the historic buildings still exist. You'll find all the pictures you want.'

She agreed eagerly and they went the next day,

driving down into the *centro storico*, as historic Naples was called. As he'd guessed, she was enthusiastic and began clicking, enchanted by the narrow, winding streets with washing strung from side to side, and the stalls selling fish and fruit.

At last they collapsed into chairs at a roadside café, and revived themselves on cake and coffee.

'I'm so glad you thought of this,' she sighed blissfully. 'It's been wonderful. This place is almost too picturesque to be true.'

Dante nodded. 'Naples has its modern districts, places full of soulless, efficient buildings. But it also has these corners where people can still be human instead of cogs in a wheel. People here don't just know each other, they're neighbours, practically family. A lot of them *are* family. You tend to get whole apartment-blocks populated by relatives. Let's have some—'

He stopped as a wild scream came from somewhere nearby. Suddenly there was chaos. People were running down the little streets, waving their arms and indicating something behind them.

'*Incendio!*' they screamed. '*Incendio!*'

'There's a fire somewhere,' Dante said.

Following the pointing hands, they began to run until they came to a five-storey building on one side of a narrow alley, where the ground was entirely made of steps. Smoke was billowing from the windows and people were streaming out, shouting to each other.

'They've called the fire brigade,' Dante said, picking up a few words. 'But these lanes are too narrow for the machines. The nearest they'll get is that corner, then they'll have to carry the ladders into this street and set them on the ground. Let's hope their ladders are long enough. Luckily, everyone seems to be escaping the buildings fast.'

Behind them a woman was screaming, 'Piero, Marco, Ginetta, Enrico—*mio dio*!'

From the bags cast aside on the pavement, it seemed that she had been shopping when the news had reached her and had run back to her children. Now they were hurling themselves into her arms and she was sending up frantic prayers of relief.

'*Salvo,*' she wept. Safe. '*Oh, dio! Salvo. Ma no! Dove Nico?*'

Nico? People began to look around. Nico? Where was Nico?

One of the boys said something and recoiled as his mother slapped his cheek.

'What is it?' Ferne asked, horrified.

'Nico was coming down with them, but they lost sight of him,' Dante explained. 'She's blaming them for going on without him.'

'Nico!' the woman screamed, gazing up at the building. '*Nico!*'

Suddenly there was a mighty rumble followed by a crash from inside the building, and smoke billowed out of the windows.

'The inside has collapsed,' Dante said grimly. 'Let's hope Nico got out.'

But the next moment there was a shout of horror. Everyone looked up to see a little boy standing on a rickety wrought-iron balcony at the top, looking down.

'Nico!' his mother screamed again. 'Come down.'

She was too hysterical to realise that this was impossible, but everyone else understood, and groans went up at what seemed inevitable.

People were running to fetch ladders which they leaned up against the wall, but the boy was five storeys up and nothing reached him. Another ominous rumble from within the building warned how close danger was.

'Move that ladder!' Dante yelled. 'Push it over here.'

'But it's not long enough,' someone protested.

'Don't argue,' he roared. 'Just do as I say.'

Impatiently he yanked the ladder from their hands and set it up against the wall.

'Hold it,' he snapped.

Recognising the voice of authority, they scurried to obey. This was a new Dante, one Ferne had never seen before, a man of grim determination; his eyes were hard, his attitude set, brooking no argument, and woe betide anyone who got in his way.

She ventured to say, 'But what will you do when the ladder runs out?'

For a moment he looked at her as though he'd never seen her before.

Then recognition kicked in, and he said curtly, 'I'll climb.'

He turned away without waiting for her reply and the next moment was climbing the ladder swiftly, two rungs at a time, until he reached the base of the third balcony. Seizing the wrought iron, he managed to haul himself to the upper rim while the crowd below gasped. Ferne gazed in awe, thinking how strong his arms must be to manage that.

Having mounted the balcony, he climbed up onto the rail and leapt upwards. It was only a small distance, but it was enough to take him to the base of the next balcony where he did the same thing, managing to climb up there too.

One more to go. Thank goodness, Ferne thought, that he was so tall and so long in the leg. A shorter man could never have managed those leaps.

Now he was there, soothing the child. But how was he going to descend with him? Those watching below saw Dante take a hard, considering look down, then nod as though the decision was made. He turned and knelt down so that the child could climb onto his back; his arms wound tightly about Dante's neck. The next moment he'd swung over the balcony, going down the iron railings inch by inch until he reached the bottom and hung there.

Everyone below held their breath, wondering what he could possibly do now. He soon showed them, swinging back and forth until he could risk releasing the rail, and taking a flying leap onto the balcony below. It seemed an impossible trick, yet he managed it, throwing himself forward at the last minute so that he landed on his knees, and that the child on his back was safe and unhurt.

Nearly done. One more leap before they reached the safety of the ladder. Could he make it, or would they both plunge to earth? Down below hands were raised up as if everyone feared the worst and would try to catch them.

Dante didn't hesitate, swinging over the balcony, working his way down the railings, then taking the leap. A roar broke from the crowd as he landed safely.

A man had climbed the ladder and now reached out to take Nico, helping him down to safety while Dante remained on the balcony, breathing hard. Cheers and applause broke out as the child reached the ground, but nobody could relax until his rescuer was also safe. At last Dante reached for the ladder and climbed down to a deafening roar.

Ferne felt the tears pouring down her cheeks. She couldn't have said why she was weeping, whether it was fear for Dante or pride in him, but she was filled with feelings that threatened to explode.

He gave her a brief smile and went to the mother, who was in transports of delight, uttering passionate thanks that seemed to embarrass him. She was clinging to the child, who seemed dazed and unresponsive, but who suddenly seemed to awaken and look around him, searching for something. When he didn't find it, he began to scream.

'Pini?' he cried. 'Pini! He'll die—*he'll die!*'

'Is that another child?' Ferne asked. 'Does he mean someone's still in there?'

'No, Pini is his puppy,' said his mother. 'He must be out here somewhere.'

'No, *no*!' Nico sobbed. 'He's still in there. He'll die.'

His mother tried desperately to soothe him.

'*Caro*, it can't be helped. Nobody can risk their life for a dog.'

Nico began to scream. 'Pini! Pini, Pini…!'

'He's probably dead already,' somebody said. 'He must have been overcome by the smoke—he won't have suffered.'

'No, *there*!' came a shout from the crowd.

Everyone looked up, gasping at the sight of the little dog appearing at the window. He was barking and looking around him in fear and bewilderment. Screams rose from the crowd as his inevitable fate approached, and Nico began to struggle, trying to escape.

'Pini, Pini—I'm coming!'

'No!' cried his mother, clutching him tightly.

'Stay there,' Dante said sharply. 'Just don't move.'

The next moment he was running headlong back to the building.

There were more screams from the crowd as they realised what he meant to do.

'He's crazy—does he want to be killed? Does he know what he's doing? Stop him!'

But Ferne had seen the reckless determination in his eyes and knew that nothing could have stopped him. Terrified, she watched as he reached the house and began climbing up the ladder through the smoke that now seemed to surround everything. Every time he vanished, she was convinced she wouldn't see him again, but somehow he always managed to reappear, higher and higher, closer to the place where the dog was looking down, yelping with terror.

By now two fire-engines had arrived, but had to stop at the end of the narrow street. Seeing what was happening, the firemen came running along the street with a detachable ladder and sent it shooting up towards Dante. Mercifully it was longer than the first one, but when they shouted at him to climb onto it he merely glanced down at them, shook his head and turned back, heading up again.

He'd reached the last balcony, but now his luck ran out. As soon as he seized it, the wrought iron pulled away from the crumbling brickwork so that one end came completely free, swinging down violently. Screams came from the crowd as Dante hung from the iron, seemingly with no way to save himself. The firemen were working the ladder, trying to get it closer to him.

Ferne watched, her heart in her mouth, unable to endure looking, yet equally unable to turn away. It was surely impossible that he could come through this alive?

Then he kicked against the wall hard enough to swing out and up. From somewhere he found the strength to reach higher, and begin to climb up the swinging balcony. He did it again and again, inching closer to the window where the dog was shivering.

Cheers rose as he finally made it, but as he reached for the dog the animal vanished into the building. Dante hauled himself in, also vanishing, and everyone below held their breath. The next moment there came a crash from inside. Smoke billowed from the window, and an appalled hush fell over the onlookers. He was dead. He must be.

Ferne buried her face in her hands, praying frantically. He couldn't die. He mustn't.

Then a shout of triumph went up. *'There he is!'*

Dante had reappeared at another window,

further down, with the dog in his arms. Now he was closer to the ladder with the fireman at the top. A little more manoeuvring, and it was near enough for him to reach down and hand the animal to the fireman, who began to back down the rungs, leaving the top of the ladder free for Dante to follow.

It was nearly over. He reached the ladder, climbed onto it and started the descent. In another moment, he would be safe.

But then something seemed to halt him. He froze and stayed there, clinging on, leaning against the metal, his eyes closed, his head hanging down.

'Oh heavens, he's passed out!' Ferne whispered. 'It's the smoke.'

The fireman passed the dog to another man further down, then climbed back up to Dante, positioning himself ready to catch him if he fell, reaching up to touch him.

To everyone's relief Dante seemed to come out of his trance and look around him. At last he managed to move and complete the journey down.

As he reached the ground, the cheers broke out again. He shook his head as though to clear it and, seeming to return to reality, took the dog from the fireman and carried it to the child, who screamed in ecstasy.

If the crowd had cheered him before, they now went completely mad. A man who risked himself for a child was a hero; a man who took the same risks for a dog was a wonderful madman.

Yes, a madman, Ferne thought, trying to still her thumping heart. A glorious madman, but still a man who didn't live on the same planet as everyone else.

He seemed strangely unwilling to enjoy the praise he'd won. They tried to hoist him shoulder-high, but now all he wanted was to escape.

'Let's go,' he said, grasping her hand.

CHAPTER FIVE

THEY ran from the crowd, dodging the out-stretched hands, darting through street after street until they were lost and their pursuers were far behind.

'Where are we?' she asked.

'Who cares? Anywhere.'

'And where's the car?'

'Anywhere. What does it matter?'

'Will you talk sense?' she laughed. She was on a high of relief.

'No. Why talk sense? When was it ever sensible to be sensible?'

'Never for you; I can see that,' she said tenderly. 'Come on, let's get you somewhere safe.'

'Wherever you say. Lead on.'

She suddenly felt protective. Taking his hand as she might have taken the hand of a child, she led him until they found a small café with a table on the pavement where they could let the sun drench them.

'I need this,' he said, 'after all that smoke. I also need a drink, but I suppose I'd better not have one since I have to drive home—when we find the car.' He began to laugh. 'Where are we going to find it? Where do we start?'

'I think I remember the street. Don't worry about it now.'

When the waiter had taken their order, he leaned back, looking at her. There was exhilaration in his eyes.

'Dante, for pity's sake,' she said, taking hold of his hand again. 'Will you come down to earth?'

'I thought that was what I'd just done.'

'You know what I mean. You're up in the stratosphere somewhere. Come back down to the same planet as the rest of us.'

'What for? I like it up here.' He turned his hand so that now he was holding her. 'Come up here with me. It's a great life. I've never had such fun.'

'Fun? You could have died!'

'Well, the strangest things can be fun if you look at them the right way.'

'You could have died,' she repeated slowly, as if to an idiot.

'But I didn't. I could have, but I didn't. Don't you understand? It's been a great day.'

'How can you *say* that?' she exploded. 'How can you sit there as if it was nothing? Of all the mad things to do! To save a child, yes, that's wonderful. But to take such a risk for a dog— what were you thinking of?'

'I'm a dog lover. And that little boy would have been broken-hearted if I'd left his dog to die.'

'And what about you? Don't you mind if you live or die?'

He shrugged. 'I don't worry about it. It'll happen when it happens.'

'It'll happen a lot sooner if you take crazy risks.'

'Maybe it will, maybe it won't. What's wrong with taking risks? Life's better that way. Think of it as doing the quick-step with fate as your partner. You go faster and faster, never knowing which of you is going to reach the edge first. Everything is possible; it's the only way to live. And, if not, better to die like that than, well, some of the other ways.'

'You nearly came to grief,' she reminded him. 'When you were on top of the ladder you seemed to collapse. You just clung there and I thought you were going to fall. What happened?'

'Nothing. You imagined it.'

'But I didn't. You slumped against the ladder.'

'I don't remember. There was smoke everywhere and a lot of things passed me by. It doesn't matter now. Let's leave it.'

'I don't think we ought to leave it. You may have been affected in some way that isn't obvious yet. I want a doctor to have a look at you.'

'There's no need,' he said in a voice suddenly full of tension. 'It's over.'

'But you don't know that,' she pleaded. 'You passed out on the top of that ladder and—'

'*How the hell do you know?*'

The sudden cold fury in his voice was like a slap in the face, making her flinch back.

'You weren't up there; you don't know what happened,' he snapped. 'You saw me close my eyes against the smoke and give myself a moment's rest before climbing down the rest of the way. *And that's all!* Don't start dramatising.'

'I didn't mean— I'm just worried about you.'

'Do I look as if I need worrying about?' he asked in a voice that was now quiet and steely.

Ferne was struggling to come to terms with the terrible transformation in him, and she had to take a deep breath before she could reply bravely, 'Yes, actually, you do. Everyone needs worrying about. Why should you be any different? Something dreadful has happened to you. It might have made you ill and I simply want to find out. Why should that make you angry?'

'Why does any man get angry at being fussed over? Just leave it, please.'

His voice was still quiet, but now there was something in it that was almost a threat.

'But—'

'I said *leave it*.'

She didn't dare to say any more, and that word 'dare' told her what a dreadful thing had happened. The mere thought of being afraid of Dante was incredible, and yet she was. This was more than masculine irritation at being 'fussed over', it was bitter, terrifying rage.

But he was recovering himself. Before her eyes, the temper drained out of him.

'I'm sorry,' he said. 'I'm not quite myself. I'll be all right soon. Just promise me one thing— you won't say anything about this at home.'

'Not tell them about the fire? I think that story will get around somehow.'

'I don't mean that. I meant the other thing, that I had a bad moment on the ladder. Hope worries easily. Say nothing.'

When she hesitated he said, 'You *must* give me your word.'

'All right,' she said quickly. She had a fearful feeling that his rage was on the verge of rising again.

'You promise faithfully?'

'Yes, I promise.'

'Fine. Then everything's all right.'

Everything was far from all right, but she couldn't say so. She could never forget what she'd seen.

But now his mood was lightening, changing him back into the Dante she knew.

'Look on the bright side,' he said. 'Think what exciting pictures I must have given you.'

Pictures. Stunned, she realised that she'd never once thought of them.

She, to whom photography was such a part of her DNA that even her own lover's treachery had been recorded for posterity, had forgotten everything the moment Dante had started to climb.

'I didn't take any pictures,' she whispered.

'What do you mean?' he asked in mock outrage. 'You take pictures of everything. How come I'm not considered worth the trouble?'

'You know the answer perfectly well,' she

snapped. 'I was too worried about you to think of photography.'

He shook his head. 'I don't know what the world is coming to,' he said sorrowfully. 'My great moment and you missed it. Shall I go back up and give you a second chance?'

'Don't bother,' she said crisply. 'The second take is never as effective as the first.'

They both knew what they were really talking about. The woman who let nothing get in the way of a good picture had missed this because she'd forgotten everything but his being in danger.

Now he would know, and how he would love that! But when she met his eyes she saw in them not triumph, but only bleak weariness, as though a light had gone out. He was struggling to present his normal, jokey self, but it was an effort.

'Come on,' he said tiredly. 'Let's go home.'

They found the car and drove back in silence. At the villa he immediately went for a shower. While he was away, Ferne outlined the events to the family but, remembering her promise, said nothing about what had happened at the end.

'Trust Dante to go back for the dog,' Hope said.

'He loved it,' Ferne said. 'It was as though risking his life gave him some sort of kick.'

'His father was the same,' Toni sighed. 'Always finding excuses to do crazy things.'

'Yes, but—' Hope began to speak, then stopped.

Puzzled, Ferne waited for her to continue. Then Hope met her husband's eyes and he gave an almost imperceptible shake of the head.

'If a man is like that, he's like that,' she finished lamely. 'I'll just go up and see if he's all right.'

She returned a moment later saying, 'I looked in. He's asleep. I expect he needs it.'

Then she deftly turned the conversation, leaving Ferne again with the impression that where Dante was concerned there were strange undercurrents.

Next morning he'd already left for town when she rose. She tried not to believe that he was avoiding her, but it was hard.

Her new credit cards arrived in the post, and news came from the consulate that her passport was ready. She drove down and collected it, then went to a café by the water and sat, considering.

Surely it was time to move on? Her flirtation with Dante had been pleasant but it would lead nowhere. Forgetting to take pictures was an ominous sign, because it had never happened before. But the mere thought of a serious affair with him was madness, if only because of his habit of withdrawing behind a mask.

On the surface he was a handsome clown who could tease his way into any woman's heart. But, when she'd given him her heart, what then? Would she be confronted by the other man who concealed himself inside, and whose qualities were beginning to seem ominous? Would he frighten her? Or would Dante keep her at bay, allowing her only to see what suited him? Either prospect was dismaying.

She thought of their first meeting on the train when they had sat together, thundering through the night, talking about the circles of heaven and hell. It had seemed a trivial conversation, but now she had the conviction that Dante was mysteriously acquainted with hell. Yesterday he had looked into its fiery depths not once but twice. Unafraid. Even willing.

Why? What did he know that was hidden from the rest of the world? What was his hell, and how did he confront it?

She was sunk so deep in her reverie that it took a while to realise that her mobile phone was shrieking.

'Ferne—at last!'

It was Mick Gregson, her agent, a cheerful, booming man.

'You've got to get back here,' Mick said. 'There's a great job coming up, big time, and I've put your name forward.'

He outlined the job which was, indeed, 'big time'. Following Sandor's example, a major Hollywood actor had just signed up for a West End play, seeking the prestige of live theatre. Next to him Sandor Jayley was peanuts.

'The management wants only the best for the pics, and when I mentioned you they were very interested.'

'I'm surprised anyone wants me after last time,' she observed wryly.

'I've heard that they value your "self-sacrificing honesty". Don't laugh; it's doing you a world of good. Seize this chance, sweetie. Gotta go.'

He hung up.

So there it was, she thought, staring at the silent phone: the decision was made for her. She would say farewell to Dante and return to England, glad to have escaped.

Escaped what?

She would have to learn to stop wondering about that.

The phone rang again. It was him.

'Where are you?' he asked in a voice that sounded agitated. When she told him, he said, 'Don't move. I'll be there in a few minutes.'

She was waiting for him, baffled, when he drew up at the kerb.

'Sorry to hassle you,' he said as she got in. 'But I need your help urgently. I've had a call from a man who owns a villa a few miles away and wants me to sell it. I'm going up there now, and I need a great photographer, so of course I thought of you.'

'I'm flattered, but my experience is showbiz, not real estate.'

'Selling a house can be a kind of showbiz, especially a house like this. In the nineteenth century, it was notorious. The owner had a wife and three mistresses and kept each one in a different wing. Then he was murdered.'

'Good for them.'

He laughed. 'It's odd how people always assume that it was the women.'

'If it wasn't, it should have been,' Ferne said without hesitation.

'It probably was. The police never found out. I want you to bring out the drama, while also making it look a comfortable place to live.'

After an hour they came to the villa, set on a

hill with an extravagant outline, as though it had been built as part of a grand opera. Inside, the place was shabby with few modern comforts. The owner, a tubby, middle-aged man, followed her around, pointing out what he considered the attractions, but she soon left him behind and made her own way. The atmosphere was beginning to get to her.

It took three hours. On the way home, they stopped off for a meal and compared notes. Now Dante was a serious businessman. His notes were thorough, and he was going to do a first-class job with the house.

'My text, your pictures,' he said. 'We're a great team. Let's get back home and put it all on my website.'

'Fine, but then I've got something to tell—'

'Naturally, I'll pay you.'

'So I should hope.'

'Of course, I can't afford your usual fees. I expect you get top-dollar now for the *right* kind of picture.'

'I'll ignore that remark.'

'But you're the best at this kind of thing, and I could sell these houses much faster with your help.'

'I'm trying to tell you—'

'I'm going to leave soon, driving all over this

area, drumming up business. Come with me. Together we'll knock 'em all dead.' When she hesitated, he took her hands in his. 'Say yes. It's time to have a little fun in your life.'

This was the Dante she'd first known, the chancer who faced life with a smile. The darkness of the recent past might never have been.

'I don't know,' she said slowly.

She was more tempted than she wanted to admit. Just a little longer in his company…

'Look, I know what you're thinking,' he said persuasively. 'But you're wrong. I've accepted your rejection.' His voice became melodramatic. 'Bitter and painful though it is.'

Her lips twitched. 'Oh, really?' she said cynically.

'Why don't you believe me?'

The mere idea of Dante meekly accepting rejection was absurd. It was a ploy, telling her that he was settling in for a long game, but if she admitted that she would be conceding a point in that very game. If there was one thing she knew she mustn't do, it was let him win too easily.

'Are you seriously asking me to believe that you'll act like a perfect gentleman at all times?'

'Ah, well, I might not have been planning to

go quite that far,' he hedged cautiously. 'But nothing to offend you. Just friendly, I promise.'

'Hmm,' she observed.

'Hmm?' he echoed innocently.

'Hmm.'

In this mood, he was irresistible. On the other hand there was the promise of the biggest job of her life, maybe a trip to Hollywood eventually.

'I'll think about it,' she said.

'Don't take too long.'

They drove back to the villa and spent a contented hour at the computer, marrying his text and her pictures. The result was a triumph, with Ferne's flair for the dramatic balancing Dante's factual efficiency. He sent a copy to the owner, who promptly emailed back, expressing his delight.

At the end of the evening Ferne went out onto the terrace and stood looking up at the stars, wondering what she was going to do. It should have been an easy decision. How could any man compete with such a career opportunity?

She knew what would happen now. Dante would have seen her come out here, and he would follow her, trying to charm her into doing exactly what he wanted.

Just *friendly*, indeed! Who did he think he was kidding?

She could hear him coming now. Smiling, she turned.

But it was Hope and Toni.

'Dante has gone to bed,' Hope explained. 'He wouldn't admit it, but I think he has a headache.'

'Is something wrong?' Ferne asked. Something in the older woman's manner alerted her.

'He tells us that he wants you to travel and work with him,' Hope said.

'He has asked me, yes. But I'm not sure if I should agree. Perhaps it's time for me to be getting back to England.'

'Oh no, please stay in Italy for a while,' Hope said anxiously. 'Please go with him.'

Ferne's first thought was that Hope was match-making, but then she got a closer look at the other woman's expression and her amusement died. Hope's face was full of strange fear.

'What's the matter?' she asked. 'It's something serious, isn't it?'

Again that disconcerting silence; Hope glanced at her husband. This time he nodded and she began to speak.

'I'm going to confide in you,' she said,

'because we trust you, and we both think that you must learn the secret.'

'Secret?' Ferne echoed.

'It's a terrible one and it weighs on us. We try not to believe it, but the truth is—' She took a deep breath and spoke with difficulty. 'The truth is that Dante might be dying.'

'What?' Ferne whispered, aghast. 'Did you say—?'

'Dying. If that should happen, and we could have done something to prevent it and had not— But he will not have it spoken of, you see, and we don't know what to do.'

Ferne forcibly pulled herself together.

'I don't understand,' she said. 'He must know if he's ill or not.'

She could hear fearful echoes in her head. They were filled with warnings and told her that she was about to discover the dark secret that made Dante unlike other men.

'On his mother's side, he's a Linelli,' Hope explained. 'And that family has a hereditary problem. There can be a weak blood vessel in the brain that can suddenly start to bleed. Then the victim will collapse, perhaps go into a coma, perhaps die.'

'This has happened to several of them over

the years,' Toni said. 'Some have died, but even the ones who survived have often been unlucky. His Uncle Leo suffered a major haemorrhage. His life was saved by surgery, but his brain was damaged. Now he's little more than a child, and to Dante he's an awful warning. He refuses even to consider that he might have inherited this illness and need treatment.'

'But has there ever been any sign?' Ferne asked. 'Or are you just afraid because it's hereditary? After all, not everyone in the family will have it.'

'True, but there was one frightening moment about two years ago. He had a headache so bad that he became confused and dizzy. This can mean a minor rupture of the blood vessel, and if that's ignored it can lead to a major one. But he insisted that he was perfectly recovered, and nothing else has happened since. That might mean nothing is wrong, or it might mean that he's been very, very lucky. He could go on being lucky for years, or…' Hope broke off with a sigh.

'But wouldn't it be better to find out?' Ferne asked.

'He doesn't want to know,' Toni said sombrely. 'He isn't afraid of death, but he is afraid of surgery, in case he ends up like Leo. His attitude is that, if death comes, it comes.'

'Doing the quick-step with fate,' Ferne murmured.

'What was that?'

'Something I've heard him say. I didn't understand it before. But I can't believe he'll go so far. Surely he'll be better having a diagnosis?'

'He's determined not to,' Hope said in despair. 'He doesn't want the family pressuring him to have surgery, even though it might not be so much of a risk. Surgical techniques have greatly improved since Leo's operation nearly thirty years ago, and Dante could easily come out of it well and whole, but he won't take the chance. He wants to get the best out of life while he can, and then, well…'

She gave a despairing sigh. Ferne was transfixed. This was worse than anything she'd feared.

'If only we knew for sure, but there's no way to be quite certain,' Hope resumed. 'Unless there's a definite symptom, like a dizzy spell. Have you ever seen him grow faint without warning?'

'Yes,' Ferne said, remembering with horror. 'He seemed to get dizzy when he was coming down the ladder when he saved the dog. But it seemed natural after what he'd been through—all that smoke.'

'It probably was natural,' Hope agreed. 'And his headache tonight is probably natural, just a delayed reaction to what he went through. But we always wonder. It's hard to say anything for fear of enraging him.'

'Yes, I've seen that,' Ferne murmured. 'I wanted him to see a doctor, and he was very angry. He made me promise not to say anything to the family, or I would have told you before. He got so furious that I had to give in. I could hardly believe that it was him.'

'He's going off alone,' Hope said. 'Please, Ferne, go with him.'

'But what could I do? I'm not a nurse.'

'No, but you'd be there, watching out for him. If anything worrying happens, you won't dismiss it as a stranger would. You can summon help, perhaps save his life. And you might even persuade him that he doesn't have to live this way.'

'He won't listen to me,' Ferne said. 'He'll probably suspect me from the start.'

'No, because he's invited you to go with him, so it will all seem natural to him. Please. I beg you.'

Ferne knew the decision had been made. This

woman who had come to her rescue and asked so little in return was now imploring her.

'You don't need to beg me,' she said at last. 'Of course I'll do it. You must tell me all you can about this illness, so that I can be of most use.'

For answer, Hope flung her arms about Ferne's neck in a passion of thankfulness. Toni was more restrained, but he laid a powerful hand on Ferne's shoulder and squeezed tightly.

But Ferne was shaking, wondering what she'd let herself in for.

CHAPTER SIX

A SOUND from inside the house made them look
up quickly, but it was only Primo, come to say
goodnight before taking Olympia back to their
apartment. Ferne took the chance to slip away
among the trees. She needed to calm her
thoughts and, more than that, calm her emotions.

For now there was a howling wilderness inside
her, and she wanted to scream up to the heavens
that it couldn't be true. It mustn't be true, for if
it was true she couldn't bear it.

She'd wanted to know Dante's secret, and here
it was. He was probably dying, and he knew it.
At any moment of the day or night he could
collapse without warning. That was the fact he
lived with, refused to duck from, even laughed at.
That was the quick-step he was dancing with fate.

Now she understood why he'd gone back into
the burning house when anyone wiser would have

stayed away. Inwardly he'd been yelling, 'Go on, then, do your worst!' to the gremlins who haunted him, trying to scare him, not succeeding.

If he'd died that day, he'd have called it a blessing compared with the fate he dreaded: permanent disability, being as dependent as a child, pity. To avoid that he would do anything, even walk into the fire.

This was why he chose light relationships. He couldn't allow himself to fall in love, nor would he risk a woman falling in love with him. He was at ease with her because she fended him off with laughter and seemed in no danger of serious feelings, which was just what he liked; it was safer for them both.

But he'd miscalculated, she thought in anguish. The news of his being in danger had brought a rush of emotion to her heart. Deny it though she might, the misery of knowing that he might be brutally snatched from her at any moment was tearing her apart.

She should fly this place now, run from him while she might still have even a little control over her feelings. Instead she had agreed to stay in his company, to watch over him, vulnerable to his charm which seemed even more potent now that she understood the tragedy that lay behind it.

She would probably fall in love with him despite her determination not to. And how would she bear what might happen next?

Flee! said the voice in her mind. *Forget what you've promised.*

'I can't,' she whispered, resting her head against a tree.

To go was to abandon him to whatever was waiting, leave him to face it alone. The fact that he'd chosen it that way would make it no less a betrayal.

'No,' she murmured. 'No, no, *no!*'

Suddenly she knew she couldn't keep her promise to Hope. She'd been mad to say yes, and there was still time to put it right. She would hurry back now…

'There you are,' came Dante's voice. 'Why are you hiding?'

She turned to see him walking towards her. He had the rumpled look of a man who'd recently been asleep.

'I came out for some air,' she said. 'It's lovely out here at night.'

'It is beautiful, isn't it?'

He didn't put his arms about her, but leaned against the tree, regarding her quizzically.

'Are you all right?'

'Yes, fine,' she said hastily. 'What about you? How's your head?'

'There's nothing wrong with my head. Why do you ask?'

'When you went to bed early, Hope thought—'

'Hope's a fusspot. My head is fine.'

Was his voice just a little bit too firm? She shouldn't have raised the subject. It was a careless mistake, and she must be more careful.

'You can't blame her for fussing,' she said lightly. 'You of all men, going to bed early! What kind of earthquake produced that?'

'I'm probably still suffering a touch of smoke inhalation. Even *I'm* not superman.'

'Now, there's an admission!' she said in as close to a teasing voice as she could manage.

She longed to take his face between her hands, kiss him tenderly and beg him to look after himself. But anything like that was forbidden. If she stayed she would have to guard every word, watch and protect him in secret, always deceive him. The sooner she was out of here, the better.

'Dante,' she said helplessly. 'There's something I must—'

'Oh yes, you were trying to tell me something this afternoon, weren't you? And I never gave you the chance. Too full of myself as always. Tell me now.'

It would have to be faced soon, but before she could speak blessed rescue came in the form of a commotion. Ruggiero's toddler son, Matti, came flying through the trees as fast as his short legs would carry him. From behind came Ruggiero's voice, calling to him to come back, which he ignored.

'I used to escape at bedtime just like that,' Dante said, grinning. 'Some rotten, spoilsport grown-up always grabbed me.'

He seized Matti and hoisted the toddler up in his arms, laughing into his face.

'Gotcha! No, don't kick me. I know how you feel, but it's bedtime.'

'It was bedtime hours ago,' Ruggiero said breathlessly, reaching them. 'Polly looked in on him and he made a run for it.'

'Parents can be a pain in the neck,' Dante confided to the tot. 'But sometimes you have to humour them.'

Reluctantly Matti nodded. Dante grinned and handed the child to his father.

'You really know how to talk to him,' Ruggiero

said. Then, fearing to be thought sentimental, he added, 'I guess it's because you're just a great kid yourself, eh?'

'Could be,' Dante agreed.

Ferne, watching from the shadows, thought that there was more to it than a joke. Dante was part-child, part-clown, part-schemer, and part something else that she was just beginning to discover. Whatever it might turn out to be, he was a man who needed her protection. Somewhere in the last few moments the decision had been made.

'Now we're alone again,' he said, 'what were you going to say?'

Ferne took a deep breath and faced him with a smile.

'Just that I really enjoyed working with you. When do we leave?'

Be careful what you say in jest: it may return to haunt you.

That thought pursued Ferne over the next few days.

She'd teased Dante about being a perfect gentleman at all times, and he'd responded with an encouraging dismay. But as time passed she began to realise that he'd taken her seriously and was being, as he'd promised, 'just friendly'.

He bought a car, a solid, roomy vehicle designed for serious travel, and quite unlike the frivolous choice she might once have expected him to make. They headed south to Calabria, the rugged, mountainous territory at the toe of the Italian peninsular. One of Dante's techniques was to seek out places that had been on the market for a long time and offer his services.

'There are three villas there that my research tells me have been for sale too long,' he said. 'Let's try our luck.'

Their luck was in. The owners were getting desperate and were eager for Dante to add their properties to his books. They spent several days working up a sales pitch for each house, complete with glorious pictures. At the end of it, Ferne was exhausted.

'I seem to spend my life climbing stairs and walking mile-long corridors,' she complained. 'If I'd known it was going to be this tiring, I wouldn't have come.'

Dante himself didn't seem at all tired, and was clearly in such blazingly good health that she wondered if she was crazy to be watching out for him. He had a fund of funny stories which he directed at her over dinner, reducing her to tears of laughter, after which he would take her hand to lead her upstairs to their separate rooms, kiss her on the cheek and bid her goodnight.

No man could have behaved more perfectly. No man could have been more restrained and polite. No man could have been more infuriating.

For this she'd turned down the chance of a lifetime?

Mick Gregson hadn't been pleased.

'What were you thinking of?' he'd bawled down the phone. 'This man carries influence in film land. If he'd liked your work, you could have done anything you wanted.'

But I'm doing what I want, had been her silent thought.

'Ferne, I can't go on representing you if you're going to act like this.'

'That's your decision, Mick, and of course I respect it.'

They had parted bad friends.

Now she was on the road with a man who'd promised 'just friendly', and who seemed infuriatingly determined to keep his word.

There was no justice.

But one thing had changed—now she understood the true reason for Dante's restraint. He wouldn't make advances to her because his personal code of honour forbade him to ask for love when he might die without warning.

Here was the explanation for the way he slipped quickly in and out of relationships, never getting too close to any woman. It was his way of being considerate.

And he was right, she assured herself. If she wanted more from him, that was her problem.

'Where do we go next?' she asked as they turned north again, leaving Calabria behind.

'A place near Rome that I've promised to take a look at. There are some two-thousand-year-old ruins, plus a huge villa that the owner insists on calling a *palazzo*, that's "only" six centuries old. It may not be easy to shift.'

'If it's antique and historical, won't the atmosphere of romance help to sell it?'

'An atmosphere of romance is all very well in theory, but people tend to want decent plumbing as well. I know the owner, Gino Tirelli, and he assures me that it's in a good state of repair—but he might, just possibly, be biased. Luckily I'm not due there until next week, so we can give ourselves a few days by the sea.'

'That sounds lovely. This heat is really getting to me.'

'Of course, we could always go sight-seeing

in Rome. There are some really interesting historical buildings.'

'The sea, the sea,' she begged faintly.

He laughed. 'The sea it is, then. Let's go.'

A few hours' driving brought them to the Lido di Ostia, the beach resort about fifteen miles from Rome. It was a sunny place of level, pale-yellow sands that were adorned not only with umbrellas and loungers but the other trappings of civilization: wine bars and cafés.

Their hotel was close to the sea with a view over the ocean.

'They've got single and double rooms available,' Dante told her after a talk at the desk. 'A double room's cheaper.' In reply to her raised eyebrows, he said, 'How long can a man behave perfectly?'

'I think I can afford a single room.'

'You don't give an inch, do you?'

'You'd better believe it,' she said, laughing.

Not for the world would she have admitted her relief that his defences were finally crumbling.

The hotel had a shop that sold beach items. She lingered over a bikini that—for a bikini—was relatively modest, and a respectable one-piece. Dante eyed her hopefully as she hovered between them.

'Why don't you try it?' he suggested, indicating the one-piece.

She was slightly surprised that he urged her to try the modest garment rather than the revealing one. Afterwards, she realised that she should have been more suspicious.

In the dressing-room she donned the costume, regarded herself in the mirror and sighed. It was elegant and showed off her figure, but didn't do her total justice. No one-piece could have done that. But, until she was sure how far along this road she was going to let Dante whirl her, she couldn't risk being a tease. That wouldn't be fair to him.

Nor was it fair on her, she realised, trying to calm the pleasure that fizzed through her as she thought of his eyes dwelling on her nearly naked body. It wasn't the only pleasure she was denying herself right now, and soon she must decide why.

She dressed again and went out, handing the costume to the assistant for wrapping. 'I'll take this.'

'I've already paid for it,' Dante said, whisking it out of her hand and putting it into a bag he was carrying. 'Now, let's be off.'

'I can't let you pay for my clothes,' she said

as they crossed the road to the beach. 'It wouldn't be proper.'

'If we're going to have another discussion about propriety, I'd rather do it later over champagne.'

'Oh, all right.'

The sand was glorious, soft and welcoming. He hired a hut, two loungers and a huge umbrella, then handed her the bag with her purchase and stood back to let her enter the hut first.

When she opened the bag, she was reminded that this man was a talented schemer.

'They've given me the wrong costume,' she said, going outside again. 'Look.' She held up the bikini. 'But I don't see how it happened. I saw you put the other one into the bag.'

'I guess this one must have already been in there,' he said, eyes wide and innocent.

'But how…?' Light dawned and she stared at him indignantly. *You didn't?*'

'If you've learned anything about me, you know that I did,' he said unanswerably. 'I bought the bikini while you were in the changing room.'

'But how dare you?'

'A case of necessity. You were going to buy that middle-aged thing that doesn't do you justice, so I paid for them both and slipped the bikini into the bag before you came out.'

'But what about the one I chose? Where is it?'

'No idea. It must have escaped.'

'You—you devious—'

'No such thing. Just a man who doesn't like wasting time. Now, are you going to get in there and change, or are you going to stand here all day talking about it?'

'I'm going to get in there and change,' she said promptly. And vanished.

It might not have been modern and liberated to let a man make her decisions, but that was a small sacrifice in return for the look in his eyes. He'd behaved disgracefully, of course, but all things considered she would forgive him.

The mirror in the hut promised everything to the beauty who gazed back, wearing just enough to be decent. Restrained as the bikini was, it didn't hide the way her tiny waist developed into curved hips, or the fact that her skin was perfect. Turning, she studied her rear view over her shoulder, noting that perhaps her behind was a fraction too generous.

Or, then again, perhaps not.

At last she was ready to make her grand entrance. Throwing open the door, she stepped out into the sunlight, only just resisting the temptation to say, 'Ta-Da!'

He was nowhere to be seen.

Oh, great!

'Ah, there you are,' he said, appearing with cans of liquid. 'I've been stocking up on something to drink. We can keep these in the hut until we're ready.'

'Do I look all right?' she asked edgily.

'Very nice,' he said in a courteous voice that made her want to thump him.

But his smile as he studied her told another story, so she forgave him.

While she waited for him to emerge, she let her eyes drift over the other men on the beach. Sandor had once told her that there were few men who appeared at an advantage in bathing trunks. He'd spoken with self-conscious grandeur, from the lofty heights of physical perfection.

But when Dante appeared she forgot everything else. He didn't show off; he didn't need to. His tall, lean figure was muscular without being obvious, and he seemed to have the tensile strength of whipcord.

Ferne's brief contacts with his body had hinted at power, not flaunted but always in reserve.

Now she saw the reality and it pleased her, especially the long legs that moved with a masculine grace that hinted at his ability as a dancer.

For a moment she was back in his arms as they danced across the floor, feet between feet, spinning and twirling with never an inch out of place, because his control had been perfect. Watching him now, his body almost naked, she felt again the excitement of that night begin in the pit of her stomach and stream out to her fingertips.

'Shall we go in?' he asked, reaching out.

She took his hand and together they ran down the beach, splashing into the surf. She yelled aloud with ecstasy as the water laved her, and joined him in a race out to the horizon.

'Careful,' he said. 'Don't go too deep.'

But she was beyond caring. The feel of the water was so good that she wanted more and more.

'*Yee-haa!*' she cried up to the sky.

He laughed and plunged after her, keeping close, ready for the moment when she pulled up, treading water and puffing.

'All right now?' he called. 'Got it out of your system?'

'No way. Here goes!'

Kicking hard, she projected herself up as high as she could go, then dropped down deep into the water, down, down, until at last she kicked to start rising again.

But she was deeper than she'd guessed, and she didn't seem to be climbing fast enough. She became alarmed as her breath began to run out.

Suddenly there was an arm around her waist and she was being yanked up to the surface fast, until mercifully her head broke free and she could breathe again.

'All right, you're safe,' came Dante's voice. 'What were you thinking of, you crazy woman?'

'I don't know—I just wanted to— Oh, goodness!'

'Steady. Relax. I've got you.'

He trod water while keeping her well above the surface, holding her tight against him, his hands almost meeting about her waist.

'All right?' he said, looking up.

'Yes, I—I'm fine.'

It was hard to sound composed when the sensation of her bare skin against his was so disturbing. Her thighs were against his chest, his mouth was just below her breasts, and the waves were moving them about so that their contact constantly shifted; with every new touch the tremors went through her.

'I'm going to let you down,' he said. 'You can't

touch the ground, but don't worry. Just hold onto me. Down—easy.'

She knew he meant only to be gentle and reassuring by lowering her slowly, but the feeling of her flesh gliding against his was just what she didn't need right now, she thought frantically. Control. *Control*.

'Ouch!' he said.

'What?'

'You're hurting me, digging your nails into my shoulders.'

'Sorry!' she said wildly. 'Sorry—sorry.'

'OK, I believe you. Let's get back to shore. Can you swim, or will you hold onto me?'

'I can manage fine,' she lied.

They made it back to the shore without incident, and she set her feet down on the sand with relief.

'All right?' Dante asked.

'Yes, thank you. You can let me go now.'

'I'll just support you until we reach the lounger. You had quite a shock.'

Her legs felt weak, but that was natural after her alarm. It surely couldn't have anything to do with her burning consciousness of his left hand about her waist while his right hand clasped hers?

What happened next was really annoying. By sheer ill-luck an unevenness in the sand made her stumble so that Dante had to tighten his grip to stop her falling.

'Let's do it the easy way,' he said, lifting her high into his arms and carrying her the rest of the distance.

This was even worse. Now she had no choice but to put her arms about his neck, which positioned her mouth close to his and her breasts against his chest, something a sensible woman would have avoided at all costs.

At last he eased her down onto the lounger and dropped on one knee beside her.

'You gave me a fright,' he said. 'Vanishing below the water for so long. I thought you'd gone for good.'

'Nonsense,' she said, trying to laugh it off. 'I'd have been bound to float up eventually.'

'Yes, but it might have been too late.'

'Then it's lucky for me that you were there. You do the "rescuing damsels in distress" thing really well.'

'It's my speciality,' he said lightly. 'And, just to show you how good at it I am, let me dry you off.'

He tossed the towel around her shoulders and began to dab.

'I can manage, thank you,' she said in a strained voice.

'All right. Do it properly, and I'll get you something to drink.'

He poured her some wine in a plastic container.

'Sorry it's a bit basic, but the wine is good,' he said.

She drank it thankfully, wishing he'd move away and not kneel there, so kind, so sweetly concerned, so nearly naked.

'Thanks,' she said. 'I feel better now. You don't need to hover over me.'

'Am I being too protective? I can't help it. I keep thinking what it would have been like without you, and I don't like that thought at all.'

'Really?' she asked quietly.

'Of course. How could I manage without your brilliant pictures?'

'My pictures?'

'You really enhance my work in a way that nobody else has managed to do. We make a great team, don't you think?'

'Fantastic,' she agreed dismally.

'So I'll just keep on watching out for you.'

Her head shot up. 'What—what did you say?'

'I said I'm watching out for you. You obviously need someone being protective. Hey, careful. You've spilled wine all down yourself.'

She seized the towel out of his hands and dabbed at her bare torso. Her head was in a whirl, and her senses were in an even worse whirl.

'Did you say you're keeping a protective eye on me?' she said.

'I think I need to, don't you? And it's what friends do, isn't it?'

'Oh yes, of course they do,' she babbled.

'It's time you had a rest.'

'Yes,' she said with relief. 'I think that's what I'll do.'

CHAPTER SEVEN

She was glad to escape by stretching out and closing her eyes. His words had unnerved her, reminding her that it was she who was supposed to be watching out for him.

She dozed for a while and awoke to find herself alone. Dante was further down the beach, kicking a rubber ball around with some boys. For a while she watched him through half-closed eyes, unwillingly admiring the lines of his body, the athletically graceful way he moved.

She was no green girl; Sandor hadn't been her first lover. At twenty-eight, she knew her own body well, knew how it could be most totally satisfied, knew exactly what it wanted.

But that could be a problem when it couldn't have what it wanted.

It would have been easier to observe Dante leaping about the beach if she didn't have to listen to the voice inside whispering how well he would move in bed, how subtle and knowing his caresses would be.

How fine would his tall body feel held close against her own long body? When she saw him give a mighty kick, she thought of his legs between hers. When he reached for the ball at an impossible angle, she could almost feel his hands against her skin, exploring her tentatively, waiting for her with endless patience, knowing exactly how to…

She sat up, trembling and annoyed with herself. What was the matter with her?

'Just friendly'. That was the matter.

When Dante returned, he found her fully dressed.

'I've had enough of this,' she said fretfully. 'I think I'll go into town.'

'Great idea,' he said. 'I'll show you the shops, then we'll go to dinner.'

She ground her nails into her palm. Why couldn't he at least show some ill temper, like any other man, thus giving her the chance to feel annoyed with him?

But the wretch wouldn't even oblige her in that.

Because he wasn't like any other man.

At least she'd made him put his clothes on.

They spent the rest of the day sedately, buying

the odd garment, and also buying computer software. In one shop she discovered a superb programme that she hadn't expected to be available for another month, and snapped it up. Over dinner, she enthused about it to Dante, who listened with genuine interest. It was the high point of the day.

On reflection, she thought that said it all.

Afterwards he saw her to her door but made no attempt to come in.

'Goodnight,' he said. 'Sleep well.'

She went in, restraining herself with difficulty from slamming the door.

Furiously she thought of the signals he'd sent out that day, signals that had said clearly that he wanted her and was controlling it with difficulty. But the signals had changed. Now he might have been made of ice, and it was obvious why.

He was scheming. He wanted her to be the one to weaken. If either of them was overcome with desire, it must be her. In his dreams, she succumbed to uncontrollable lust, reaching out to entice him.

Hell would freeze over first!

Next day they promised themselves a lazy time in the sun.

'I could happily stay here for ever,' Dante said,

stretching out luxuriously. 'Who cares about work?'

It was at that exact moment that a voice nearby called, '*Ciao*, Dante!'

He started up, looked around, then yelled, '*Gino!*'

Ferne saw a man in his fifties, dressed in shirt and shorts, advancing on them with a look of delight on his broad face.

'Is that…?'

'Gino Tirelli,' Dante said, jumping up.

When the two men had clapped each other on the shoulder, Dante introduced Ferne.

'Always I am pleased to meet English people,' Gino declared. 'At this very moment, my house is full of important English people.'

'So that's why you asked me to delay my arrival,' Dante said. 'Who've you got there? Members of the government?'

'A film company,' Gino said in an awed voice. 'They're making a film of *Antony and Cleopatra* and shooting some scenes in the ruins in my grounds. The director is staying with me, and of course the *big* star.'

'And who is the big star?' Ferne asked, suitably wide-eyed.

Before Gino could reply there was a squeal from behind them, and they all turned to see a

young man of about thirty with curly, fair hair
and a perfectly tanned body strolling along the
beach in a careless way, suggesting that he was
unaware of the sensation he created.

But he was fully aware of it, as Ferne knew.
Sandor Jayley always knew exactly what effect
he was creating.

'Oh no!' she breathed.

'What is it?' Dante asked her in a low voice.
'Good grief, it's—?'

'Tommy Wiggs.'

The young man came closer, pulling off a light
shirt and tossing it to a companion, revealing a
muscular body sculpted to perfection, now
wearing only a minuscule pair of trunks.
Regarding him grimly, Dante was forced to
concede one thing: as Ferne had said, he did
have magnificent thighs.

'I've got to get out of here before he sees me,'
she muttered. 'That'll really put the cat among
the pigeons.'

But it was too late. Sandor had seen his host
and was starting up the beach towards him, doing
a well-honed performance of *bonhomie*.

'Gino,' he called. Then, as he saw Ferne, his
expression changed, became astonished, then
delighted. 'Ferne! My darling girl!'

Arms open wide, he raced across the sand and, before she could get her thoughts together, she found herself enfolded in a passionate embrace.

It was an act, she thought, hearing the cheers around them. For some reason he'd calculated that this would be useful to him so he was taking what he wanted, selfishly indifferent to the effect it might have on her. For she was terrified in case she reacted in the old way, the way she now hated to remember.

Nothing happened. There was no pleasure, no excitement. Nothing. She wanted to shout to the heavens with joy at being free again!

'Tommy—'

'Sandor,' he muttered hastily. Then, aloud, 'Ferne, how wonderful to see you again!' He smiled down into her eyes, the picture of tender devotion. 'It's been too long,' he said. 'I've thought of you so often.'

'I've thought a few things about you too,' she informed him tartly. 'Now, will you let me go?'

'How can you ask me to do that when I've got you in my arms again? And I owe you so much.'

'Yes, those pictures didn't do you any harm, did they? Let me *go*!'

Reluctantly he did so, switching his attention to Gino.

'Gino, how do you come to know this wonderful lady?' he cried.

'I've only just met her,' Gino said. 'I didn't realise that you two were—are…'

'Let's say we're old friends,' Sandor said. '*Close* friends.'

Ferne became awkwardly aware of Dante standing there, arms folded, regarding them sardonically. After everything she'd told him about Sandor, what must he be thinking?

A little crowd was gathering around them as news went along the beach that the famous Sandor Jayley was among them. Young women sighed and regarded Ferne with envy.

'Sandor,' she said, backing away from him, 'Can I introduce you to my friend, Signor Dante Rinucci?'

'Why, sure.' Sandor extended his hand. 'Any friend of Ferne's is a friend of mine.'

Dante gave him an unreadable smile.

'Excellent,' he said. 'Then we're all friends together.'

'Let's all sit down.' Sandor seated himself on her lounger and drew her down beside him.

He was in full flood now, basking in the warm glow of what he took to be admiration, oblivious to the fact that one of his audience was embarrassed and another actively hostile.

'Just think,' he sighed. 'If that house where we were going to shoot had come up to scratch, we'd never have moved to Gino's *palazzo* and we—' he gave Ferne a fond look '—would never have found each other again.'

'There were rats,' Gino confided. 'They had to find somewhere else fast, and someone remembered the Palazzo Tirelli.'

'Why don't you join us?' Sandor said suddenly. 'That's all right with you, isn't it, Gino?' Asking the owner's permission was clearly an afterthought.

Far from being offended, Gino nearly swooned with delight.

'And it will give Ferne and me the chance to rekindle our very happy acquaintance,' Sandor added.

'Sandor, I don't think—' Ferne protested quickly.

'But we have so much to talk about. You don't mind if I take Ferne away from you for a few days, do you?' he asked Dante.

'You mean Dante isn't invited too?' Ferne asked sharply. 'Then I'm not coming.'

'Oh, my dear, I'm sure your friend will understand.'

'*He* may, I won't,' Ferne said firmly. 'Dante and I are together.'

'So loyal,' Sandor cooed in a voice that made Ferne want to kick him in a painful place. 'Signor Rinucci, you're invited too, of course.'

'How kind!' Dante said in a voice that revealed nothing. 'I'll look forward to it.'

Ferne turned horrified eyes on him. 'Dante, you don't mean that?' she muttered.

'Of course I do. Getting really acquainted with the place may help me with the sale.'

'How? You've never needed it before.'

'Well, perhaps I have my own reasons this time,' he said, his eyes glinting.

Sandor didn't hear this exchange. Champagne had arrived and he turned to lift two glasses, one of which he handed to Ferne, saying, 'It's all settled, then. Here's to our reunion!'

A young girl detached herself from the swooning crowd on the beach and asked him for an autograph, handing him her lipstick so that he could write his name on her back. Beaming, he obliged, then gave Ferne a questioning look.

'No camera today? Not like you.'

'I left it in the hotel.'

'You? The lady who never moves without her camera? Well, well.'

His look was heavily significant, clearly meant to recall the last time she had turned her camera on him. She faced him back, her eyes full of anger.

Dante watched them and said nothing.

Having established the scene, Sandor didn't linger over the champagne. Indicating the crowd, he said modestly, 'You see how it is—wherever I go. I'll leave now, and see you at the villa this evening.'

He strode away, pursued by adoring fans, plus Gino.

'So that's him,' Dante said. 'He's exactly as you said, except worse.'

'I don't know what's going on here,' she said wildly. 'When we last met, he couldn't find words bad enough for me.'

'But that was three months ago, and he did pretty well out of it. He's a bigger star now than he was before, thanks to you. So clearly he wants to shower you with his favours. Tonight you'll be his honoured companion.'

'Are you trying to be funny?' she asked stormily. 'Do you think that's what I *want*?'

He gave a strange smile. 'Let's say I'm interested to find out. I didn't mean to offend you. Let's get going.'

It was late afternoon when they reached the Palazzo Tirelli, a magnificent edifice. Grander still were the ruins that lay nearby, dating back nearly two-thousand years. Ferne could just make out a film crew looking them over, making notes, rehearsing shots.

Gino came to meet them and show them over the place with its long, wide corridors and stone arches. In every room he was able to describe some notable historical episode, which sounded impressive until she saw Dante shaking his head.

Their rooms turned out to be on different corridors, the only ones left, according to Gino. His manner was awkward, and Ferne guessed he was acting on instruction.

At supper she was seated next to Sandor, with Dante on the opposite side of the table several feet down. There were about fifty people at the long table, most of them film crew and actors. Everyone was dressed up to the nines, making her glad she'd chosen the softly glamorous dress of honey-coloured satin that paid tribute to her curves, yet whose neckline was high enough to be tantalising.

'Beautiful,' Sandor murmured. 'But why aren't you wearing that gold necklace I gave you? It would go perfectly with that dress.'

'I'm afraid I'd forgotten it,' she said.

His self-assured smile made her want to

thump him. She glanced down the table to see how Dante was taking it, but he wasn't looking at her.

He was having a good evening. Dinner jacket and bow-tie suited him, as the ladies nearby made clear. Ferne would have signalled her admiration if she'd been able to catch his eye, but he seemed happy with the full-bosomed creature who was laughing so uproariously at his jokes, that her attractions wobbled violently in a way that Ferne thought extremely inappropriate.

For a moment, she was nostalgic for Dante's jokes; sharing laughter with a man brought a special closeness. It was something she'd never known with Sandor, and it meant that she was always on Dante's wavelength, always inhabiting his world, even when they were bickering. In fact, the very bickering was a sign of that closeness, because they could always trust each other to understand.

As Dante had predicted, Sandor treated her as his honoured guest.

'I owe you so much, Ferne. If it hadn't been for what you did for me, I'd never have got the next step up.'

'That's not what you said at the time,' she observed wryly.

'I didn't appreciate your skill in turning a difficult situation into something that would benefit me.'

She stared at him, wondering how she'd ever taken this conceited booby seriously.

'Sandor, what are you after?' she demanded.

He regarded her soulfully. 'Destiny works in mysterious ways. We were fated to meet on that beach. Everyone was staggered by those pictures you took of me. Between us, we produced something of genius, and I think we could be geniuses again.'

She stared at him in outrage. 'You want me to…?'

'Take some more, as only you can. We'll go out to the ruins, and you tell me exactly how you want me to pose. I've been working out in the gym.'

'And I'm sure you're as fit and perfect as ever.'

'What did you think when you saw me today?' he asked eagerly.

It would have been impossible to tell him the truth, which was that he had seemed 'too much', because her ideal was now Dante's lithe frame.

To her relief, the maid appeared to change the plates for the next course. For the rest of the meal she concentrated on the elderly woman on her other side.

Afterwards the great doors were opened onto the garden, where coloured lights hung between the trees. People began to drift out to stroll beneath the moon. Sandor drew Ferne's arm through his.

The crowd congregated near the ruins, where blazing lights had been switched on, illuminating them up to the sky. The director, an amiable man called Rab Beswick, hailed Sandor.

'I like this place more every time I see it,' he said. 'Just think what we can make of these…' He indicated several walls, some of which stood at right angles to each other with connecting balconies.

'Just the right place to make a speech,' came a voice behind them.

It was Dante, appearing from nowhere.

'Antony was known for his ability to make the right speech at the right time,' he said. 'And his genius for picking the place that would be most effective.'

The director looked at him with awe.

'Hey, you're Italian,' he said, as though nothing could be stranger than finding an Italian in Italy. 'Are you an expert about this?'

'I've made a particular study of Marc Antony,' Dante said.

'Well, I'd be glad of anything you could tell me.'

'Let's not get carried away,' Sandor interrupted peevishly. 'This film isn't meant to be an historical treatise.'

'Certainly not,' Dante said suavely. 'Its selling point will be the personal charms of Signor Jayley.'

From somewhere there was a smothered choke. Sandor turned furious eyes in a vain attempt to detect who was making fun of him. Unable to locate a suspect, he turned back to Dante.

Which was what Dante had intended, Ferne thought. Whatever was he up to?

'Height is always effective,' Dante continued smoothly. 'If Antony was to make a great speech up there, silhouetted against the sky—'

'That's not in the script,' Sandor said at once.

'But it could be written in,' Dante pointed out. 'I'm not, of course, suggesting that you yourself should go up there. That would be far too dangerous, and naturally the film company won't want to risk their star. A double could be used for the long shot.'

Sandor relaxed.

'But it could look something like this...' Dante finished.

Before anyone realised what he was doing, he

slipped out of sight, and a moment later reappeared on one of the balconies.

'You see?' he called down. 'What a shot this would make!'

'Great!' the director called up.

Ferne had to admit that Dante looked magnificent, standing high up, bathed in glittering spotlight. She only prayed that the balcony was strong enough to hold him and wouldn't start crumbling.

This time she really wished that she'd brought her camera, but one of the production staff had his and was snapping away madly. Sandor was livid, she was fascinated to notice.

'Come on down and we'll talk about it,' Rab called. 'Hey, be careful.' Dante was hopping down like a monkey, ending with a long leap to the floor, where he finished with a flourish.

'You're right, that's a great shot. You'll help us work on it, won't you?'

'Sure thing,' Dante said. 'I can show Mr Jayley how to—'

'It's getting late,' Sandor said hastily. 'We should be going inside.'

'Yes, let's go and look at the pictures,' Rab said eagerly. 'Come on, everyone.'

As the rest of them drifted away, Ferne murmured to Dante, 'What did you do that for?'

'You know exactly what I did it for,' he murmured back. 'I haven't enjoyed myself so much for ages. He's ready to kill me.'

His whole being was flooded with brilliance, as though he'd reached out, taken life by the hand and was loving every moment.

'Didn't anyone ever tell you not to repeat a trick?' she asked severely. 'Just because you climbed up into that building the other week, doesn't mean you have to keep doing it. You were just showing off.'

He grinned, and her heart turned over. 'You won't insult me by calling me a show-off. Too many have said it before you. As for repeating the trick? Sure, it was the memory of the fire that gave me the idea. It was actually a lot easier to get up there than it looks, but your lover wouldn't have tried it if you'd offered him an Oscar.'

'He is not my lover.'

'He wants to be.'

'Come on,' someone yelled from the retreating crowd. 'They're going to show the pictures.'

She would have argued further, but he slipped his arm about her, urging her forward irresistibly until they reached the villa, where someone had linked up the camera to a computer and had projected the pictures onto a screen.

There was Dante, high up, splendid, laughing down at them. Whether his triumph lay in making the climb, or in making Sandor look absurd and diminished, only Ferne knew. One thing she was sure of—he'd done it in style.

She looked around for Sandor, wondering how he was taking this.

'He retired,' Gino explained. 'He's had a long day.'

Translation: he's sulking like a spoilt child, Ferne thought. Dante had hit the bull's eye.

Dante himself seemed oblivious to his success. He was deep in conversation with Rab, and by now Ferne was sufficiently in tune with his mind to recognise that this was another move in the game. He wouldn't say anything in front of an audience. But later…

'I've had a long day too,' she said. 'Goodnight.'

She slipped away and hurried up to her room. Sooner or later there was going to be a visitor, and she wanted to be ready.

First she needed a shower to wash the day off her. She turned it on as hard as she could and stood there, head back, arms wide, just letting it happen. It felt good.

She could have laughed aloud when she thought of how Dante had achieved his revenge—an Italian revenge—not violent, but skilled; a lithe, dancing movement, a quick thrust of the stiletto, unseen by anyone but his adversary, who had slunk away, humiliated.

Now she realised that she ought to have feared for Dante's safety when he'd been up high, but she hadn't, because she was under the spell he cast. And she was still under his spell, she thought happily.

She finished under the shower, pulled a robe around her and stepped out into the bedroom. But what she found there made her stop sharply.

'*Sandor!*'

He was leaning against the door, his arms folded, a look of happy expectation on his face. He'd removed his shirt so that his magnificent chest was presented for her approval in all its naked perfection, smooth, muscular, evenly tanned.

'What are you doing here?' She sighed.

'Oh, come on, sweetie. We both knew this was going to happen.'

'Tommy, I swear, if you try to touch me I'll thump you so hard you'll see stars.'

'You don't mean that.'

'Don't tell me what I mean. I'm warning you.'

He laughed and sauntered easily over to her, the king claiming his rights.

'I think I might just put that to the test—*Aargh*!'

He yelped as her hand struck his face.

'You bitch!' he wailed. 'I could get a swollen lip.'

She opened her mouth to reply, but before she could speak there was a knock on her door. She darted to open it and found Dante standing there. He was wearing dark-blue pyjamas, and his face had an innocent look that filled her with suspicion almost as great as her relief.

'I'm so sorry to trouble you,' he said, 'but there's no soap in my bathroom and I wondered if you'd mind— Oh dear, am I disturbing something?'

'Nothing at all,' Ferne said. 'Mr Jayley was just going.'

Dante regarded Sandor with apparent surprise, seeming not to have noticed him before, but Ferne wasn't fooled. He knew exactly what he was doing. In his own way, he was as much of an actor as Sandor, but a more subtle one.

'Good evening,' he said politely. 'Oh dear, you seem to have suffered an injury. You're going to have a nasty swollen lip.'

'Eh!' Sandor yelped. He tried to make for the bathroom, but Dante was blocking his way so that he was forced to turn away and retreat from the room altogether, slamming the door behind him.

'That should keep him occupied,' Dante said with satisfaction.

CHAPTER EIGHT

'BUT how did you know? I didn't hit him that hard. He didn't have a swollen lip.'

'No, but he was afraid of it. I was just outside the door and I heard everything.'

'And was it coincidence that you were there?'

'Certainly not. I was lurking in the corridor. When I saw him go in, I listened. After all, you might have welcomed him.'

'And then you'd have just gone away, I suppose?' she said sardonically.

Slowly Dante shook his head, and there was something in his eyes she'd never seen before.

'No way. If you'd welcomed him, I'd have come in and thumped him myself a lot harder than you did. But there was no need. You dealt with him very efficiently—I'm glad to say,' he added softly.

'You didn't really think I wanted him, did you?'

He made a wry face. 'I hoped not, but I needed

to know. When I saw how easily he entered, I did wonder.'

'I was in the bathroom, or he'd never have got in.'

'Are you really over him?'

'Of course I am. I just wish we'd never come here.'

'You were a big hit at dinner.'

'You weren't doing so badly yourself,' she flung at him.

'Just passing the time, keeping an eye on you, making sure you didn't misbehave. I had to know how you feel about him. It mattered.'

'And now you know.' She met his gaze, silently urging him on.

But the man who'd dismissed his enemy with a master stroke suddenly seemed to lose confidence.

'What happens now?' he said. 'It must be your decision. Do you want me to go?'

'I don't know what I want,' she said distractedly. It was almost true.

'Ferne.' His voice was quiet and suddenly serious. 'If you don't know, neither of us knows.'

'That's not fair.'

'Fair?' His voice was edgy. 'You stand there half-naked, doing heaven knows what to me, and *I'm* being unfair?'

The towel robe had opened just enough to show her breasts, firm and glowing with the need she could no longer hide. While she hesitated, he took the edges of the material and drew them apart, revealing the rest of her nakedness.

'*That* is being unfair,' he said in a shaking voice.

She couldn't move. Her whole being seemed to be concentrated on him, on his touch and the thought of where it would alight next. The feeling was so intense that it was as though he was already caressing her everywhere. It was almost a shock when he laid his fingers lightly at the base of her throat, leaving them there, seeming to wait for something.

She drew a long breath. None of Sandor's dramatic caresses had affected her one tenth as much as Dante's patience.

'Tell me,' he said softly.

'Tell you…?'

'Tell me what to do. Ferne, for pity's sake, if you want me to stop say so now, because I don't have that much control left.'

Her smile was deliberately provocative. 'Perhaps a man can have too much control. Maybe he even talks too mu—'

Her words were silenced by his mouth on hers.

It was too late now, past the point of no return. Her own kiss was as fervent as his, speaking of desire held in too long, of frustration released in giddy, headlong joy.

While he kissed he was pulling at the robe until it fell to the floor and there was no barrier to his hands caressing her everywhere, setting off tremors that shocked her with their intensity. She managed to return the compliment, ripping away at his clothes until he was as naked as she.

Neither of them knew who made the first move to the bed. It didn't matter. They were running down the same road, seeking the same triumphant destination.

She had anticipated his skill, but her imagination had fallen far short of the reality. He made love as he did the quick-step, unfailingly knowing the right touch, the right movement, always in perfect understanding with his partner. Her body felt as though it had been made for this moment, this loving, this man, and only this man.

At the last moment he hesitated, looking down into her face as though seeking one final reassurance. By now her breathing was coming fast, and any delay was intolerable. She wanted him and she wanted him *now*.

'Dante,' she whispered urgently.

He gave a quick sigh of satisfaction, hearing something in her voice that he'd needed to know, and the next moment he was inside her, glorying in being part of her.

After he looked different. The teasing clown who enchanted her was also the lover who instinctively knew the secrets of her body and used them for his purpose in a way that was almost ruthless. He'd known what he wanted and been determined to have it, but what he'd wanted was her joyful satisfaction. Now he had it, which meant he knew his power over her, but she had no fears about that power. She trusted him too much for that.

She wondered if she looked different to him too. Then she caught the faint bewilderment in his eyes and knew that she did. That delighted her, and it was she who moved towards him for their second loving, caressing him in ways that had never occurred to her before, because he was like no other man. He laughed and settled himself against her, implicitly inviting her to do whatever she liked, an invitation she accepted with vigour.

Later, when they had recovered, he propped himself on his elbow, looking down at her lying beneath him with a mixture of triumph and delight.

'What took us so long?' he whispered.

How could she give him an honest answer

when she was only just now facing the truth in
her own heart?

*It took time because I've been holding back,
fearful of having too many feelings for you. I
knew if I got too close I was in danger of loving
you, and I don't want to. To love you is to risk
heartbreak, and I don't have the courage. Even
though—even though it may already be too late.
Too late for me? Too late for you?*

There was no way to say that.

She just opened her arms and drew him in so
she could enfold him protectively until they fell
asleep in the same moment.

As the first touch of dawn came into the room,
Dante rose from the bed, careful not to waken
her, and went to stand by the window. From here
he could see the sun rising behind the ruins,
casting its promise over the new day.

A new day. It was a feeling he'd thought he
would never know. The circumstances of his life
had bred in him a wary detachment, making it
easier to stand back, observe himself wryly,
often cynically, and sometimes with a melancholy that he fought with laughter.

But this morning the melancholy had lifted.
Detachment was gone, leaving him at peace.

Peace: the very last quality he associated with Ferne. She teased him, haunted him, jeered and provoked him. Sometimes he wondered if she'd known how she tempted him, but then he would see the look in her eye—assessing, challenging, taking him to the next stage of the game they were playing.

The game was called 'who will blink first?' She'd played it with consummate skill, enticing him into indiscretions like buying her a bikini. That had shown his hand too obviously, and she'd played on it, luring him to the edge, closer to the moment when he'd had to abandon the control that ruled his life.

The luck of the devil had been on her side. Nobody could have predicted the arrival of Sandor and the fierce jealousy that had stormed through Dante. Seeing them together on the beach, Sandor's hands actually touching her body—the one he thought of as his own personal possession—he'd come close to committing murder.

She'd tried to refuse the invitation to stay here, but why? A demon had whispered in his ear that she was afraid to be in Sandor's company lest the old attraction overwhelm her. He'd insisted on accepting, driven by the need to see more of them together and know what he was up against.

It had been no satisfaction that so many lures had been cast out to him last night. There were at least three bedrooms at which he could have presented himself, sure of a welcome. Instead he'd haunted her door until inevitably Sandor had appeared, bare-chested, for seduction, and entered without knocking.

The moment when he'd heard her slap the man's face had felt like the beginning of his life.

It meant that in the game they were playing she'd won and he'd lost. Or possibly the other way around. Whatever! He couldn't have been happier.

He returned to the bed, sitting down carefully so as not to disturb her. He wanted to watch her like this, relaxed and content, breathing almost without making a sound. A wisp of hair had fallen over her face and he brushed it back softly. Somehow his hand stayed, stroking her face.

Her lips moved in a smile, telling him that she was awake. The smile turned into a chuckle and she opened her eyes to find him looking directly into them.

'Good morning,' he whispered, settling beside her and drawing her close.

No passion now, just her head on his shoulder in blissful content, body curled against body, and the sense of having come home to each other.

'Good morning,' she murmured.

'Is everything all right?'

'Mmm!' She hid her face against him.

'Me too,' he agreed. 'Very much all right.'

After a while she opened her eyes again to find him sunk in thought.

'What are we going to do now?' he wondered.

'Leave this place behind,' she said at once. 'Sandor will throw us out anyway.'

'A pity. Part of me wants to stay around for a while just to poke him in the eye. He had his turn making me jealous. Now it's my turn to pay him back.'

'Jealous? You?'

'Don't play the innocent. You knew exactly what you were doing to me. You loved seeing me on hot coals.'

'I'll admit it had its entertaining moments,' she mused. 'But that was because you were trying to play hard to get. Not always successfully, mind you, but you tried.'

'Of course,' he said, sounding shocked. 'Don't forget that I promised "just friendly", and a gentleman always keeps his word.'

'Gentleman? Huh!'

'Let's have that discussion later,' he said hastily. 'The point is, I couldn't break my word, so I had to get you to break it for me. You forced me into retreat, so I'm innocent.'

'Oh, *please*!' she jeered. 'The one thing I can't imagine is you being innocent. You are a scheming, manipulative, double-dealing, tricky— Oh, the hell with it! Who cares if you're a bad character? What are you *doing*?'

'What does it feel as if I'm doing? Hush now, while I prove what a bad character I am.'

Laughing, he proceeded to do exactly that with such vigour that she was left breathless.

'I suppose I ought to be grateful to Sandor,' Ferne said when they had recovered. 'He might be a clumsy oaf, but he did us a favour. Do you know, he actually wanted me to take some more pictures of him?'

'What, after you…?'

'Yes, apparently my photographs flattered him as nobody else's did. Heavens, how did I ever fancy myself in love with that twerp?'

He suspected another reason why Sandor had tried to seduce Ferne. Such was the man's vanity that he wanted to believe that he could reclaim her whenever he liked. But about this Dante stayed tactfully silent.

'I suppose we should get up,' he said at last. 'It's a beautiful day.'

Gino was waiting for them downstairs, clearly on hot coals.

'Sandor had a restless night and he's gone for a walk in the grounds. He says he doesn't feel up to seeing anyone.'

'I wonder what could have brought that on?' Dante said sympathetically.

'Artistic sensibility,' Gino sighed.

'I understand,' Dante said solemnly. 'A true artist sometimes needs to be alone to commune with the universe. Did you speak?' This was to Ferne, who was displaying alarming symptoms of choking. She managed to shake her head and he continued. 'We'll leave at once. Give me a call when the filming has finished and I'll come back then.'

They didn't even stay for breakfast. Tossing their things into bags, they fled the Palazzo Tirelli like children making a dash for freedom.

As the car swung out of the gates Ferne caught a glimpse of a tragically noble figure standing on a hill, watching their departure with a look of passionate yearning. Not that she could see his expression at this distance, but she would have bet money on it.

'It's like your Shakespeare said,' Dante

observed. 'Some men are born twerps, others achieve twerphood, and some have it thrust upon them. Well, something like that, anyway.'

'You've really got your knife in to Sandor, haven't you?' she chuckled.

Dante grinned. 'I did once. Not any more.'

Ferne leaned back in her seat, smiling. The jokey note of the conversation suited her exactly. This was a man to have fun with, nothing more. The gleam of danger was still far off on the horizon, but she knew it was there, throwing its harsh light over everything in anticipation. The only answer was to look away.

'Where are we going?' she asked after a while.

'Anywhere away from here.'

Safely out of Rome, he turned south and hugged the coast for about a hundred miles. There they found another beach, quiet, simple and delightfully unglamorous. The town was the same, a good place for strolling and buying toothpaste before retreating to their modest hotel and the room they shared.

'Thank goodness Sandor wasn't able to organise our accommodation this time,' Dante chuckled as they lay together in a cosy embrace late that night. 'It wasn't an accident that we were put miles apart.'

'Yes, I kind of worked that out. Low cunning.'

'Fatal mistake. I'm the master of low cunning. Someone should have warned him.'

'You're also an old-fashioned male chauvinist, now I come to think of it.'

'It took you long enough to find that out. When did you see the light?'

'You said that if I'd welcomed Sandor into my room you'd have come in and thumped him.'

'Good 'n' hard.'

'But who gave you the right to veto my lovers? What about my right to make my own choice?'

'My darling, you have an absolute right to choose any man you want.'

'Good.'

'As long as the one you choose is me.'

'And you think I'm going to put up with that nineteenth-century attitude?'

In the darkness she heard him give the rich chuckle of the triumphant male.

'Yes, because I'm not going to give you any option. Now, come here and let me make the matter plain to you.'

So she did. And he did. And after that they slept in perfect harmony.

Ferne had known from the first evening that there was more to Dante than met the eye. How many men discussed *The Divine Comedy* with a woman they'd known only a couple of hours, even if they were named after the poet?

Hope had mentioned that he had three academic degrees, and from odd remarks he dropped in their conversations she realised that this was no idle boast. His brain was agile and well-informed, and she could easily guess his horror at the thought of losing his high-powered skills.

Since she'd learned the truth about the threat to Dante's life, she'd come to see him as two men—one always standing behind the other, a permanent warning. When he was at his funniest, she was most conscious of the other man, silently threatening in the shadows, never allowing Dante to forget that he was there.

Sometimes it broke her heart that he must face his nemesis alone, and she longed to take him in her arms, not in the light-hearted passion that they usually shared, but with tender comfort. Then she remembered that he had chosen his isolation, however bitter it might be, and he wanted no comfort. Without her help, without anyone's help, he was complete and whole.

One evening he was unusually quiet, but he seemed absorbed in a book, so she'd put it down to that. Later that night she woke suddenly to find him sitting by the window, his head buried in his hands. He was completely still and silent, in such contrast to his normal liveliness that she knew a twinge of alarm.

Slipping out of bed, she went to kneel beside him.

'Is everything all right?'

'Yes, fine.' But he seemed to speak with an effort.

'You don't look well.'

'Just a bit of a headache.'

'Have you had it all evening? You haven't said much.'

'It'll go away. Just give it time.'

'Have you taken anything?'

'Yes.'

'And it doesn't work?'

'It will, in time.'

'Come back to bed. A sleep may do you good.'

'Later. Leave me now. I don't want to talk.'

'I'm only worried for you.'

'Will you drop the subject please?'

Dante's tone was light, but Ferne saw in his eyes something that reminded her of that other time. There was a steely anger, and a determination not to yield, no matter what the cost to himself or anyone else. Hastily she backed off, remembering Toni's words that to persist would be to endanger Dante, not help him.

She returned to bed, pulling the covers over her head so that she could huddle down and be alone with her thoughts. She lay awake for a long time, telling herself that this must be just an ordinary headache, the kind everyone had.

It seemed that she was right, because the next day he was his normal self. Perhaps it was only her imagination that the 'other' Dante had been there, hostile, rejecting.

One evening they bumped into Mario, an old friend from Dante's college days. The two men plunged into academic conversation, occasionally remembering their manners, apologising and drawing her in. She laughed, not at all offended, fascinated by this new angle on Dante.

When he went to fetch more drinks, Mario said, 'We all thought he'd be head of the college by now.'

'Is he really that clever?' Ferne asked.

'He could think and write rings around anyone else. I know they offered him a professorship, but he wanted to go off travelling.'

Next day she claimed tiredness, urging Dante to spend some time with Mario. He said she was the nicest, most understanding woman he'd ever known—which made her feel guilty, because she had an ulterior motive.

When she was safely alone she opened her laptop, accessed the Internet and looked up all she could find about his ailment. She had already done this once, on the day before they'd left Naples, but now she had a driving need to know far more.

A sudden bleeding into the space between the brain and an area of the lining that surrounds it; a weak blood vessel that suddenly ruptures.

Sometimes there are warning symptoms, such as headache, facial pain and double vision. This can happen minutes or weeks before the main rupture.

She read everything that she could find, forcing herself to understand every detail. The picture that kept returning to her mind was Dante going back into the burning building to rescue the dog, knowing that it might cost him his life.

When you lived with the possibility of death every moment, how much would you actually fear it? Welcome it?

There were three files that she needed to read again. Quickly she downloaded them, put them

in a folder, titled it 'ZZZ', then shut everything
down quickly. Finally she called Hope.
Describing the headache, she said, 'I was worried
at first, but he's been fine ever since, so maybe it
was normal. He seems full of beans.'

'Thank you,' Hope said fervently. 'I can't tell
you what it means to us to know you're with him.'

'I've got to go now. I can see him returning
with his friend. I'll call again soon.'

Looking out of the window, she hailed the two
men, who waved back and pointed up the street
to a restaurant.

'Coming,' she called down.

It took a moment to slip the printed file into
her drawer, then she was ready to leave.

The three of them spent a convivial evening,
but at the end Mario seemed to forget Dante and
become more interested in looking at Ferne's
plunging neckline. After which, Dante said he
needed an early night and swept her off to bed.

Mario departed next morning, but he left a
legacy in Dante's mind. Stretched out on the
beach, Ferne was startled to look up and find
him doing a crossword puzzle in Latin.

'It's not difficult if you're Italian,' he demurred
when she expressed her admiration. 'The two
languages are so similar.'

'What's that?' she asked, pointing at a clue.

He translated for her and said, 'The answer is *quam celerrime*. It means "as quickly as possible".'

'*Quam celerrime,*' she mused. 'It has a nice, flowing sound, doesn't it? What a pity I was always useless at languages. What's the Italian version?'

'*Il più rapidamente possibile.*'

'No, I definitely prefer *quam celerrime*. Not that I could do anything with *celerrime* at the moment. I'm half-asleep.'

'Bad night?'

'No, it was a wonderful night, thank you. I just didn't get any sleep.'

He laughed, and she settled down. She was deep in happy slumber when the sound of her mobile phone reached her from a distance.

'Someone wants you,' Dante said, reaching into her bag for the phone. 'Here.'

It was a text:

Never thought you were the one to turn down the chance of a lifetime. The offer's still open and this time I want the right answer. Money, money, money. Mick.

'Who's Mick?' Dante asked, reading over her shoulder.

'Can't you tell?' Ferne asked sleepily. 'He's my

sugar-daddy. He wants to cover me with diamonds and buy me an apartment in the West End, but I told him no. That stuff is old-fashioned.'

'Now I remember; he's your agent, isn't he? You mentioned him on the train the night we met.'

'Uh-huh!'

She was trying to sound half-asleep, but inside she was alert and wary. She didn't want Dante asking questions about why she'd refused a big job, in case he stumbled on the truth. Diverting him was going to be tricky.

'Why is he mad at you?' Dante asked. 'What have you turned down?'

She sighed as if it was too boring to be discussed.

'He wanted me to go back to London and do another theatre shoot with a big star who's condescending to do a live play. Sandor Jayley with knobs on. No way!'

'Who's the star?'

She told him. Dante stared.

'You rejected *him*? Just think what you might have—'

'He's bringing his fiancée with him,' she said, trying to sound petulant. 'No chance for me to be vulgar and unprincipled there.'

Dante grinned, slipping an arm around her.

'Can I flatter myself that you prefer to be vulgar and unprincipled with me?'

'I can't stop you flattering yourself,' she observed indifferently. 'Some men are so conceited.'

'Not me. I can't believe you'd choose me over the chance to make a lot of money.'

'You forget,' she said languidly. 'I already made my fortune with Sandor.' She drew a light finger down his bare chest. 'Now I'm in the mood to spend some of it on, er, the *pleasures of the moment*.' She uttered the last words in a seductive whisper.

'Oh, really?' he said, speaking with some difficulty, she was pleased to note.

'*La grande signorina* gives her orders?'

'Definitely. And she's very demanding.'

'So I'm here only for your pleasure?'

She surveyed him with wicked glee. 'Well, what else did you imagine you were here for? I expect my every whim to be obeyed.'

'I'm your willing slave.'

'And my first whim is to swim. Into the sea with us.'

'I was hoping for something better.'

'Hmm! Being my willing slave didn't last long, did it? Come on.'

She wriggled free of him and ran down the beach, hearing him just behind her. Once in the surf, he seized her and drew her further in, until the water was up to their chests; nobody else could have seen the way his hands were wandering.

'Just what do you think you're doing?' she challenged.

'Only my duty. I wouldn't want to disappoint you.'

'But you can't do *that* in public.'

'It's not in public, it's under water. Perfectly respectable.'

'There is nothing respectable about what you're doing,' she gasped.

After that she became incapable of speech and could only cling onto him, digging her nails into his shoulder in a way that left marks for days.

When they finally returned to their loungers, she asked him to fetch her a drink. While he was gone she texted Mick with shaking hands.

Sorry, can't change my mind. Am out of action for a while.

She switched off the phone and hid it away safely, silently thanking a merciful providence for helping her get away with it this time.

Hopefully Mick wouldn't trouble her again, whatever he might guess.

Oh, to blazes with Mick and what he might think! To blazes with everything, except getting Dante back into her bed *quam celerrime*.

They played it out in the before sending the nanny moved. The final experiment

CHAPTER NINE

THE 'willing slave' fantasy kept them entertained for a while. Unlike many men, Dante was totally relaxed with it, his masculine confidence too powerful to be disturbed by such a joke.

They played it out in the bedroom, with her indicating her requirements and him following to the letter, both enjoying the challenge, laughing, not thinking any further. That was how they both preferred it.

One morning as they were preparing to go out the phone rang, and it was Gino.

'The film crew have left,' Dante informed Ferne when the call was over.

'Already?'

'There was some sort of a kerfuffle; Sandor threw a fit and everyone was out in an hour. Now we're needed to sell the place.' He looked at her, smiling. 'Ah, well, I guess it was too perfect to last for ever.'

'Nothing lasts for ever,' Ferne said lightly.

'That's what I say.' Then he sighed and added ruefully, 'But sometimes it would be nice if it did.'

They spent two days at the Palazzo Tirelli before heading back to Naples, where they moved into a small apartment belonging to a friend of Dante who was currently away.

On the first night back they went to dinner at the Villa Rinucci. Hope broadcast the event to the family, inviting everyone to drop in. But for her the real point of the evening was to see with her own eyes that Dante was in good health, and even better spirits.

'He's told me all about it,' she said when she and Ferne had a moment alone in the kitchen. 'You actually slapped Sandor Jayley's face because you prefer Dante?'

'I'd have slapped his face anyway,' Ferne protested. 'It had nothing to do with Dante.'

'Oh, come! What about that big offer you turned down?'

'Well, I had to, after I made you a promise. Hope, Dante and I are ships that pass in the night, we both know that. We're having fun, but it can't last. He's not in love with me, and I'm not in love with him.'

Hope didn't reply in words, but her cynical gaze was answer enough. A moment later Toni called, and they both went out to where everyone was lounging in the garden as the evening wound down.

Ferne wished she could speak openly to Hope and tell her that love was impossible because she simply wouldn't allow it to happen.

She knew she had been lucky as few women were ever lucky. Dante was a gentle and considerate man. If she was tired, he would urge her to bed, kiss her gently and either hold her until she slept or creep away, leaving her in peace.

When they talked, he listened to her with every appearance of real interest. His own conversation was fascinating. Beneath the sometimes clownish exterior was a thoughtful, educated man who might well have been a professor in some serious subject.

In bed he was a skilled and tender lover, giving her a physical pleasure she had never dreamed possible, and treating her like a queen. On the surface no woman could have asked for more.

But in her heart she had the melancholy feeling that it was all a sham, an illusion, because he was hiding the most important part of himself from her. And while that was true it would protect her from falling deeply in love with him.

She reassured herself about that many times.

Their apartment was high up on the fifth floor of a block overlooking the Bay of Naples. From their bedroom window they could see the great volcano Vesuvius in the distance. Several times she woke to find him on the window seat, contentedly watching the full moon across the bay casting its glow on the volcano.

One night he stayed up late, leaving her to come to bed alone. She'd waited for him, then fallen into a half-sleep. Somewhere in that doze she'd thought she felt a gentle kiss on her cheek, but when she opened her eyes she was alone.

She'd slept again, and had finally woken to find him sitting by the window. This was different from last time, when he'd sat with his head in his hands, clearly in pain. Now he seemed content, gazing out, still in the same thoughtful mood as before. When he saw that she was awake, he didn't speak but held out an arm for her to come and join him.

'Do you remember when we looked at this before?' he murmured.

'Yes, and you told me you'd once heard it

rumble and longed to hear it again,' she said. 'There's nowhere to get away from it, is there? Wherever you are in Naples, it's always there.'

'You think you're used to it,' he murmured. 'You know it in all its phases, but you can still be taken by surprise.'

She watched him, wondering what he would say next. He'd been in a strange mood for the last couple of days, with less to say than usual. He didn't seem sad or unwell, merely thoughtful. Occasionally she would look up to find him watching her with eyes that were almost puzzled, as though something had disconcerted him. If he caught her glance, he would smile and turn quickly away.

'What have you been taking for granted?' she asked him now.

'Everything, perhaps. You think you know how things are, but suddenly it's all different. You're not the same man you were—whoever that was.'

He gave a brief, nervous laugh, sounding mysteriously as though he had no self-confidence. 'I'm talking nonsense, aren't I?' he said.

'Mmm, but go on. It sounds good.'

'Yes, nonsense can sound very impressive. I learned that long ago. You can even impress yourself with it for a while. But—then the volcano rumbles and reminds you of things you've always known, and maybe wish you didn't.'

Ferne held her breath. Was Dante finally going to tell her the truth about himself, thus letting her come really close to him at last?

'Are you afraid of the volcano?' she whispered. 'I mean, the one inside?'

'Yes, although I wouldn't admit that to anyone but you. I've never even admitted it to myself before, but I feel I could tell you anything and it would be all right. I need never be afraid again.' He added wistfully, 'Could that ever really be true?'

'I suppose it would depend how much you wanted it to be true,' she ventured. 'If you trusted me…'

'I trust you as I've never trusted anyone in my life. If not you, then who?'

He took her hands in his, bending his head to kiss the palms.

'You have such tiny, delicate hands,' he whispered. 'Yet they're so strong, so welcoming. When they reach out, they seem to contain all the world.'

'I would give you the world if I could,' she said. It was a dangerous thing to say, but the words seemed to come out of their own accord. 'If it were mine to give.'

'Perhaps it is and you don't know it.' He stroked her face with tender fingers. 'Sometimes I think I know more about you than you know about yourself. I know how loving and honest you are, how brave, how open-hearted.'

'It's an illusion,' she said. 'That's a fantasy figure you've created.'

'Why do you say that?'

'Because nobody could be the way you see me.'

'Why? Because I think you're perfect?'

'That proves it's an illusion.'

'No, it proves I'm a man of insight and good sense. Now, don't argue with me. If I say you're perfect, you're perfect—and I do say it. I know you could never perform a deceitful or underhand action.'

His words, spoken so warmly and with such emotion, gave her a bad moment. The knowledge of her deception, however well-meaning, seemed to hang over them, poisoning the moment.

'Dante—'

His finger lightly touched her mouth. 'Don't spoil it.'

Don't spoil it. The words were like a bitter reproach.

But it wasn't her fault, she thought wildly. She was protecting him, but that innocent desire had led her up this path, fraught with danger.

'Let me say what I want to before I lose my nerve,' he murmured.

'I can't see you ever losing your nerve.'

'That's an act. Inside I'm a coward. If you only knew how much of a coward, you'd run away. And that's what you ought to do.'

'Isn't that for me to decide?'

'How can you, when you don't know the worst of me?'

'Then tell me the worst. I'm braced for anything.'

'You make a joke of it, but there are things…'

'Yes?' she said eagerly.

'Ferne…' She felt a tremor go through him. 'Have I imagined what's been happening to us?'

Now her heart was beating so hard that she couldn't speak, only shake her head.

'I know I said "just friendly",' he whispered. 'But I say a lot of things that are nonsense. I guess you know that by now. When we talk—and I've never talked to anyone the way I talk to you—I always feel that you understand everything I'm not saying. With you, I don't have to worry. I can be at peace.'

He made a wry face, aimed at himself. 'I never thought the day would come when I saw peace as a virtue. I was always one for racketing around. Yes, you knew that, didn't you?' His soft laughter joined hers. 'I don't suppose there's much about me you haven't worked out: clown, idiot, self-deceiver, overgrown schoolboy.'

'I could add a few others,' she teased.

'I'll bet you could.'

'Then how can you say I don't know the worst of you? I probably think you're worse than you are. Why don't you put me right?'

'Tell you what a hero I am? What a strong, solid, upright character who never cut corners or skirted around the truth in his life?'

'No, I don't think I could quite believe that.' She was teasing him along the road, inviting him into the place where he would feel safe enough to tell her everything. When there was total honesty between them, the way would be clear for whatever lay in the future.

She wanted there to be a future. She could admit that now. She'd hidden her feelings, even from herself, behind a barrier of caution and sensible reasoning. But now Dante himself was demolishing that barrier. If she was only a little patient, there would be happiness soon.

'It you presented yourself as a stuffed dummy full of virtue I think I'd just laugh,' she admitted. 'And then I'd send you on your way, because I'd have no use for you.'

'For the stuffed-dummy part or the virtue?' he asked lightly.

'Guess.'

He smiled, but then his smile faded as emotion swept him.

'Oh, Ferne, don't change,' he said desperately. 'Promise me you'll never change, and then maybe I can dig deep in myself and find a little courage. Only it's going to take more than just a little. It's going to take a lot to show you myself as I really am, stupid and pig-headed, blind to what matters.'

'Stop,' she said, putting her fingers lightly over his mouth. 'Don't run yourself down.'

He didn't argue, just took hold of her fingers and moved his lips against them. His eyes were almost desperate. She stroked his face, willing him to take the last step that would join their hearts in the closeness that only honesty could bring.

'Dante,' she whispered. 'Please—please.'

Suddenly he gripped her tightly, drawing her to him and burying his face against her.

'Help me,' he said huskily. *'Help me.'*

She held him eagerly, flooded with emotion that made it impossible to speak. His carefully constructed armour was cracking, revealing the vulnerability he'd striven so hard to hide, and she wanted only to enfold him, to offer him the help he'd finally sought. Now the moment had come, she was almost dizzy with joy and gratitude.

'What's this?' he said, touching her face. 'You're crying.'

'No, I'm not, not really. I'm just—'

'Don't cry.' He was lightly brushing her tears away. 'I didn't mean to upset you.'

'I'm not upset.'

He took her face between his hands, looking down at her tenderly before dropping his mouth to hers. She kissed him back eagerly, trying to tell him silently that she was his in any way he wanted. If only they could take the next step.

'I'm so lucky to have you,' he said. 'If only…'

'If only…?' she echoed wistfully.

'If only I were worth it. There's so much I want to say to you, but not just now. My head's in a muddle—as usual,' he finished, turning it into a joke.

But she wouldn't let him get away with that.

'I don't think this is your usual muddle,' she persisted.

'No, I'm getting worse. Be a little patient with me.'

'All right,' she said, trying not to sound sad.

'Let's go to bed,' he said. 'We've got a long drive tomorrow.'

She was stunned, hardly able to believe that the emotion of a moment ago had vanished to nothing. They had come so close, and to see the prize snatched away at the last minute was hard. But she let him lead her unprotesting to bed. One incautious word from her, and the chance could be lost for ever.

He pulled the clothes up over her and got in beside her, holding her briefly before kissing her goodnight. Then he turned over and went to sleep.

She lay staring into the darkness, trying to come to terms with what had happened. It was disappointing to sense his withdrawal, yet she felt she understood. He'd meant to tell her—she was convinced—but he'd backed off, perhaps appalled by so nearly abandoning the caution of a lifetime.

Now she must be patient and it would surely happen, for there had been something in his manner that had never been there before, a new trust and tenderness. His eyes had shone with a different light, and somewhere Ferne had sensed a door opening.

How long had she loved him—right from the start? The signs had been there when he'd gone into the burning building and she, who'd coolly photographed Sandor's betrayal, had forgotten everything but Dante's danger.

She'd deceived herself, believing she was only doing this for Hope, when the truth was she yearned to be with Dante. How could she ever have imagined that it was possible to be with this man night and day and not love him?

The sadness had been to love him and hide from him, as he was hiding from her. But now that would soon be over, and she was feeling happy again as she fell asleep.

Next day they drove miles to a villa that was going to take all their joint skills to sell. But the challenge was exhilarating, and they returned home in a triumphant mood. On the drive back, Dante was in high spirits.

'We'll stop for a meal,' he said. 'But only a quick one. Let's not be late home.'

He said nothing about the day before, but there was something in the happy atmosphere that told her everything was different. He'd come to the edge of saying the words that would bind them closer, that it was almost as though they had already been said. Looking up, she saw him watching her with a contented smile that told her she was right.

When they reached home there was work to do, and they both settled down at computers.

'It's coming on really well,' he said, looking over her shoulder. 'How did I ever sell houses without you?'

'You don't have to butter me up,' she said sleepily. 'You're stuck with me, whether you want me or not.'

'That's what I like to hear. Why don't you go to bed?'

'I think I will.' She shut down her computer.

'Leave it,' Dante said. 'I'll put it away with mine.'

She kissed him and drifted away, yawning.

He watched her go, wondering if she would think it strange that tonight he didn't come to bed with her. In fact he was hatching a plan—reprehensible, no doubt, but he didn't think she'd mind too much when she found out.

She had never done as she'd promised and emailed him the pictures he had taken of her.

Now he proposed to conduct a raid and claim them. Waiting until he could see that she'd turned the bedroom light off, he switched her computer back on.

He located the folder without difficulty, and within moments was looking at the pictures he'd taken. He'd thought he knew them, but now they struck him with new force. So much had happened since then. He hadn't meant to grow so close to her, but it had happened despite his resolutions. Perhaps it was fate. He, a man who believed in fate, had to believe in this possibility.

Now he couldn't understand why he hadn't seen her clearly before. Entranced by her loveliness, he'd overlooked the strength and honesty in her face. It was this, as much as her passionate body, that had broken down his defences, so that only a day ago he'd been on the verge of telling her things he'd never told another living soul, things he'd sworn never to tell anyone in his life—however long or short that life might be.

He'd come to the very edge, then backed off. But not very far. The thought was still there in his mind that if he plucked up courage he could tell her everything, beg her to risk the future with him. If not her, then nobody, for there was nobody else in the world that he trusted as much.

She was smiling at him from the screen, her eyes wide and clear, offering hope where there had been none before, a future where there had been only blankness.

Quickly he connected the laptop to his portable printer and printed out a copy of the picture.

That was enough for now. Tomorrow he would confess what he'd done and they would laugh together, revelling in their private world where nobody else was allowed, and where they kept each other safe.

He was about to log off when he noticed the file called 'ZZZ'.

Through her light sleep Ferne was vaguely aware of the sound of the printer coming from the next room, then a long silence, until she heard the printer again. When it ended there was another silence that dragged on and on. Without knowing why, she was suddenly filled with fear.

Moving slowly, she left the bed at the same moment that Dante entered the room. Strangely, he too was moving slowly, as though struggling to recover from some terrible blow. He switched on the light, and she saw he was holding some papers, which he tossed onto the bed. She drew a sharp breath as she recognised some of the files about his condition that she'd stored on her computer.

At the sight of Dante's face filled with cold rage, her heart nearly failed her. It was the face of a stranger.

'I printed them off your computer,' he said. 'What are they?'

'Just—something I've been reading.'

'Just something you *happened* to be reading?' His voice was calm but as cold as ice. 'I don't think so. There are at least a dozen downloads in that folder. You've been searching the Internet for anything you could find on this one subject, and you didn't just chance on it by accident, did you?' When she hesitated, he added, 'Don't lie to me, Ferne.'

If only he would return to being the Dante she knew, and not this frightening stranger. She tried to find some warmth in his eyes, but there was only a cavern of emptiness that filled her with dread.

'I won't lie to you, Dante. I knew you had a problem.'

'Who told you? Hope, I suppose?'

'Yes, she was worried about you. You had that funny turn on the ladder the day of the fire, and then a bad headache.'

'And you both put two and two together and came up with five. I was sick with smoke that day, but you had to make a big thing of it.'

'All right, you think we were fussing about nothing, but people who care about you *do* fuss. That's how you know they care. You told me once that Hope has been the nearest thing to a mother that you've known since your own mother died. Well, mothers fuss. They may have to hide it, but it's what happens.'

'So, she told you—when? How long ago?'

'I—'

'How long ago?' he repeated relentlessly. 'Before we came away together?'

'Yes.'

'You've known all this time?' he said softly. 'There was I, like a fool, thinking I could guard my privacy, never dreaming you were spying on me.'

'I wasn't spying.'

'*This* is spying.' His voice was like the crack of a whip, making her flinch back.

'Is it wrong to care for you, to want to see you safe?'

'My safety is my own affair.'

'Not always,' she said, beginning to get angry. 'What you do affects other people. You can't spend your life cut off from everyone.' She drew a sharp breath. 'But that's what you've tried to do, isn't it?'

'That's my business.' His face was deadly pale, not white but grey. 'Is that why you came with me? As a kind of guardian, watching over me like a nurse with a child—or worse?'

'I never thought of you like that.'

'I think you did—someone so stupid that he has to be kept in the dark while he's *investigated* behind his back.'

'What did you expect me to do when you kept the truth from me?' she cried.

'*You've* been hiding secrets from *me*,' he shouted.

'I had to, but I didn't want to. I always hoped that you'd come to trust me.'

'But that's the irony; that's the ugly joke. I *did* trust you. I've never felt so close to anyone.'

'Then you were fooling yourself,' she said hotly. 'How could we be close when you were concealing something so important? That's not real closeness. That's just a pretence of it on your terms.'

'Exactly: "how could we be close when you were concealing something so important?" That says it all, doesn't it? When I think of you watching me, judging me, adjusting your actions to keep me fooled…'

He drew a sharp breath, and she saw sudden, bitter understanding overtake him. 'That's the real reason you refused to take that job, isn't it? And there was I thinking that maybe you wanted to be with me as much as I— Well, it just shows you how a man can delude himself if he's stupid enough. I must remember to pay you back the money you sacrificed for me.'

'Don't you dare say that!' she cried. 'Don't you *dare* offer me money.'

'Do you feel insulted? Well, now you know how I feel.' His voice rose on a note of anguished bitterness. 'But can you also understand that at this moment *I can't bear the sight of you*?'

CHAPTER TEN

As if to prove it, he turned away and began to pace the room, talking without looking at her.

'What a laugh I must have given you!'

'You don't really think that?' she said. 'You can't. I have never laughed at you.'

'Pitied, then. That's worse. Can't you understand?'

Wearily, she understood only too well. Dante was staggering under the weight of humiliation as he realised how close he'd come to opening his heart to her. For years he'd held off, never risking deep emotion and trust, until he'd met her. Now he felt betrayed.

She'd known that he guarded his privacy, but it was worse than that. He shut himself away from the world's eyes in a little cave where he dwelt alone, and even she wasn't allowed to venture. She thought of his loneliness in that bare cave, and shivered.

'I've always wanted to talk to you about it,' she said. 'I hated deceiving you. But I'd have hated it more if you'd died, and you might die if you don't have it properly checked.'

'What is there to check? I know the chances.'

'I wonder if you know as much as you think you do!' she said in a temper. 'You're a conceited man, Dante, proud, arrogant and stubborn, in a really stupid way. You think you know it all, but medical science moves on. If you'd let the doctors help you, something could be done. You could be fit and strong for years ahead.'

'You don't know what you're talking about,' he said harshly. 'Don't tell me what happens with this, because I know more about it than you ever will. I've watched what it's done to my family, the lives it's ruined; not just the people who suffer from it, but those who have to watch them die. Or, worse, when they don't die, swallowing up the lives of the people who have to care for them. Do you think I want that? Anything is better. Even dying.'

'Do you think your death would be better for me?' she whispered.

'It could be, if it set you free, if I'd made the mistake of tying you to me so that you longed for my death as much as I did.' A withered look came into his face. 'Except that I wouldn't long for it, because I wouldn't understand what was happening to me, wouldn't know. Everyone else would know, but I'd know nothing. I'd just carry on, thinking I was a normal man. *And I would rather be dead.*'

Then he stared at her in silence, as though his own words had shocked him as much as they had her. When the silence became unbearable, Ferne said bitterly, 'What about what I want? Doesn't that count?'

'How can you judge when you don't know the reality?'

'I know what my reality would be like if you died. I know it because I love you.'

He stared at her with eyes full of shock, but she searched them in vain for any sign of pleasure or welcome. This man was dead to love.

'I didn't mean to, but it happened. Did you ever think of what you were doing to me?' she pleaded.

'You weren't supposed to fall in love,' he grated. 'No complications. We were going to keep it light.'

'And you think love is like that? You think it's so easy to say "don't" and for nothing to happen? It might be easy for you. You arrange things the way you want them, you tell yourself that you'll get just so close to me and no further, and that's how things work out, because you have no real heart. But I have a heart, and I can't control it like you can.

'Yes, I love you. Dante, do you understand that? I *love* you. I am deeply, totally in love with you. I didn't want that to happen. I told myself the same silly fantasies that you did—how it could be controlled if I was sensible. And it crept up on me when I wasn't looking, and, when I did look, it was too late.

'Now I want all the things I swore I'd never let myself want: to live with you and make love with you, marry you and bear your children. I want to crack jokes with you, and hold you when you're sleeping at night.

'You never thought of that, did you? And you don't think it matters. I wish I was as heartless as you.'

'I'm not—'

'Shut up and listen. I've listened to you, now it's my turn. I wish I didn't love you, because I'm beginning to think you don't deserve to be loved, but I can't help it. So there it is. What do I do now with this love that neither of us wants?'

'Kill it,' he snapped.

'Tell me how.'

His face changed, became older, wearier, as though he had suddenly confronted a brick wall.

'There is a way,' he murmured. 'And perhaps it's the best way, if it will convince you as nothing else could.'

'Dante, what are you talking about?'

'I'm going to kill your love.'

'Even you can't do that,' she said, trying to ignore the fear that was growing inside her.

'Don't be so sure. When I'm finished, you'll recoil from me in horror and run from me as far and fast as you can. I promise you that will happen, because I'm going to make sure it does. When you look back on this time, you'll wish we'd never met, and you'll hate me. But one day you'll thank me.'

The brutal words seemed to hang in the air between them. Ferne stared at him hopelessly, vainly looking for some softening in his face.

He checked his watch. 'We have time to catch a flight if we hurry.'

'Where are we going?'

'Milan.' He gave a frightening smile. 'I'm going to show you the future.'

'I don't understand. What is there in Milan?'

'My Uncle Leo. Have they told you about him?'

'Toni said he was a permanent invalid.'

'*Invalid* doesn't begin to describe it. They say

that in his youth he was a fine man, a banker with a brain like a steel trap that could solve any problem. Women basked in his attention. Now he's a man with the mind of a child.'

'I'll take your word for it. I don't need to see him.'

'I say that you do, and you're going to.'

'Dante, please listen—'

'No, the time for that is passed. Now *you* listen. You wanted me to show you how to kill your love, and that's what I'm going to do.'

She tried to twist away but his hands were hard on her shoulders.

'We're going,' he said.

'You can't make me.'

'Do you really think I can't?' he asked softly.

Who was this man who stared at her with cold eyes and delivered his orders in a brutal *staccato* that brooked no argument? Why did he have Dante's face when he wasn't Dante, could never be him?

Or was he the *real* Dante who had lived inside this man all the time?

'Go and pack your things,' he said in a voice of iron.

She did so, moving like an automaton. When she came out with her bag, he was waiting.

'The taxi will be here in a minute,' he said.

Neither spoke on the way to the airport; there was nothing to say. Ferne had the feeling of coming to a huge bridge stretching so far into the distance that she couldn't see the other side. It led to an unknown place that she feared to visit, but to turn back now was impossible.

Worst of all was the sensation of travelling there alone, for there was no comfort to be found in the steely man beside her.

Then she caught a glimpse of his blank face, and remembered that he was the one in need of comfort. But he would accept none, especially from her.

On the flight to Milan, she ventured to say, 'What kind of place is he in?'

'A care home. It's clean, comfortable, kind. They look after him well. Sometimes his family visit him, but they lose heart after a while, because he doesn't know them.'

He added wryly, 'One strange thing that you may find useful, he still speaks excellent English. With all the damage that was done to the rest of his brain, that part has remained untouched. The doctors can't say why.'

At the airport he hailed a taxi to take them to the home, where a nurse greeted them with a smile.

'I've told him you called to say you were coming. He was so pleased.'

That sounded cheerful, Ferne thought. Perhaps Uncle Leo was better than Dante imagined.

She followed them through the pleasant building until they came to a bedroom at the back where the sun shone through large windows. A man was there, kneeling on the floor, solemnly decorating a Christmas tree. He looked up and smiled at the sight of them.

He was in his late sixties, plump and grey-haired, with twinkling eyes and an air of friendly glee.

'Hello, Leo,' said the nurse. 'Look who I've brought to see you.'

'I promised to come,' Dante said to him in English. 'And I brought a friend to see you.'

The old man smiled politely.

'How kind of you to visit me,' he said, also in English. 'But I can't talk for long. My nephew is coming, and I must get this finished.' He indicated the tree, immediately returning to work on it.

'It's his latest obsession,' the nurse said. 'He decorates it, takes it all down then starts again. Leo, it's all right, you can leave it for the moment.'

'No, no, I must finish it before Dante gets here,' Leo said urgently. 'I promised him.'

'I'm here, Uncle,' Dante said, going to him. 'There's no need to finish the tree. It's fine as it is.'

'Oh, but I must. Dante will be so disappointed otherwise. Do you know Dante, by any chance?'

Ferne held her breath, but Dante was unfazed. It seemed that he was used to this.

'Yes, I've met him,' he said. 'He's told me all about you.'

'But why doesn't he come?' Leo was almost in tears. 'He keeps saying he will, but he never does, and I so long to see him.'

'Leo, look at me.' Dante's voice was very gentle. 'Don't you know me?'

'No.' Wide-eyed, Leo stared at him. 'Should I?'

'I've often visited you before. I hoped you'd remember me.'

Leo's gaze became intense. 'No,' he said desperately. 'I've never seen you before. I don't know you—I don't, I don't!'

'It's all right, it doesn't matter.'

'Who are you?' Leo wailed. 'I don't know you. You're trying to confuse me. Go away! I want Dante. Where's Dante? He promised!'

Before their horrified eyes, he burst into violent tears, burying his face in his hands and wailing. Dante tried to take the old man in his arms but was violently pushed away. Raising his voice to a scream, Leo barged his way out of the room, racing across the lawn towards the trees.

The nurse made to follow him, but Dante waved her back. 'Leave this to me.'

He hurried out after Leo, catching up with him as they reached the trees.

'Oh dear,' Ferne sighed.

'Yes, it's very sad,' the nurse said. 'He's a sweet old man, but he gets fixated on things, like that tree, and things just go round and round in his head.'

'Is it normal for him not to recognise his family?'

'We don't see much of them here. Dante comes more often than anyone else. He's so gentle and kind to Leo. I shouldn't tell you this, but he pays the lion's share of the expenses here, plus any special treats for the old man; he gets nothing back for it.'

'And Leo has been like this for how long?'

'Thirty years. It makes you wonder how life looks from inside his head.'

'Yes,' Ferne said sadly. 'It does.'

'I suppose he doesn't really know, and that makes it bearable for him, poor thing. But then Dante visits him, and it brings him no pleasure because he never recognises him.'

Heavy-hearted, Ferne wandered out into the gardens, heading for the trees where she'd seen them go. She could understand the way Dante flinched from being reduced to this, being pitied by everyone. If only there was some way to convince him that her love was different. Inside her heart, hope was dying.

She heard them before she saw them. From somewhere beyond the trees came the sound of weeping. Following it, she came across the two men sitting on a fallen log. Dante had his arms around his uncle, who was sobbing against his shoulder.

He looked up as she approached. He said nothing, but his eyes met hers in a silent message: *now you understand. Be warned, and escape quickly.*

'Stop crying,' he said gently. 'I want you to meet a friend of mine. You can't cry when a lady is here—she'll think you don't like her.'

The gentle rallying in his voice had its effect. Leo blew his nose and tried to brighten up.

'*Buon giorno, signorina.*'

'No, no, my friend is English,' Dante said. 'We must speak English to her. She doesn't understand foreign languages as we do.' He emphasised 'we' very slightly, clearly trying to create a sense of closeness that would comfort Leo. 'Her name is Ferne Edmunds.'

Leo pulled himself together. 'Good evening, Miss Edmunds.'

'Please, call me Ferne,' she said. 'I'm so glad to meet you.' Floundering for something to say, she looked around at the trees. 'This is a lovely place.'

'Yes, I've always liked it. Of course,' Leo added earnestly, 'it's a lot of work to keep it in good condition. But it's been in my family for such a long time, I feel I must—I must—' He broke off, looking around in bewilderment.

'Don't worry about it,' Dante said, taking his hand and speaking quietly. 'It's all being taken care of.'

'I so much wanted everything to be right when he came,' Leo said sadly. 'But he isn't coming, is he?'

'Leo, it's me,' Dante said urgently. 'Look at me. Don't you recognise me?'

For a long moment Leo gazed into Dante's face, his expression a mixture of eagerness and sadness. Ferne found herself holding her breath for both of them.

'Do I know you?' Leo asked sadly after a while. 'Sometimes I think—but he never comes to see me. I wish he would. He said once that he was the only person who really understood me, and he'd always be my best friend. But he doesn't visit me, and I'm so sad.'

'But I do visit you,' Dante said. 'Don't you remember me?'

'Oh no,' Leo sighed. 'I've never seen you before. Do you know Dante?'

At first she thought Dante wouldn't answer. His head was bowed as though some terrible struggle was taking place within him, consuming all his strength. At last he managed to say, 'Yes, I know him.'

'Please, please ask him to come to see me. I miss him so much.'

Dante's face was full of tragedy, and Ferne's heart ached for him. He'd been right; the reality was more terrible than anything she could have imagined.

'Let's go back inside,' he said, helping Leo to his feet.

In silence they made their way back across the lawn. Leo had recovered his spirits, as if the last few minutes had never been, and was chatting happily about the grand estate he believed was his.

The nurse came out onto the step, smiling kindly at Leo, welcoming him inside.

'We've got your favourite cakes,' she said.

'Oh, thank you. I've been trying to explain to my friend here about Dante. Look, let me show you his picture.'

From a chest of drawers behind the bed Leo took a photo album and opened it at a page containing one picture. It was Dante, taken recently. He was sitting with Leo, both of them smiling and seeming content with each other. Leo looked at it with pride.

'That was taken— Well, you can see that he's nothing like…' He looked at Dante sorrowfully.

Ferne felt her throat constrict and knew that in another moment she would be weeping. The picture was clearly Dante, and the fact that Leo didn't recognise him told a terrible story about his mental state.

'You see what a nice boy he is,' Leo said, running his fingers over the face on the page. 'He was always my favourite. Look.'

He began turning the pages, revealing earlier pictures. Ferne gasped as she saw Leo as a young man before his tragedy, sitting with a little boy on his knee. Even at this distance of years she could recognise Dante in the child. His face was the one she knew, bright and vivid with intelligence, gleaming with humour.

But the greatest tragedy of all was the fact that the man's face was exactly the same. Their features were different, but their expressions were identical. In his day, Leo had been the man Dante was now, dazzling, charmingly wicked, capable of anything.

And he had come to this.

Turning the pages, Leo revealed more pictures, including one of a beautiful young woman.

'That was my wife,' he said softly. 'She died.'

But Dante shook his head, mouthing, 'Left him.'

There was the child Dante again, with a man and a woman.

'My sister Anna,' Leo said proudly. 'And her husband, Taddeo Rinucci. They died in a car accident years ago.'

He switched back to the modern picture of Dante and showed it to the real man.

'You see? If you could remember what he looks like, and then—?' Tears began to roll down his face.

Ferne's heart broke for Dante, sitting there regarding this tragedy with calm eyes. When he spoke to Leo, it was with tender kindness, asking nothing, giving everything.

'I'll remember,' he said. 'Trust me for that. And I'll try to find some way of making things nicer for you. You know you can rely on me.'

'Oh yes,' Leo said brightly. 'You're always so good to me—who are you?'

'It doesn't matter,' Dante said with an effort. 'As long as we're friends, names don't matter.'

Leo beamed.

'Oh, thank you, thank you. I want—I want—'

Suddenly he was breathing wildly and shuddering. His arms began to flail, and it took all Dante's strength to hold him in his chair.

'You'd better go,' the nurse said tersely. 'We know what to do when he's like this.'

'I'll call later,' Dante said.

'By all means, but please go now.'

Reluctantly they did so.

'What happened to him?' Ferne asked as they left.

'He had an epileptic seizure,' Dante said bluntly. 'That's another thing that happens with his condition. He'll lose consciousness, and when he awakens he won't remember anything, even our visit. Once this happened and I insisted on staying, but my presence only distressed him. Possibly it's my fault he had the seizure, because seeing me agitated him.'

'That poor man,' she said fervently.

'Yes, he is. And, now you know, let's go to the airport. You've seen all you need to.'

She agreed without argument, sensing that Dante was at the end of his tether.

They spoke little on the short flight back to Naples. Ferne felt as though she never wanted to speak another word again. Her mind seemed to be filled with darkness, and she could see only more darkness ahead. Perhaps things would be better when they got home and could talk about it. She tried hard to believe that.

But, when they reached home, he stopped at the front door.

'I'm going for a walk,' he said. 'I'll be back later.'

She knew better than to suggest coming with him. He wanted to get away from her; that was the truth.

And perhaps, she thought as she opened the front door, she too needed to be away from him for a while. That was the point they had reached.

The apartment was frighteningly quiet. She'd been alone there before, but the silence hadn't had this menacing quality because Dante's laughing spirit had always seemed to be with her, even when he was away. But now the laughter was dead, perhaps for ever, replaced by the hostility of a man who felt he'd found betrayal where he'd thought to find only trust.

It had all happened so fast. Only hours ago, she'd been basking in the conviction of his unspoken love, certain that the trouble between them could be resolved and the way made clear. Then the heavens had fallen on her.

No, on them both. Even when Dante had been at his most cruel, she had recognised the pain and disillusion that drove him. Her heart cried that he should trust her, but life had taught him that the traps were always waiting at his feet, ready to be sprung when he least expected it.

In desperation she'd told him that she loved him, but now it hit her with the force of a sledgehammer that he hadn't said as much in return. He'd spoken only of killing her love, and had done his best to do it. With all her heart she longed to believe that he'd been forcing himself, denying his true feelings, but she was no longer sure what those feelings were. At times, she'd thought she detected real hatred in his eyes.

Perhaps that was the real Dante, a man whose need to keep the world at bay was greater than any love he could feel. Perhaps the cold hostility he'd turned on her was the strongest emotion he could truly feel.

She sat there in the darkness, shaking with misery and despair.

In the early hours she heard him arrive, moving quietly. When the door of the bedroom opened just a little, she said, 'I'm awake.'

'I'm sorry, did I wake you?' His voice was quiet.

'I can't sleep.'

He didn't come near the bed but went to stand by the window, looking out in the direction of Vesuvius, as they had once done together.

'That was what you meant, wasn't it?' she asked, coming beside him. 'Never knowing when it was going to send out a warning.'

'Yes, that was what I meant.'

'And, now that it has, we're all supposed to make a run for it?'

'If you have any sense.'

'I never had any sense.'

'I know.' He gave a brief laugh. 'Nobody who knew us would imagine I was the one with common sense, would they?'

'Certainly not me,' she said, trying to recapture their old bantering way of talking.

'So I have to be wise for both of us. I should think what happened today would have opened your eyes. You saw what's probably waiting for me at the end of the road.'

'Not if you take medical help to avoid it,' she pressed.

'There is no avoiding it, or at least so little chance as not to justify the risk. To become like Leo is my nightmare. Maybe one day it'll happen, and if we were married what would you do? Would you have the sense to leave me then?'

Ferne stared at him, unable to believe that he'd really spoken such words.

'You'd want me to leave you—just abandon you?'

'I'd want you to get as far away from me as possible. I'd want you to go where you'd never have to see me, or even think about me, again.'

Shattered, Ferne stepped back and looked at him. Then a blind rage swept over her and she drew back her hand, ready to aim at his face, but at the last minute she dropped it and turned away, almost running in her fear of what she had been about to do.

He came after her, also furious, pulling her around to face him.

'If you want to hit me, do it,' he snapped.

'I ought to,' she breathed.

'Yes, you ought to. I've insulted you, haven't

I? Fine, I'll insult you again. And again. Until you face reality.'

The rage in his voice frightened her. Part of her understood that his cruelty was a deliberate attempt to drive her off her for own sake. Yet still it stunned her in its intensity, warning her of depths to him that she had never understood because he had never wanted her to understand.

'Reality means what you want it to mean,' she said. 'Maybe I see things differently.'

'Marriage? Children? Holding hands as we wander into the sunset? Only I wouldn't just be holding your hand, I'd be clinging to it for support.'

'And I'd be glad to give you that support, because I love you.'

'Don't love me,' he said savagely. 'I have no love to give back.'

'Is that really true?' she whispered.

The look he gave her was terrible, full of despair and suffering that she could do nothing to ease. That was when she faced the truth: if she had no power to ease his pain, then everything was dead between them.

'Try not to hate me,' he said wearily.

'I thought you wanted me to hate you as the quickest way of getting rid of me.'

'I thought so too, but I guess I can't manage

it. Don't hate me more than you have to, and I'll try not to hate you.'

'Hate *me*?' she echoed. 'After everything we've— Could you hate me?'

He was silent for a long moment before whispering, 'Yes. If I must.'

He looked away again, out of the window, to where the dawn was breaking. The air was clear and fresh; the birds were beginning to sing. It was going to be a glorious day.

She came up close behind him, touching him gently and resting her cheek against his back. Her head was whirling with the words that she wanted to say, and yet no words would be enough.

She could feel him warm against her, as she'd known him so often before, and suddenly, irrationally, she was filled with hope. This was Dante, who loved her, no matter what he said. They would be together because it was fated. All she had to do was convince him of that.

'Darling,' she whispered.

His voice was hard, and he spoke without looking at her.

'There's a flight to England at eleven this morning. I've booked your seat.'

* * *

He came with her to the airport, helping her to check in and remaining with her as they waited for the first call. There was no more tenderness in his manner than there had been before. He was doing his polite duty.

She couldn't bear it. Whatever might happen, there was no way she could go one way and leave him to go another, at the mercy of any wind that blew.

'Dante, please.'

'Don't.'

'Tell me to stay,' she whispered. 'We'll make it work somehow.'

He shook his head, his eyes weary and defeated. 'It's not your fault. It's me. I can't change. I'll always be a nightmare for any woman to live with. You were right. I shouldn't have lived with you and not warned you. I made the terms but didn't tell you what they were. Doesn't that prove I'm a monster?'

'You're not a monster,' she said fervently. 'Just a man trapped in a vicious web. But you don't have to live in it alone. Let me come inside, let me help you.'

His face was suddenly wild.

'And see you trapped too? No, get out while you can. I've done you so much damage, I won't do more. For pity's sake, for *my* sake, go!'

He almost ran from her then, hurrying into the crowd without looking back even once. She watched as the distance between them grew wider, until he vanished.

But only from her sight. In her mind and heart where he would always live, she could still see him, making his way back to the empty apartment and the empty life, where he would be alone for ever in the doubly bitter loneliness of those who had chosen their isolation.

CHAPTER ELEVEN

IT WAS late at night when Ferne reached her apartment, to find it gloomy and cold. Locking the door behind her, she stood in the silence, thinking of Dante far away, locked in a chill darkness that was more than physical.

She'd eaten nothing all day, and after turning on the heating she began to prepare a meal, but suddenly she stopped and simply went to bed. She had no energy to be sensible.

Where are you? she thought. *What are you doing? Are you lying alone, your thoughts reaching out to me, as mine to you? Or are you passing the time with some girl you picked up for the evening? No, it's too soon. You'll do that eventually, but not just yet.*

She slept for a little while, awoke, slept again. Sleeping or waking, there were only shadows in all directions. At last she was forced to admit that a new day had dawned, and slowly got out of bed.

Her first action was to call Hope. She'd managed to keep her up to date about the disaster, Dante's discovery of her files, their trip to Milan and her return to England, and Hope had asked for a call to say she'd arrived safely.

'I meant to call last night, but I got in so late,' she apologised.

'Never mind. How are you? You sound terrible.'

'I'll be fine when I've had a cup of tea,' she said, trying to sound relaxed.

'How are you really?' Hope persisted with motherly concern.

'I'll need a little time,' she admitted. 'How's Dante?'

'He'll need time too. Carlo and Ruggiero went round to see him last night. He wasn't at home, so they trawled the local bars until they found him sitting in a corner, drinking whisky. They took him home, put him to bed and stayed with him until morning. Carlo just called me to say he's awake, with an almighty hangover, but otherwise all right.'

They parted with mutual expressions of affection. A few minutes later the phone rang. It was Mike.

'I've been hearing rumours,' he said. 'They say you might be back in the land of the living.'

She almost laughed. 'That's one way of putting it. I'm back in England.'

'Great! I have work piling up for you.'

'I thought you dumped me.'

'I don't dump people with your earning potential. That job you turned down is still open. They tried someone else, didn't like the result and told me to get you at any price. It's fantastic money.'

The money was awesome. If the Sandor episode had propelled her into the big time, her refusal of an even better offer had given her rarity value.

'All right,' she interrupted Mike at last. 'Just tell me when and where, and I'll be there.'

Later that day she went to the theatre, where the major star and his equally famous fiancée were rehearsing. From the first moment everything went well. They liked her, she liked them. Their genuine love for each other made them, at least for the moment, really nice people. They praised her pictures and insisted that she must take some more at their wedding.

The tale of her meeting with Sandor in Italy had got out. She began to receive offers to 'tell all' to the press. She refused them, but Sandor had heard rumours and become nervous, having given a self-serving interview to a newspaper, illustrated with several of Ferne's notorious pictures. Her fame had increased. So had her price.

All around her, life was blossoming.

No, she thought, not life. Just her career. Life no longer existed.

She talked regularly with Hope and gained the impression that Dante's existence was much like her own, outwardly successful but inwardly bleak.

But there was no direct word from him until she'd been home for a month, and then she received a text:

> Your success is in all the papers. I'm glad you didn't lose out. Dante.

She texted back:

> I lost more than you'll ever know.

After that there was silence. Desperately she struggled to reconcile herself to the fact that she would never hear from him again, but then she received a letter.

> I know how generous you are, and so I dare to hope that in time you will forgive me

for the things I said and did. Yes, I love you;
I know that I shall always love you. But for
both our sakes I can never tell you again.

Night after night she wept with the letter
pressed against her heart. At last she replied:

You don't need to tell me again. It's enough
that you said it once. Goodbye, my dearest.

He didn't reply. She had not expected him to.

Her sleep was haunted by wretched dreams. In
one she found that time had passed and suddenly
there he was, older but still Dante. She reached
out eagerly to him but he only gazed at her
without recognition. Someone took him by the
arm to lead him away.

Then she knew that the worst had happened, and
he'd become the brain-damaged man he'd always
feared. She longed for him to look back at her just
for a moment, but he never did. She'd been blotted
from his mind as if she had never been.

She woke from that dream to find herself
screaming.

Struggling up in bed, she sat fighting back her
sobs until suddenly her whole body seemed to
become one gigantic heave. She flung herself out

of bed and just managed to dash to the bathroom in time.

When it was over, she sat shivering and considering the implications.

It could be just a tummy bug, she thought. *It doesn't mean I'm pregnant.*

But it did. And she knew it. A hurried visit to the chemist, and a test confirmed it.

The discovery that she was to have Dante's child came like a thunderclap. She'd thought herself modern, careful, sensible, but in the dizzying delight of loving him she'd forgotten everything else. In a moment her life had been turned upside down. Everything she'd considered settled was in chaos.

A child of Dante's, born from their love, but also born with chance of the hereditary illness that had distorted his life: a constant reminder of what she might have had and had lost.

The sensible answer was a termination, but she dismissed the thought at once. If she couldn't have Dante, she could still have a little part of him, and nothing on earth would persuade her to destroy that. Fiercely she laid her hands over her stomach, still perfectly flat.

'I won't let anyone or anything hurt you,' she

vowed. 'No matter what the future holds, you're mine, and I'll keep you safe.'

Then she realised that she'd spoken the words aloud, and looked around the apartment, wondering who she'd really been addressing. One thing was for sure: Dante had a right to know, and then, perhaps…

'No, no!' she cried. 'No false hopes. No fantastic dreams. Just tell him and then—and then?'

Once her mind was made up, she acted quickly, calling Mike and clearing the decks at work. Then she got on a plane to Naples, and booked into a hotel. She told nobody that she was coming, not even Hope. This was between Dante and herself.

It was still light when she walked the short distance to the apartment block and stood looking up at his windows, trying to discern any sign of life. But it was too soon for lamps to be on.

She took the lift to the fifth floor and hesitated. It was unlike her to lack confidence, but this was so vital, and the next few minutes so important. She listened, but could hear nothing from inside. The silence seemed a bleak forecast of what was to come. Suddenly her courage drained away and she stepped back.

But her spirit rebelled at the thought of giving up without trying, and she raised her hand to ring the bell. Then she dropped it again. What was the point? Dante himself had believed that you couldn't buck fate, and now she saw that he was right. Fate was against them. Defeated, she headed for the elevator.

'Don't go!'

The words were almost a scream. Turning, she saw Dante standing there in his doorway. His hair was dishevelled, his shirt torn open, his face was haggard and his eyes looked as though he hadn't slept for a month. But the only thing she noticed was that his arms were outstretched to her, and the next moment she was enfolded in them.

They held each other in silence, clasped tight, not kissing, but clinging to each other as if for refuge.

'I thought you were never going to knock,' he said frantically. 'I've been waiting for you.'

'You knew I was coming?'

'I saw you standing down there. I didn't believe it at first. I've seen you so often and you always vanished. Then I heard the lift coming up, and your footsteps—but you didn't ring the bell, and I was afraid it was just another hallucination. I've had so many; I couldn't bear another. So many times you've come to me and vanished before I could wake and keep you here.'

He drew her into the apartment, and enfolded her in his arms again.

'Thank God you're here,' he said, words that carried her to the heights.

But his next words dashed her down again.

'I've longed to see you just once more. We parted badly, and it was my fault. Now at least there can be peace between us.'

So in that he hadn't changed. He was no longer denying his love, but in the long term he was still determined to keep apart from her.

She took a deep breath. Relief at finding him here had undermined her resolution, but now the moment had arrived.

'It isn't that simple,' she said, stepping back and regarding him with loving eyes. 'Something's happened. I came to tell you about it—but then I'll go away if you like, and you need never see me again.'

His mouth twisted. 'That doesn't work very well.'

'No, with me neither, but when you hear what I have to say you might be so angry that you want me to leave.'

'Nothing could make me angry with you.'

'You were once.'

'I stopped being angry a long time ago. Most

of it was aimed at myself. I forced you into an impossible situation, I know that. I should have stayed clear of you from the start.'

'It's too late for that. The time we had together has left me with more than memories.' Seeing him frown, she said, 'I'm going to have a baby, Dante.'

Just for a moment she saw joy on his face, but it was gone in an instant, as though he'd quenched it forcibly.

'Are you sure?' he breathed.

'There's no doubt. I did a test, and then I came here to tell you, because you have the right to know. But that's it. I don't expect you to react in a conventional way because I know you can't.'

'Wait, wait!' he said fiercely. 'I need time to take this in. You can't just— A baby! Dear God!'

'I did dare to hope you'd be pleased,' she said sadly. 'But I suppose you can't be.'

'Pleased—at bringing another child into the world to spend a lifetime wondering what was happening inside him? I thought we were safe, that you were taking care; hell, I don't know what I thought. But I always swore I'd never father a child.'

'Well, you've fathered one,' she said quietly. 'We have to go on from there. You can't turn the clock back.'

'There is one way.'

'No,' she said firmly. 'Don't even mention that. If you think for a moment that I could destroy your child, you don't begin to know me. I told you I love you, but I could easily hate you if you ask me to do that.'

But she couldn't stay angry as she looked at him, saddened by the confusion in his face. He'd always insisted on being in control, quick-stepping with fate to the edge, but now he'd reached an edge he'd never dreamed of and he was lost. The thought gave her an idea.

'Fate doesn't always do what we expect,' she said, slipping her arms about his neck. 'It's had this waiting for you quite a while, and it's probably been laughing up its sleeve, thinking it's found the way to defeat you. But we're not going to let it win.'

He rested his forehead against hers. 'Doesn't fate always win?' he whispered.

'That depends who you have fighting with you.' She stepped back, taking his hand and laying it over her stomach. 'You're not alone any more. There are two of us backing you up now.'

He stared. 'Two?'

'Two people fighting on your side.' She gave

a faint smile at the stunned look on his face, and pointed to her stomach. 'There is actually someone in there, you know. A person. I don't know if it's a boy or a girl, but it's yours, and it's as ready to defend you as I am. When you get to know each other, you'll be the best of friends.'

He was very still, and she sensed him holding his breath as he struggled to come to terms with ideas that had always been alien to him.

'It won't be easy,' she urged, speaking with gentle persistence. 'It may have your family's inherited illness, so we'll find out, and if the news is bad at least you'll be there to help. You can explain things that nobody else can. The two of you will probably form an exclusive society that shuts me out, but I won't mind, because you'll have each other, and that's all you'll really need.'

'No,' he said softly. 'Never shutting you out, because we can't manage without you. But, my love, you don't know what you're letting yourself in for.'

'Yes, I do: a life of worry, always wondering how long the happiness will last.'

'If you know that—'

'But the other choice is a life without you, and I choose you. I choose you for me and as a father for our child, because nobody else can be the father you can. Nobody else knows the secrets you do.'

He held her close, where she belonged, where she'd dreamed of being all the long, lonely weeks. They neither kissed nor caressed, but stood still and silent, rediscovering each other's warmth, coming home. At last he led her into the bedroom and drew her down onto the bed.

'Don't worry,' he said quickly. 'I won't try to make love to you.'

'Darling, it's all right,' she said shakily. 'I'm in the early stages. It's quite safe.'

'Safe,' he whispered. 'What does "safe" mean? You can never be sure, can you? And we won't take any risks.' He gave a sharp, self-critical laugh. 'Listen to me, talking about not taking risks. But I'm such a selfish beggar; I've never had to think about anyone else's health before. I guess I'll have to get working on that.'

She kissed him in a passion of tenderness.

'You're almost there now,' she murmured.

'Almost?'

'There's something I want you to do,' she said, speaking quietly, although her heart was beating hard. 'We're going to find out the truth about your condition. I can't live with the uncertainty.'

'And if the worst is true?' he asked slowly.

'Then we'll face it. Not just for our sake, but for our child's too. This is your baby, born into the same heritage, and I want to know what it may face. If I don't know the truth, I shall worry myself sick, and that isn't a good thing for the baby. Do this for me, my love.'

In the long silence she sensed his agony and enfolded him protectively, trying to speak of her love without words.

'Be a little patient,' he begged at last. 'Don't ask me just yet.'

She understood. She was asking him to overturn the rules on which his whole life had been lived, and it was hard. All his major decisions had been taken alone. Now she'd told him that he had two supporters, but he was still struggling to adjust to that idea, or even understand it.

'Take your time,' she whispered.

They slept without making love, and when she woke at first light it was no surprise to find him sitting by the window, as he had often done before. She went to join him, sitting quietly. He didn't turn his head, but his fingers entwined with hers.

'It's still waiting there,' he said, indicating the silent volcano. 'I guess it finally gave me the rumble I wasn't prepared for. And, as I always feared, I have no answer. Why don't you despise me, run a mile, kick me out of your life?'

'Because without you I'd get bored,' she said, with a note of their old teasing. 'And, when our child asks where Daddy is, what do I tell her?'

'Say you chucked him out with the rest of the rubbish. Or you might recycle me into a sensible man.'

'Then how would I know it was you?' she asked with a hint of a chuckle.

'And what's this *her* business? Since when did she become a girl?'

'I've decided it's going to be a girl. We're better at being practical.'

He cocked a humorous eyebrow. 'I need another woman nagging me?'

'That's definitely what you need. Hope and I aren't enough. It's a task for three.'

Then her smile faded as she saw something on a nearby table and reached out for it. 'That's one of the pictures you took of me when I first came here.'

'We went to the consulate to get you a new passport,' he recalled.

'But how do you come to have it? I never did remember to give them to you.'

'No, and I raided your computer for them. This was the best, so I printed it out to keep.' He stopped and watched her for a moment, remembering. 'I'd never loved you as much as I did then. That previous night, I came to the edge of telling you everything.

'I backed off at the last minute, but when I went through those pictures and saw how you looked at me I knew I had to tell you, because you were the only person I could ever trust with the truth. Suddenly it was all clear, and I knew I could tell you everything.'

'Oh no,' she whispered, dropping her head into her hands. 'And then you found that folder and realised I'd betrayed you. No wonder you were so terribly hurt.'

'You didn't betray me. I've known that for a long time, but I was in such a state of confusion that I couldn't wait to be rid of you. You made me think, and I didn't want to think. It was only after you'd gone that I realised what I'd done—chosen safety and predictability over life. I kept that picture with me to remind myself what I'd lost.'

'But why didn't you call me and ask me to come back?' she asked.

'Because I thought I had nothing to offer you, and you were better without me.'

'That will never be true. I want you with me all my life.'

'If only…' he said longingly.

'My love, I know what I'm asking of you is hard, but do it for me. Do it for *us*.'

Without speaking, he slipped to his knees and laid his face against her, his hand gently touching her stomach. Ferne caressed him, also in silence. Nothing more was needed. He had given his answer.

Hope was in ecstasies as they reached the villa that evening, greeting them both, but especially Ferne, with open arms.

'Welcome to the family,' she said. 'Oh yes, you're a Rinucci now. You're going to have a Rinucci baby, and that makes you one of us.'

Ferne couldn't help smiling at the way she'd been taken over. Then Hope went even further.

'I'm so looking forward to another grandchild,' she said blissfully.

'But Dante isn't actually your son, is he?' Ferne said, startled.

'Oh, son, nephew, what does it matter? He's a Rinucci, and now so are you.'

Next day, she took over the preparations for Dante's tests, telephoning a contact at the local hospital. He moved fast, and Dante was admitted that day for a lumbar puncture and a CT scan. From behind a window, Ferne watched as he prepared for the scan; he kept his eyes on them until the last minute, as he was swallowed up in the huge machine.

After that the minutes seemed to go at a crawl until they were given the results. During that endless time, Ferne realised that she had always known what the truth would be.

'The tests show that you've already had one mild rupture quite recently,' the doctor said. 'You were lucky. You came through it. You might even go on being lucky. Or you could have a major rupture in a few weeks and possibly die.'

Dante didn't reply, but sat in terrible stillness, as though already dead. After a lifetime of avoiding this moment, he was forced to confront it.

'But surgery can make it all right?' Ferne's voice was almost pleading.

'I wish I could say that it was as simple as that,' the doctor replied. 'The operation is very difficult, and there's a high death-rate. But if he goes into a coma first then the rate is even higher.' He addressed Dante directly. 'Your best chance is to have it now before things get worse.'

Dante had been sitting with head sunk in hands. Now he looked up.

'And if I live,' he said, 'can you guarantee that I'll still be mentally normal?' He choked into silence.

Gravely the doctor shook his head.

'There's always a chance of complications,' he said. 'I wish I could give you a guarantee, but I can't.'

He walked out, leaving them alone, holding each other in silence. After all the dancing with fate, all the arguments, there was only the bleak reality left. With the operation or without it, the possibility of death was high. And, with it, there was a real chance of something Dante considered far worse.

Why should he choose to walk into the unknown? Ferne knew that there was only their love to make the risk worthwhile, but was that enough? Now he was really dancing to the edge of the abyss, but not with fate, with herself, trusting her to stop him plunging over. But even she had no power to do that.

At that moment she would not have blamed him for walking away.

'What am I going to do?' he asked desperately. 'Once I would have said that dying didn't worry me, and it would have been true. But now there's you—and her.' He pointed downwards, and a wry smile twisted his mouth. 'Who'd have thought that having something to live for could be so scary?'

She waited for him to say more. The only words that mattered would come from him.

'I've used my illness as a way of avoiding responsibility,' he said after a while. 'I didn't see it like that at the time. I thought I was doing the sensible thing. Now it just looks like a form of cowardice. My whole life has been a sham because I couldn't face the reality.'

He looked at her in agony, whispering fiercely, 'Where do you get your courage? Can't you give some to me? Because I don't have any. Part of me still says just walk away and let it happen as it will.'

'No!' she said fiercely. 'I need you with me. You've got to take every chance of staying alive.'

'Even if it means becoming like Leo? That scares me more than dying.'

She drew back and looked into his face.

'Listen to me. You ask me to give you courage, but can't you understand that I need *you* to give *me* courage?'

'Me? A clown, a chancer?'

'Yes, a clown, because I need you and your

silly jokes to shield me from the rest of the world. I need you to make fun of me and trip me up, and take me by surprise and get the world in proportion for me. You made me strong and whole, so that now I need to be able to reach out and hold your hand for *my* protection, not yours.'

He searched her face intently, trying to discern the answer to mysteries. At last he seemed to find what he needed, for he drew her close, resting his head on her shoulder.

'I'll do whatever you wish,' he said. 'Only promise to be there.'

CHAPTER TWELVE

THE doctor emphasised that there was no time to lose, and a date was set for the next day.

They spent that evening at the villa, where the family had gathered to wish Dante well. He had apparently recovered his spirits, even making a joke of his new deference to Ferne.

'I don't believe this is Dante,' she said. 'It's so unlike him to keep agreeing with me.'

'He's turning into a Rinucci husband,' Toni said. 'However strong we look to the rest of the world, at home we all obey orders.'

Nobody knew which of the wives murmured, 'So I should hope,' but the others all nodded agreement, and the husbands grinned.

'But he's not a husband,' Hope pointed out. 'Perhaps it's time that he was.'

'You'll have to ask Ferne,' Dante said at once.

He smiled up at her with a hint of the old, wicked humour. 'I just do as I'm told.'

'Then you'll be a perfect Rinucci husband,' she said in a shaking voice.

'But when is the wedding?' Hope asked.

'As soon as I come out of hospital,' Dante said.

'No,' Hope said urgently. 'Don't wait so long. Do it now.'

Everyone knew what she meant. It might be now or never.

'Can it be arranged so quickly?' Ferne asked.

'Leave it with me,' Hope said.

She had contacts all over Naples, and it was no surprise when after a few phone calls she announced that an emergency service could be arranged for the next day. The wedding would be in the afternoon, and Dante would enter the hospital straight afterwards.

It was all achieved in double-quick time, and Ferne was left worried that Dante felt he was being hustled into marriage. Her fear increased when he was quiet on the way home.

'Dante?'

'Hush, don't speak until you've heard what I have to say. Wait here.'

He went into the bedroom and searched a drawer, returning a few moments later with two small boxes. Inside one, Ferne saw two wedding-rings, large and small. Inside the other was an engagement ring of diamonds and sapphires.

'They belonged to my parents,' he said, taking out the engagement ring. 'I never thought the day would come when I'd give this to any woman. But then, you're not any woman. You're the one I've been waiting for all this time.'

He slipped it onto her finger, dropped his head and kissed the spot. Ferne couldn't speak. She was weeping.

'And these,' he said, turning to the other box, 'are the rings they exchanged on their wedding day. They loved each other very much. He got up to mad tricks, and she tried to stick with him whenever she could. She was afraid that he'd vanish without her.

'I used to blame her for that. I felt resentful that she took risks without thinking of me, left behind. But I understand now. I've come to understand a lot of things that were hidden from me before.'

His voice shook so much that he could barely say the last words. He bent his head quickly, but not quickly enough to hide the fact that his cheeks were wet. Ferne held him tightly, fiercely glad that in her arms he felt free to weep, and that she too had come to understand many things.

That night they made love as if for the first time. He touched her gently, as though afraid to do her harm. She responded to him with passionate tenderness, and always the thought lay between them: perhaps never again; perhaps this was all there would be to last a lifetime. When their lovemaking was over, they held each other tenderly.

Next morning a lawyer called with papers for Dante to sign, and also some for Ferne.

'They're in Italian. I don't understand a word,' she said.

'Just sign them,' he told her. 'If I become unable to manage my own affairs, this will give you complete control.'

She was a little puzzled, since surely as his wife her control would be automatic? But perhaps Italian law was more complicated. She signed briefly, and returned to her preparations.

There was no lavish bridal-gown, just a silk, peach-coloured dress that she already knew he liked. In a dark, formal suit, he looked as handsome as she'd ever seen him. Standing side by side, looking in the mirror together, they made a handsome couple.

Both of them tried not to look at the suitcase he would take with him, which contained his things so that he could go on to the hospital when the wedding was over.

At last the lawyer departed and they were alone, waiting for the taxi.

'I think it's here,' she said, looking out of the window. 'Let's go.'

'Just a moment.' He detained her.

'What is it?'

'Just one more thing I have to know before we go ahead,' he said quietly. 'I want to marry you more than anything on earth, but I can't face the thought of being a burden in your life. Will you give me your word to put me in a home if I become like Uncle Leo?'

'How can I do that?' she asked, aghast. 'It would be a betrayal.'

'I can't marry you to become a burden on you. If you don't give me your word, the wedding's off.'

'Dante…'

'Understand me, I mean it. One way or another, I'll leave you free.'

'And your child?'

'We just signed papers that will give you complete control, whether we're married or not.

So you'll have everything that's mine to support you and our child.'

'Did you think I was talking about money?' she asked with a touch of anger.

'No, I know you weren't, but you have to know that my arrangements will look after you both, even without a wedding.'

She sighed. Even now he was setting her at a little distance.

'Do I have your word,' he asked again, 'that if I become *incapable*…?' He shuddered.

'Hush,' she said, unable to endure any more.

'I don't want people to see me and pity me. I don't want my child to grow up regarding me with contempt. Do I have your word that if this goes wrong you'll put me away?' He took her hand in his. 'Swear it, or I can't marry you.'

'*What?*' She stared, appalled at this unsuspected ruthlessness.

'I'll call it off right now if you don't give me your word. I can't go through with it unless I'm sure. You've never really understood what that dread means to me, have you? And I've never been able to make you.'

'I know it means more to you than I do!' she said wildly.

This should have been their most perfect

moment, when they could be happy in their love despite all the problems. But she was saddened at his intransigence.

Perhaps he saw this, because his voice became gentler.

'Nothing means more to me than you,' he said. 'But try to understand, my love; you've done so much for me. I beg you to do this one thing more, to give me peace.'

'All right,' she said sadly. 'I swear it.'

'Promise on everything you hold dear and sacred, on the life of our child, on whatever love you have for me—*promise me*.'

'I promise. If it comes to that—' she paused, and a tremor went through her '—I'll do as you wish.'

'Thank you.'

The wedding was in the hospital chapel. All the Rinuccis who lived in Naples were there. The women of the family lined up to be the bride's attendants. The men scrapped for the privilege of waiting on Dante.

Toni gave her away, escorting her down the aisle with pride. Dante watched her approach with a look that took her breath away, and that she knew she would remember all her life. As she reached him and laid her hand in his, the problems seemed to melt away. Even the promise he'd imposed on her could not spoil this moment. She was marrying the man she loved, and who loved her. There was nothing else in the world.

Holding Dante's hand in hers, she declared, 'I, Ferne, take you, Dante, to be my husband. I promise to be true to you in good times and in bad, in sickness and in health. I will love you and honour you all the days of my life.'

She knew he wasn't quite ready to understand that. She could only pray for the miracle that would give her the chance to show him.

Then they exchanged rings, the ones that had belonged to his parents, who'd chosen never to be parted. One after the other they recited the ritual wedding-vows, but then the priest looked a silent question, asking if they wished to add anything of their own. Dante nodded, took her hand and spoke in a clear voice for everyone to hear.

'I give you my life for whatever it's worth—not much, perhaps, but there's no part of it that isn't yours. Do with it whatever you will.'

It took her a moment to fight back the tears, but then she said in a shaking voice, 'Everything I am belongs to you. Everything I will ever be belongs to you, now and always—whatever life may bring.'

She said the last words with special significance,

hoping he would understand, and she felt him grow still for a moment, looking at her, questioning.

Then it was over. It was time to turn and make their way out of the little chapel, followed by the family.

Instead of a wedding feast they all accompanied Dante to his room, where a smiling nurse showed them in. There was a bottle of champagne to stress that this was a party, but before long the laughter and congratulations faded, as they all remembered why Dante was there.

One by one they bid him goodbye, all of them knowing that it might be final. Hope and Toni embraced him heartily, then left them alone.

'You must rest well,' the nurse told him. 'So go to bed now, and drink this.' She held up a glass. 'It will help you sleep.'

'I want to stay with him,' Ferne said.

'Of course.'

She helped him undress, and suddenly it was as though a giant machine had taken over. It had started, and nobody could say how it was going to end.

'I'm glad you stayed with me tonight,' he said. 'Because there's still something I need to say to you. I want to ask your forgiveness.'

'For what?'

'For my selfishness. I've had a good look at myself, and I don't like what I see. You were right when you said I shouldn't have let you get so close without telling you the truth.'

'We were supposed to keep it light,' she reminded him.

'But that wasn't under our control. You and I could never have met without loving each other. I loved you from the start, but I wouldn't admit it to myself. Instead I selfishly found excuses, pretending that it wasn't what it was, and I led you into danger.'

'Don't talk of it as danger,' she interrupted him. 'You've been the best experience of my life, and you always will be, whatever happens. Do you understand that? *Whatever happens*.'

'But say you forgive me,' he said. 'I need to hear you say it.' He was already growing sleepy.

'I'll forgive you if you want, but there is nothing to forgive. Please—please try to understand that.'

He smiled but didn't answer. A moment later, his eyes closed. Ferne laid her head down on the pillow beside him, watching him until her own eyes closed.

This was their wedding night.

* * *

In the morning the orderlies came to take him to the operating theatre.

'One moment,' Dante said frantically.

As she leaned over him, he touched her face.

'If this should be the last time…' he whispered.

It hit her like a blow. This might really be the last time she touched him, looked into his eyes.

'It isn't the last time,' she said. 'Whatever happens, we will always be together.'

Suddenly he reached out, as though trying to find something.

'What is it?'

'Your camera,' he said. 'The one you always keep with you.'

Now she understood. Pulling it out, she fixed it to take a picture after a few seconds' delay, and set it up a little distance away. Then she took him into her arms, looking into his face.

His own eyes on her were quiet with a peace she had never seen in them before.

'Yes,' he said. 'We'll always be together. I may not be there again, but my love will be, until the end of your life. Tell me that you know that.'

She couldn't speak, only nod.

Then it was time. The orderlies wheeled him

away. Suddenly it was all over; she might never see him alive again.

'Suppose he dies?' she said to Hope, distraught. 'Dies in an operation that he only had because I made him? He might have lived for years without getting sick. If he dies, I'll have killed him.'

'And if it goes well, you will have saved his life and his sanity,' Hope said firmly.

How slowly the hours passed. Many times she took out the camera and studied the last picture she'd taken. It was tiny, but she could see Dante's face turned towards her with an expression of adoration that startled her. Had it been there before, and had she just never noticed? Would it be the last of him that she ever saw?

What had she done to him?

She seemed to see her life stretching before her, with an empty place where he should have been. There was her child, asking where her father was, and not understanding that her mother had sent him to his death.

The years would pass and their child would grow, become a success, married. But without a father to show his pride and love.

'I took it away from him,' she mourned.

'No,' Hope said. 'You have to understand that

Dante was right about doing the quick-step with fate. He's giving himself the best chance, or rather, you've given it to him. You were fate's instrument. Now it's out of our hands.'

At last he was wheeled out of the operating theatre, his head swathed in bandages. He looked pale, ghostly, and completely unlike the Dante they knew. But he was alive.

'It went well,' the doctor told them. 'He's strong, and there were no complications, so we were able to support the wall of the weak artery with less difficulty than usual. It's too soon for certainty, but I expect him to live.'

'And—the other thing?' Ferne stammered.

'That we'll have to wait and see. It's a pity he delayed treatment for so long, but I'm hopeful.'

That qualification haunted her as she sat beside Dante's bed, waiting for him to awaken. She didn't know how long she was there. It was a long time since she'd slept, but however weary she was she knew she couldn't sleep now.

Hour after hour passed. He lay terrifyingly still, attached to so many machines that he almost disappeared under them. Part of his face was invisible beneath the huge plug clamping his mouth and attaching him to the breathing machine.

She had seen him wicked, charming, cruel, but never until this moment had she seen him totally helpless.

Perhaps it was for ever. Perhaps she had condemned him to this, although he'd begged her not to. He'd asked her forgiveness, but now, in the long dark hours, she fervently asked for his.

'I may have taken everything away from you,' she whispered. 'You tried to warn me, but now, if your life is ruined, it's my fault. Forgive me. Forgive me.'

He lay motionless and silent. The only sound in the room was the machine helping him to breathe.

Dawn broke, and she realised that she'd been there all night. A doctor came to detach the breathing machine, saying, 'Let's see how well he manages without it.'

Ferne stood well back while the plug was removed from his mouth and the machine pulled away. There was a pause, while time seemed to stop, then Dante gave a small choke and drew in a long breath.

'Excellent,' the doctor declared. 'Breathing normal.'

'How long before he comes round?' Ferne asked.

'He needs a bit longer.'

He departed and she settled back beside the bed, taking Dante's hand in hers.

'You've made a great start,' she told him.

Could he hear her? she wondered. Hearing was supposed to outlast all the other senses. Perhaps if she could reach him now she could even help to keep his brain strong.

'It's going to be all right,' she said, leaning close. 'You're going to wake up and be just the same as I've always known you—scheming, manipulative, dodgy, a man to be avoided by a woman with any sense. But I've never had any sense where you were concerned. I should have given in the first day, shouldn't I? Except that I think I did, and much good it did me. Do you remember?'

He lay still, giving no sign of hearing.

She went on talking, not knowing what she said or how much time passed. The words didn't matter. Most of them were nonsense, the kind of nonsense they had always talked—but he must surely hear the underlying message, which was an impassioned plea to him to return to her.

'Don't leave me alone without you; come back to me.'

But he lay so still that he might already have gone into another world. At last, leaning down, she kissed him softly on the lips.

'I love you,' she whispered at last. 'That's all there is to say.'

Then she jerked back, startled. Had he moved? She watched closely. It was true; he moved.

A sigh broke from him, and he murmured something.

'What did you say?' she asked. 'Speak to me.'

'Portia,' he whispered.

'What was that?'

After a moment, he repeated the word. 'Portia—I'm so glad you're here.'

She wanted to cry aloud in her despair. He didn't know her. His brain was failing, as he'd feared. Whoever Portia was, she was there inside with him.

Slowly he opened his eyes.

'Hello,' he murmured. 'Why are you crying?'

'I'm not—I was just happy to have you back.'

He gave a sleepy smile. 'You were calling me names—scheming, manipulative, dodgy. Never mind. My little friend will stand up for me.'

'Your little friend?' she asked, scarcely daring to breathe.

'Our daughter. I've been getting to know her. I want to call her Portia. She likes it. Darling Ferne, don't cry. Everything's going to be all right.'

* * *

It took time to believe that his recovery was complete, for the news seemed too good to be true. But with every hour that passed Dante showed that his faculties were as sharp as ever.

'We played fate at his own game,' he told her. 'And we won. Or, rather, you did. You were the player. Before you came, I never had the nerve to take that game on. Without you, I should never have had it.'

He touched her face.

'I see you there so clearly, and everything around you; all the world is clear. I hadn't dared to dream that this would happen.'

'It's what I always believed,' she said.

'I know, but I couldn't be sure. There was always the chance that you might have had to put me in an institution.'

Ferne hesitated. It would have been so easy to let this moment slip past and be forgotten, but something impelled her to total honesty, whatever the risk.

'Oh no,' she said. 'I would never have done that.'

He frowned. 'But you promised, don't you remember?'

'I know what I promised,' she said calmly. 'But nothing would have made me keep that promise. Even now I don't think you begin to understand how much I love you. Whatever happened, I would have kept you with me. If you were ill, that would have been more reason to love you, but you were in no state to understand it then. So I had to practise a little deception.'

He looked stunned, as though the full power of her declaration was only just dawning on him.

'But,' he whispered at last, 'you promised on everything you hold dear and sacred.'

'I lied,' she said calmly. 'You wanted to be kept out of sight, so that's what I would have done—but you would have been in our home, where the world couldn't see you, but I could see you every day. Whether you were yourself, or whether your mind had gone, you would have been my husband and I would have loved you until the last moment of my life.'

Suddenly, shockingly, she found her temper rising. Why should she have to explain all this to him?

'So now you know,' she said. 'I lied to you. I wanted to marry you so much, I'd have said and done anything. I made that promise without the most distant intention of keeping it, because I loved you with all of my heart and all of my *life*—but you just couldn't realise, could you?

'Can you see it now? Or are you just too proud and arrogant—and too *stupid*—to understand? You think love is a matter of making bargains, and you can't get it into your head that love has to be unconditional. If it isn't unconditional, it isn't love.'

She waited to see if he would say anything, but he seemed too stunned to speak. Was she being foolish? she wondered. Was she risking their marriage for the satisfaction of getting this off her chest?

But she had no choice. If they were to stand a chance, the air must be clear between them.

'So now you know the worst about me,' she said. 'I tricked you into marriage by deceit. I'm a shameless, dishonest woman who'll do anything to get her own way.'

When at last Dante spoke, he said only two words, and they were the last words Ferne expected to hear.

'Thank goodness!'

'What was that?'

'Thank goodness you're a liar, my darling! Thank goodness you had the courage to be shameless and deceitful. When I think of the disaster that could have befallen me if you'd been truthful, I tremble inside.'

'What—what are you talking about?' she said, half-laughing, half-afraid to believe her ears.

'I never felt I had the right to marry you, knowing what I might be leading you into. It was my way of setting you free. If you'd refused to promise, I'd have forced myself to refuse the marriage, although to be your husband was what I wanted with all my heart. In life, in death, or in that half-life I dreaded so much, I want you, and only you, to be there with me.

'But that felt like selfishness. I demanded that promise because I believed I had no right to trap you and blight your life.'

'But you could never blight my life,' she protested. 'You *are* my life. Haven't you understood that?'

'I guess I'm just starting to. It seemed too much to hope that you should love me as much as I love you. I still can't quite take it in, but I know this: my life belongs to you. Not only because we married, but because the life I have now is the life you gave me.

'Take it, and use it as you will. It was you who drove the clouds away, and you who brings the sunlight. And, as long as you are with me, that will always be true.'

* * *

Two weeks later Dante was discharged from hospital, and he and Ferne went to spend a few weeks at the Villa Rinucci. Even when they returned to their apartment they lived quietly, the only excitement being the delayed wedding-breakfast, celebrated when the whole Rinucci family was present.

After that everyone held their breath for the birth of the newest family member. Portia Rinucci was born the next spring, a combination of her mother's looks and her father's spirit. At her christening, it was observed by everyone that it was her father who held her possessively, his face blazing with love and pride, while her mother looked on with fond tolerance, perfectly happy with the unusual arrangement.

If sometimes Ferne's eyes darkened, it was only because she could never quite forget the cloud that had retreated but not completely vanished. As her daughter grew, it might yet darken their lives again—but she would face it, strengthened by a triumphant love and a happiness that few women knew.

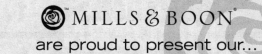

MILLS & BOON
MODERN™

proudly presents

DARK-HEARTED DESERT MEN

*A kingdom torn apart by scandal;
a throne left empty;
four smouldering desert princes…
Which one will claim the crown – and who
will they claim as their brides?*

March
***WEDLOCKED: BANISHED SHEIKH,
UNTOUCHED QUEEN***
by Carol Marinelli

April
TAMED: THE BARBARIAN KING
by Jennie Lucas

May
FORBIDDEN: THE SHEIKH'S VIRGIN
by Trish Morey

June
SCANDAL: HIS MAJESTY'S LOVE-CHILD
by Annie West

"I felt the knife against my throat and thought I was going to die."

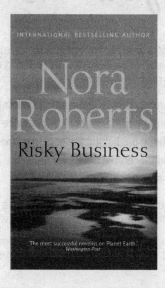

When Liz Palmer finds the body of her newest employee, his brother, Jonas, shows up asking questions. Then someone breaks into Liz's apartment, intent on her murder.

Now Jonas's quest to unravel his brother's murky past draws them both into a dangerous criminal underworld that could cost them both their lives…

Available 5th March 2010

www.silhouette.co.uk

millsandboon.co.uk Community

Join Us!

The Community is the perfect place to meet and chat to kindred spirits who love books and reading as much as you do, but it's also the place to:

- Get the inside scoop from authors about their latest books
- Learn how to write a romance book with advice from our editors
- Help us to continue publishing the best in women's fiction
- Share your thoughts on the books we publish
- Befriend other users

Forums: Interact with each other as well as authors, editors and a whole host of other users worldwide.

Blogs: Every registered community member has their own blog to tell the world what they're up to and what's on their mind.

Book Challenge: We're aiming to read 5,000 books and have joined forces with The Reading Agency in our inaugural Book Challenge.

Profile Page: Showcase yourself and keep a record of your recent community activity.

Social Networking: We've added buttons at the end of every post to share via digg, Facebook, Google, Yahoo, technorati and de.licio.us.

www.millsandboon.co.uk

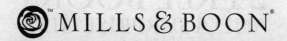

2 FREE BOOKS
AND A SURPRISE GIFT

We would like to take this opportunity to thank you for reading this Mills & Boon® book by offering you the chance to take TWO more specially selected books from the Romance series absolutely FREE! We're also making this offer to introduce you to the benefits of the Mills & Boon® Book Club™—

- **FREE home delivery**
- **FREE gifts and competitions**
- **FREE monthly Newsletter**
- **Exclusive Mills & Boon Book Club offers**
- **Books available before they're in the shops**

Accepting these FREE books and gift places you under no obligation to buy, you may cancel at any time, even after receiving your free shipment. Simply complete your details below and return the entire page to the address below. You don't even need a stamp!

YES Please send me 2 free Romance books and a surprise gift. I understand that unless you hear from me, I will receive 5 superb new stories every month including two 2-in-1 books priced at £4.99 each and a single book priced at £3.19, postage and packing free. I am under no obligation to purchase any books and may cancel my subscription at any time. The free books and gift will be mine to keep in any case.

Ms/Mrs/Miss/Mr_____ Initials _____

Surname _____

Address _____

_____

_____ Postcode _____

Send this whole page to: Mills & Boon Book Club, Free Book Offer, FREEPOST NAT 10298, Richmond, TW9 1BR